To Gary

The Unraveling
A NOVEL

God Bless

A NOVEL

Mark A. Gudmunson

TATE PUBLISHING
AND ENTERPRISES, LLC

The Unraveling
Copyright © 2012 by Mark A. Gudmunson. All rights reserved.

No part of this publication may be reproduced, stored in a retrieval system or transmitted in any way by any means, electronic, mechanical, photocopy, recording or otherwise without the prior permission of the author except as provided by USA copyright law.

The opinions expressed by the author are not necessarily those of Tate Publishing, LLC.

Published by Tate Publishing & Enterprises, LLC
127 E. Trade Center Terrace | Mustang, Oklahoma 73064 USA
1.888.361.9473 | www.tatepublishing.com

Tate Publishing is committed to excellence in the publishing industry. The company reflects the philosophy established by the founders, based on Psalm 68:11,
"The Lord gave the word and great was the company of those who published it."

Book design copyright © 2012 by Tate Publishing, LLC. All rights reserved.
Cover design by Jan Sunday Quilaquil
Interior design by Joana Quilantang

Published in the United States of America

ISBN: 978-1-62024-458-6
Fiction / Christian / Suspense
12.08.07

Endorsements

Mark Andrew Gudmunson's sequel to *Priceless* is well written and thought provoking. What an inspiring message of hope in the midst of trials and personal spiritual crisis. The twists and turns of this story are captivating and will grip the reader until the very last page. A must-read.

—Sissy J. Austin, teacher's assistant and pastor's wife church of the Nazarene, NC

Eagerly anticipating the renewal of Jay and Anna's story from *Priceless*, I was not let down with this sophomore prose of kidnapping and terror based in modern-day Mexico. I was hooked by the second chapter. Mark Gudmunson definitely breathes a bit of fresh air and intrigue into the Christian fiction market. All I can say is, I can't wait to see what comes next!

—Inger Koppenhaver owner Badlands café, creative writer, Terry, MT

Wow! What an amazingly powerful yet beautiful story! Mark Gudmunson has a God-given talent that is beyond words.

—Casey Garland, administrator and creator of Faithbook on Facebook

The Unraveling is a modern parable of God's grace and mercy that will capture a reader's imagination. From page one I was caught up in a story I couldn't set aside until I finished it, and months later I still find the story fresh in my mind. This book is a must-read!

—Susan Sukraw, pastor COTN-District Assignment with North Platte Area Youth for Christ

Mark Gudmunson has written a compelling story of how a young missionary couple's world collides with pure evil. *The Unraveling* is a gripping story of Christian love, faith, perseverance, and trust in the most extreme circumstances. There are many life lessons learned from the characters as they live out this epic adventure. There are so many twists and turns in the story it keeps you in suspense throughout!

—Laurie Davis, graphic artist, Grass Valley, CA

Foreword

My brother, Mark Gudmunson, has the gift of observing the many struggles and difficulties associated with growing to maturity in the Christian faith and addressing them in parable form. Once again we see the contrast between the struggles in the life of Jay Bilston in regards to the surrendering of control in life to a sovereign God and walking by faith and Jay's bride, Anna, who has total confidence that whatever happens in a life surrendered to God will be what is most beneficial.

This novel, like *Priceless*, the first novel about Jay and Anna, is an enjoyable and often suspenseful means of delivering some deep spiritual truths that can help any Christ-follower in their daily walk.

As we follow Jay and Anna on their journey to answer the call to "go into all the world and preach the gospel," many can identify with the struggles Jay faces with fear, issues of trust, and total surrender to a loving heavenly Father. I believe Jay, like many of us, falls into the trap of feeling his own unworthiness of God's care and keeping. He is plagued with the idea that God will surely care for those great men and women of God we hear about. After all, they are doing great things for Him.

"But I'm just a nobody." Jay forgets about God's immeasurable love and grace and the fact that no one is worthy without the miracle of God's grace. He also has a difficult time grasping the inherent value of each life of God's adopted children.

Anna, on the other hand, understands and embraces the privileges of being a joint-heir with Christ. Her response is not "What if God doesn't care for me in a time of struggle?" but rather "I wonder how God is going to take care of me and bring beauty out of ashes."

As I read these novels, it is no mystery to me why Mark's ministry is effectively reaching young people for Christ. God has truly given him a gift of communicating truth through observations about everyday happenings. As you read, do not just expect to enjoy a suspenseful storyline. Expect to learn and be challenged in your own faith journey.

—Reverend Thomas Charles Gudmunson, Miles City Wesleyan Church, Terry Wesleyan Church, Miles City, Montana

Chapter 1

Oppressive summertime heat brought all life to a halt on the high plateau desert of central Mexico. Sharply rising steeps cut with jagged, abrupt draws gave depth to a flat landscape that went on forever, as far as the eye, or one's imagination, could see. Pale greens and grays met the contrasting brilliant blue of the enormous sky as it extended infinitely over the horizon. Soft, wispy clouds white as snow lapped across the sky, moved by currents of air like waves across the ocean. Dull gray, light blue, and dim violet were the dominant color schemes of the sparse plant life covering the gravelly soil of the desert floor.

The soil—visible through the trees, cacti, and brush—was a rust color. Rugged edges of the wrinkled draws held little vegetation. Abrupt horizontal cuts, some with a depth of over one hundred feet, revealed the composition of the desert soil—a thin top layer of light gray ash mixed with reddish soil, giving the ground a mottled pattern. Layers of nearly white ash repeated itself every twelve to fifteen feet in depth, testimony to volcanic eruptions in the region. Neither animal nor insect seemed to be present, and if they were, some shady patch of ground, nook, or cranny served as refuge from the hot desert sun. Wave upon distorted wave, created by the intense heat, rose up from the desert floor. Extended travel was difficult at best during the hottest part of the day.

This was a God-forsaken country unable to sustain more than small villages and outposts built around sparse and sometimes bitter water sources. Life in these parts was bleak at best.

Massive space filled with sparse population bred lawlessness in most of the region. Human inhabitants were, for the most part, illiterate; surviving generations with learned knowledge and superstition passed down from one family member to another.

Religion of the region was dominated by talismans and charms designed to ward off demons, witches, and evil spirits. An occasional mention of Christ or the living God was sometimes referenced, learned long ago from Roman Catholic missionaries from Spain, long since gone. An incomplete understanding and lack of education lent to the gross distortion of Christianity, which was often combined with pagan religions of the native population.

Bands of outlaws preyed on the simple people, oftentimes stealing their children either to supply their chain of human trafficking or provide slave labor for criminal enterprises, with drug manufacturing and trafficking being the largest enterprise by far in this remote and desolate country.

Little help, if any, came from the central Mexican government. Lack of resources, regional corruption, and spotty communication were the fruits of failed policy that dated back more than a century. All of this created a perfect recipe for lawlessness and anarchy, lending credence to the saying, "Only the strong survive."

Just recently, a new Light was beginning to shine in the region. A Light that brought hope and love to the repressed people of the countryside. It was spreading, slowly at first but more rapidly with the passing of each day. The source of the Light was nothing less than the love of Jesus Christ, brought to these people by those called by God to bring His Word and His plan of salvation through grace to those whom time neglected in this remote, nearly uninhabited region. Only God could know the far-reaching effects His Light would have on both those receiving and those who delivered the Living Word.

Chapter 2

The midday sun bore down on the tall, dark man standing behind a large juniper tree. From his vantage point, he could survey a small compound of houses and businesses more than a hundred yards in front of him. Heat waves were rising off the desert floor, giving the small village an eerie composition as the stranger peered through them. The tree, which was shielding him from both the glaring rays of the overhead sun and from the view of anyone within the compound, stood in the center of a large outcropping of sage brush and scraggly mesquite trees that topped out at roughly four and a half feet, nearly shoulder height. The man had direct sight into the small compound through a front gate that blocked a small red-dirt road, actually nothing more than a large worn path. The trail continued on through the compound, past the gate, and out a similar gate on the opposite end of the compound, bisecting it directly in the center with a seemingly equal amount of small buildings on either side.

Most of the buildings were constructed out of cinder blocks with flat roofs made out of concrete. Bundles of rebar were sticking up at the corners like antennae. It gave the buildings an appearance of a swarm of army ants clustered together. On top of some, he could see where people had set up makeshift kitchens with open fire pits right on the gray concrete. A couple had large pots of water boiling in preparation for the washing of clothes. Sagebrush and weeds grew up around the small dwellings.

Some of the shacks had windows of single pane glass, although the vast majority had nothing more than square openings covered on the inside by some sort of canvas or similar stiff cloth. A six-foot-high fence constructed out of the same cinder block material encircled the small village. The blocks had been crudely laid, some recessed in and others protruded out, a testimony to the unskilled labor that had placed them.

Sagebrush pushed up on either side of the wall, giving it the appearance of being supported by the bushy plants. A courtyard in the center of the little compound teemed with activity, though he couldn't tell who or what was going on. Sounds of chickens clucking and squawking mingled with the squeals and grunts of pigs could be heard over the din of life inside the fenced village. On several occasions he watched as poor peasants worked their way up the worn path and into the village. Some of the travelers pulled small thatches bearing produce, cheeses, or other kinds of goods to be traded or sold in the village that day. More fortunate ones led donkeys burdened down with goods into the village. On one occasion, he watched as an old flatbed truck billowing charcoal color smoke out of its tailpipe sped down the road and into the village to deliver its precious cargo of clean five-gallon water-filled bottles to the people inside who were waiting for their daily supply of the precious liquid.

Several little shanty buildings dotted the landscape around the outside of the compound and served as houses for the less fortunate among them. These houses were constructed of whatever materials the peasants were able to salvage from the nearby countryside. Some were no more than sticks and twigs tied together to form crude walls covered with a grass thatch ceiling. The floors of the little shacks consisted of nothing more than hard dirt worn smooth from constant use. To describe these little huts and their occupants as impoverished would be an understatement of gigantic proportion.

Smoke rose up from a few pit fires in front of a couple of the shanties as old ladies bent over them, oblivious to the oppressive midday temperatures that easily reached triple digits. They were busy cooking hand-ground corn tortillas on flat and smooth stone griddles warmed by radiant heat from the nearby flames.

A constant scowl adorned the man's face, revealing a mood that was souring with the passing of each minute. A steady rage of fire, which had been burning inside him, continued to build as he waited for someone or something to emerge from the complex. Large, dark veins stood out on his neck and temples as he fought to control his anger. Hate surged from his soul up through his limbs, into his head and every pore of his being. It was a feeling he welcomed, even enjoyed, as the rush of power from the adrenaline surged through his tense body. Every muscle on his torso trembled as he fought to maintain control. His eyes watered slightly. Endorphins fueled by pure hate and evil raged through him.

The amount of effort it took to balance on the fine point between immense anger and uncontrollable fury surprised him. A slight smile of anticipation appeared briefly on his dry, sun-cracked lips before giving way to his normal scowl. The desire to kill was overwhelming.

"Not yet, not now." He punctuated his thoughts with a slight shake of his head.

The need to inflict pain threatened to overtake his senses. The compelling desire to succumb to the power of hatred surging inside was nearly causing him to abandon his hiding place and rush wantonly into the village to unleash his furry on anyone with whom he should make contact. He was wound tight, ready to explode. This was supposed to be a quick little exercise, but it was turning into anything but.

"In…get the information…out, quick as that!" Those had been the only instructions to his surrogate eyes and ears.

Fifteen minutes, half an hour tops, was all the time it should have taken. Now it was dragging on and on, hour after hour, and all he could do was wait.

Maybe she ran away. Maybe she isn't coming back. Maybe she is revealing my plan. These were the thoughts that kept cycling fear-

The Unraveling

fully through his mind, only to be angrily slammed away. Doubt and underlying fear only added fuel to his ire.

Several large black flies buzzed around his head like slow airplanes circling the runway as they waited their turn to land on his long, black, matted eyelashes. Their presence seemed to have little if any effect on the man as he watched and waited.

A long, straight ditch, crudely cut into the desert floor by picks and shovels long ago, was the source of the flies. The ditch emerged from under the concrete wall of the small compound and traveled over half a mile before opening up into a circular pit no more than fifty feet in diameter. It was almost half full of raw sewage that flowed ever so slowly before emptying into the stagnant water of the slime-covered pit. An odor, suffocating to anyone who came near, rose up off the lagoon and its umbilical stream; although the man showed no indication whatsoever that it bothered him.

Joyous sounds of children playing could be heard from both inside and outside of the high fence around the compound. His furrowed brow deepened at the sounds of their happy voices.

"What gives them a right to be so happy?" He hissed angrily while casting a nervous glance around the perimeter of his hiding spot. Anger surged nearly to the point of explosion as he listened to their excited banter.

"If I could just get my hands on one of those filthy brats…"

In his mind, he could imagine himself inflicting severe pain through torturous acts on one of the innocent children. Lifelike images of agonizing pain visible on the face of some helpless soul excited him.

His heart beat wildly in anticipation of the fantasized violence. With several violent side-to-side motions, he shook the thoughts from his mind. It was neither the time nor the place for such distractions, enjoyable as they were.

No, I need to stay focused, he thought with another quick shake of the head.

A mirror of angry intensity re-emerged on his face as he reigned in the visions of violence.

Pooled deep inside wrinkled, squinty sockets, black, beady eyes constricted into a heart-piercing glare as they darted back and forth across the landscape, searching for anyone who may have discovered his concealed vantage point. Dark, chapped lips continued to quiver in anger. They remained separated just enough to reveal two rows of yellow-stained teeth clenched in fury on his weathered face. Several of the teeth were broken or missing, giving his mouth an almost picket fence-like appearance. Visibly angry, his face was a barometer of the turmoil contained within his enraged soul.

An inadvertently raised left hand rubbed a large jagged scar that ran from his left eye to just under his left ear. Grimy fingernails scratched at the edges of the war wound. Thick, matted black hair, covered in dust and sweat, absorbed the searing heat and caused little beads of perspiration to run down his neck, where they added to a sweat stain visible on the upper part of his dirt-caked, homemade burlap shirt.

Glaring eyes peered at the dry ground as he quickly kicked at the dirt with his worn cowboy boots.

"What could be taking her so long?" A golf ball-sized rock occupied his right hand and served as a stress relief as his grimy fingers rubbed back and forth incessantly over the smooth surface of the stone. Suddenly, a midsized black dog appeared from somewhere behind and to the right of his hiding place. It was an unexpected meeting, startling both him and the dog. Either seeing or smelling the man, the dog turned and began to scurry away at an angle, tail tucked between its legs, one eye always on the interloper.

Recovering from his initial surprise, the man quickly gained his senses, brought the dog around with a quick whistle while simultaneously cocking his right arm just before launching the stone at the animal. Spinning through the air with deadly accuracy, the missile caught the dog right between the eyes. The impact brought a sickening thud followed by a quick yelp as momentum from the projectile knocked the animal flat, each leg sprawling in a different direction.

The accurate throw produced a slight, brief grin before giving way to the man's normal frown. Brief elation filled his eyes as he watched the dog struggle back to its feet, yelping all the while. With tail tucked, it ran straight away from the man as fast as its long legs would carry it.

Chuckling to himself, he refocused his attention on the little village. Though the episode with the dog was an outlet for his pent-up tension, he was still angry and impatient. Just the same, hitting that dog was exactly what he had needed to gain better control over his emotions. Eyeing another round stone with the approximate dimensions of the last, he reached down and scooped up the smooth weapon with one fluid motion while maintaining a watchful eye on the compound.

Left hand to right hand and back and forth the stone went over and over as he used up some of his nervous energy. Movement at the gate brought him into a lower crouch behind the juniper. He peered out through the heat waves, trying vainly to identify whoever was approaching. Anticipation welled up inside, fueled by a mix of angry excitement and lustful hatred. It had been a long wait, and someone was going to pay.

Lower he crouched as the lone figure began to approach. Slowly it came, picking its way through the sage and the cacti. Rising heat waves distorted the person's appearance. Even so, he could tell the individual was petite, hopefully the very person he was waiting for. Closer and closer the person approached.

Blinding anger filled his head as he waited impatiently. The ten or so minutes it took for the person to reach him seemed equal in time to the hours he had already spent waiting. Frustrated, patience spent, he tightened his grip on the stone resting in his right hand.

The small person slowed with apparent apprehension as it closed to within ten feet of the dark man. A hooded cloak covered the small frame, concealing the identity of the person inside. Small, petite hands protruding from the baggy sleeves clenched tightly around a grease-soaked packet containing freshly made corn tortillas. Slowly, cautiously the hooded individual continued to approach the man until no more than a foot separated the two.

To a bystander, the two would have appeared to be having a normal, face-to-face conversation. To the smaller individual, the face-to-face meeting seemed to last an eternity.

A face contorted with hatred and anger punctuated by a deathly stare greeted the smaller of the two as they made eye contact. Every muscle on the angry body was tensed. A hollow, vacant stare from the large dark eyes of the hooded individual met the man's steely glare. Neither person said a word.

Without warning, the tall man's arm leapt up from his side in a blur as his rock-laden fist exploded onto the side of the head of the small person standing in front of him. Impact from the blow lifted the small-framed person off the ground with little resistance. Like a rag doll thrown through the air, the feather-light body rose up in an arc before slamming to the ground several feet away from the man. Dust welled up around the victim, who was stirring and scooting around in an attempt to move away.

The man yelled at the prone body on the ground, "Try to run away from me, will you!"

He walked over to the bundle and, in one fluid motion, placed a well-aimed kick right in the middle of the body of the cloaked figure.

"Aughhh" followed by a slow hiss of air was all that could be heard from the person on the ground.

Deliberately, the man walked around his victim, anger surging throughout his body. He felt powerful, whole. Violence raised his every sense to a heightened state. Voices inside his head screamed at him to continue, even escalate his violent attack. An overwhelming desire to kill was invigorating him. Slowly, deliberately the cloaked figure began to scoot away from the man.

"Where do you think you're going?"

Another quick kick punctuated his question. The muscles on his back and shoulders began to quiver, waiting to explode into action. Quickly, he reached down and, with apparent ease, yanked the small figure off the ground until the hooded head was no more than inches from the man's own face.

"You can't get away from me! I'll find you anywhere you go! I'll break every bone in your worthless body!" He shook his victim back and forth.

Violent shakes caused the large hood to slip off the helpless victim, revealing a beautiful young woman no more than twenty years of age. Long dark hair cascaded over her shoulders and reached the small of her back. It was bright and vibrant as it shone in the midday sun. A large reddish welt began to rise on the right side of her head but did nothing to mask her beauty. She was absolutely stunning.

Her face was the frame for perfectly shaped dark lips, high cheekbones, and large, distinct eyebrows, which only enhanced her most striking feature—her large dark eyes. Much lighter in complexion than her attacker, the young girl's skin was smooth and rich, light tan in color. She seemed out of place there in the middle of such a harsh environment.

"Hear me? Every bone in your body!"

Angry, spittle-filled air delivered the stench of rotting teeth and poor dental hygiene, nearly gagging the young girl.

With another quick jerk, the large man threw the small girl back to the hard ground. She landed on her shoulder and side with a thud. Pain seared her senses but not enough to keep her from rolling quickly to her left to dodge another quick kick.

"Luis, stop, I'm here. I came back," she pleaded with her attacker as she regained her feet and circled away from him. "I wasn't running from you at all. I did exactly as you asked of me,"

Hearing his name, the dark man hesitated for a moment. Then, anger still surging inside, he continued his advance on the young girl.

"You told them of my plans; you were making a pact with them against me,"

"No, Luis! It's not true! I told them of nothing. I only listened as they talked, just as you told me to!"

Scraggly sage and cacti made it difficult to move as she continued her circular berth of the man. Quick as light he moved, striking another blow across the young girl's face, knocking her to the ground. Through her cloak, she could feel the prickly spines of a small cactus poking her in the side. Dust rose up around her, sticking to the fresh blood now flowing from her mouth and left nostril. The sight of it excited him even more.

A feeling of power and invincibility flooded his senses. All concern of concealment now gone, the mad man let loose a primal, gut-wrenching roar that could be heard for a great distance. Even so, no one in the village or working at one of the small fires so much as glanced their way. Even the sound of children playing continued on, uninterrupted.

In a crouch, the madman rushed his victim, intent on tearing her limb from limb. A machine on a mission, he surged forward recklessly, hatred and fury driving him on, suffering and death the only thoughts on his mind. He closed the distance between the girl and himself in a split second. Just as he reached her, she spun around without warning and in one fluid motion tossed two handfuls of sand and gravel into the eyes of her attacker.

"Augghhhhh!" he roared.

Searing pain filled his eyes as much of the sand and dirt found its mark. Grimy hands shot to his closed eyelids in an attempt to rub the debris out. Falling to his knees, he continued pawing at the cause of his pain and discomfort.

"I'm going to kill you!" he roared in the direction of the girl. He swung his arms around recklessly in an attempt to reach her, but to no avail. Unbearable pain shot through his eyes. Several additional roars escaped his lips before he cursed at the girl and climbed slowly back to his feet. Still blinded by the grit, he pressed on, intent on inflicting painful revenge.

"Kill you—hear me?" he bellowed over and over.

Streams of tears cascaded down his cheeks, cutting little rivers through the dirt and grime caked to his face.

Opening his eyes proved to be futile. Too much dirt and sand had lodged under the eyelids to be removed very easily. He could feel the course, gritty sand as it left little scratches on his eyeballs, the excruciating pain only adding fuel to his fury.

Stumbling around blindly, he continued to grope for the girl who had long since moved from beyond his reach.

Knowing it was only a matter of time before he cleared his eyes and came at her again, she leapt into action. Picking up a boulder the size of a grapefruit, she rushed Luis from behind and struck him with all her might on the back of his head, knocking him flat and momentarily senseless. She climbed on his back and firmly pressed the blade of a dagger, drawn from inside her cloak, to his hot and sweaty neck.

"Luis, listen to me. I did exactly as you instructed me to do. For that you try to kill me? I tell you the truth, if you so much as lift a finger, raise up, or try to do anything other than what I tell you, you'll be dead within seconds. Do you hear me?"

Blood ran down his neck and dripped onto the ground beneath him. He could feel the sharp blade as it cut into his flesh. His head throbbed, and he still couldn't see clearly. The fury that had been building just moments before had begun to abate. He knew she meant what she said. Slowly he relaxed and slumped down to the ground. He had no other choice.

The girl sat atop her attacker. Deep desire to kill him was nearly overwhelming. She had suffered years and years of mental and physical abuse from this man. Yet something held her in check. Whether it was fear of being alone, fear of the unknown, or simply some strange hold Luis had over her, she didn't know. Somehow, she couldn't bring herself to end his life.

For several moments neither of them moved. Luis lay prone on the ground, while the young girl held the sharp dagger firmly to his throat. Slowly, unexpectedly Luis began to chuckle. She could feel his body convulse back and forth as his chuckle grew into a laugh and finally into nearly uncontrollable guffaw after guffaw. His movement caused the blade of the sharp knife to cut deeper into his neck, resulting in a steady flow of blood. If he felt the pain of the knife, he didn't show it. It had no effect on Luis, or his laughter, for that matter.

"Rosalita, you are a mad woman! A mad, mad woman!" he managed to spew out in-between laughter.

Unsure of how to respond or what to do, the young girl remained seated on the filthy back of her former attacker, knife held firmly to his neck. Luis's sudden shift in mood took her by surprise. Rosalita was unsure whether this was simple trickery to get her to let him up so he could continue his assault on her, or if his anger had indeed abated.

Still, he continued to laugh. Each guffaw produced an odor of decay that mingled with sweaty, grimy body odor that seemed to rise up in a cloud around her head and nearly gag her. A voice inside her head continued to tell her over and over to kill him. She detested everything about the man. Stolen by him when she was a small child, she had lived through nightmare after ghoulish nightmare. For some reason, he'd kept her for his own all these years. His normal method of operation was to discard his victims, usually with bloody violence after only a few days. Inexplicably, she was the exception to the rule.

Somehow he seemed attached, almost fond of her, if that was remotely possible for someone like him. Many times he'd nearly done away with her. He had beaten, choked, and suffocated her to the point of unconsciousness, but something had always held him back from ending her life.

It was her eyes, he'd decided, perplexed by his own inability to do away with her. It had to be her eyes. Never once had he seen fear in them. No matter the torture, the threats, or the violence he'd subjected her to over the years, they never showed fear. Hatred, contempt, and anger, yes, but fear never. It amazed and intrigued him. Over the years, he'd killed and maimed hundreds of victims, and without exception they all showed extreme fear in their eyes, some faster than others, but all of them in the end.

For more than a dozen years, he'd been her master, her authority figure, her controller. Now the roles were reversed; she was the one with the upper hand. One quick, firm slice and his hold over her, his reign of torture and abuse, would all end, and she would for the first time be a free woman.

Unable to inflict the final, mortal blow, she slowly eased the knife off the man's neck. Feeling his body tense up, she jumped, scooted, and shuffled away from him as fast as she could, dagger still in hand. Standing some ten feet away, she watched as Luis slowly climbed to his feet, brushed off the dust and grime, and rubbed his eyes as he continued to laugh. Shaking his head side to side in disbelief, he quickly felt first the wound on his neck and then the source of the throbbing pain on his head. Blood coated his fingers from the two wounds. After looking them over through blurry eyes, he stuck them in his mouth to suck off the sticky fluid.

"Rosalita, you've grown up," he stated between laughs.

Reaching down, he quickly snatched up one of the spilled corn tortillas that now littered the ground and with two quick bites began chewing, gumming the fire-cooked dough around in his mouth. Rosalita remained vigilant, knife at the ready, should he charge her again.

"Come now. We have places to go." He turned from the village and headed down a ravine, to a waiting Jeep 4x4.

Rosalita watched for a moment or two before scrambling to gather up the rest of the tortillas. Sliding the dagger back into its hiding place, she made her way after Luis. Several minutes later, she caught up to the man who only moments before had tried to kill her. Without saying a word, they made their way the final half mile to the vehicle and climbed into the seats.

"What did you learn?" Luis's hands were on the steering wheel as he surveyed the trail in front of them.

Rosalita remained silent for a moment or two before answering him. "In two weeks, the Americans are coming."

Luis turned the key in the ignition. The Jeep quickly roared to life. He maneuvered the vehicle around a large boulder and headed back down the trail opposite the way it had faced just moments before. He shifted the lever through the gears with expert ease, and the vehicle gained speed as it bounced down the trail.

Luis grew excited. "Two weeks! Two weeks and one of the gringos will be mine!"

For the first time, Rosalita raised her hand up to the throbbing welt on her face. She rubbed it gingerly and checked her fingers for blood. Satisfied there was none, she slouched down into the seat and withdrew into her own dark and gloomy world.

Luis continued to maneuver the vehicle over the rough terrain, back toward their hideout, his own thoughts forming a hideous fantasy of what was soon to come. "Two more weeks!" He was filled with gleeful anticipation.

Chapter 3

Jay gazed out the window as he lifted the handle to the kitchen faucet in the little yellow house he and Anna had called home for the past two years. The house was situated on top of a tree-covered hill on the northeast end of Colorado Springs where he and Anna had just finished up their studies at the missionary school.

The bright colors of the early morning sky were absolutely mesmerizing and were punctuated by the rays of the morning sun as they shone brightly through large raindrops that fell in the east. Several of the drops were landing on the leaves of the massive aspen and oak trees in the front yard where they were hanging suspended above the earth. Brilliant rays of light passed through the clinging drops, causing them to glisten and shine like bright diamond fruit on some new type of exotic tree.

Parts of the western horizon were visible to Jay from his little window, and it stood in complete contradiction to the bright rays of sunshine radiating from somewhere directly behind him.

Nearly charcoal in color, the sky seemed to extend outward to where the land melted into the horizon. Visible was the tail end of a huge thunderstorm, the obvious source of the large raindrops as it receded to the west. Several little nearly white wispy clouds skated across the sky at a much lower altitude and higher speed than the thunderhead. The contrast in size and color to the massive frontal system gave the large storm a three-dimensional appearance.

The nearly black sky was absolutely amazing to Jay. It was the base color of a living canvas on which God used trees, rain, grass, and other living elements to layer the amazing live painting. Rays of the sun shining under the clouds from the east added

24

a color and element of lighting that no artist could ever duplicate. Individual beams of sunlight shining through falling drops of rain caused each drop to shine and glisten like individual missiles of quicksilver falling from the heavens. An occasional flash of lightning could be seen descending out of the dark clouds, which served to heighten the visual effect of the wondrous picture that God was creating. Right at that moment, nothing else existed to Jay but the private show God seemed to be displaying just for him.

Tears filled his eyes and joy filled his soul as he watched the beauty of God's natural artwork unfold and change before his very eyes.

"I wish Anna was awake to see this," he whispered, oblivious to the water rushing out of the kitchen faucet.

"Thank you, God, for the beauty of this moment. It is truly a blessing to me."

The "creak-clunk" of a closing door, followed by the vibrating-piston slamming sounds of galvanized plumbing as it filled with water brought Jay back to the moment. Anna was up and taking her morning shower. Startled back to reality, he filled his glass with water, turned off the kitchen faucet, and paused for a moment longer to soak in the beautiful picture. Finally, tearing himself from the window, he bent to making coffee and a small breakfast of scrambled eggs and toast to share with Anna.

With a large plop, Jay seated himself on the hard wooden kitchen chair, scooted his open Bible across the table, and began to read several verses in the Psalms. Except for the sound of the shower and the gurgling of the coffee pot, quietness filled the house. Every few minutes, a low rumbling of thunder could be heard and sometimes seemed to shake the small house.

At first it was nothing more than a tedious chore, but Jay had come to love his early morning Bible reading and reflection time. It helped him get in a "right frame of mind," as Anna liked to say. He could hardly imagine a day going by without it.

Thoughts of the previous several days' activities ran through his mind. A smile crept across his face as he recalled the proud looks and teary eyes of their parents when he and Anna had walked to the podium to receive their diplomas. Laughing out loud, he could envision his best friend Bill as he stood up and yelled, "Way to go, dog!" much to the surprise and delight of the conservative gathering of people.

Bill's outburst even elicited a small chuckle from Dr. Whitson, dean of theology at the school. Dr. Whitson was a very stoic and conservative professor who seemed to have very little, if any, sense of humor.

Jay and Anna were both pleasantly surprised when Nancy and Bob Johnson, Anna's aunt and uncle from Washington, showed up for the ceremony along with Chet Ingle and his wife, Veronica. The two couples had traveled the long trip together by automobile.

"It gave us a good excuse for a vacation," Chet explained. "Besides, I've always wanted to see some of those air force gliders they use down here in action. For that, the pain of sitting through your graduation ceremony was a small price to pay," he added wryly.

Everyone laughed except Veronica, who smacked Chet on the shoulder.

"You're going to make Jay and Anna think we don't like them."

"Anna already knows we like her," he added with a wink.

Chet and Jay had become acquainted four years earlier when Chet had saved Jay's life after an automobile accident. A strong friendship had developed between the two almost instantly. As soon as Jay had recovered enough from his injuries, Chet made a point of visiting him a couple times a week for an impromptu Bible study.

At first it was nothing more than an annoyance, but Jay endured it just so he could spend time with his new friend and mentor. After a few months, he actually found himself looking forward to the Bible studies. He was amazed at the amount of knowledge and understanding of God's Word he was gaining.

Chet's biggest priorities were to help Jay through his slow rehab and to spur on his personal growth with God. He had grown to look at Jay as a son and found it very difficult emotionally when Jay and Anna had moved away from Pullman, Washington. Leaving Pullman and Chet had been nearly as emotional for Jay. Were it not for Anna, he would never have been able to leave. Life without her was an unimaginable nightmare he dared not visit.

Jay heard the opening of the bathroom door followed by soft footfalls on the old, worn hardwood floor. Affectionately, he arched his back and neck into Anna's embrace as her slender, slightly tanned arms draped over his shoulders from behind. Quickly, he placed a well-aimed kiss on her cheek as her small hands playfully rubbed his chest. Twisting his body in the chair, he turned his head toward her and planted a proper good morning kiss.

"Good morning."

Anna kissed him again. "Good morning, my love. Why are you up so early?"

Jay stood up. "Old habits are hard to break, I guess."

Jay quickly pulled out a chair for Anna and began filling two large cups with steaming coffee. Two spoons of sugar and just enough milk turned the coffee the color of muddy water. A huge smile met Jay as he handed Anna one of the cups.

"Thank you, my love."

"Why, you're mighty welcome."

Leaning down, he gave her another quick kiss before turning his attention to the stove and the waiting scrambled eggs. After a quick stir, four pieces of potato flour bread were fed into a nearby chrome toaster.

Moving back to the eggs, he plated equal portions of the scrambled eggs onto waiting Little Mermaid-theme plates

The Unraveling

before placing them on the table. Turning his attention back to the toaster, he looked down at the bread with impatience. He was annoyed that he always seemed to start the toast either too early or too late to accompany the main course while it was still hot. Impatience finally winning over, he pushed the button and automatically ejected the bread from the toaster. It wasn't quite finished. Shaking his head in frustration, he pushed the lever back to the toast position and waited.

Irritation filled his voice as he turned his attention toward Anna. "This stupid thing. It takes forever and a day."

"It's all right, honey. It'll be done soon."

Jay whined, "I know, but the eggs are getting cold, and no one likes cold eggs."

She added with encouragement, "They'll be just fine. Besides, the toast will be hot."

Jay turned back to the toaster and popped the toast up again.

He gingerly removed the hot toast from the toaster. "Close enough." Moving quickly across the floor, he half juggled, half tossed the toast from one hand to the other before practically throwing it onto a small plate.

Anna grabbed up the toast and slathered a generous portion of butter on Jay's while only placing a little on her own. When she was finished, she extended her arms across the table, palms upward, toward Jay. He returned the gesture, palms down, and took her hands in his own. Anna quickly thanked the Lord for their meal and for their life together and for His continued blessing, followed by a quick amen. Instead of releasing her grip on Jay's hands as usual, Anna continued to hold them until Jay's eyes met her own.

Anna gently squeezed Jay's hands. "I love you so much!"

Looking in her large sparkling eyes, Jay responded by telling Anna, "I love you too." His gaze remained locked onto Anna until she released her grip and picked up her fork. Following suit, Jay picked up a piece of toast with his vacant left hand.

"It's not much, but better than nothing, I suppose." He placed a fork full of egg on the toast before taking a bite.

"It's absolutely wonderful!" Anna exclaimed with mock enthusiasm as she chewed her first bite.

They continued eating their breakfast, Jay ravenously and Anna more daintily as she carefully poked her fork through the rubbery scrambled eggs. The overdone and now cold eggs were less than appetizing, but she cheerfully ate them nonetheless. This had been their morning routine since they had married four years earlier. Even though Anna had never been much of a morning meal person, nor Jay much of a cook, the look of enthusiasm and joy on his face each and every morning was too great a reward to tell him any different. Thus their first tradition was born.

After breakfast, Jay poured them both another cup of coffee and doctored it up just the way they liked it.

Sitting across from each other, they reminisced about the previous evening's events as they enjoyed their coffee. Neither could believe how fast the past two years had flown by, let alone the four they'd been married. Excitement and apprehension filled them as they wondered what their future would hold. The fact that they would be leaving in a couple days for the mission fields in Mexico was extremely exciting to Anna but just the opposite for Jay. His mind was filled with apprehension and fear most of the time. Praying with Anna for courage and peace, his fears had subsided somewhat. Still, the thought of going to a foreign country, speaking a foreign language, and learning to live among a different ethnic group created a fear that was proving very hard to overcome. Voicing his fears and concerns about their upcoming deployment to the mission field to Anna was quickly becoming a morning tradition for Jay.

Anna had repeatedly told Jay, "Look at it as an adventure."

"An adventure to me is driving across town during rush hour."

The Unraveling 29

"Just remember, we're going out of obedience to God, and in return He has promised to bless us. Besides, we'll be together the whole time."

"I know. I keep reminding myself of that every day, but for some reason I have an extremely uneasy feeling about all of this."

Anna teased Jay, "Honey, you have an uneasy feeling about everything."

Frowning dejectedly, he slowly and deliberately began his last hope of an unarguable fact.

"Yeah, but remember what Doctor Philmore said about abductions and kidnappings in the region?" Jay paused to let this terrible bit of information sink in. "Numerous people have either been killed or simply never found."

Anna smiled as she reached across the table to his fidgeting hands.

"Honey, they have to tell us anything and everything that could happen," she stated in her most soothing voice. "Besides, he also said our compound had never seen even a single incident," she answered almost defensively.

Jay gloomily retorted, "Yeah, well, the odds have to catch up some day."

Anna smiled at Jay as he pouted. For several moments neither person said a word as they drank their coffee in silence.

A giant rumbling precipitated a house-jarring shaking that lasted for several seconds as a new storm made its presence felt.

A look of fear and concern spread across Anna's face. "Ooh thunder!"

"I know, isn't it great?!"

Excitement filled his eyes, reminiscent of those of a small child's as they eagerly scanned the presents under a Christmas tree on Christmas morning.

Anna shuddered in synchronicity to another large clap of thunder. "To you it is, but not to me!"

Tears of joy filled her eyes as she watched Jay peering eagerly out the kitchen window and up into the turbulent skies over Colorado Springs. Every day she thanked God for bringing him into her life. His love and devotion to her was more than she ever imagined possible. It had been a joy to witness firsthand the changes God had made in Jay's life the past several years. More exciting yet was the realization that like herself, Jay too was now a missionary dedicated to furthering the work of God's kingdom.

"Lightning," he stated matter-of-factly to himself as much as to Anna as a large flash lit up the landscape. "Another one! Ooh that was a good one!"

Pullman, Washington, had its fair share of thunderstorms, but nothing in comparison to Colorado Springs, one of the most active areas in the United States for thunderstorms and lightning strikes.

Anna walked across the floor and grabbed Jay by the hand.

"We have nothing to do all day until our dinner at church this evening." She tugged on his hand. Jay continued watching out the kitchen window with anticipation.

"What do you want to do?" he asked halfheartedly without turning his head, content to watch the storm.

Anna continued to tug playfully on his hand. She teased, "I'm going back to bed. You could always join me, unless that thunderstorm is more interesting," while rubbing her hand up and down his arm.

Anna turned, Jay's hand in hers, and started down the hallway toward their bedroom. Jay's eyes lit up, and he smiled as he turned from the window and obediently followed her down the hall and into their room.

"If you insist," he said, entering the room and closing the door while fear and unease over their immediate future nagged away at the back of his mind.

The Unraveling   31

Chapter 4

The turbulent sky of the morning had given way to a brilliant blue "skyscape" dotted with cotton ball-shaped clouds, stragglers from the morning thunderstorms. The clouds were little puffs of color that scooted across the horizon, each one seemingly a different color, varying from brilliant white to charcoal gray and every color in between. Dozens of thin, white lines streaked across the sky from north to south, residual effects of fighter planes making training flights from nearby Peterson Air Force Base to destinations unknown.

A crescendo of voices could be heard from a nearby, meticulously groomed grass field where children were busy playing the games that children play. The field sat adjacent to a small, well-kept red brick building trimmed in lima bean green. Taupe-colored steel ribbed roofing completed a picture-perfect southwestern Hacienda.

Four older sedan-style cars were parked, one in each corner of a large gravel parking lot that lay directly in front of the small brick building. Each car had a thin, white string attached to its rear bumper that ascended up into the sky. Attached to the end of each string was a large, multicolored kite that swayed back and forth in a synchronized, rhythmic dance set to the music of the gusting winds.

Two well-dressed young men of Spanish descent were standing on stepladders, one on each side of the entryway to the brick building. Each was gripping a rope that was attached to a large white banner with large black lettering that read: "Congratulations, Jay and Anne."

An older man dressed in a light tan cotton suit stood in front of the banner and directed the two young men to move the large banner first this way and then that. Seemingly satisfied, he ordered the young men to tie the banner off to the large posts of a portico roof covering the entryway. He, too, was of Spanish descent.

Several vehicles of different makes and models, vintage and condition began arriving in an almost steady stream until the large gravel parking lot was nearly full. Each car was seemingly full to capacity of smartly dressed, upbeat and festive families bearing food and small gifts for the special occasion.

Jay and Anna were nearly the last to arrive as usual and had to park on the street next to the sidewalk across the busy road from the church. Looking both ways, they quickly navigated the busy highway and headed toward the small building full of waiting people. Amazement spread across Jay's face as he turned to Anna.

A chuckle escaped Jay's lips. "Can you believe all of this?"

Eyes wide and shining, she surveyed the kites and decorations the people had put up for them. Smiling broadly, tears filled her eyes as she took in the whole scene.

"Unbelievable," was all she could manage, followed by a giggle of her own.

She couldn't remember ever seeing the parking lot so full of cars. Joy and appreciation surged inside of her as they made their way to the little building.

Anna prayed silently, "Thank you, Lord, for the many blessing you have and are bestowing on our lives."

A loud clamoring of voices could be heard as the double doors to the church burst open, allowing a horde of well-dressed young boys and girls to descend upon Jay and Anna.

"Miss Anna, Miss Anna!" the children proclaimed excitedly. Their voices rose in pitch as excitement continued to build. The throng of children circled around Anna and Jay, stopping them several yards short of the church. A steady, shrill stream of both

The Unraveling

English and Spanish chatter filled their ears as the children continued to mob the honored guests. Responding with hugs, Anna greeted every child she could reach with unbridled enthusiasm.

A half grin complemented an amused and bewildered look on Jay's tanned face.

Jay surveyed the children mobbing Anna. "I can't believe it! Every time! It never fails!"

After dozens of hugs, Anna was free from the throng. For several moments she stood, smiling, as she joyfully watched the children scurry back and forth at play. Already, the departed throng was being replaced by a group of adoring adults, each eager to give them a hug, kiss on the cheek, or clap on the back. Many greeted them in broken, heavily accented English, but a large majority greeted them in their native Spanish. This made it extremely difficult for Jay to follow, so he mostly smiled and nodded his head whenever someone spoke to him.

Anna seemed unfazed by the mixing of the two languages, however, as she conversed with each and every person in Spanish, regardless of which of the two languages they addressed her in. Her mastery of both languages absolutely amazed Jay. He still struggled with the very basics of the Spanish language after more than three years of studies, barely able to labor through the simplest of conversations. It had been a nightmare for him when they first started to attend the little, Hispanic church shortly after their arrival at Colorado Springs. Surprisingly, the communication gap had barely gotten any better over time. He shuddered every time he remembered their first visit to the church…

～ ～ ～ ～

As they approached the church for the first time, Anna repeatedly exclaimed, "It's close to home, and besides, we can polish up our Spanish before we head to the mission field."

"How can we polish up on Spanish if we can't even speak Spanish?" he countered.

It mattered not the amount of his protests; her mind was made up and that was all there was to it. At first, their unannounced and uninvited attendance at the church was met with cold, suspicious stares as the congregation strained to see this foreign couple in their midst. Compounding their discomfort, the only empty pews in the plain, almost drab sanctuary seemed to be up at the very front. Undaunted by the collective, unfriendly gazes, Anna took Jay by the hand and with the most gregarious smile she could muster began the seemingly endless walk to the front of the church. Discomfort growing with each step, a very self-conscious Jay obediently followed, slumped shoulders, eyes directly on the floor in front of him like an obedient puppy that had just received a healthy dose of punishment from its master.

Shortly after they were seated on the cold, hard, wooden pews, a smallish, middle-aged Hispanic man walked to the podium and began speaking in Spanish while gesturing toward Jay and Anna. Anna smiled and nudged Jay with her right elbow as she waved to the congregation with her left hand in an attempt to get him to emulate her. Standing up, she pulled a very reluctant and disgruntled Jay with her as she turned to the congregation and introduced themselves in Spanish.

Whatever she said must have been funny, because the congregation started to laugh and clap as the pastor began to speak again. It was obvious to Jay that the pastor was welcoming them, but the speed with which he spoke made it impossible for him to understand even a single word. He strained, hoping to hear something, anything that he might recognize. The pastor may as well have been speaking Martian as far as Jay was concerned. On the other hand, Anna seemed to fully understand what was being said, even answering the pastor on more than one occasion.

Jay was shocked and nearly horrified when the congregation, after a quick prayer by the pastor, rushed to the pew he and Anna were sitting in and began hugging and speaking to them in Spanish. Anna smiled and joyfully spoke to each and

The Unraveling   35

every person as they received their hugs. Jay on the other hand, just smiled and nodded, unsure what anyone was saying to him. Several small children gathered in front of Jay and Anna and nervously pointed and laughed at Jay and his inability to communicate until a couple of embarrassed mothers shooed them off toward the back of the church, where they continued their laughing and pointing.

To Jay, the spontaneous greeting time went on for what seemed like an eternity, but was in fact only a few minutes before the congregation made their way back to their pews as the pastor began the service in earnest. Jay felt lost as the service proceeded. Every aspect was foreign to him. Some of the music sounded familiar as the congregation sang hymns, but he couldn't understand any of the words and didn't recognize the music well enough to determine which hymns they were.

The pastor was very animated as he delivered his sermon. He caused Jay to jump with a start on more than one occasion as he slammed the palm of his hand onto the pulpit, emphatically driving home whatever point he was trying to make with all the skill of any Southern revival evangelist. The congregation was very attentive and emotional. They participated with what Jay decided were lively "amens" throughout the service. Several responded to an altar call at the benediction, most with tears streaming down their faces.

Their departure from the church after the service was worse than their entrance. Several different families approached them in greeting, some even extending a lunch invitation. Jay was lost. He felt claustrophobic as more and more people surrounded them.

Anna, on the other hand, seemed to really be enjoying herself. Conversing in Spanish with ease, she seemed to be talking just as fast as their new friends. Much to Jay's dismay, Anna accepted a lunch invitation extended to them from the pastor and several other families. They decided to eat right there in the church fellowship hall and quickly took up seats at several long folding tables, while several of the women rushed to retrieve their Sunday dinners, which were waiting for their families at home.

Jay watched Anna in amazement as she continued her lively conversation with the others. He was startled and surprised, pleasantly so, when the pastor sat down across from him and began speaking in English, "Kind of overwhelmed, Señor Jay?"

"Yeah, you could say that." Jay was relieved that he could actually understand someone.

"About half of my people can speak English rather well," the pastor added. "They are self-conscious, but their English is getting better all the time." Jay nodded, unsure what else to say.

"You are welcome here. My people are very happy to have you. We are all excited to hear that you and Anna will be soon going to Mexico to spread God's Word. There is much need there."

Jay nodded in external agreement, a forced smile on his face, while a turbulent storm of doubt, fear, and apprehension gnawed away and grew on the inside, as it did each time he was reminded of their future path.

Jay countered, "Well, it'll still be a couple years, at least, before we go anywhere."

"Oh, those few years will go by faster than you can imagine. Time will absolutely fly by. You'll see," the pastor encouraged.

Jay nodded with artificial enthusiasm as he muttered a reply, hoping the conversation would head in a different direction. One thing he didn't want or need was to be reminded constantly of what his future held. Anna already reminded him of that daily, it seemed.

〰 〰 〰 〰

Over the past couple of years, her excitement and passion seemed to grow with the passing of each minute, while his seemed to diminish. It seemed to Jay that going on the mission was all Anna talked about. She was so positive and excited all the time, and so exuberant, that even his constant grumbling and objections did little to bring her down. Occasionally, when his objec-

The Unraveling

tions became overly strong, bordering on obnoxious, Anna would comment about his "attitude."

She would say quietly, "I just don't see how you can be so negative all the time." Her face would be a barometer of the hurt his words were causing. "You told me you felt called to this ministry, but you sure are being negative about it."

The words were true, and Jay knew it. In no way was he acting obedient to God's will for his life. It wasn't that he didn't want to; he was just scared to let go, to let God direct their life together. Quite simply, he just couldn't bring himself to trust God fully. His constant grumbling and disobedience threatened to drive a wedge between him and Anna.

Fortunately for him, Anna was extremely patient and forgiving. She knew God's will and recognized Jay's disobedience. Choosing to be positive instead of confrontational, Anna encouraged Jay constantly, seldom saying a negative word that might cause conflict between them. Unbeknownst to Jay, Anna lifted him in prayer all day, every day. She knew that God would answer her prayers and that eventually Jay's heart would be softened.

Whenever discouragement crept in, she reminded herself, "In God's time, not mine..." In time, Jay began to keep his fears and doubts to himself. The last thing he wanted was to drive a wedge between him and Anna. Slowly, a small part of himself withdrew into a dark, well-guarded compartment deep in his soul—an area of unrest, resentment, and building tension.

∽ ∽ ∽ ∽

Jay shook his head again in disbelief. The time had finally come, and here they were at a going-away party in a church that had fully accepted them as one of their own. They made their way through the throng and into the small church. There were people everywhere waiting to greet the young couple as they were led to the fellowship hall and kitchen. Jay smiled as he read several of the large banners on the walls, most of them written in Spanish, congratulating the two of them. His eyes scanned the room and came to rest on a large table in the center that was nearly over-flowing with smartly wrapped and ribbon-covered packages, presents for him and Anna. A couple of teenagers were hanging around the table, moving the presents around in an attempt to identify whatever prize waited inside.

They had felt several of the packages before an elderly grand-mother weighing no more than eighty pounds dripping wet and four and a half feet in height, with weather-wrinkled brown skin, gray hair, and a toothless frown spied them from the kitchen. She rushed toward them waving a wooden spoon while letting loose a rapid-fire string of Spanish that Jay couldn't understand. In spite of her small stature, whatever she said was effective as the youngsters turned and fled to the far end of the room as fast as they could while the elderly grandmother marched around the table, wooden spoon raised in defense of the island of goodies. She continued her vigilant stand for several more moments as she scanned the room, daring anyone to come near the precious cargo she was guarding. Satisfied that all was safe, she turned and slowly made her way back to the kitchen and waiting pot where she resumed stirring whatever was inside.

Overwhelmed with emotion, Anna grabbed Jay by the hand and half dragged and half pulled him from first one brightly colored banner to the next, until every single decoration and ban-ner had been visited. Several of the people along the way took the opportunity to hug and take pictures with the two of them as they made their way around the crowded little room. Jay couldn't help but smile as their tour stopped directly in front of the table bearing all of the gifts.

"Just look at all of this! I can't believe there is so much stuff. Why, there are more gifts here than we had at our wedding."

Anna smiled as she surveyed all of the bright packages piled high on the table. She was speechless as she stood there, shaking her head in disbelief.

The two of them jumped a little as Pastor Fillipe tapped a fork against a glass in an attempt to get everyone's attention. Speaking very rapidly in Spanish, he welcomed everyone to Jay and Anna's going-away fiesta. Everyone clapped and roared their approval for several moments before turning their attention back to the pastor. Once the room was quiet, Pastor Fellipe blessed the food before directing Jay and Anna to the front of the line. He then instructed someone near the door to bring in all of the children for dinner. It was a festive and lively celebration. The noise level increased as everyone raised their voices in an attempt to be heard, one above the other.

Laid out on two tables covered with red and yellow tableclothes was enough food to feed two or three times as many people as were present. Food prepared by hand and with Spanish influence was the predominant theme, although there was a basket of fried chicken from a deli just down the road. Jay and Anna were at the front of the very impatient line of people as they began moving parallel to the table of food.

The colors and aroma of the food always enticed Jay to take more than he should, resulting in a filled plate before he was even halfway through the line. Being much more conservative, Anna took tiny portions and a lot more variety. They made their way to a couple of waiting chairs at a table decorated in their honor. Someone brought them glasses filled with green punch that had lime ice cream islands floating around on the top. Recognizing the punch, Jay took a large gulp before turning his attention to the food on his plate. Although he was unable to name most of the dishes, every one of them was extremely delicious.

The line through the buffet moved along quickly, and before long everyone was sitting at a table and eating their dinner. Almost everyone made a second trip through the line, and a few even went back for a third helping, including Jay. Feeling stuffed, he leaned back in his chair and took several long, deep breaths and placed his hands behind his head.

He asked Anna, "Why did you let me eat so much?" as he continued to maneuver his body around in an attempt to gain some room for his stomach to expand. Anna had only gone through once and hadn't even eaten everything on her plate. Never a big eater, even the temptation of a large buffet no more than a few feet away failed to entice her.

Anna chided, "Well, you silly! You do this every time we have a potluck. You didn't even save room for dessert."

He rubbed his protruding belly. "Oh, there's always room for dessert, especially if it's ice cream. Ice cream just fills in all the cracks, no problem."

People had begun milling around the room, visiting with one another. Several people approached Jay and Anna to take their picture or have a picture taken with the two. Everyone was polite, and all seemed sincerely sad knowing that the two of them would be leaving very soon. It was a bittersweet moment for Anna and a dreadful moment for Jay. Both realized that this going-away party signified both an end to a chapter in their lives and also a new beginning. A new beginning filled with hope and excitement for one, fear and dread for the other.

A couple of ladies moved to the center of the room. Both were in their middle forties, and both had several children in the church. Aracelis was a rather large woman and had known Anna the longest. Rachelle was much shorter and petite and had only begun attending the church four months earlier. She had met Anna at a homeless shelter where she, her husband, and four children lived. They had entered the United States through a works program but had been unable to find a home or apartment to rent.

Neither Rachelle nor her husband, Riccardo, knew very much English. They loved being in the United States but found the language barrier intimidating. Upon hearing of their plight, Anna introduced herself to the family and helped find them an apartment on the outskirts of Colorado Springs. They were forever grateful for the help and kindness she had shown them, so when Anna invited them to attend her little church, they eagerly accepted, even though they both had a Roman Catholic background. Amazed at how quickly they were accepted by the congregation, the family had attended faithfully every time the church doors were open.

Aracelis addressed the crowd of people, "Ahem, excuse me please! Excuse me!" She repeated herself several times until everyone in the room was quiet with their attention focused on the two ladies.

"This is Jay and Miss Anna's party, and we have several presents for the two of them." She gestured toward Jay and Anna. "We just want you to know how much we love you and are going to miss you! You will always be a part of our family, and you will always be in our prayers." She paused as the room erupted in applause for what seemed like several minutes.

"Now it's time for you to open your gifts!" Rachelle walked over and grabbed Jay and Anna by the hand and led them to the table with all the gifts. Sitting in chairs that had been placed there just for them, they timidly began opening the presents one by one. Brightly colored hand-knitted blankets and homemade quilts dominated the gifts given to them by the congregation, bounty that would come in handy for them once they were relocated in Mexico.

Collective "oohs and aahhs" echoed in the room as the bright wrapping paper was ripped away from each present, revealing the prize inside. One of the last gifts they opened was a large photo album that had been decorated inside and out and was filled with pictures of Jay and Anna and many of the people in their church family as they worshiped and fellowshipped together over the past three years. When the last gift had been opened, Anna stood with emotion choking her voice and thanked everyone present for their kindness and thoughtfulness. "Jay and I will cherish these gifts from the heart forever!" she said as the people stood and clapped.

When the clapping had subsided, Aracelis returned to the table of gifts and turned to Jay and Anna. "We are not yet done here. We have one more gift for each of you. First, for you, Señor Jay, we have this gift that will hopefully touch your heart. I know it will touch your stomach!" Aracelis turned and motioned toward the kitchen as three teenagers worked their way toward Jay and Anna. They were gingerly carrying a large cake, larger than any single cake Jay had ever seen before. It was a square design and had been decorated in the shape of an open Bible. Someone had even inscribed the Psalm 23 with black frosting. It was magnificent to look at.

"It's an ice cream cake. We all know how much you love ice cream," Aracelis told an astonished Jay as he made his way over to the cake. He was amazed at how intricate the lettering was. Someone with a very steady hand had gone to a lot of work.

"Thank you so much!" Jay smiled brightly. "I don't think I'll ever be able to eat all of it, though." He smiled again and winked.

The room erupted in laughter as Jay grabbed a serving spoon from the food table and feigned taking a large bite. Someone yelled from the crowd, "You have a big enough mouth to fit that spoon!"

Aracelis added sarcastically. "We were hoping that maybe you would want to share it. That is, if you think there's enough."

Jay deadpanned back, "I think there might just be enough… maybe…"

One of the women in the crowd walked up and handed Aracelis a brightly wrapped package. Aracelis turned and raised the package toward the crowd. "And now, we have this last gift for you, Miss Anna." She turned and handed Anna the package. "It is a gift made from our hands but full of our hearts! We love you and cherish you and hope that whenever you wear this, you will remember us."

The Unraveling

Anna gingerly received the package. Turning it over and over in her hands, she marveled at the beauty of the homemade wrapping paper that had been decorated with vibrant purples, blues, yellows, and reds. It was almost too pretty to open.

"Open it! Hurry…open it," a voice pleaded from the crowd.

"I don't want to rip the paper." Anna gingerly loosened the scotch tape. "I'm going to save this paper forever." Anna slowly worked on the package. Bit by bit the tape was removed and paper pulled back until the prize inside was exposed for all to see.

Gingerly, Anna removed her present from the paper. In her hands, she held a beautiful hand-woven dress made of the finest Alpaca wool available. It was softer than any wool she'd ever felt before. Anna was amazed at the craftsmanship and skill that had gone into the beautiful garment. More amazing still were the hand-dyed colors. It had horizontal lines varying in size and color. The colors of the lines alternated between dark purple and a light violet. It was breathtaking.

"I don't know what to say. It's absolutely beautiful." Tears filled her eyes. "I'll definitely cherish this forever!" She clutched the dress to her body. "It's so beautiful and soft."

Several of the women came forward to admire the new dress. Aracelis shared with Anna how the dress had been hand woven and that the darkest purple on the dress was called periwinkle. The dye that had been used came from sea snails found only off the coast of Mexico. She continued to explain that the Mexican people held that color in high regard, only wearing it for extremely special occasions and that most Mexican people would never have anything this fine their entire lives. Anna was nearly overcome with emotion. She had no idea the length of time it had taken to hand make a garment this fine but knew it had to be substantial. She quickly gave Aracelis and anyone else within reach a hug.

"Any clothing with this color is believed to bring safety and good will to all who wear it. Wear it with confidence and with the

Love of God and nothing will ever harm you!" she added with a laugh.

Anna replied, "I'll wear it with pride and cherish it forever."

Jay replied impatiently, "I think we should all have ice cream, err, cake! You know, before it melts away."

"I think you're right." Aracelis made her way to the table and began cutting the cake and placing the pieces on little paper plates. Everyone made their way toward the dessert table and waited patiently for their piece of Jay's ice cream cake.

The remainder of the evening went quickly. Jay and Anna visited with all of the people for several hours until the crowd thinned. Several of the teenage boys helped carry their presents to Jay and Anna's car. Jay and Anna gave hugs to the remaining people as they headed out the door. A new life awaited them. A life filled with adventure.

Chapter 5

Bright afternoon sunrays became distorted splotches of light as they shone through the leaves of the giant oak rising up directly in front of the house. Each splotch glinted brightly across the dull-silver colored threshold separating inside from out. A six-paneled door stood open to the outside world, allowing the sunlight to reflect onto the floor just inside the doorway. A warm, gentle wind rippled the leaves of the oak, bringing the splotches to life as they moved in tandem with the breeze, back and forth across the bright metal.

In the middle of the threshold, as if on the center of a stage, a reddish-orange lady bug with small black spots made its way back and forth across the metal, inside to out and then back again. Back and forth it went across the three-foot opening, one side to the other, never in a direct line, its movements mimicked a blood hound hot on a scent.

Just when it appeared to have made up its mind to go either inside or out, even advancing down onto first the linoleum with its front feet before retreating to the opposite side and waiting concrete slab, it would stop dead in its tracks as if its back feet could advance no farther. Intent on breaching an invisible barrier, the tiny bug would rise up on its spindly hind legs and flail at the air with its front legs as if it were pawing at an invisible foe.

The ensuing battle raged on for several minutes until the little bug halted in the middle of the threshold, appeared to shudder just long enough for the reddish orange shell with small black spots to separate, revealing small translucent wings that extended out from under the shell. Defying gravity, and in spite of its lack of aerodynamic design, the small wings sprung to action and the little round bug achieved lift-off, rising several feet off the ground, where it hovered for a moment or two before speeding off through the thin, mile-high air for destinations unknown.

Less a result of fascination and more sheer boredom, Jay watched from his vantage point on a small fold-up metal chair just inside the front door until the little bug disappeared from view. There was nothing better to do with his time, and he had nowhere else to go. The rest of the house he and Anna had called home for a little over two years was now empty except for Jay and his small chair. Everything else was gone, given to friends from their church. What was left of their worldly possessions was contained in several large black suitcases and a few blue, Rubbermaid totes with taped-on lids, which were sitting on the sidewalk just outside the front door.

Placing his head in his hands, Jay could scarcely believe it had come to this, nearly penniless with little worldly possessions. He had argued with Anna to no avail that they should keep at least part of their belongings in storage for whenever they returned home from the mission field.

She kept telling him over and over, "God will provide all we need, now and in the future. Besides, we can't afford the storage payment anyway." This ended all argument from Jay. It wasn't that he really wanted the few items they had and would not be taking with them. It was the finality of the commitment they had made to God many years before. With their possessions gone, the next phase of their new life had begun.

Jay ran his skinny fingers through his shiny black hair. Glancing through the open doorway, he watched and waited as Anna made her way back from the curb and the waiting maroon-colored Chrysler mini van. The rusted top of the vehicle was adorned with a white and black checkered neon sign on top. The sign read TAXI and flickered on and off, a testament to faulty wiring connections.

A short, middle-aged man with a portly belly hanging over his belt followed Anna. His hair, what little he had, was dark and greasy and was combed over the large bald expanse that made up the top of his head. A scowl adorned his pockmarked face. Jay couldn't help but notice how round the man's head was, almost bowling ball round. Beady black eyes darted back and forth nervously as he sized up the luggage and containers waiting to be loaded.

His fat, greasy fingers pulled at his multicolored, striped T-shirt in an attempt to cover his protruding belly. "Shall I get these for you, miss?"

Turning back to the man, Anna smiled brightly. "Anna! You can call me Anna, and this is my husband, Jay."

The man blushed, a wide smile breaking out on his face revealing dark, tobacco-stained teeth and two gold crowns. "Well, um, Anna, would you like me to load these for you?" he asked before casting a nervous glance at the despondent Jay.

Punctuating her statement with her ever-ready smile, Anna replied, "That would be great, Leo! Thank you so much!"

Unused to being treated so nicely, Leo smiled again and quickly grabbed up the waiting luggage, turned, and headed toward the van with his heavy cargo.

Turning to Jay, Anna smiled and threw up her hands. "Well, honey, it's that time! Are you going to help me with these containers or just sit there?"

Jay had been sulking all morning, his mood souring with the passing of every hour. Slowly tipping the metal chair back onto all four legs, Jay pulled himself up in a slow, meticulous manner as his body continued its semiprotest over the turn of events. His gray eyes were constricted in a glare, and the corners of his mouth turned down ever so slightly, revealing his ever-souring mood.

"Come on, grumpy, it's going to be fun! A life adventure! Just think of the memories we'll make and the lives we will affect!"

Jay nodded unconvincingly as he made his way over to one of the totes. Without saying a word, he bent down, grabbed the sides of the container, and lifted it to his shoulder.

"It's not that bad, Jay! We'll be together the whole time!" Anna reminded him as she affectionately rubbed his back.

Jay shrugged as he struggled toward the van. He wasn't going to say anything to Anna. She had been patronizing him all morning, and he wasn't going to give in to her charm now just to make her feel better. *Let her stew awhile,* he thought as he reached the van and clumsily placed the container in the back. He knew he was being silly, didn't even really know what he was pouting about, but somehow it made him feel a little more in charge of what was going on in their life.

"Well, that's everything," Leo stated through labored breathing as he placed the last blue container roughly in the back of the van.

"Thank you so much, Leo! What would we ever do without you?"

Leo smiled once again. "Well, we better head out if we hope to beat the traffic. We got about twenty miles or so to the airport, and if we leave right now I think I can get you all there with a little time to spare." Leo added with growing confidence.

Opening the door for Anna, Jay mumbled, "Take all the time you can," before sliding in beside her.

Leo got in the front and headed off down the road toward the airport. Jay turned in his seat and watched with a lump in his throat as the little yellow house he and Anna had called home quickly disappeared from view. Sensing his distress, Anna grabbed Jay's hand and squeezed it tightly in her own. Although Jay enjoyed the affectionate attention, her warm touch did little to raise his spirits.

Looking out the side window of the van, Jay continued to watch all of the familiar landscapes come and go as the van

The Unraveling   49

sped on toward the airport and the new life waiting for the two of them.

Unused to passengers taking even the slightest interest in him, Leo continued to talk as if they were long lost friends. Anna's friendly dialogue only fed his desire to visit all the more. Much to Jay's annoyance, it wasn't long until Leo was telling them his whole life's story. Anna didn't help matters any as she continued to both answer Leo's questions and retort with sincere questions of her own. Real concern and empathy were gaining her insight into the lonely life this man led. Before they were halfway to the airport, Anna was witnessing to her new friend and even took a moment to pray for his ailing wife. Under normal circumstances, Jay would have been watching Anna's witness with amazement and pride, but not this day. Nothing but fear and longing filled his senses.

What if something bad happens to us? To Anna? What would I do? How would I ever survive?

These thoughts cycled themselves over and over through his mind as they drew ever closer to the airport and their destiny with the unknown.

Leo wheeled up directly in front of the airline curbside check station. "Well, here ya go! Told ya I'd get ya here, and with time to spare!"

Opening his door and exiting the cab in one fluid motion, Leo practically ran to the rear of the van and began unloading the luggage. Anna's eyes sparkled with excitement as she joined Leo on the sidewalk. "You are so helpful! We are absolutely blessed to have gotten you today!" she exclaimed as an unencumbered grin broke out on Leo's face.

"Here, this is the pastor's number at the church I was telling you about! You get hold of him right away. You and your wife need people that care about you. I'll let him know you'll be calling."

People rushed by back and forth, either coming or going. Leo seemed unaware as his face turned red and tears filled his eyes. Anna took his hand, asked him if she could pray for him, and began without waiting for an answer. Squeezing his hands as she finished her prayer, Anna asked, "How much do we owe you?"

"You don't owe a cent! This ride is on the house." Leo held up his hands in protest as he moved to the front of the van. "You guys take care!" Leo jumped in the van, turned on his taxi sign, and headed off down the road.

Anna waved to the shrinking van before turning to Jay. "Well, we'd better get these bags checked and go find our plane!"

The enthusiastic tone of her voice only added to Jay's souring mood. *How can she be so happy? Doesn't she realize what we are leaving behind?* With the help of a concierge, Jay slid the bags to a waiting check station and collected a baggage claim ticket for each.

"Well, I guess that's that," he exclaimed as he handed Anna the tickets. "It's still not too late to turn back, though," he half pleaded.

"Don't be silly. The adventure has just begun!" Anna retorted, unaware how prophetic her words would prove to be.

Chapter 6

The large plane circled out over the Gulf of Mexico. Large thunderheads were rising up far to the south as far as Jay could see. Ripples on the water could be seen, even from more than fifteen thousand feet. Jay was amazed at all the ships, boats, and oil platforms visible from his vantage point. Even more amazing was the edge of the gray smog bank rising up from the city of Houston. It extended out into the gulf about a mile from the shoreline.

Peering through the thick layer gave the water an uninviting dirty brown appearance, while just outside the acrid cloud the water was emerald blue and enticing. The difference was stark and appalling. Never in his life had he imagined smog so thick and filthy could ever be witnessed in his own country. It was definitely an eye opener.

As the plane banked away from the water and back over the city, Jay's heart rate quickened. Even though they would not be departing the plane, just knowing they were going to land one last time in the United States before heading south of the border raised his spirits. It was silly, he knew, but somehow landing gave him a false hope that they still had more than one option ahead of them.

Squeezing his hand slightly, Anna leaned over and gave Jay a quick kiss on his cheek and whispered in his ear, "Almost there." Try as he might, Jay couldn't stay angry at her. She was his whole world.

"Almost to Houston?" he asked hopefully.

"No silly, almost to Mexico!"

Jay's eyes fell to the floor as an emotional lump filled his throat once again. Beads of sweat broke out on his forehead and his stomach began to churn, either from the motion of the airplane, the sudden drop in elevation, or the finality of their immediate future. Maybe a combination of all three.

Slowly the plane leveled out and began an even more rapid descent. A stewardess made a quick trip through the cabin, reminding everyone to raise their drop-down trays back to their locked position.

Closing his eyes tightly, Jay sat back firmly in his seat. This was the part he hated most—the hard landing. Not an experienced flyer, he wondered how so many people seemed to be at complete ease during this part of flight. Here they were, hundreds of people flying through the air in a vehicle—a missile, even—traveling several hundred miles per hour toward the earth with many, many gallons of jet fuel on board. That realization only added to his fear.

I can't believe some states are actually passing laws making it mandatory to wear bike helmets while riding a bicycle, yet in an airplane all we have for safety is a little seatbelt strap, a floating seat back, and drop-down oxygen mask. Some help that would be in an emergency.

Distinct mechanical whining followed by several clunking noises, which could be felt as well as heard, indicated the landing gear was down and locked into place. *It won't be long now.*

With whitened knuckles, Jay continued to grip Anna's hands tightly. If his grip was painful, she never once let on. Feeling sick to his stomach, Jay's whole body tensed up as the wheels on the plane made contact with the concrete tarmac.

The large bird bounced back up into the air a couple feet before settling down on the three small wheels bearing the jet's entire weight as it cruised down the runway at more than a hundred miles per hour. Opening his eyelids slightly, Jay peered out the small side window at the landscape speeding by.

Quickly, the jet decelerated as its brake flaps extended up out of the wings. It was impressive how quickly the big machine

The Unraveling

slowed down. Slowly, his body relaxed, including his hand as he realized just how tightly he was gripping Anna. Sweat glistened on his palms, and he could feel the clamminess as he rubbed them briskly together.

Anna asked quietly, "Feel better?"

Nodding his head, Jay indicated he did.

"That's good, silly head," Anna teased as she playfully rubbed his dark hair.

Jay didn't respond but instead kept his eyes locked intently on the fast-approaching airport. Bright sunlight reflected from the large pane glass windows of the approaching terminals caused his steel gray eyes to draw down into a squint.

Planes of all sizes could be seen as they either approached or began their departure from the airport. Men with orange flags seemed to be scurrying about in chaotic pandemonium as they waved their flags back and forth or up and down in some sort of language that none but the giant planes could understand.

Anna attempted to get Jay to respond to her. "See? That wasn't bad at all."

A shrug of the shoulders was all the response she could get.

Long walkways extended from the airport out to the waiting tarmac and the arriving planes. "Dry docks waiting for an air ship to connect with," Jay told Anna as they both peered out the window.

A final thud could be felt as well as heard as the plane made connection. People began rising out of their seats and grabbing luggage from the overhead storage compartments in anticipation of departing the plane. Jay watched in amusement at the people as they waited impatiently for the stewardess to open the front doors to the plane to allow them to get off. Most of the passengers stood, bent over at the waist at a forty-five degree angle to keep from banging their heads on the storage bins above. They looked as if they were holding a choreographed position for a musical. Jay couldn't help but notice the impatient frowns that adorned most of the passengers' faces. *Maybe they're going on a mission too!*

A smile broke out on his face at the thought. The first real smile in a long time.

The collective mass of people began to move ever so slowly as the door to the plane was finally opened. Like cattle in a chute, the people began to move forward one at a time until all that were going to had deboarded the plane.

"I think we should get off, even for just a little while," Jay pleaded with Anna. "We could get a Big Mac or something. We have time."

"We don't have time, silly. Besides, we just ate about two hours ago."

"I know, but I'm kind of hungry, and this could be our last chance for a long time. If you don't want a hamburger, we could get some ice cream or something,"

"Jay, we only have fifteen or twenty minutes before the plane departs. Not nearly enough time to navigate a busy airport."

Shoulders sagging, Jay hung his head in defeat. Anna watched for a moment or two, unsure what she could say or do to make him feel any better. Never had she seen him so despondent in all the years she had known him.

"Jay, what's the matter? Why are you acting this way?"

Anna's words brought an immediate irritation to Jay's voice.

"Acting which way? Just because I want some ice cream or a Big Mac, you think something is wrong?"

"That's not what I'm talking about at all!"

Jay continued to sulk. He didn't want to have this conversation and especially didn't like Anna questioning him. Even though he knew he was being silly, he couldn't help himself, not that he wanted to. Sitting back hard in his seat and crossing his arms in defiance across his chest, Jay screwed on the best pouting look he could muster and replied smugly, "I don't know what you're talking about!"

The Unraveling

Anna replied quietly, "I'm talking about you sulking about, acting as if the whole world is coming to an end. It just doesn't make sense to me, and I don't understand it."

An awkward silence fell between the two of them. Squirming uncomfortably in his seat, Jay cast a quick glance at Anna's face. Her dark features were striking as the sun filtered into the cabin directly onto Anna. Sadness and frustration tugged at the corners of her eyes, and her small lips gave way to the slightest of frowns. Stabbing guilt filled his heart at the sight of her discouragement. She was all he really cared about in the entire world, and in no way did he want to disappoint her. Slowly he reached out his right hand to cover her petite, olive-colored hands folded in her lap. When she didn't respond to his touch, he began gently stroking her soft skin in an attempt to soothe the one he loved.

"I'm sorry, I just can't help myself. I can't get over the fact that we are leaving our whole life behind. Besides, it could be dangerous, and I can't stand the thought of anything happening to you. I don't think I could survive without you," Jay finally confessed to Anna as people began filtering back onto the airplane.

Anna paused for several moments to gather her thoughts. A stewardess came through the cabin with a small garbage bag. With a smile, Anna handed her Jay's empty Coke can before turning back to Jay.

"Jay, nothing is going to happen to me. Besides, God has us in His hands! He'll protect us," she stated quietly but with confidence.

"How do you know that, Anna? How do you know God will keep us safe?"

"Because He promises to always be with us, to protect us, and He always keeps His promises!"

"But what about the people that trust Him and bad stuff still happen in their lives? Did God keep His promises with them?"

Anna turned her hands over and grabbed Jay's in her own and demanded firmly, "Jay, look at me." Slowly Jay's gray eyes locked onto hers. "I don't have all the answers to every situation that has ever happened, and I don't need to have an explanation for all the things that have gone wrong in the lives of the faithful. I have no right to question God or His plans. He can see perfectly all that has and all that ever will happen, and if we are faithful and obedient to His will, whatever happens will be the best for us every time."

"That doesn't comfort me very much. Besides, how do I really know that we are following God's will? Maybe we're following our own will. If that's the case, then bad things will most definitely happen."

"Oh, Jay, how could you not know we're following His plan for us? We began this journey over four years ago while we were still in Pullman. If it wasn't God's plan, He would have let us know long before now."

Fixing his eyes on the lighted walkway, Jay mulled over Anna's last words. In his heart, he knew she was right in everything she had just said; still, he didn't like it. The fear of the unknown just wouldn't be stilled as it pressed down like a heavy weight on his soul. Try as he might, he just couldn't banish it as it raged on through frightening images played over and again in his mind.

Looking up, Jay scanned every inch of Anna's pretty face. Her distinct dark eyebrows and large brown eyes had a mesmerizing effect on Jay every time. Kindness, love, and comfort met his gaze as he searched her face for an elusive answer or calming reassurance. Unsure what to say or how to tell her what was on his heart, Jay just soaked in her beauty for several moments.

Reaching his large hand to her face, Jay caressed her soft skin before taking her chin in his hand.

"I'm just so afraid of losing you. I know it's God's will for us, but I just can't bear the thought of ever being without you again in my life. You're my whole world, Anna."

"I'm not going anywhere! I'll always be here with you, Jay! I love you!"

The Unraveling

Reaching for a microphone, one of the stewardesses welcomed all the passengers to the flight before informing them of the safety rules and procedures. Oblivious to her speech, Jay continued to gaze intently at Anna, waiting for some assurance, some wisdom that would assuage his fears. With a small jolt the plane began to move slowly down the tarmac to get in line on the runway for takeoff.

Smiling broadly, Anna reached up and placed her hand on one of Jay's broad shoulders.

"Nothing is going to happen to me. We're going down together to an established mission where all of the people of the region will welcome us with open arms! Besides, we've already visited it twice before! Nothing happened then and nothing will happen now!"

Casting his eyes back to the floor, Jay sulked for a moment or two. "But what if it does? I have a bad feeling about this trip. I don't know what it is, but I have a bad feeling."

"Oh, you silly, you're just upset about being gone for more than a couple weeks. It's not as if we will never come back to the States. We'll still come back, we have family here, our church is here, and our support group is here. We'll be back from time to time."

"No, you don't get it! I don't care where we're at as long as I'm with you," he lied. "I just have a bad feeling about this whole thing, like something bad is going to happen to you…or to us."

Anna sat back in her chair and closed her eyes as the plane began to speed down the runway. She kept Jay's hand in her own as the big bird began to accelerate up into the air at more than a forty-five degree angle. Any argument no matter how logical was futile, and she knew it.

Quickly the plane climbed up through the altitudes until it was more than five miles in the air when it leveled out. Quick and efficient, the stewardesses made their way through the cabin as they passed out soft drinks and peanuts. Jay quickly opened a fresh Coke and took a quick gulp. A mask of frustration covered his face as he placed the Coke into the cup holder in front of him.

"Anna, I love you, and I know you think I'm being paranoid or something, but I seriously have a very bad premonition about all of this. I'm not just making it up to argue with you. I wish I could make it go away, I've tried to make it go away, believe me! I've prayed about it and asked God to give me a sense of assurance; so far, my unease hasn't lifted one little bit. If anything, it's gotten far worse."

Smiling brightly, Anna reached up and stroked Jay's cheek again. "Jay, we all have fears and unease from time to time. Anything less wouldn't be human, but we have to have faith and trust God. He has a perfect plan for our lives if we will just be obedient and faithful to His will. We simply have to give everything to Him—our possessions, our lives, and even the ones we love. Just place everything in His hands and then the little fears that run our life won't have any power over us. When we do that, God can and will do mighty things through us!"

Jay hung his head in defeat. He knew the words Anna was saying were true. Knew them by heart, he'd heard them so many times in his life. Putting them to practical use, well, that was another matter.

Ding! The fasten seatbelt sign came on, signaling the approach to their destination was at hand. Looking out the small window, Jay could see Mexico City far below and slightly ahead of the plane. The size of the city was staggering from the air. Once again, a dark cloud of smog could be seen only minutes ahead of the plane as it approached its destination, only this time the smog appeared much thicker and darker than it had in Houston.

Leaning her head over toward Jay's until they just touched, Anna whispered, "Jay, I love you so much! You're the love of my life too. Even so, I've given you and your well-being to God, placed you in His hands. I can take comfort in the fact that He'll protect you and guide you. As hard as it can be, I have chosen

The Unraveling

to trust Him with your life, my life and our life together. I know He has great plans for us, and I'm ready for whatever challenges come our way. Would you pray with me and ask God to take away your burden?"

Jay nodded in agreement.

"Then I'll pray for us. Dear Heavenly Father, Protector of our lives, I ask that you take this burden from Jay. Please, Lord, help him with this struggle. Reassure him through your Holy Spirit that you are indeed in control and have us in the palm of your hand. Lord, I ask that you send a calming reassurance to Jay. Let Him know your presence is always with us; in your heavenly name, amen."

With her left arm, Anna gave Jay a hug, followed by a quick kiss. They could feel the plane drop rapidly in elevation, descending on Mexico City. Jay's ears needed to pop as he forced a yawn. Looking out the window, he was surprised how close they already were to the ground. Busy streets filled with cars and busses grew closer and closer until Jay thought they were going to hit the unsuspecting travelers.

Everywhere he looked people scurried to and fro. Narrow streets crammed full of one kind of vehicle or another seemed to be in gridlock everywhere he looked. Garbage littered the ground, and loose papers tumbled down the streets as the wind sent them on their way.

Welcome to my new life, Jay thought as the large plane touched down.

Chapter 7

Struggling against the weight, Carlos raised a stout, wooden staff worn smooth from years of constant use and laden with terra cotta buckets onto his narrow shoulders. Cloudy water lapped over the top of the vessels, spilling onto the ground on either side as he balanced his load. Sweat ran down his forehead and dripped onto the red gravely soil path he was following as hunger pangs raged in his belly.

It had been two days since he had last eaten, and he was famished. Scanning the horizon, Carlos was overjoyed to see large billowing thunderheads as they rose up to meet the brilliant blue sky. Monsoon season was just beginning and although sometimes dangerous, this was his favorite time of year.

Wiping sweat from his brow with one hand while holding up his raggedy pants with the other, Carlos began struggling up the narrow, red dirt path toward the net-covered grow plots more than half a mile away. His shoulders screamed in protest as they bore the heavy and unstable load. On either side of his neck, large calluses worn raw from the wooden staff began seeping a reddish fluid, staining the worn burlap shirt that covered them. No less than ten other boys were in front of him, spread out roughly fifty yards apart as they struggled with their own burdens full of water.

Once they reached the grow plots, up a crudely constructed ladder they climbed until reaching a storage trough more than twenty feet in the air where they would dump their loads, one pot at a time. Connected to the trough were dozens of PVC pipes that extended out over the ever-thirsty plants growing below.

Small holes had been drilled in the pipes to allow the water to escape as it filled the lines. Gravity forced the water to flow from the tank into the PVC pipes, while subsequent pressure caused the water to shoot out through the small holes over the waiting plants below. It was a crude but effective watering system, evident by the lush vegetation growing beneath. Once lightened of their load, the boys would descend down the ladder and return to the main water source—a dug well—via another path worn just as smooth as the first, only to begin the process all over again.

Up the hill they traveled; dumped their water; back down the hill, over and over again in a never-ending task that had no reward other than the ability to live another day. The humidity was high and growing, making the task at hand even more difficult. With hopeful anticipation, Carlos scanned the sky again, hoping for a sign of good news.

Happiness filled his large brown eyes at the sight of the rapidly growing storm front. Thunder could be heard in the distance as the storm quickly approached. With a little luck, this would be his last trip of the day. A large storm meant a lot of rain. A lot of rain meant a lot of water. A lot of water nullified the need to water the precious plants growing in their protective plots. Maybe, just maybe, he would receive a small reprieve from his daily duties. Even so, any chance of food would almost definitely be gone if they were not working, a trade off that was worth it as far as Carlos was concerned, as long as the rain didn't last for several days. That long of a respite would give him much too much time to think about his hunger. Times like that were almost overwhelming for the young man.

Carlos had nearly caught up to another boy directly in front of him, who was struggling up the path with his load. Fear seized him as the boy continued to labor. In no more than twenty steps, Carlos would overtake and pass the boy.

Carlos hissed as the boy lagged behind even more, "Miguel, hurry up! I'm right behind you! Miguel, you must not stop. The rain is coming; then you can rest." If he heard, Miguel didn't acknowledge the words Carlos said. Instead, he sobbed and moaned over and over again as his burden became more than he could bear.

Reaching out his hand while scanning the horizon, Carlos grabbed Miguel by the arm and helped him along, up the path. *Pound, pound, pound* went his heart, fed by fear of retribution. This was no place for slackers, and none would be tolerated. If one couldn't carry his burden, death was the only punishment. The rules were clear and simple: carry your water and avoid contact with the other workers. Failure to do so would result in certain death.

"Miguel, go on, get up there," Carlos half pleaded, half demanded as he pushed the boy in front of him.

High winds began to blow red dust into their eyes as a large dust devil kicked up dried grass and dirt directly in front of them.

Carlos pleaded, "Miguel, hurry up, you'll get us both into trouble." Under normal circumstances, any boy lagging would simply be passed up by those behind until one of the bosses spotted the tail-dragger. After that, it was most generally too late. The offender was usually beaten to a gruesome and bloody death before being fed to the hogs back at the compound. A public demonstration intended to motivate, and it worked. In this world, it was usually each man looking out for his own welfare. Not many would risk their own neck for the sake of a neighbor. They all feared the bleak outcome that each of them ultimately faced. None of them had any hope in their lives other than the hope for a little rain and a rare meal. Everything else was survival by instinct in the cruel world in which they lived—the only world they knew.

Carlos was different from the rest. Something inside, whether conscious, instinct, or purely a sense of something greater than himself fed a small but constant hope in his life. Daily, before beginning the repetitive task of delivering water, tending the plants, or cultivating a new plot, Carlos would scan the horizon with an expectation of something greater than all he knew or

The Unraveling

had ever known. Somehow he drew comfort from that hope, a sustained comfort that carried him through all the days of torture and strife that ruled his young life.

A comfort that separated him, made him different from all of the others in the compound. It was as if he was at peace, constant peace that even he could not explain. The other boys noticed it. Some of them called him the dreamer, but most rallied around him, drawn to him by that sustained hope—a hope that was apparent in everyday actions of kindness and compassion toward his comrades.

Without lobbying for position, Carlos had become the quiet leader of his little group of slaves. On more than one occasion his compassionate heart had prompted him to carry the load or to plead for leniency for one of the others. A beating or whipping from one of the guards, his only compensation. Even so, he couldn't turn his back on one in need. Once again, his compassionate heart put him directly in the line of fire.

"Miguel, they'll kill you if you don't go. Come on, you can do it." Miguel's head hung down as he labored to take each painful step. Out of energy from lack of nourishment, his body would not go on.

"Miguel, it's going to rain. Then you can rest. One more trip. That's all you must make."

Miguel's eyes were bloodshot and vacant. His mouth hung open as he labored through each difficult breath. Saliva, thick and white dripped from his mouth and foamed up around his chapped and dry lips. He was on his last legs of life, the flame of desire to live nearly extinguished.

Carlos had seen this look many times before and knew there was little one could do to encourage the individual. Yet still he tried. Wrapping his right arm around his struggling friend, Carlos practically carried the young boy up the path toward their destination. Wind pounded them in the face as the storm drew ever nearer. Big muddy drops of rain stung them on their faces as they labored forward. Hope surged inside of Carlos as he drew nearer the waiting water trough—one hundred, fifty, thirty-five, twenty yards to go to drop their cargo. The rain was falling in sheets now. Somehow they were going to make it.

Crraaack the air exploded around the two frail bodies. *Crraaack* again as they fell to the now muddy ground. The sky had grown dark, nearly black from the large thunderstorm now directly over them, *crraaack*, again.

At first Carlos thought they had been struck by lightning. The deafening noise and ensuing pain made him believe he was dying right then and there. Confusion and agony filled his senses as the loud cracking continued over and over. Then he heard it, the unmistakable laughter that sent chills up his spine. Glancing up out of the corner of his eyes only confirmed his fears.

Directly in front of them, less than five feet away and through flashes of lightning, he could see the silhouette of a large man with a sizeable bull whip in his hand. It was the head boss. Somehow he'd seen the two of them struggling along and had taken it upon himself to punish them, making them examples for the rest of the young men laboring away. Rumor had it that this man was a son of Satan himself; pure evil ran through him. His lust for blood, torture, and death brought fear to even the guards. He loved to torture and loved to inflict pain to the point of agonizing death. Once he started, his victim didn't stand a chance. In all the years Carlos had been at the compound, never once had he seen this man grant mercy to a single victim. The more a victim pleaded for his life, the more he enjoyed it. "Walking Death" was the nickname given him by the prisoners. They all feared the day they would cross his path.

With practiced skill, the man pumped the whip back and forth, gaining speed and momentum until, with a violent downward jerk and an evil, harrowing laugh, he cracked the whip and sent the sizzling end directly onto the back of his intended victim. Miguel shuddered as the frayed end of the whip, traveling

The Unraveling

more than one hundred miles per hour, cut through burlap, skin and flesh on his back.

Blood surged to the surface and began staining the young boy's light-colored shirt, which only added to the man's violent frenzy. Over and over the whip sizzled through the air before striking the helpless boy up and down his frail torso. Blood splattered everywhere with each blow. Carlos lay in the mud, frozen with fear. The rain poured down over he and Miguel as the whip continued to find its mark. Water red with blood flowed from Miguel's prone, lifeless body and pooled under Carlos. Raising his large brown eyes ever so slightly toward Miguel, Carlos was greeted by a lifeless stare from his young friend's black eyes.

Burying his head in the mud, Carlos covered the back of his head with his arms and tried to scoot away. He knew what was in store for him, but instinct told him to get away as fast as he could. The rain was coming in torrents now. Carlos could barely breathe from all the water. Still, the whip cracked through the air as it continued to inflict damage on the body of its young victim. Slowly, slowly Carlos inched away.

Maybe, just maybe I'll get away.

A shrill and unnatural laughter rose above the roar of the rain. "Where do you think you're going, my pretty?" the large man yelled, followed by a guttural roar.

Crack! went the whip as the end found its mark on Carlos's back. Pain unimaginable screamed through his senses. *Crack!* over and over again, faster and faster as the man worked himself into a murderous frenzy. *Please don't, Luis. I was working! Please don't,* Carlos's mind screamed silently.

Skin and flesh began to shred as the whip found its mark again and again and again. Carlos didn't know how much more he could take. He could feel his consciousness ebbing away.

Please help me! Save me! Carlos's mind screamed out again. *I don't want to die!*

Just then, as if on cue, the sky opened up and hail the size of quarters began to pelt down from above. Carlos squirmed with pain as the ice missiles, followed by the whip struck his injured body over and over. As the storm increased in intensity, the blows from the whip became less frequent until his tormentor quit his attack with a curse and ran for the nearest shelter. Carlos lay prone on the ground, arms covering his head as the ice continued to pelt down on him. The ground for as far as he could see was white with hail several inches thick.

Carlos moved his head to the side and glanced at Miguel's lifeless body now covered in several inches of blood-stained ice. He could feel the hail on his body, and he welcomed the relief the frozen water gave his tattered back. The cold compression was exactly what his body needed as it constricted his damaged flesh and ebbed the flow of blood.

He looked around. Luis and the others were nowhere to be seen. For another five minutes the hail continued to fall. Shivers racked his frail body in an attempt to keep it warm. Slowly the storm subsided and the wind died down.

I have to get out of here before Luis comes back.

With every ounce of energy he could muster, Carlos rolled over on his side, dumping the blood-laden ice off of his back. The sight of so much blood caused him to wretch uncontrollably as he struggled to get up. Failing in his attempt, Carlos fell onto his injured back and screamed silently from the pain. Tears streamed down his face as he fought for composure.

Fixing his eyes on the swiftly moving clouds, Carlos tried to divert his attention from the pain. Amazement filled his eyes as the clouds parted, revealing the bright blue sky directly above. In the center of the patch of blue, Carlos could see the white bottom of a jet liner as it streaked across the sky. Watching it until it disappeared behind clouds, Carlos wondered what kind of magnificent bird could fly so high and free.

The Unraveling

After a few more moments of rest, Carlos struggled to his feet and gingerly made his way back to his cell and all of his cellmates. Somehow against all odds he had lived to see another day.

Chapter 8

Once off the plane, Jay and Anna scanned the busy airport for their connecting party. Feeling conspicuously out of place, Jay glanced around at the people as they passed by. Some of the natives pointed, some laughed, but most just stared at the foreigners in their midst. Trying to act normal, his heart rate sped up when his eyes connected with those of one of the military guard's standing against the wall opposite him and Anna. Even though they had visited Mexico before, he could not get used to the armed guards stationed throughout the facility.

"I thought Mexico was a free country." They made their way to the luggage terminal.

"They're here for our protection as much as anything, silly." Anna smiled broadly to one of the guards as they passed by. Returning her smile with an ever-so-small nod, the guard continued staring straight ahead.

Slowly they made their way through the throng of people to pick up their bags all the while searching for their connection. Small children rushed up to them trying to sell little packets of Chiclets, a type of chewing gum readily available in America as well as Mexico. Taking a small bag of change out of her purse, Anna began handing coins out to the little hands, palms up, waiting for a handout.

At first she refused the little packets of gum but relented when it became apparent the children would not accept the money otherwise. Materializing from thin air it seemed, children continued to mob her until all of the change was gone. Once it became apparent no more money was to be had, the children moved on to more promising prospects.

69

With a loud clang, the first bags and suitcases slammed into the metal turnstile at the bottom of the conveyor where they began their journey around and around the merry-go-round until their rightful owners claimed them. Dozens of bags came down, one after the other before Jay spotted the first piece of their luggage. Retrieving it before it passed by, he was relieved to see the rest of their luggage as it made its way down the ramp. With Anna's help, they claimed the rest of their belongings, placing them on the side of the conveyor.

"Now what do we do?" Jay asked with building annoyance in his voice. "Wasn't someone supposed to meet us here?"

"I'm sure they'll be here shortly, if they're not already."

"It's not like we're early or anything! What are we supposed to do with our luggage, just leave it sitting here?"

"We're not going to leave it here, silly. Besides, we're not going anywhere."

Looking around, Anna spotted a brass luggage rack, similar to the style used in motels, just across the large room. Without saying a word she walked away from a wide-mouthed Jay to retrieve the cart. Stopping long enough to gain permission, Anna returned with her prize.

"Voila!" She began loading their luggage onto the cart. Reluctantly, Jay began helping her with the task until every box, suitcase, and container they owned was stacked high on the wheeled cart.

Moving through the busy airport was no easy task. People were everywhere, coming and going in a rush, each seemingly in a different direction and all talking at the same time. Their speech was so fast that Jay couldn't understand a single word anyone was saying. All it sounded like to him was a small roar, which was adding to his blossoming headache. On several occasions people ran smack into him as he pushed the cart through the busy airport.

"Did you see that? They deliberately hit me," Jay complained to Anna as she led them toward a counter with a large sign above it that read *customs*.

Providing their papers, Anna helped Jay place their luggage up onto the counter where it could be inspected by one of the dozens of agents busy waiting on people. Even though he had nothing to hide, Jay could feel his anxiety level rise as the young man behind the counter poured over their paperwork and asked several questions of them: where they were going, what the reason was for their visit, and for how long. Once satisfied, the officer handed their papers back and waited impatiently for them to get out of the way so he could help the next traveler.

They quickly loaded their luggage and once again entered the busy melee of people in an attempt to find whoever was supposed to meet them. Once across the airport, Anna noticed a group of people, all with placards bearing the names of individuals they were supposed to meet. Grabbing Jay by the arm, she half pulled him and the luggage toward the throng. Sure enough, in the middle of the pack stood a smartly dressed young man holding a placard that read simply *Bilston*.

They quickly learned that the young man's name was Ramón and that he had been sent by the mission to retrieve Jay and Anna.

"I'm so glad to find you, I thought I was late and had missed you," the young man nervously explained.

I wonder where he thought we would have gone? Jay thought glumly.

"Nope, we're here, and you're just on time!" Anna exclaimed with a disarming smile.

Grabbing the cart, Ramón quickly wheeled it out of the airport and directly to an old 70's vintage Volkswagen van parked right next to the sliding glass entrance doors and began practically throwing the luggage in the back.

The temperature was moderate, but the humidity seemed very high to Jay as he handed the last of the luggage to Ramón.

The Unraveling

Checking out his surroundings, he was amazed at all the vehicles speeding past, many honking their horns nonstop, it seemed. Most of the vehicles were older vintage, and nearly all seemed to spout dark gray smoke out their tail pipe. The exhaust really got bad when three large passenger busses sped by, leaving a dark blue, almost black cloud of diesel fumes to mark their passage.

"Well, everyone ready?" Ramón asked while walking to the front of the van. "It's a seven-hour drive so we better get going," he explained.

Opening the sliding side door, Jay and Anna climbed in and sat down on the only other seat in the van. The passenger front seat had been removed, and in its place were three small crates containing several large, white chickens in each container.

Waving his hands as he talked, Ramón explained the fowl were for the mission and would be used for brood stock in hopes that they would soon be able to raise their own eggs and poultry. The rear two seats had been removed also to accommodate luggage and to haul a dozen or more bags of chicken feed.

"Nothing like being cooped up," Jay laughingly told Anna.

With a grind of gears and a jerky start, the van leapt out into the steady stream of traffic while eliciting several blares from the horns of the other vehicles. Finding seatbelts was futile, so Jay and Anna clung to each other and prayed as traffic whizzed by at alarming rates of speed.

The streets were narrow and the lanes narrower yet. Jay couldn't see how four lanes of traffic were able to navigate such a tight place. Yet somehow they did.

With all the skill of a racecar driver, Ramón nosed the van into the outside lane as they entered a busy roundabout built with a large water fountain in the center. Cars, trucks, and busses sped around the interchange, weaving in and out of each other chaotically until they found the street they needed to take. Most of the vehicles had turn signals, although Jay hadn't seen a single one used up to that point.

With a quick turn of the wheel, Ramona guided the van down a blacktop highway full of traffic. Row upon row of flat-top two-story apartment buildings lined either side of the street. Dilapidated exteriors and dirt yards were the decorative theme of most of the buildings they drove past. The row houses were finished with dingy-looking stucco and had a Spanish or European look to them. Most of the windows were arch topped and many had wooden shutters.

Large rooftop gardens lush with vegetation were visible on the top of some of the buildings they passed by. Here and there, Jay could see street vendors busily preparing food on their wood-fired grills. Pedestrians were lined up waiting to purchase the delicious-smelling food at every stand they passed, reminding Jay that once again it was mealtime.

The scenery around Mexico City was nothing short of spectacular; although more than 7000 feet in elevation, mountains rose up in a circle around the sprawling city with Popocatepetl and Iztaccihuatl being the most prominent of the bunch. All of the mountains surrounding Mexico City were part of an active chain of volcanoes, and Jay could hardly imagine what it must be like living in the shadowy ring of so many explosive giants.

Jay watched out his window at the ever-changing scenery—the one constant being endless house after house. It seemed as if they had traveled for over an hour, but they still seemed to be in the middle of city. The traffic was growing heavier, but no one slowed down. The road they were on snaked around through the buildings with no rhyme or reason.

"Just think, we only have seven more hours of this," he exclaimed to Anna.

Anna smiled and hugged Jay's arm. "Just think of it as an adventure!"

"What an adventure," Jay groused.

Ramón spotted a Golden Arches and turned in without slowing a bit. How he missed an oncoming car was beyond Jay. "I'll

The Unraveling   73

bet they couldn't have fit a playing card between the two of us!" Jay exclaimed nervously.

Anna agreed as they pulled up to the drive-thru window and placed their order. Ramón called out, "Last stop for a bathroom break!" as they waited for their food.

"Sounds like a good idea to me!" Anna exclaimed as she and Jay exited the van and headed inside.

Jay waited for Anna just inside the door of the restaurant. The place was packed, and people stared openly at the foreigners. Fidgeting nervously while glancing at his wrist, he realized he had no idea of the time here in Mexico. *What could be taking her so long?* he thought as he nervously glanced around.

After a few minutes, Anna returned from the rest room. She was pale and looked tired. He gave her a hug as they made their way back to the van. Once safely situated back on their seat, Ramón handed them a bag containing their Big Macs, fries, and Cokes. Jay was happy that McDonald's had gone global; it made him feel a little more at home.

No one spoke as they consumed their food. Ramón ate with one hand and drove with the other. Traffic seemed even more hectic than before, but if it bothered him, it didn't show. Jay practically inhaled his food and finished more than half of Anna's. Still feeling ill, she ate only a few bites and nestled down close to Jay to try to get a little sleep.

Jay continued watching the changing scenery with very little, if any, conversation with Ramón. He didn't know what to say and didn't want to try talking over the noisy chickens anyway.

The van continued climbing up the high desert plateau. It was hard to believe they were close to two miles above the sea and still going up. Traffic continued to be heavy as the road continued getting narrower, eventually dropping down to one lane going each direction.

At first, the road was well paved with brightly painted lines, but the farther they traveled, the bumpier and more beat up it became. Centerlines consisted of a faded white dash separating the two lanes, and they were sparse at best.

The hours drug on, and the terrain became more rural the farther they went with only small villages visible from time to time. Anna stirred awake after several hours of sleep and was discouraged to learn they still had more than three hours to go to reach the mission.

"Why do we even have a mission clear out here in the boondocks? It's not like there are even that many people around here."

Anna responded, "Well, there are people around here, and they need God in their lives too! Besides, it's not that much different here than where some of your family live in Eastern Montana. Some of the towns there are hours apart. They still have churches…and God."

Jay smiled as memories of his family and time spent together came rushing back into his mind. He could picture his young nephew out chasing a deer or antelope around the massive landscape that made up Eastern Montana. Hunting was a way of life there, and his nephew fully embraced that tradition. Looking out the window, Jay could see the similarities between the two places. Stark, barren landscape filled with sage, cacti, and not much else made up the terrain.

Jay smiled. "That's what I'll do, just pretend it's Montana."

"That's the spirit!" She smiled back as she moved her black hair out of her eyes. She loved Jay with her whole heart and so wanted him to be happy. She knew he would be okay if he would just trust God and give this new life of theirs a chance.

After several hours of travel marked by only a fuel stop and a couple of checkpoint stops, they finally arrived at a point where three roads converged. Which way should they go? The answer was simple—right there in the middle of nowhere, a twenty-five-foot tall, purple statue resembling Barney the dinosaur rose up from the desert floor, arm extended out, pointing down one of the three dirt roads.

The Unraveling

Jay and Anna got out and walked around the strange roadside attraction as Ramón shared with them how a church youth group from Florida had raised the money to purchase the purple dinosaur for the children of the mission. After making it through customs and eventually through the countryside of Mexico, it arrived at the mission. The people there had no idea what to do with the odd gift. After several weeks of debate, it was decided the creature would be used as a roadside direction marker to show people the way to the mission. There was a little dedication plaque on the front of the beast that simply said, *A Gift for the Children, Enjoy! Four Lakes Community Church of Four Lakes Florida! God bless.*

Anna walked past the purple beast and asked, "Isn't that an odd gift?"

"Yah, I never would have imagined anything like this, ever." Jay surveyed the oddity.

"Well, it's been here several years now, and it points to the mission," Ramón explained and added with a chuckle, "We bring the children here a couple times a year to look at the gift. I guess you could call it a field trip of sorts."

Ramon called out, "Thirty more miles!" as they piled back into the van. "Thirty hard miles!"

Circling the purple statue one last time, Ramón nosed the van down the middle road toward the Mission. It became evident right away why he had told them the thirty miles would be hard. The road was all washboards and rutted, marked with deep potholes every couple of feet. Up and down, side to side the van pitched and jumped as it hit obstacle after obstacle on the unmaintained road. Jay and Anna had to hold on for dear life to keep from being thrown from their seat.

The last thirty miles seemed as if they would take forever. They watched the shadows grow as the sun slid down behind the horizon. The high desert sky was spectacular, dominated by orange and yellows splayed across the horizon. Jay and Anna watched with amazement and joy at the changing scene. With more than twenty miles to go, it had become apparent they most definitely would arrive at the mission in the dark.

Down the trail they continued. The farther they went, the paler Anna became from all the back-and-forth motion. Just five miles from the mission, she had to have Ramón stop due to car sickness. Jay felt sorry for her as she vomited in the grass on the side of the road. He had gotten out to help her and handed her a few napkins to wipe her mouth as she returned to the van. He was shocked to see how red her eyes had become. The contrast between her pale skin and red eyes really made them stand out.

As they climbed back into the van, Anna exclaimed, "All the travel has taken its toll on me, that's for sure."

A worried look crossed Jay's face, "Well, we're almost done traveling for the day."

Ramón took the last five miles extremely slow to accommodate Anna the best he could, although it wasn't much help. Finally, the last mile and a half smoothed out as they reached a fairly flat portion of the plateau. Speeding up, Ramón became visibly more excited the closer they came to the small village and waiting mission. As they crested the last rise, Jay could make out lights from the houses inside the wall-enclosed town on the horizon. His heart sped up in anticipation of their arrival.

Ramón had to roll to a stop just outside the gate to the town. Their way was blocked by candle-waving people singing greetings to their new missionaries. Jay turned his attention to Anna as a large smile broke out on his face. Anna's smile was equally as large as tears of joy filled her weary eyes.

Ramón turned in his seat and gestured wildly to the throng. "This is for you, your welcome song. The whole town has shown up for this glorious day!"

The Unraveling   77

Chapter 9

Wispy gray shadows danced across the stark concrete block wall as wind-blown curtains filtered the sun through the living room window and created a kaleidoscope of images that shifted and shape-changed at the whim of the breeze. The small room was actually a common room used for eating, resting, and reading in the little hacienda.

A tiny kitchen blended into one end, distinguished only by the small stainless steel sink and antique burner top stove. Acting as both a cutting table and counter space, a small, painted cabinet with a wooden countertop not more than two-feet square lined the wall between the stove and the sink. *Drip, drip, drip,* went an old tarnished sink faucet as it constantly fed a growing rust stain that circled the drain.

Rickety and worn from years of use, a small wooden table with two mismatched wooden chairs took up nearly half of the small room and acted as a boundary between the dining and living areas. Unopened boxes with large, hastily written words scrawled across their side like, *kitchen, pictures, pots, pans,* lined the walls as they waited to be unloaded.

Each living unit was fully contained, allowing them complete privacy from others. All of the walls were constructed out of concrete or pumice block and did very little to deaden the noise from the other units. Even the floor was concrete with a few throw rugs placed in the dining room/kitchen area. Only the ceiling was finished with a rough stucco texture.

A single, naked light bulb hung from the ceiling, suspended by a black insulated wire, the only source of light other than the window in the small room. Above the bulb, a four-blade fan had been added by an industrious visitor years before. *Thuwhumph, thuwhumph, thuwhumph,* went the fan, over and over as the poorly balanced blades churned the thin air.

Two days had passed since their arrival at the mission. A busy two days it had been, with very little time for sleep. Much of the past forty-eight or so hours were spent joyously greeting each resident as they came to meet them. It was a festive atmosphere that filled Jay with amazement. Everyone was so gracious and friendly he could scarcely believe it. Although exhausted from travel, he and Anna patiently entertained each and every villager until the wee hours of their first morning with only a few hours to themselves that first day.

Jay yawned and began to lay down for a nap. "I guess this is our siesta time."

With music blaring and people bantering excitedly, the whole process began anew their second evening and stretched clear through the night. Finally, long after the sun had risen over the horizon, they were left alone in the small common apartment building they shared with three other families. Too exhausted to unpack, they had lounged around all afternoon before turning in early for the night, their first uninterrupted sleep in three days' time.

Jay listened to the noisy fan as he and Anna lay in their bed. The rhythmic melody of the paddles had a soothing effect on him. Finally rested after a long night of sleep, he was content to just lie there and listen to Anna's timed breathing, mixed with the constant noise from the ceiling fan in the other room. *Thuwhumph, thuwhumph, thuwhumph,* went the fan, followed by Anna's breathing, over and over, perfectly in time.

Rolling to his side, Jay gently slid his legs over the edge of the bed and slowly got up to keep from disrupting her. She had been feeling ill ever since their arrival, residual effects of the lengthy travel, they surmised. Her eyes had been bloodshot and weary and her complexion pale, although her temperature remained

The Unraveling 79

normal. As long as Jay had known Anna, he couldn't remember a single time she had been ill, other than the sniffles on a couple of occasions. This new turn of events had him very worried, and he fussed over her like a new parent fusses over a newborn child.

For several moments, he just stood and watched her sleep. He couldn't believe Anna was his wife, even after all these years. His heart fluttered with joy and an overwhelming sense of love.

What would I ever do without her? he thought as he made his way to the kitchen.

Glancing out the window, Jay was surprised to see most, if not all the children of the mission gathered around the wrought-iron fencing that surrounded the courtyard of the apartment. The head of each child was pressed against the opening between the vertical bars in hopes of catching a glimpse of their new missionaries.

The bars were evenly spaced close enough for the children to rest their cheeks against comfortably and were thick enough to hide their ears. Their narrow faces reminded Jay of minnows and other small fish he used to spend hours observing in the aquarium his family had when he was growing up.

He shook his head in amazement at the sight before turning his attention on the ancient refrigerator in the corner. It was an old, round-top style that was popular in the United States in the 1950s. At one time it had been white, but now most of the paint had flaked off, leaving only a few, off-white abstract splotches on a dark gray canvas. Opening the door with a spring-loaded pull handle, he retrieved an ice-cold Coke that he had placed near the exposed cooling coils in the back of the unit. Thick frost had accumulated over the coils and was already building up on the thick, steel sides of the cooler. *Nothing like stepping back in time!* he thought as he let the door close on its own with a thump.

At least we have Coke.

Popping the top of the can, he watched as little atoms of Coke rose up through the opening, riding on bubbles of carbonated gas. Sampling the beverage satisfied him that it was Coke indeed.

He gulped down a third of the can in one big drink and enjoyed the burning sensation building in his throat, all the way into his stomach. The carbonation elicited a large, satisfying belch that echoed in the small room and burned all the way up into his sinuses. *That was a good one!* he thought as he placed the can on the old rickety table and sat down.

The Coke did little to sate his appetite but would have to do as Jay looked around the room again. The kitchen was stocked with food, but he had no idea what he would make since the toaster was still packed and tortillas seemed to be the only bread in the house. He finally decided it would be best to wait for Anna to think up something for their morning meal.

He could hear the voices of the children as they continued their vigil just outside yet resisted the temptation to go talk to them until Anna was up and around. She was always at ease, and Jay followed her around like a scared puppy, even when he knew he was being silly.

She would tell him over and over, "They're just people, and they want to get to know us." Still, he resisted any interaction unless she was right there to hold his hand.

It was true. All of the people were friendly, almost to the point of being irritating to him. It wasn't that he didn't like them or like the attention they gave; he just didn't like the amount. Since their arrival, they had had very little time to themselves. That was the part he didn't like. Anna was everything to him, and he wanted to spend time with just her. As he thought about it, he realized he was just a little jealous of the time and attention she gave to the people.

Carefully leaning back in the chair, Jay polished off his Coke in two large drinks. *Tastes like home,* he thought as he crushed the can in his hand. With a toss, the empty can landed on the center of the table and slid clear to the other side, stopping only inches from the edge while leaving a sticky trail of dark fluid in its wake. Jay continued to balance on the back two legs of his chair while using his legs to stabilize himself. He watched as a black bug, probably a roach, crawled out from under the fridge and scurried across the floor, only to disappear under the stove. *What in the world have we gotten ourselves into?* he thought, bringing the chair back to all fours with a thud.

Slowly he rubbed his hands back and forth across his forehead and with his fingertips massaged the skin under his thick black hair. His temples rested against his palms, and he began to work them in a circular motion. It felt good, and he could feel the stress and unease abate somewhat. They were at the mission, but that didn't mean he had to like it.

He continued his head massage for several minutes and slowly moved to his eyes, which he rubbed vigorously with curled-up index fingers. Although he knew it wasn't good for them, he continued to rub with a substantial amount of force. The pressure felt good and relieved his stress too. Finally, with a large stretch, as far as his arms could reach, he arched his back and yawned. It felt good to work his muscles around.

Feeling better already, he decided to take a shower while he waited for Anna and moved quickly to the tiny bathroom, which consisted only of a small corner shower, toilet, and small pedestal sink all jammed tightly together. A small plate of mirrored glass about one-foot square had been glued to the wall directly over the sink. It was so low Jay had to bend down just to use it. *They must have built this bathroom for midgets.*

Even the shower was small. The showerhead was rustic and protruded out of the wall no more than four feet off the floor. It dripped constantly, leaving a reddish rust stain on the floor drain. Working the water control faucet back and forth failed to produce anything but lukewarm water from the faucet whether on the cold side or turned all the way to hot.

Irritated, Jay got in the shower and began to lather up with soap brought from home. The pressure was minimal and only added to his frustration. On top of that, the water had an oily feel that coated the skin and left him feeling anything but clean. *Just another thing to ruin my day!*

Happy to keep the shower short, Jay got out and quickly toweled off. He dressed rapidly and combed his long, skinny fingers through his wet hair. Even though the water wasn't hot, the mirror was steamed over, which prevented him from using it. *What kind of place is this?* he asked himself in frustration. *Short showers, rusty water, appliances from the 1950s, mirrors that steam over from lukewarm water... I can hardly wait to see what comes next.*

Returning to the living area, Jay grabbed another Coke and popped the top. This time he was content to sit at the table and just sip on the Coke. He was still hungry but decided to let Anna sleep for a while longer. A long rest was just what she needed to make her feel better.

Shaking his head in disbelief, he ran the events of the past several days through his mind. Everything seemed surreal to him, like a dream, or nightmare. Although the past several years had been spent preparing for this moment of their lives, he had never quite admitted that it would truly come to fruition. To him, it had been more like a dream that might come true someday, while it had been the whole world to Anna. She had committed to this ministry from day one and had been unwavering in her dedication and determination. In a way, he admired her for it, but mostly it just irritated him.

Although he had signed on, taken the schooling necessary, and attended the little Hispanic church in Colorado Springs, he had never accepted in his heart the fact that this would one day be their life's work. Throughout the years, he had felt certain that life would get in the way of their calling or "God's calling on their life," as Anna often reminded him. Yet here they were, smack dab in the middle of nowhere, Mexico, to do God's work.

It wasn't as if they had no idea what they were getting into, they had both been on several mission trips before, including to a mission not five hundred miles from this one. But that had been different. Those trips were simply that—trips. Going into those, he knew that in two short weeks after arrival they would be going home again. This time, home came with them.

Taking another sip, Jay realized how quiet the room had become. He could still hear the fan but realized something was missing. There was no other noise to be heard. Sliding his chair back just far enough, he peered out the window expecting to see the children waiting just outside the fence for him and Anna to emerge. No one was there. Even the section of normally busy street visible from their window was empty. "That's odd." He slid his chair back even farther.

Unable to see any more, he got up and walked to the window. An empty, dirt street was all that was visible. Curious, he made his way out the front door to the wrought-iron fence. The houses across the street were devoid of any life or activity. A black-and-white mutt slinked up the center of the dirt road, turning every twenty feet or so to see if anything was following. Nothing else stirred. The town was silent, a ghost town.

An uneasy feeling began to fill Jay's stomach. Something just wasn't right. A sense of panic and dread filled his heart. Moving quickly, he re-entered the house and walked to the bedroom. The solid wooden door was half open, just like he had left it. *Thuwhumph, thuwhumph, thuwhumph,* went the fan over and again. *Drip, drip, drip,* went the kitchen faucet.

Sliding in through the open doorway, fear gripped his mind as a rumpled and vacant bed with the covers thrown back and sheets laid bare was all that met his gaze. Anna was gone.

Chapter 20

Like red-hot lava, fear flowed through every fiber of his being. For a moment, paralysis gripped his legs; they became heavy and weighted down as if they were part of the concrete floor he was standing on.

Gasping for air, his heart quickened and lungs constricted, making it difficult to breathe. Beads of perspiration formed on his forehead, caused by an unjustified fear. Even so, no sense of reason or logical thought was possible. His mind could focus on one thing and one thing only. Anna was gone, and he had no idea where to find her. Several moments passed as dread surged through his heart, only to be replaced by sheer panic.

A voice that sounded foreign, stiff, choked with emotion, rising both in crescendo and tone as panic raged inside, seemingly exited Jay's mouth, "Anna, Anna, where are you?" Moving slowly across the room, he checked the floor on the other side of the bed, no Anna. He could see his hands and arms shake but wasn't even certain they were his own. They didn't feel like his, anyway.

Leaving the room, he continued to call out to Anna in the strange falsetto voice that had taken over his body. Knowing it was in vain, he checked the little bathroom and one small linen storage closet just next to the bathroom door. She wasn't there. Back to the bedroom, still no Anna, and no sign of her either. Fear was feeding panic, which was driving him on faster and faster.

Moving rapidly now, he left the small house, ran through the small courtyard before stopping at the edge of the street. Still no one was visible. As quickly as he could, he moved around the entire perimeter of the common-row houses that made up his building. A jarring *crunch, crunch, crunch, crunch* could be felt as well as heard in his ears and throughout his whole body as each desperate step impacted the course, eroded volcanic soil. The sound and feel reminded him of chomping on a milkless mouth full of Captain Crunch cereal when he was a boy.

Four small apartments made up the small row house, each apparently empty, void of life except for a small, wiry-haired dog on a thinly braided rope chain that yapped noisily as he ran past, three pink-and-black mottled piglets in a fenced yard, and a large green-and-red parrot on a stick stand in one of the front windows of the adjoining houses. The morning sun was already high in the light blue sky and burning hot. Wispy white clouds were flowing up from the south in rows, like soldiers marching in columns.

Indecision and strange surroundings held him fast in the middle of the red dirt street just outside of his apartment. What to do? Where to go? Lengthy glances, first up, and then down the roadway revealed nothing. Tears of frustration and desperation began to pool in his lower eyelids. Shaking his head side to side, he re-entered the small apartment and searched again for Anna. She wasn't there, and he knew it.

Through clenched teeth, Jay said to himself, "Just get a hold of yourself. What am I doing? She's got to be around here somewhere," he added in an attempt to ease his own anxiety.

Gripping the back of one of the kitchen chairs hard until his knuckles turned white from the pressure, Jay leaned his head down until his chin rested on his chest. "I'm being paranoid! She has to be here! She just has to."

Sucking air through parsed lips, he expanded his lungs and exhaled slowly to gain some composure. With his right hand, he ran his fingers back and forth through his dark curly hair as he concentrated his mind on Anna.

He prayed out loud, "Lord, help me find her. Keep her safe and keep me sane."

For several more moments he repeated the prayer until he could feel the tension in his body relax somewhat. The noisy ceiling fan continued its rhythmic serenade. All else seemed calm in this new world he now called home. He scuffed his foot back and forth and watched a river of red dust slide off his sneaker and onto the floor. Unsure what to do or where to go, he paced around the room.

Several moments passed as indecision gave way to determination; he had to find her. With a new resolve, he left the apartment and made his way back to the center of the street. For a moment he did nothing, just stood there trying to decide which direction to go, left or right, north or south. The only two choices he really had.

Settling on north, he slowly began to make his way up the street. The end of the mission compound was visible to him but still no sign of life. Slowly he passed house after house, surveying each and every one, all with the same result, nothing. Finally, reaching the closed northern gate of the city, he turned slowly around, resurveyed each building. Nothing. The only telltale sign bearing evidence of life was the smoke rising up from cooking pits in front of some of the units. Even so, not a person was in sight. It was an eerie scene that caused chills to run up and down his spine and reminded him of an ancient episode of the television show *Twilight Zone*.

Moving back to the gate, Jay peered out into the vast desert beyond the walls. He could see very little other than the red dirt road, which seemed to extend forever and upward, across the terrain, to where land melted into the horizon, almost as if it led directly to the heavens.

Turning back to the village, he took a couple steps. Clouds of fine red dust rose up around him before falling quickly back to the earth as he waited, unsure what to do next. After a slight hesitation, he moved back through the village until he arrived in front of his own house.

Discouraged, he could feel the tide of fear rising up from the depths of his soul. A hopeful glance toward their small unit yielded no new news, so he began the slow walk toward the south end of the compound. Dust continued to bellow up in front of him, blown ahead by the slight north wind, which was directly at his back. The reddish cloud cast a dark hue on everything he looked at. The taste of dust filled his mouth as it built up in his sinuses.

Clearing his throat, he turned his head and tried to spit the taste from his mouth as he continued slowly through the town. A faint sound halted him in his tracks. Straining with all his might, he turned his head one way and then another in an attempt to pick up the noise again, nothing. *It must be my imagination!* he thought as he vigorously shook his head back and forth in an attempt to clear his mind.

The air was silent, stunting the flicker of hope the sound, imagined or real, had given birth to. Where was she? Where were all the people?

Moving forward again, he didn't have to wait long for an answer; sounds of children's voices began to make their way to his ears. At first he didn't really trust the noises, believing them to be a creation of his own desire and imagination, nothing more than a sound mirage, but the farther he traveled, the louder they became. Rushing faster now, Jay found himself nearly running toward the voices. Hope sprang up anew as he made out distinct laughter and other sounds that could be made only by children at play.

Tears of hope and a suppressed joy filled his eyes and distorted his sight, but he didn't care. He had found people, and hopefully Anna.

Moving unabated, Jay approached the last few buildings near the southern gate. Paying them no heed, he traveled right through a flock of white chickens that were squawking and scratching around in the dirt. With loud cackles protesting his intrusion, the flock scattered toward the yards of the nearby houses. Jay continued on, honed in on the sounds like a bloodhound on a scent, a resolve of determination in his heart.

As he neared the south gate to the compound, he could tell the sounds were festive, which raised his hopes. They were coming from his right, behind the last two homes on the street. He followed them down a narrow road that ran between the two houses and ran alongside a large field covered in rocks. Out in the center of the field, more than thirty children were kicking around a soccer ball. They laughed and yelled as they ran up and down the field, chasing after the ball. A red cloud of dust hung suspended above the field.

A new church building stood at the far end, and a large group of people could be seen milling around the entry doors, which were wide open. The walls were brilliant white stucco which caused the church to really stand out in the bright sunlight. A roof-covered veranda ran the entire length of the front of the church and was at least ten-feet wide.

Rust-colored half-round tile roofing on the awning roof reminded Jay of waves on the ocean and stood out against the white stucco siding above. Cutting diagonally across the field, Jay headed directly for the rough-hewn, solid wooden doors, hoping to find Anna inside. But soon the children noticed him and abandoned their game of soccer to run over and greet their newest missionary. Jay's momentum came to a halt as the excited children circled around, undeterred by the scowl which had settled on his face.

"Señor Jay, Señor Jay," they clamored over and over in unison as they reached their small hands out in an attempt to touch the American.

Even though his mind was focused on finding Anna and nothing else, Jay took the time to stop and greet the children for several moments before pushing on through the crowd. With the children now part of his posse, he continued his assault on the

The Unraveling

church mission until no more than twenty feet separated him from the other people.

It seemed as if the whole town was present, which startled him but also answered the question of where all the people had gone. Slowing to little more than a crawl, he scanned the faces in hopes of catching a glimpse of Anna. A sea of smiles met his glances as the people began moving toward him, not one of them familiar. *Pound, pound, pound,* went his heart as anxiety continued to build. *Where is she? She has to be here somewhere!*

Garbled voices began filling his ears as the people all began speaking to him at once in their native tongue. Their speech was so rapid that Jay could make out only a word or two, so he just smiled and nodded. Once again, unable to move, Jay shook the hand of each and every person he met with a forced smile.

He plead hopefully, over and over again, hopeful that the people would understand, and direct him to his better half, "Anna, Miss Anna!"

Smiling and nodding their heads, everyone continued to reach out to touch him. Their joy was apparent and would have been flattering under normal circumstances, but bent on finding Anna, it was little more than an irritation to Jay.

Pushing through the throng, Jay reached the open doors of the church. Bright sunlight behind him made the inside of the church seem extremely dark. Scanning around the room, he was able to make out several more people congregated up toward the front, near the raised platform. High-pitched laughter told him the group was primarily women. Moving slowly through the doorway, he paused just long enough to allow his eyes to adjust to the low light. His heart leapt with joy as he made out the distinguished laughter of the one he loved.

Chapter 11

Jutting up off his forehead, Jay's eyebrows were scrunched into an abrupt mountain range as he put on his best scowl before approaching Anna and a small group of women from the village. Long, black, and frayed, her unkept and static-charged hair danced out in every direction from her head as if trying to escape whatever bonds kept them in place. That, coupled with the fact she still had on her pajamas from the night before, indicated a hasty departure from their house.

Smiling and gesticulating wildly with her hands, Anna was right in the middle of an animated conversation. Sparkling brightly like large jewels, her eyes lit up even more when she caught sight of him coming across the sanctuary with a group of children and adults in tow. The pronounced scowl on his face was not lost on her. For a moment she was concerned, but the excitement of her conversation eroded any misgiving she had.

Two large ceiling fans with four-foot wooden paddles turned in tandem and caused a slight breeze in the dark room. Nine hard wooden pews were lined up in rows on either side of a three-foot center isle. The floor was cold, gray concrete that had been treated with some type of sealant, which caused it to glisten as if it were wet. A large, crudely made wooden cross hung on the wall behind the wooden pulpit. Stretching across the room, a wooden altar, no more than two feet in height, served as a barrier between the main floor and the stairs, which led up to the stage.

Anna and her little group were crowded around both sides of the altar. Anna was petite in her own right, but Jay was amazed at the small stature of all of the women gathered around her. Stopping no more than a few feet from the group, he strained to hear what they were talking about. Their rapid speech coupled with their tendency to all talk at once made understanding very difficult for him, although he was fairly certain "fiesta" was said several times.

Flowing around him like water around a stone, the children pushed up to the group of women and began chiming and clamoring for Anna's attention, pushing him even farther back to the fringe of the small gathering. To the left and up on the stage, Jay noticed a young lady intent on keeping to herself. She was petite and light skinned. Pools of light shimmered on the raven black hair that hung halfway down her back. She had on a simple dress made out of a course material that looked like burlap. Large pockets had been crudely sewn onto the front of the dress, and a large hood hung down the back. Simple, laced sandals were all that covered her feet. Jay guessed her to be no more than twenty years of age.

She could be Anna's twin, or at least her sister.

Feeling his eyes on her, the young girl raised her gaze to his for several moments before quickly turning away with not so much as a smile. Jay wasn't sure, but he thought he could detect a hint of contempt in her large brown eyes, and he made a mental note to ask Anna about the young lady.

By now, Anna was pushing forward toward Jay. Wrapping her arms around his neck, she leaned over and whispered in his ear, "There you are. I knew you'd find me!"

Everyone was still talking and laughing, so Jay simply nodded and mumbled under his breath.

Pulling away from him, Anna motioned toward the ladies, closest one first. "Jay, this is Anabel, Chelyn, Dez, Elennel, and Eniale," she said without any hesitation. "These are my newest friends!"

The ladies beamed at the mention of their name. Jay forced a smile and nodded back at each one of them as they shyly made eye contact. There was no way he was going to remember their names so easily, so he decided not to even try. About that time, a middle-aged man dressed in taupe khakis and an off-white, cotton button-up shirt with no collar and sleeves rolled to the elbows approached and began speaking to the group. Jay noticed the man was confident but gentle in his manner and was somewhere in his midfifties, judging from the prominent gray streaks in his thick hair.

Turning to greet him, Anna began speaking very rapidly in Spanish. Jay tried to follow along, but with all of the simultaneous conversations he couldn't keep up. Rubbing his forehead, he realized he was developing a headache. Wishing he were anywhere else, he began to shift his sight and weight back toward the doorway while gently pulling Anna after him in an attempt to get her to leave.

If she knew what he was doing, she paid it no heed as she continued her excited conversation with the gentleman. They spoke for several moments before Anna turned quickly toward Jay. She told him excitedly. "Jay, this is Jesse. He's the resident pastor here. He's going to be spending some time with us to get us acclimated."

Once again, with forced smile, Jay greeted the smiling man.

"Señor Jay, we are so happy to have you here with us," Jesse greeted him in fluent English. "It can be kind of overwhelming right at first, but I think once you have been here for a little while, you will find that you are right at home. All of the people are so excited to have you here! My family and I are so excited to have you here! We praise God every day, many times a day, for sending you and Anna here to be with us! We are so very grateful."

Jay didn't know how to respond. Although pleased by the heartfelt welcome, he wasn't sure he shared the same enthusiasm.

He finally managed halfheartedly, "Well, we're glad we're here."

"Jay, Jesse and all the ladies, all the people, actually, are planning a huge welcome party for us. I'm so excited! Doesn't that sound wonderful?"

Surprised, Jay once again answered halfheartedly, "That sounds great, but I thought we already had a welcoming party our first night here."

Jesse explained, "Oh no, that was not a proper party. We're going to have a large fiesta with a parade, a special meal, followed up with a celebratory church service. All of the people have been waiting and planning this for some time."

By now everyone was pressed up against the three of them, bantering back and forth excitedly. Everyone except the strange young lady, but even she was pushed up close enough to hear what was going on.

"That's why I wasn't at the house. While you were in the shower, I got up and saw all of the children pushed up against our gate. When I went out to tell them good morning, they pulled me from our courtyard and began to march us down to the church. Before I knew it, the whole mission had joined in. I couldn't believe it. All everyone kept talking about was the celebration. It took me a while to figure out they were talking about a celebration for us. Isn't it exciting?"

Once again, Jay nodded less than enthusiastically. For some reason a party just didn't seem all that appealing to him.

Probably because I'm still upset with Anna, he thought to himself. *Oh well, a party won't be that bad, and besides, they'll probably have some really good food.*

They continued to talk for some time. Jay was surprised and even humored as the conversation shifted from English to Spanish and back again as first one person, followed by another, added their two cents worth into the conversation. Even more surprising was the fact that he was beginning to understand what they were saying.

They stood there for more than a half of an hour planning the upcoming party. It was finally decided they would hold the party the following Saturday and that it would begin about four o'clock in the afternoon.

Jesse loudly explained, "That way, all of the festivities can be over and done with early enough for everyone to get enough sleep before our regular church service on Sunday! We do not want to miss our regular church service. People come from all over the countryside to take part. You will be surprised just how many people attend!"

"Then it's settled. We'll have the party in three days! Saturday at four p.m. it is!" Anna exclaimed excitedly.

They continued talking for several more moments. Everyone was too caught up in the excitement to notice the strange young lady in the burlap dress had pulled her hood up over her head and slowly worked her way to the back of the church. As she sidled up to the open doorway and silently slid into the outside world, not one person looked her way.

～ ～ ～ ～

As they reached their little house, Anna turned to Jay. "Saturday is going to be a wonderful day, a day to remember forever!"

With a note of sarcasm, Jay replied, "I can hardly wait."

"Oh, Jay, you'll love it, and you'll learn to love all the people too."

He pouted. "Just don't leave me here alone again without telling me where you're going. I about had a heart attack."

"It's not as if I could go far. This mission isn't all that big, you know. Besides, you need to become less dependant on me and interact more with the people. I mean, think about it, really. What could possibly happen to me?"

Sitting down hard in the kitchen chair, Jay continued to sulk. Lacking any inspirational comebacks, or arguments, he decided to let the matter drop.

As Anna made her way into the bedroom, he stated quietly without conviction, "Well, you never know."

Emerging with a towel and her change of clothes, Anna bent down and pecked Jay on the cheek. "You're so cute. What would I ever do without you?"

The Unraveling

"Leave me here alone again, you just might find out," he answered under his breath as she closed the bathroom door.

Chapter 12

Slithering and twisting it came, back and forth through the shrub and cacti-covered terrain. Slowly but steadily the rust-colored snake made its way over the ridge, head first, wider body and finally, smaller and fading tail as it crested the northern edge of the basin where the dull greens and grays bordered the emerald blue sky.

From his vantage point, he watched. Tempered excitement and anticipation leapt in his chest as he waited patiently. Rough, grimy fingers worked their way back and forth over the smooth surface of the heavy, palm-sized stone that rested in his right hand. Constricted eyes not only helped him see better but also produced a concentrated scowl that broadcast danger. This was the moment he'd been waiting so long for.

Rising from his seat, he moved away from the tree and its forgiving shade under which he'd been sitting and into the unforgiving, late-afternoon summer sun. Monsoon season was now upon them, raising the humidity level substantially. Beads of sweat popped up on his neck and forehead almost immediately and fed little rivulets of water as they raced down his face and fell to the parched ground below. If he noticed, he showed no indication, lost instead in concentration at what approached.

Slowly it continued, zigzagging back and forth as it bisected the basin floor in front of him. Unable to hide its reddish color, it stood out starkly against the blues and greens that surrounded it, and still it approached.

Anticipation growing even greater, the man ran several yards and climbed on top of a large outcropping of rock that rose more than ten feet into the air and bordered the pathway of the approaching prey. Working his way right to the edge, he crouched down like a cougar, ready to pounce, and waited.

Twisting and turning, it reached the near edge of the ravine and started creeping up the hill, back and forth as it approached, almost as if it had no care in the entire world. Slowly, slowly it continued, making its ascent toward the top as if destined for this moment and whatever fate awaited it.

Large, billowing, black clouds were beginning to form and stack up on each other directly behind the man as if they too were waiting for this moment in time.

Craning his neck, he could make out the round eyes on the head of the approaching beast as it drew ever nearer. With heart pounding wildly, every muscle in his body tensed up.

The unblinking, bright yellow eyes were a sharp contrast to the rust-colored body and had an almost hypnotic effect on him.

Closer it came, full speed ahead, intent on a destination known only by itself.

With heart pounding even more, the man continued to wait for just the right moment, causing his excitement and adrenaline to surge even higher. Timing was everything, and margin for error was nearly nonexistent. Counting down from ten under his breath, he prepared to pounce.

Every physical sense was at full alert as he readied himself. Little rocks and streams of dirt cascaded down the massive rock wall before piling up at the base of the outcropping as his foot disturbed the soil near the edge. In one fluid motion, his muscular legs sprang upward and outward as he launched himself off his vantage point to the trail below. Senses still at high alert, he could feel the wind as it filled up his loose shirt with a blast of air that felt cool as it rushed over his sweat-laden body. Arms out to his sides for balance, he landed in a crouch in the soft, thick dust on the trail below as if he had been dropped out of the sky.

The sudden appearance of the man in the path directly in front of the advancing beast caused it to veer sideways as it attempted to stop before reaching him. It continued its slide for a moment or two before turning back to face him head on. At just the last possible moment, the large Jeep slid to a stop mere inches from the human barricade now in its path. The red snake of dust following the car quickly enveloped both the vehicle and the man and hung in the air for a few moments before settling back to the earth from which it was born.

Ignoring the taste and smell of dust in his mouth and nostrils, the man threw back his head and let loose a guttural laugh that echoed throughout the valley.

Gaining his composure, he roared, "Scared you to death, didn't I, Rosalita?"

Looking out at him from behind the large steering wheel, Rosalita's eyes were dark, nonreflective pools that masterfully masked the mood in her heart.

"I could have run you over, no problem, and no one would ever have known what happened to the great Luis," she stated quietly.

Again he roared, knowing in his heart that what she said was the truth.

"What's the matter? Did I give you a start?" he asked, trying to draw some sort of response from the young girl.

"I always expect the unexpected from you," was all she replied as she climbed from the hot vehicle.

"I suppose you do!"

Luis watched her with veiled admiration as she moved toward him fearlessly. She was, to the best of his recollection, the only person who showed little, if any, fear of him. It was for that reason that he had kept her around for so long. He had tested her many times over, always with the same result—contempt and hatred, but no fear. Abuses too great to mention and beyond any man's imagination he'd inflicted upon her. The visible proof lay in the many scars her body bore—war wounds, unspeakable horrors that had caused such damage and disfiguration, not to mentions the harm done to her spirit. Inner turmoil raged, unseen, in her soul.

To say she fascinated him could not even begin to express his interest in this girl. Deep in his heart, he knew one day that he would kill her. Kill her just as he killed all of the others. For now, though, he was content to keep her around. Test her, use her, find her breaking point, and break she would just as they all did. A day he had fantasized and dreaded about countless times. It was during those times that he was the most violent, spurred on by sick and twisted images that played themselves out, over and over in his imagination, driving him mindlessly on.

Slowing with caution, Rosalita drew within a couple feet of Luis. Eyeing the smooth stone clutched in his right hand, she moved toward his left side, out of striking distance before stopping.

If he noticed what she was doing, he gave no indication other than a slight grin, which seemed out of place on his scarred and angry face. Missing and broken teeth gave him a comical, almost disarming appearance, but Rosalita knew just how dangerous he really was.

Gusting winds picked up the light reddish dust in a choreographed dance set to the moaning winds that were sweeping in, wave after wave from south to north. Missiles of cold moisture cratered the soft dirt at their feet as the heavy and roiling thunderclouds began to release their cargo.

Shivering abruptly from the contrasting cold water on his back, Luis grabbed hold of Rosalita, drawing her near. "What did you find out?" he questioned impatiently.

Lightning flashed from the dark clouds directly behind him and matched the lightning intensity in his nearly black and evil eyes as he peered at the young girl.

Matching his glare, Rosalita answered him in an unemotional and monotone voice. "Three days from now there will be a party welcoming the gringos. The whole village and the surrounding countryside, for that matter, will be attending. It would be a good time to take one of them, I think."

"These gringos, do they have names?" he asked with growing excitement.

"Doesn't everyone?"

Jerking her arm hard, he pulled her to himself. "This isn't the time to be smart, Rosalita!" he warned.

She knew his warning was real, that she was toying with danger, so she resisted the urge to reply sarcastically.

"Their names are Jay and Anna."

Relaxing his grip, Luis's face lit up at this new revelation. "Jay and Anna, Jay and Anna; I wouldn't mind having a Jay or an Anna. Preferably an Anna, I think," he mused to himself.

Rosalita wrenched herself free from his grasp and began walking back toward the Jeep. Lightning continued to flash, followed almost instantly by large, booming thunder that seemed to go on forever and ever.

"If we don't get out of here now, we may never get out of here."

As if on cue, the storm clouds let loose a torrent of cold water, which pounded down relentlessly and began turning the red, dusty soil into a thick, muddy mess.

With catlike speed, Luis ran to the Jeep's dry sanctuary just as Rosalita started the engine. Rosalita jerked the shifting lever into first gear, shifted the rig into four-wheel drive, and gave the beast just enough gas to finish the climb to the top of the quickly rutting roadway.

"We better wait this one out right here," she exclaimed as she scanned the dark and angry sky overhead.

Though midday, the sky was as dark as night, lit up only by flashes of bright lightning strikes, which were happening with great frequency and followed quickly by deafening thunder that seemed to roll on and on for several seconds, oftentimes with no distinguishable break between claps.

"What violence!" Luis admired.

The Unraveling

The storm raged on for more than an hour, plenty of time for Luis to hatch an insidious plan bent on altering the lives of two unsuspecting and innocent people.

Chapter 13

Arching his back into the hard wooden slats of the well-worn kitchen chair, Jay balanced the rickety furniture on its hind legs while spreading his bare legs out across the unstable kitchen table. A clammy film covered his bare torso as the high humidity that came with the monsoonal season caused his skin to sweat out of every pour, or so it seemed.

He reached into the large pocket of his baggy Bermuda shorts with one hand while running the long, skinny fingers on his other through his dark, damp hair like a comb. Fishing around in the pocket, he could feel the hard ruggedness of the heavy pewter cross attached to the heavy metal chain the townspeople had given him as a gift just a day before. It was cool to the touch, and the cold hardness of the cross felt good in his hand.

Retrieving it from his pocket, he began to spin the heavy crucifix first one way then another as it wound its way around his index finger. The air whirred as the chain and cross cut a path through it. Back and forth it went with great speed, skill he had achieved from hours of practice.

It moved in tandem to the rhythmic soprano voice of Anna, coupled with the running water of the shower. Unable to contain himself, Jay broke out in a large smile as joy surged in his soul.

I could be content to just sit here and listen to her for hours.

The sudden clank of a small pebble hitting the glass on their front door window brought him out of his bliss but elicited an even larger smile as he slid his legs off the table, slammed the wooden chair to the ground, and spun around, all nearly simultaneously, to face the source of the noise. Squealing with delight as they ran around the corner of the building, Jay caught sight of the guilty intruders as they made their rapid getaway.

Crouching down to the ground as low as he could get, he crept to the inside of the front door and rolled to the side, out of view of the children. Waiting for several moments, he peeked out the corner of the window in time to see the children sneaking back to their original post just behind the flower-covered trellis in the small courtyard. Catching sight of him, the children once again made a hasty, squealing retreat back to the outside corner of the small home, where they regrouped and began to approach the front of the home, and Jay, with as much stealth as a half dozen kids could garner. Sometimes they would come from different directions, sometimes crawling, sometimes running, but each time, Jay would pop up in either the kitchen door window or the living room window just as the children neared the front of the home, sending them giggling on their hastily bid retreat once again.

They had played this game for hours the previous couple of days. Jay was amazed at the length of their attention span and stamina. To make things more interesting, he had even slipped out the front door and hid right next to the corner of the building where he knew they would soon emerge. Emerge they did, and what a sight to behold as their little feet ran in thin air with fright for several moments right after Jay had let out his longest and loudest roar he could muster right before falling on his side, shaking uncontrollably with laughter.

The children laughed just as hard at this new turn of events. Jay had upped the ante, and they loved it. Anna had watched in amazement and joy as this little game of cat and mouse began drawing Jay out of the gloomy mood that had taken over his life. *Leave it to children*, she thought as she sat witnessing the rebirth of her old Jay right before her very eyes. At first, Jesse protested and chased the children off. "You are disturbing them. Let there be some privacy," he scolded the downcast faces as they slowly headed toward their own homes.

Motioning toward Jay with her eyes, Ann exclaimed, "It's all right, let them play. It's good for us!"

After several moments, Jesse understood Anna's message and allowed the children to return. Return they did, continuing their game for many more hours before heading home for the evening. Bright and early the next morning, they began again, right where they left off. It was a good distraction for Jay. They played their little game off and on for the balance of the second day and were now right back for more of the same.

Today would be different. Jay watched and waited, ready to surprise the children as they made a new approach at their assault on him and Anna. Smiling, he could hear their little voices and the sound of their little feet as they tromped along in the loose dirt just around the corner of the building. For some reason, anticipation always seemed to build in his stomach right at this point even though he knew just what to expect next. He knew it was silly but didn't care. For the first time in a long while, he was just enjoying having fun. Time, however, was not on their side this day. In less than an hour they were all due for the large welcoming party the mission was holding in Jay and Anna's honor.

Sneaking out the door, Jay watched and waited as the little bodies began their approach on the house—small silhouettes through the little pink flowers growing on the vine-covered trellis. Jay waited, hiding behind the small brick-lined flower garden and watched as they drew nearer and nearer. Ten feet, eight feet, five feet, three feet, Jay continued to wait, stealthlike, ready to pounce. Just when it seemed they would certainly discover his hiding place, he sprung into action.

"Rooaarrrr," he bellowed at the top of his lungs, arms thrown high in the air.

Gasping for air, he began to choke with laughter as the children shrieked with joy and tried to run away from this new, fron-

The Unraveling

tal assault. The look of surprise on their faces was more than he could take. Gaining their footing, the children scurried off to the end of the building to collect themselves and begin anew.

"Jay! Look at you! You're all dirty," Anna exclaimed from behind, startling Jay just as badly as the children had been only moments before.

"It's just a little dust," he exclaimed less than convincingly as little rivers of sweat cut through the grime that had accumulated on his bare chest and legs.

"Now you're going to need another shower!"

Turning to face the children who were once again making a new approach, Anna brought them up short. "You all need to go home and get ready for the party," she reminded them.

Disappointment covered their grimy faces at the news but was quickly replaced with smiling anticipation as Anna reminded them all that there would be piñatas at the party and they would most surely be loaded with candy and treats, enough for everyone.

Turning to Jay, and with the sternest voice she could muster, she ordered him back to the shower to wash off the grime. "And make it quick," she demanded as sternly yet unconvincingly as possible.

Like a child, shoulders hunched up in disappointment, Jay obediently trudged to the bathroom to take another shower.

Feeling accomplished and a little mischievous, Anna added, "And don't forget to wash behind your ears, mister!"

Jay smiled as water poured over his body on its way to the drain. Even though he still had reservations about being at the mission, he was starting to feel much more at ease than when they had first arrived. It seemed that everyone there absolutely loved him and Anna. They were all so friendly and outgoing all of the time, almost as if they were part of a big, new family. Even so, small doubt still lingered in the back of his mind, hanging there, unwilling to leave him. Try as he might, he just couldn't completely rid himself of the burden. Even Anna was no help as he had shared with her the previous evening of his mood and doubt.

"You just have to give it to God and give it time! You have to trust that He has our best interest at heart, that He has a wonderful plan for us! Worrying will not add one minute to your life," she reminded him. "Besides, look how much better you already feel! Give it a little more time and you'll be feeling great, excited even about being here!" she encouraged.

A little more time! A little more time! All I have is time! he thought as he dried off from the shower.

Emerging from the steamy bathroom, Jay stopped in his tracks as Anna stood, back toward him looking out the kitchen window as a steady stream of festively clad villagers made their way down the main road toward the church at the far end of the mission. Black and long, her shiny hair hung more than halfway down her back, pulled together and held in place by a white scrunchy. It swayed back and forth as she hummed a song under her breath moving her body back and forth in rhythm to the song.

Nearly touching the floor, her beautiful, one-of-a-kind dress only accentuated the slight movement of her hips. It was the beautiful, handmade dress she had received from their church back in Colorado Springs, and it looked splendid on Anna.

Letting out a loud whistle, Jay teasingly showed his approval of his beautiful wife.

Turning into his waiting embrace, she smiled and said, "You probably whistle like that at all the pretty girls."

"Just the really pretty ones," he teased back, closing his arms around her.

"I love you, Jay Bilston."

"I love you too, Miss Anna!"

They stood in embrace for several moments, Anna resting her head on Jay's chest. Jay rubbed her arms, eager for the embrace, reassured by her touch. Slowly he stroked her slightly damp hair.

The Unraveling

"Promise never to leave me! Not for any reason. I know I would die without you!"

"Well, we don't want you to die now, do we? Besides, I'm not going anywhere, silly man!"

Somehow her confident retort had a less than calming effect on him. The uneasy feeling in the back of his mind continued to produce a lingering annoyance every bit as real as a pebble in a shoe.

"Well, we better get to the chapel. I think most of the people are already there. Besides, I'm really hungry,"

Raising her lips to his, she gave him a long, emotional kiss. "You're not going dressed like that, Mr. Bilston," she as much told as asked.

"Might as well. I could never keep up with Miss Anna! Besides, you're the one everyone has come to see."

"Oh, pshh!" she teased as she separated from his embrace and headed toward the door. "At least wear some nice jeans and a nice shirt. Jesse says this will be the party to remember for the rest of our lives!"

Chapter 14

Jesse and the ladies had worked hard all day preparing for the festive occasion. Normally banquets were held in the chapel only on special holidays—Christmas, Easter, Cinco de Mayo—with all other events held in the small, single-room schoolhouse just behind the new church. Not this day. This was more than a special party; this was the official introduction and installation of their new missionaries from America.

The entire village would be in attendance, along with everyone that had either been invited or had heard of Jay and Anna's arrival from miles around the mission. None would be turned away. With so many guests, the schoolhouse would just not be large enough to accommodate all, so the decision had been made to hold the banquet in the church.

Brightly colored streamers, banners, and welcome signs written in both Spanish and English covered nearly every bit of wall space in the small church. Colorful, lifelike piñatas hung just above head height from ropes strung over the large metal beams and were tied off to the steel supports that held up the ceiling. The piñatas swayed back and forth as the large overhead fans far above churned up the air.

The wooden seating pews had been moved from the center of the building and now lined the walls of the church. In their place were several long tables arranged in a *U* shape and were covered with starched white tablecloths and were laid with colorful pans and vessels containing enchiladas, tamales, rice dishes, vegetables, tortillas, mole sauce, and nearly every other traditional Mexican dish imaginable.

One table on the end held a very special and rare treat for such a poor community; spread out on a large wooden platter every bit as big as the table itself was a splendid pig, pit roasted, hooves, head and all. The skin was a reddish, smoke color, which shined brightly in the indoor light. The steaming hot pig even had an apple in its mouth.

The room was abuzz with activity, women carrying more and more platters of food to the waiting tables, old men sitting in the wooden pews, visiting with one another while young men claimed one corner of the building, pushing and working each other for position at the back of their group while eyeing a group of young ladies doing likewise in another corner. As soon as one was shoved to the front, shyness and panic began to set in until the young man or woman broke free and scurried back to the rear safely behind their friends. All were dressed in their finest clothes—women in long, colorful dresses, all hand sewn, while the men wore their nicest pants and whitest shirts they had. For many, their outfit was one of only two they owned, if they were so fortunate.

When Jay and Anna entered the building through the large, wooden doors that had been propped open for ventilation, all activity stopped as the crowd reacted with a collective cheer. The response was embarrassing to Jay, but Anna just beamed as they made their way into the center of the building, where they were met by a throng of people rushing to greet them. Most of the women and young ladies rushed up to Anna to admire her hand-made dress. It was by far the most beautiful garment they had ever seen with its vibrant shades of purple contrasting against the white and off-white cloth that had been used in the pattern. Anna explained to them how the women in her church back home had spent countless hours making her dress as a going-away gift. It truly was one of a kind and fit for royalty.

Watching from afar, Jay admired the beauty of his wife, her long black hair pulled into a ponytail as it swung back and forth across the back of her dress. Smiling to himself, he couldn't help but notice a radiance that seemed to envelope her as she interacted with the people.

She really loves everyone! he thought as a group of men, including Jesse, approached him and began pumping his hand in greeting while ushering him to the center of the room to join Anna.

After garnering everyone's attention, Jesse formally introduced Jay and Anna, which produced another long round of cheering. Silencing the group with outstretched arms, Jesse blessed the food before herding Jay and Anna to the front of the line.

"As our guests of honor you must go first," he announced to the pair.

Not knowing where to start, Jay just stood there, admiring the spread for a moment. "I think I died and went to heaven," he exclaimed.

"Silly man, I knew you, er…your stomach, would like this."

They filled their plates with enchiladas, tamales, sausages, vegetables, salads, and roasted pork.

"I'll take some of the skin too!" Jay told Anna, who passed the word on in Spanish to the man in charge of the pig.

"I can't believe you eat the skin," Ann responded to Jay as he crunched down on the brittle morsel.

"It's the best part!" he exclaimed between bites.

They were ushered to the head table to a pair of seats that had been reserved just for them. The people streamed by as they ate, each stopping to welcome them, which in turn made it difficult to eat their food. The constant interruption began to annoy Jay.

"What's the use of letting us go first if they're going to keep us from eating our food?" he grumbled under his breath to Anna.

"Go ahead and eat your food. No one will mind."

People were everywhere, many more people than lived at the mission compound. Jay wondered where they had all come from. The desert terrain seemed vacant, but for the few shanties built around the outside of the mission walls. There wasn't even a town within nearly one hundred miles in any direction.

"It's like they sent out alerts of this party clear across the country or something," Jay said between bites.

"I know, isn't it wonderful? Look at all these people we can impact," Anna replied.

I am not going out looking for all these people! he thought to himself.

The food was every bit as good as it looked and smelled, and amazingly, they didn't run out of a single thing as person after person went through the long line.

Eating till he was stuffed and his plate was empty, Jay pushed his chair back a bit and began watching the people as they interacted with one another. He noticed Anna's plate, which had been pushed far from her, food barely touched.

"Are you all right?" he asked with genuine concern in his voice. "You hardly ate anything."

Anna gave him the best smile she could muster. "I don't feel well at all," she managed as tears welled up.

Leaning her head on his shoulder, Anna began to cry, bringing Jay to a near panic. Leaning his head down to hers, he kissed the top of hers while breathing in the clean smell of her freshly washed hair. The scent of her shampoo coupled with a slight hint of her vanilla musk perfume was nearly intoxicating to him.

"What in the world is the matter?" Jay asked as he lifted Anna's chin with his hands until their eyes met.

"I'm sorry. I'm being such a baby and I don't know why," she said, embarrassed. "Food just doesn't taste good to me at all right now, and it hasn't since we began our travels. At first I thought it was just a touch of the flu or some virus, but now I'm beginning to think I have something wrong with me. And now, for no reason at all, I started to feel overwhelmed and really sad! I don't know what's going on,"

112   Mark A. Gudmunson

Finding himself in an unusual position, Jay did his best to console Anna, to assure her that all was well and would be all right. The more he tried, the more his own voice sounded less and less convincing, even to himself.

"Just try and enjoy the evening. If you start feeling too bad, we'll make an early evening of it and head home. Everyone will understand. You're just overwhelmed with all that's going on right now. You'll feel better tomorrow, you'll see."

"I can't leave early, everyone would be so disappointed. Look at all the trouble everyone has gone to just for us. Leaving early just wouldn't be the right thing to do."

People were finishing their meals and beginning to move around, visiting with one another. Small, smartly dressed children ran from one piñata to another, hoping that somehow one would drop down from the ceiling low enough for them to reach it and the goodies contained within. Conversations mixed with the sounds of children playing, a mariachi band performing, and people moving to and fro began to raise the decibel sound level until it was nearly impossible to hear the persons sitting right next to them, which only perpetuated the noise problem as people began speaking louder and louder to one another just to be heard.

The noise was only adding to Anna's discomfort. Jay couldn't help but notice how pale her olive complexion had become. Even more alarming to Jay was the manner in which Anna's large brown eyes were drawn down into a squint, a sure sign of a massive headache.

"You're not feverish," he stated hopefully as he moved his hand across her clammy forehead.

"I feel like I'm going to throw up," she said just before rushing to the women's restroom across the building.

Worry lined Jay's face as he watched her make her way across the floor. Anna had never been sick before, save for a few colds and sniffles, so this was something new for him to contend with.

The Unraveling   113

Seeing the worry on his face from across the room, Jesse made his way over to where Jay was sitting, waiting for Anna to return.

"Is everything all right?" he asked with deep concern in his voice.

"Yeah, everything is okay. Anna is just feeling a bit under the weather is all," Jay explained.

"Is there anything we can do for her?" Jesse asked.

"Well, I'm not sure what's wrong with her. Maybe if you have some Pepto Bismol or some antacid of some type, and an aspirin. That would probably be helpful."

Jumping to his feet, Jesse headed off toward the offices at the back of the church. "I'll see what I can find for her," he called out over his shoulder.

With deepening concern, Jay watched the bathroom door for any sign of Anna. *What could be taking her so long?* People passing back and forth between him and the door obstructed his view. Just when his view cleared, a group of children stopped directly in front of Jay and congregated under a piñata resembling a colorful goat. Jumping as high as they could, the children attempted to touch the swinging treasure but missed by several feet. Their lack of success did little to damper their enthusiasm, however, which only added to Jay's annoyance.

Returning with a small cardboard box, Jesse rushed up to Jay. "We have mucho medicine," he stated as he dumped the contents of the box on the table in front of Jay.

Little white pills spilled everywhere as the lid to the aspirin bottle came off the small bottle that contained them. Jay caught site of Anna emerging from the bathroom as he bent down to retrieve a roll of antacid that had fallen to the ground. Bent slightly at the waist, Anna wrapped her arms around her midsection as she made her way slowly across the floor to Jay.

"My stomach is really upset," she announced to both Jay and Jesse.

"That does it. You're going home to bed," Jay demanded, taking Anna into his arms.

"I can't go right now. We haven't even had dessert or hit the piñatas," Anna protested. "Besides, everyone will be so upset if I leave right now."

"We'll be just fine; besides, it's not as if you are going anywhere! We will all have time to visit you for days, months, and years to come!" Jesse settled the issue.

"Well, I'll go, but you should stay and enjoy yourself," she argued with Jay. "Besides, they are going to hold the installment ceremony for us. At least one of us should be here."

"That's right; we could have one of the ladies take Anna home to help her to bed. No need for both of you to leave us," Jesse agreed.

"I don't know. I would feel funny having Anna go home alone or with a complete stranger. Maybe I could take her home then come back and join the party once I know she's settled and all," Jay argued.

"Nonsense, she'll be just fine! Besides, we're all like one big family here at the mission. Everyone here knows everyone else. There are no strangers amongst us."

Feeling a bit overwhelmed, Jay had little choice and reluctantly agreed to let a couple of the young ladies take Anna home. She was his security blanket, and he did not enjoy being separated from her one bit.

"It'll be all right. I'll be all right! Just stay and enjoy yourself. Let the people welcome you with the ceremony they have planned and then come home. I'll be right there in bed waiting for you. Besides, what could ever happen?" Anna reassured Jay as the young ladies gathered her up and led her toward the open doorway.

"Well, all right, but I won't be long, I promise," Jay told Anna as he gave her a quick embrace and kiss.

The Unraveling

The small group paused at the doorway for a moment and eyed the ominous thunderheads that were building from the south.

"Looks like we're in for a big one," Jesse announced as his eyes scanned the skies.

Strong winds were beginning to kick up the red dust, blowing it across the soccer field, north to south.

A couple children were outside playing tag or some other playground game. Turning to wave good-bye, Anna reassured Jay that she loved him and that all would be fine. With a lump in his throat he waved back as the first drops of rain began to mottle the red dirt just outside the door.

"Shall we break some piñatas?" Jesse asked as he led Jay back into the church. "It's about that time, I think," he added as they approached another group of children who were trying in vain to untie the rope supporting the piñata.

"Yeah, I guess we should start before these kids tear them down," Jay added, his misgivings about Anna's departure fading to the back of his mind.

∾ ∾ ∾ ∾

Sitting at the back of the church by herself, Rosalita's ever-vigilant gaze saw everything as it unfolded. Taking a bite of food from her plate, she smiled and thought to herself, *They're making this much too easy on me.*

She had been waiting, scheming, all evening long for a way to get Anna by herself, away from all of the rest—a task that at the beginning of the evening had seemed all but impossible. Now, here she was, ready to take advantage of what fate had presented.

Setting her plate aside, she pulled the hood of her cloak up over her head, rolled up a dozen or so tortillas from a platter sitting next to her, placed them in a large pocket on her cloak, and made her way toward the open doorway.

Turning quickly back toward the crowd, she surveyed the room until satisfied that no one was watching her, slipped out the door and around the building, out of sight, directly toward Jay and Anna's.

Chapter 15

Trudging across the dirt playground, Anna did her best to keep from getting red mud on her garment by holding her dress up to her knees, a task proving to be fruitless as the three of them made their way back toward her house. Just enough rain was falling to ensure the blowing dust would plaster itself on their clothes, arms, faces, and even hair—whatever it made contact with. Large flashes of lightning illuminated the dark sky and cast an eerie shadow on the vacant town as they made their way down the main street toward home.

Howling wind made it impossible to talk, and darkened sky made it almost as difficult to find their way down the narrow street. Everything had the same vacant look, empty and unwelcoming. There were no lights in any of the houses, no pit fires from which to set a landmark, just row house after row house.

A sudden flash of lightning revealed a dark, hooded figure as it darted across the street behind the girls, cut to the rear of a line of row houses and actually passed the trio as they continued their way gingerly to their destination. Wind and rain prevented any of them from detecting the interloper.

Rain had begun pounding down on them with enough added force that the large, cold drops stung the skin. Anna wondered, *Where is that house?* as nausea renewed its grip on her.

Dusk blinded them from seeing anything more than a dozen feet away. They were traveling on instinct and knowledge the girls had gained from years of inhabiting the small town. Anna was essentially blind to her surroundings and relied on the other two every step of the way. Her head was swimming in dizziness, and her stomach was anything but placid. She hoped she'd be able to make it to her home before vomiting. Stopping to catch her breath and still her tormented stomach, she grabbed on to Gabie and Rosanne for support. Surprise and concern filled their eyes.

"Are you all right, Miss Anna?" Gabie asked with audible concern in her voice.

"We don't have much farther to go," Rosanne added with as much encouragement as she could muster.

"Yes, just give me a moment to gain my senses."

"Maybe we should pray," Gabie offered.

"That sounds like a good idea. Would you like to pray for us?"

Without missing a beat, Gabie began to pray for Anna, for her stomach, and for whatever ailment was bothering her, asking God to please help them make it to the house where Anna could get to bed. Only a moment or two had passed, and Anna, feeling much better, informed them she was ready to continue on their way.

$$\sim \sim \sim \sim$$

Slipping quietly behind the houses, Rosalita began running for the north gate as quickly as possible. Visibility was poor at best, resulting in several trips to the muddy earth. Still, she pressed on as fast as humanly possible. A slight window of opportunity had presented itself, and she was determined to take advantage of it. Her heart raced with anticipation as she reached the north gate and scanned the land beyond it as far as she could see, which wasn't far at all.

Where are they?

Not wanting to draw attention to herself, she hesitated from calling out into the night. It didn't take long to realize she would have to take a chance; time was slipping away.

Garnering as much air into her lungs as possible, she let out a short yell, "Hey!" and waited for a bit. Anger began to well up when there was no response. "Hey!" she yelled again and waited.

The Unraveling

Luis is going to kill me! she thought, not out of fear, but out of simple knowledge. With hope fading, she let out one final yell, "Hey!" and waited.

Several moments passed as she peered out into the night with squinted eyes. Slight movement of the distant grass caused her hopes to rise, but guardedly as she tried to add shape and form to the movement. Ducking down for fear of being seen, she tried her best to blend into the post next to the gate and waited.

It didn't take long before two figures began to take form as they scurried toward the gate in a defensive crouch. She waited until they were no more than a few feet from her, close enough to make out the familiar faces of Jalle, a muscular young man with long curly hair, and Robello, a middle-aged flunky that Luis kept around for amusement, at least that's how it seemed to Rosalita.

The two jumped from her sudden appearance as she hissed, "What took you so long?"

Opening the gate just enough to slide through, they turned to face her.

Jalle explained, "We had to make sure it was you. We couldn't see a thing."

"Well, we haven't any time to spare. Robello, you go back to the Jeep and drive it down to the gate. Stay to the side, off the road and wait for us, and no lights! Don't touch the brake either; the lights will surely give you away. Understand?"

He nodded his head in agreement. Rosalita pushed the gate back open to let him through. "If we aren't back in fifteen minutes, drive back over the rise and wait for us! Wait the entire fifteen minutes, though!"

Robello muttered under his breath and turned to leave,

Rosalita hissed as loudly as possible, "Robello, no lights! Don't forget, no lights!" as he disappeared from sight.

Rain was coming down in torrents as Rosalita turned and motioned for Jalle to follow her. Quickly she returned the way she had just traveled, but this time with Jalle on her heels. Soon she was parallel to the three young ladies as they made their way to Jay and Anna's house. Stopping just at the edge of the shadows, Jalle ran right into the back of her, almost knocking her into the open street, just feet from Anna and the girls.

She leaned forward and whispered in his ear, "What are you doing, you oaf?"

"Sorry, I can hardly see a thing."

Rosalita settled to the ground, almost in a prone position, and motioned for Jalle to do likewise. Rain was falling even harder and adding to the pool that was now forming around the two. Unsure of what to do next, they sat and waited to see what Anna would do.

~ ~ ~ ~

Though feeling very dizzy, Anna made it to her front door with the help of the others. Seldom had she seen it rain so hard. The cool drops felt good on her head and seemed to help with her queasy stomach. Upon opening the door, she told the girls to head back to the church.

"I don't need you here to help me. I'm just going to get out of these wet clothes and go to bed. There's no need for you to miss the festivities."

Both Gabie and Rosanne protested, but Anna would hear nothing different, insisting again that the two go back to the church to join the others.

"I really appreciate you bringing me home, but I don't need someone to sit here with me, and I don't want to ruin your whole evening. You could come in if you want to wait for the rain to subside first, but I really would feel terrible if you stayed with me and missed the whole evening of fun. Besides, you didn't even have a chance to finish your dinner."

After a few more weak protests, the girls agreed to go back to the party. The rain had begun to subside as they turned and headed down the sloppy road. With a wave, Anna stood half inside her doorway and watched the young ladies as they made their retreat.

"I'll see you tomorrow," she promised the two as they turned and waved one last time.

Smiling in spite of the way she felt, Anna said a quick prayer thanking God for such wonderful people as she entered the house and closed the door.

~ ~ ~ ~

Rosalita watched the scene as it unfolded in front of her with amazement, unable to believe her good fortune. She could almost reach out and touch the two girls as they passed by on their way back down the muddy road toward the church. Now that Anna had been left alone, her job had just become that much easier. Once in the clear she rose and turned toward the house, motioning Jalle to follow her.

Satisfied that no one could see them, she turned to him. "Hit me, hard."

Jalle hesitated, "Do what?"

"Hit me, hard!"

Jalle was stunned and didn't respond.

"I said hit me! Are you deaf? Hit me now!"

Jalle hesitated for a moment, and Rosalita backhanded him across the face as hard as she could. He was stunned and stepped back from the blow, shaking his head. Anger washed over him as she instructed him to hit her again. Without thinking, he cocked his arm and struck her across the face with the palm of his hand, the impact hard enough to send her to her knees, head to the ground.

"Thank you! Next time do what I say the first time I ask!" She climbed back to her feet.

Blood stained her swollen lips where he had hit her. Unsure what to do next or what Rosalita would do, he waited with clenched fists until she motioned him to follow her back to the muddy road.

"I'm going over to the house; you stay right here and watch until I motion for you. If you see someone coming, you need to make sure they never make it to the house. Do whatever you need to do! Understood?"

He shook his head affirmatively as she made her way across the street to Jay and Anna's front door. Taking a deep breath, she pounded on the door as hard as she could.

Anna was in the bathroom and had just started to undo her dress when the pounding started. Her heart leapt through her chest at the abrupt noise.

"What in the world?"

Standing as still as possible, she waited, heart pounding harder and harder, unsure of what to do next. *Pound, pound, pound*, went the door again.

Sure that it must be the girls returning for some reason, Anna headed back out to answer the door.

"Who is it?" She tried to make out someone through the sheer curtain covering the window on the door.

"Help me. I need help," came the muffled reply from the other side of the glass.

Peering through the window into the dark night was almost a fruitless endeavor, but after a moment, she could make out the distinct figure of a petite individual, possibly a girl.

She asked again, "Who is it?" with uncertainty building in her chest.

"Please, I need your help!" the voice on the other side of the door softly replied.

Satisfied that it was a girl, Anna cautiously opened the door and peered out into the dark night. Howling wind and falling rain filled the room with noise as Anna glimpsed the face of her night visitor. It was a girl, indeed. Her appearance shocked Anna; blood ran from her mouth, over her chin, and dripped into her muddy, cupped hands below. Mud-caked hair escaped a black hood that covered the girl's head and hung down over her dark eyes. Tears streamed down her cheeks.

She tried to push her way into the house as she sobbed to Anna, "Help me, please. He hit me."

With fear subsiding and motherly instinct kicking in, Anna opened the door wide. Bringing the girl inside, she asked, "Who hit you? Where did he hit you?" Anna peered out into the night for any sign of a pursuer.

The girl sobbed, "He hit me...he's after me!" as she made her way across the room as far from the door as possible.

Water ran from the girl's clothing and dripped on the floor as she huddled near the far wall. Recognition of the girl's face tugged at Anna's memory as she closed the door and locked it. Peering once again into the dark night produced no new discovery as Anna turned back to the stranger in her house. Scanning the girl's face through her memory proved to be futile as Anna failed to identify anyone she knew or should have known.

"Let me see you. Where did he hit you?" She moved to the girl's side.

Ever so shyly the young lady turned her face up to meet Anna, which stopped her briefly in her tracks.

Who is this girl? I should know who she is!

The girl appeared to be in her early twenties, although caked mud and flowing blood made it difficult to be sure.

Taking her head gently in her hands, Anna asked, "Do you have any other injuries?"

Shaking her head, the girl began to shudder as Anna delicately touched the wounded lips.

"I think you'll live," she added, relinquishing the girl's head. "Now, what did you say your name is?"

Sobbing to herself, the young girl turned her head away from Anna. With the best motherly voice she could muster, Anna answered, "Well, you'll tell me when you're ready. Right now, though, we need to get a wet washcloth on your mouth,"

Moving to the linen closet, Anna retrieved a washcloth from the shelf and wet it down in the bathroom sink with cold water.

"Here, put this on your lip. It'll sting a bit but stop the bleeding."

With delicate touch she applied the wet cloth directly to the wound, which produced a shudder from the girl.

"There, we'll leave that on for a bit before we apply some ointment to the cut."

Pulling a chair out from the table, Anna motioned for the girl to sit down.

"Would you like some hot tea or something other to drink?"

After the girl nodded her head, Anna reached into the refrigerator and removed a pitcher of fresh water. She filled up the little teapot and turned on the gas stove.

"It'll only take a couple of minutes." She pulled up a chair next to her visitor. "I wish you would tell me your name." She paused. "Well, let me take a look at your mouth," she insisted as the girl lowered the bloody washcloth.

"It's still bleeding a bit. Just hold it on there for a few more moments. Would you like to put on some dry clothes? I have some that would surely fit you. You could have them if you wish," Anna offered, hoping it would melt the girl's defenses.

The girl rejected the offer with a quick shake of her head and turned away from Anna's hovering.

"Well, I'm going to at least wrap a dry towel around you." Anna placed two thick ceramic mugs on the table before heading back to the linen closet.

With quickness and stealth, the girl tossed the bloody washcloth onto the kitchen table, grabbed one of the cups, and launched herself at Anna as she opened the linen closet to retrieve a towel.

Sensing something amiss, Anna raised her arms in defense and started to scream as the thick mug crashed down on the back of her head and shattered into dozens of pieces. All went black as her body dropped to the ground like a rock where it lay amid the remains of the broken mug.

"Rosalita! My name is Rosalita!" the young girl screamed at the prone body lying on the floor at her feet.

For an instant, hatred and the desire to kick, pummel, even kill the unconscious Anna almost overwhelmed her, but the knowledge of what would happen to her at the hands of Luis stopped her in her tracks. Never in her life had she felt such hatred and fury, and she didn't even know why. For some reason, Anna's genuine kindness triggered a hatred that frightened her.

Running to the door, she opened it and summoned for Jalle, who appeared next to her in a moment's time.

"What took you so long?" he asked while surveying the carnage on the floor. "Did you kill her?" he asked as his eyes rested on Anna's unconscious body.

"No, I didn't kill her, idiot."

A low and growing whistle began to blow out of the teapot as the water began to boil.

"Pick her up. We don't have any time to waste," Rosalita ordered as she made her way to the stove.

For a moment she thought about letting the teapot boil dry and hopefully burn down the house but thought better of it with the realization that a fire would most assuredly draw attention to Anna's absence sooner rather than later, and time was a commodity they needed at the moment.

Turning the stovetop control to off, she turned and headed out the door and beckoned Jalle to pick up Anna and follow.

Doing as instructed, the young man bent down and picked Anna up from the floor with ease and followed Rosalita out the open door into the dark rainy night.

Lightning flashed in the distance as the rain began pounding down once again on the trio as they made their way up the center of the street toward the north gate and the waiting vehicle.

Slosh, slosh, slosh, went their steps all the way to the gate, where Rosalita lifted and slid open the bolt before opening the gate just far enough to slip through.

"Hurry up," she whispered to Jalle, who was several steps behind her.

Turning to her left, she breathed easier when she caught sight of the Jeep.

"Let's go!"

With a grunt, he started through but came to an abrupt stop when the hem of Anna's dress caught on the gate. With a violent jerk coupled with the sound of ripping fabric, he forced his way through and turned to follow Rosalita.

With a roar, the Jeep came to life as Jalle threw his cargo into the rear.

"Let's get going!" Rosalita yelled over the noise of the engine.

The car lurched forward just as Jalle climbed into the seat next to Rosalita.

"I was just getting ready to leave," Robello announced as he muscled the car onto the muddy roadway.

The going was slow and treacherous, even more so because Rosalita wouldn't allow the use of the headlights.

All they could do was let the Jeep run in the deep ruts in the roadway and hope it stayed on course.

The rain continued to fall from the sky as the vehicle sped away from the mission. Howling wind pushed and pulled the gate and its newly claimed piece of cloth, flying like a flag, back and forth on rusty hinges, producing a rhythmic squeak that added tone to the musical storm.

Chapter 16

Children were screaming and running every which way to claim their prizes of candy and small toys as the rewards fell to the hard concrete floor and slid under tables, chairs, and people. Pieces of the piñata flew across the laughing crowd as the onlookers cheered their support for their newest missionary. Pulling the blindfold from his eyes, Jay surveyed the melee in front of him and handed the wooden bat to Jesse, who was holding the rope that supported the badly mangled piñata.

"I didn't think I was ever going to hit the thing," he said as a small girl approached from the side. Holding his hand out to hers, Jay accepted an offering of a small piece of homemade candy wrapped in wax paper. As he unwrapped it, he noticed that it looked similar to salt water taffy. Popping it into his mouth produced an instant pucker followed by shoulder shaking shudder as he sucked on the pliable material.

"What in the world is this?" he asked Jesse, who was laughing at the pained look on Jay's contorted face.

"It's a piece of lime or lemon plies, a type of candies the ladies make every year for Cinco de Mayo," he answered with a laugh. "Only the children are brave enough to eat the sour candy!"

Unable to spit the candy out, Jay swallowed hard and smiled at the little girl, who smiled back with a gigantic front-tooth-missing grin.

"Would you like another?" she asked, holding her other hand out to Jay.

With an emphatic "No!" Jay shook his head and told her to keep the candy for herself.

More than two hours had passed since Anna had gone home to lie down. It seemed more like ten minutes to Jay, who had been so busy visiting with all of the people, breaking piñatas, and eating desserts that time had gotten away from him. As a matter of fact, he hadn't even thought of her for more than an hour, distracted by the whole goings on, a fact that caused a guilty knot to form in the back of his mind.

"Maybe I should get back now," Jay said as he turned to Jesse. "I should check on Anna."

"What? You can't leave now! We're going to introduce you to the congregation and have a prayer service for you in just a few minutes."

Reluctantly, Jay agreed to stay there for a little while longer. With no more piñatas to break, the crowd dispersed back to their chairs or into small groups to visit with one another.

It was still raining quite hard outside, and the lights had flickered on and off on more than one occasion, results of severe thunder and lightning in the region. Even so, it was very warm and stuffy inside the small church. The sheer number of bodies added incredible heat and humidity to the mostly stagnant air. Sweat dampened the collar and underarms of Jay's shirt. He was glad he wore black so the sweat stains didn't show.

Jesse moved through the crowd, recruiting many of the young men to help break down the tables and move them to one of the vacant, outside walls of the church. A few of the old men brought homemade brooms out of a small closet near the large white hanging cross and swept all of the debris to the side of the building, where a group of ladies bearing burlap bags were waiting, ready to pick up all of the refuse. They all moved quickly, and before Jay knew it, the pews were being moved into place, transforming the building from a fellowship hall back into a sanctuary, almost as if the party had never happened.

The Unraveling

People spared no time claiming a spot of their own on one of the hard wooden pews. Once seated, conversations were taken up again right where they had left off.

With an air of confidence, Jesse marched up to the front of the church and placed the cushioned chairs in place before moving the podium back to the center of the raised stage. At about that time, a small lady with a head of black curls and dark brown eyes so large they made her look permanently surprised got up from one of the back pews and wove her way through the remaining crowd to take her place on the bench in front of the century-old upright piano. Flipping open the worn and split lid covering the age-stained keys, she began running her long, pencil-thin fingers back and forth over the ivory as "Amazing Grace" filled the sanctuary. As if on cue, the crowd of people jumped to their feet and began singing enthusiastically and with an unmistakable joy in their voices. Their arms waved back and forth and they swayed side to side in tandem singing in worship to their Lord.

Watching with awe, Jay was amazed at the demonstrative nature of the people as they worshipped. Not one of them was just going through the motions. These people with so very little were overjoyed with the simple knowledge that Jesus was their Lord and that He had died for their sins. Their passionate expression was a wonderful and amazing sight to behold.

They sang a few additional hymns and had prayer time before taking their seat as Jesse began to address the crowd. The air was electric with praise, and everyone present seemed to feel the Holy Spirit as He moved throughout the building. Shivers of excitement and joy ran up and down Jay's back as he observed the people become one with their Savior. Even though the service was in Spanish and Jay usually had great difficulty following the rapid speech, he knew exactly what Jesse was saying, which only excited him even more.

The service was no more than twenty minutes old when Jay heard Jesse announce his and Anna's name to the congregation.

Though he tried not to show emotion, a grin the size of a half moon broke out on his face as the crowd of people turned in their pews and began smiling and waiving at Jay.

"Señor Jay, it is time for you to come up front."

Nervous butterflies launched themselves in his stomach as he got up from where he was sitting and made his way to the front of the church. Numb with emotion and stiff with his awkward advance, Jay climbed on to the stage and stood next to the pulpit while Jesse continued his introduction. Unsure what to do next, Jay just stood there, as stiff as a board but smiling broadly. Before Jay knew what was happening, Jesse was stepping to the side of the podium, giving Jay his place.

Boom, boom, boom, went his heart as he looked out over the crowd. Unsure what to say, he smiled and cleared his throat nervously. The crowd silently waited in anticipation.

"Well, um, it's good to be here. I mean, we are delighted to be here and to count you as family."

The crowd roared their approval and clapped and clapped and clapped. It only added to Jay's embarrassment as he struggled to think of something more to say.

Make eye contact, make eye contact, kept running through his mind as he forced himself to look at the people, one at a time.

"Well, I'm going to be kind of a letdown for all of you; Anna usually does the talking as many of you already know, and I'm sorry she couldn't be here. It seems she has come down with a bit of the flu or something. She should be up and around in a day or so," he added nervously.

"I don't really know what to say. I'm really happy you all have welcomed us as part of your family. It's hard being so far from our home land and all, but knowing we have people here that love us, well, that makes it all right with me!"

Again the people roared their approval as Jay beamed a smile out over the crowd. Their appreciation was sincere and loving. Many of the children Jay had become acquainted with over the

The Unraveling

previous few days began chanting his name, much to the dismay of their mothers. With a feeble effort, Jay raised his hand and waved at his small fan club.

Stepping back from the podium, Jay motioned for Jesse to retain his former position behind the podium. With a handshake and a hug, Jesse closed the ceremony with a prayer of dedication.

"Give us a moment, and we will have a greeting line at the rear of the church," Jesse announced as the pianist began playing once again and the two of them made their way back to the rear of the church. Everyone clapped as he walked by, which made the experience all the more surreal to Jay. In a lot of ways, it reminded him of his wedding day.

Once Jay was in place at the rear of the church near the large wooden doors, the people began moving in rows out of the pews to welcome Jay. Most demanded a hug, although a few of the shy ones offered him their hand. Many of them had tears in their eyes, and some were openly crying, which made Jay tear up himself; he'd never felt so loved and appreciated before.

The people continued to mill around instead of heading home for the night. It was still raining hard, which was somewhat unusual for a monsoonal storm. Normally the storm would blow in and release its fury for a short while before moving off across the high dessert plateau. Sometimes one storm would hit right after another, but usually with a break in the rain between the frontal systems. But not tonight. Tonight it was just rain, wind, thunder, and lightning, and lots of it.

Nearly everyone had gone through the line when Jay's heart rate increased dramatically. Standing in line to greet him were Gabie and Rosanne, the two young ladies who had accompanied Anna home just a few hours ago.

Anxiety began to build in his mind as he pointed out the two ladies to Jesse. "I need to get back to Anna. Who knows how long she's been alone."

Jesse called the two girls over and asked why they were back at the church when he had sent them to stay with Anna.

"She wouldn't let us stay with her," Rosanne explained timidly.

"We tried to stay, really we did," Gabie added emphatically.

Lines of worry ran across Jay's forehead as the two ladies apologized over and over. "I'm sure she is all right," Jesse stated in an attempt to ease Jay's apprehension.

"You're probably right," Jay answered with little conviction in his voice.

Slowly the line moved along until Jay could finally see the tail end. Even though it had been no more than ten minutes since he'd talked to the girls, it seemed more like an hour. His heart was filled with worry and each smile was forced, although the people didn't seem to notice one bit. Sweat formed on his brow from stress over the situation he now found himself in.

A few of the children ran back and forth, playing tag amidst the pews, but most of them had played themselves out and were now sitting next to their parents, pestering them to go home so they could go to bed for the night. The crowd had moved to the doors but had stopped short of going out into the rain. Harsh wind and torrential rain motivated them to stay inside for the time being. Jay greeted the final family in line and headed toward the open doorway with Jesse no more than a step behind.

"It is raining so hard; couldn't you wait for a few more minutes to see if the rain lets up?" Jesse pled with Jay.

"No, a little rain won't hurt anyone! Besides, I really need to get home to Anna. She wasn't doing very well at all."

"Wait right here, I have something for you," Jesse yelled over his shoulder as he ran to the little office in the back of the church.

Jay waited impatiently for Jesse to return. All he wanted to do was get home to Anna. Craning his neck, he peered out the door and into the rain-filled night sky. Brilliant lightning lit up the sky like a thousand flashbulbs, brighter than any he had ever seen before. A deafening clap of thunder followed, even before

The Unraveling   133

the light had waned away. People ducked at the loud noise, and a murmur could be heard as the lights flickered on and off for a few moments.

Returning from the small office, Jesse handed Jay a flashlight and a clear plastic rain slick with an attached hood. "I thought you could use these, although the batteries in the flashlight are running low. There should be enough power left in them to get you home if you turn it on only when you absolutely need it. The raincoat has a slight leak, but it's better than nothing. I haven't used it in some time, and I almost forgot I even owned it. Take them; use them if you think they'll help."

"Thanks, I definitely can use them," Jay said as he slipped on the raincoat.

"Well, I guess I'll head home now,"

"Do you need anyone to go with you?" Jesse asked.

It took Jay only a moment to decide. "No, I'll be just fine,"

Several people had moved outside and stood just under the roof running across the front of the church. Rainwater had accumulated in the dirt road and was now running within just a few feet of the church doors. The rain was still pouring down in torrents and showed no sign of letting up.

"Looks like a flood," Jay said to himself as he clicked on the flashlight and scanned the beam of light across the hard dirt playground, which was now covered with standing water. "Wow, more like a lake."

The beam of light had already begun to dim, so Jay slid the switch to the off position as he gingerly made his way out to the edge of the playfield, or what he thought should be the edge of the playfield. It was hard to see, and he had to rely more on memory than on sight since it was so dark outside. The water was over his shoes and the ground underneath was muddy. Each step made a squishing sound and took his memory back to his childhood days when he and several cousins used to play in a small crick just outside of town where he grew up.

They always went out after the snow had melted and played in the water that had spilled out into the flat, never thinking that it might be dangerous. Their fun all ended one early spring day when a six-year-old neighbor girl followed them out into the water, got to close to the current of the flowing creek, and was washed away. They ran to their house as quick as they could and told Jay's parents. Jay's father ran out into the flat in his slippers in an attempt to find the young girl while his mother dialed 911.

In very little time the fire department, paramedics, and volunteers from the city had shown up on scene to search for the girl. It took them over twelve hours searching more than three miles of flooded stream before they found the girl's body lodged in the branches of a flooded tree. Vivid details still troubled his mind as he recalled the screams and moans of the mother of the young girl when the sheriff officers broke the news of their discovery.

Shivers ran up and down his spine at the gruesome memory from his childhood. Rainwater from above coupled with the deep run off had completely soaked him. For the first time in a long while he was actually cold as he made his way past the field and to the first set of homes on the side street that intersected the main road. Turning his flashlight on and off every thirty seconds or so kept him on the path as he made his way between the dark homes that lined the street. Water was everywhere and was actually flowing from the north to the south down the main street of the compound. Turning left onto the main street, Jay began to move with more determination as his surroundings became more familiar.

A smile of anticipation broke out on his face as he imagined Anna's reaction at the massive flow of water running through their compound. He hoped she was in bed and hadn't seen the water yet. *She's going to love this!*

No more than a couple minutes had passed when the beams of light revealed the row of houses he and Anna called home. Water was everywhere he looked and was several inches deep. Light

The Unraveling

from his kitchen was shining through the window and reflecting on the water that had accumulated in the entryway to their home. He could hear loud squeals of complaint from the neighbor's pigs as they made their dislike for the water known. His heart raced as he maneuvered into the entryway to their home and discovered the door to their house was standing wide open to the elements.

"Anna, Anna, what in the world is going on?" he called out as he reached the open door.

Panic filled his body and mind as he entered the house. His eyes scanned the room and focused on the bloody and broken ceramic mug that littered the floor near the linen closet. With lightning speed, Jay raced to the bedroom, hoping and praying that Anna was there, but the bed had not been slept in.

"Anna, Anna!" he called out as he raced to check the bathroom; no one was there.

Copious amounts of blood mixed with Anna's long black hair seemed to be everywhere he looked. This time, his panic and fear were warranted. He had no idea what had gone on here, but whatever had happened, it wasn't good. This time, Anna was gone.

Chapter 17

In spite of the rain, the entire village went into search mode for Anna as young and old alike checked every nook and cranny of the small compound, starting with Jay and Anna's house. Every home was searched, but not one clue or sign could be found other than the blood and broken mug. Rain continued its assault as thunderstorms and high winds battered the small village, making it nearly impossible to search the grounds. Worse yet, the rain washed away any possible tracks Anna's abductors might have left.

Jesse set up a command center in the church and was busy orchestrating the search from there. His first action was to place a call to the federal police to report Anna's abduction. The sergeant on the other end of the line took a report over the phone and informed Jesse that it would be at least two days before they would be able to respond because the heavy rains had washed out miles of roads in the area.

Pacing like a caged lion, Jay was a basket case, unapproachable and emotionally exhausted. On more than one occasion, Jesse tried to get him to lie down on a cot that one of the people had brought from home, but each time he refused.

Rosanne and Gabie were sitting in hard wooden chairs behind the table Jesse was using for his desk and looked absolutely terrified. They did their best to answer every question Jesse asked them. At first Jay was very suspicious of them, but each round of inquisitions brought the same set of answers from the two young ladies. Even so, Jesse asked them to stay put, just to cover his and their bases.

He kept explaining, "We believe what you are saying, but we need you to stay here so no one can have any doubt that what you are saying is the truth."

Several of the townspeople had gathered around the altar and were busy praying for Anna's safety. These same people who had been so joyous just hours before were now crying and wailing for God to intercede on their behalf. Even though they had only known her for a few days, these people loved Anna and considered her one of their own.

The mood of the entire village had changed in an instant. People were sad and frightened and didn't want to go home for fear of what might happen to them. Every townsperson had been accounted for, which prompted murmurings of evil spirits and demons that must have snatched Anna away. They could see no other possibility. Jesse did his best to dispel such notions, but superstitions had been a part of the lives of these people for generations, so the rumors continued to spread.

He kept telling the people over and over, "Trust in God and have faith!" But this had little impact.

With great reluctance, Jesse called missions headquarters to notify them of the situation.

"Besides, we need everyone possible to be interceding in prayer to the Lord," he explained to Jay.

What am I going to do? What am I going to do? What am I going to do? This was the only thought that ran through Jay's mind. Try as he might, he could focus on nothing else but those words. Fear was beginning to take its toll on him as vivid images of Anna lying in a pool of blood kept playing themselves over and over in his mind. *What if she's dead? Lord, what will I do?*

Slowly the night gave way to daylight and blue sky once again. Although slowly receding, water seemed to be standing everywhere one looked. A thin layer of fog was suspended no more than ten feet above the village, giving it a very eerie look and feel. People were beginning to get out and around to assess the damages and look for their livestock. Chickens that were normally out pecking around for insects remained roosted in the trees and shrubs, waiting for a patch of dry ground to emerge.

The group in the small church had dozed off for a little over an hour; Jay on his cot and the others lying on the pews, exhaustion finally overtaking them. The large overhead fans continued to churn the air, which had actually cooled nicely from the rainy weather. Finally, all was calm and seemed almost normal again in the little village.

Sloshing his way through the water and red mud, a young teenage boy from the mission, Lupe, ran on the balls of his feet down the center of the flooded roadway while holding a tattered looking flag over his head. He looked as if he was attempting to fly a kite with no string, which would have looked comical had anyone been around to see him. His large black eyes were pools of fear and his face a map of worry that could have given any onlooker the impression he was running from the piece of cloth he clenched firmly in his grimy right hand.

With determination and purpose he maneuvered through the town and turned right on the street leading toward the church. The mud was slick, and the standing water hid several of the ruts in the roadway, which caused him to stumble and fall on more than one occasion. Even so, he held the piece of cloth over his head, protecting it from the water as if it were some sort of valuable relic.

With the church in sight, Lupe gained his footing and gingerly traveled the last hundred yards before bursting through the open doorway and into the church.

"Jesse, Pastor Jesse, I have found her. Look what I have found!" His voice echoed throughout the building.

With a start, Jay and the others lurched awake, dazed and groggy from lack of sleep. Lupe continued waving his arm over his head, piece of cloth still firmly grasped in his fist. Muddy water dripped from his clothes and pooled out on the concrete floor.

The Unraveling

Practically jumping from his pew, Jesse asked him, "What's wrong? What are you talking about, Lupe?"

Lupe moved quickly across the concrete floor and stuck the tattered cloth practically in Jesse's face. "I found this when I was out trying to find all of our chickens."

Jay and the others had pressed around the suddenly self-conscious boy in an attempt to see what he had. Without warning, Jay yanked the cloth from Lupe's hand.

"This is Anna's," he announced with emotion rising in his voice.

Jesse asked, "Are you sure?"

"Positive!" Jay stated flatly.

The unique colors gave it away—periwinkle purple fading into various, lighter shades of purple, and finally a plain white before returning to the periwinkle color. It was a definite match, an actual part of Anna's one-of-a-kind dress that she had been wearing the previous evening.

Jay moved toward Lupe menacingly. "Where did you get this?"

Lupe looked nervous. "At the other end."

With rising desperation, Jay grabbed Lupe by the arm and demanded, "Where did you get this? Where at the other end?"

Moving quickly, Jesse stepped in and separated Jay from the boy. "You're frightening him. Give him a chance to speak."

Lupe swallowed hard and stepped back. Taking a deep breath, he started again, "I found it at the other end, at the gate. I was out looking for chickens and saw something flapping in the wind. I went to investigate and recognized the colors from Miss Anna's dress. I brought it to you as quick as I could."

Tears welled up in his eyes as he waited for a reprimand that never came. "Good job, Lupe," Jesse said as he patted the young man on the head. "Can you take us to the exact spot?"

Nodding his head that he could, the small group consisting of Jay, Jesse, Gabie, and Rosanne made their way out of the church and onto the flooded road. Jay was surprised how warm it already was as they waded up the street and made a left on the main road of the village. More of the water had subsided, leaving little islands of mud poking out of the water. They moved rapidly through the village with Lupe leading the way.

Many of the townspeople came out of their homes and followed the small group as it passed. By the time they reached the other end of the town, the majority of the people were in the group following Lupe. Feeling very important, he turned and motioned to the north gate of the city. "I found it right here, stuck on the bolt." He pointed to the bolt that secured the gate to the post.

Jay ran quickly to the gate to inspect the area to which Lupe had pointed. Sure enough, several threads of cloth still hung from the rusty iron bolt. Rising to his feet, he looked beyond the gate and down the road that led out into the high desert. Faint car tracks could be seen in the mud, although determining their age was all but impossible due to the torrential rains.

Tears welled up in Jay's eyes as he asked, "Where could she be?"

"Well, one thing is for certain, she's no longer here," Jesse announced dejectedly.

Chapter 28

With little effort, Jalle flung the limp and unconscious Anna off his shoulder and onto a rickety pallet covered with burlap bags, where she landed with a thud. Dust exploded into the air from the impact, making it difficult to breathe. In spite of being in good shape and toting a fairly light bundle, he struggled for breath from his hike and cursed Anna as he turned to go. Reaching the doorway, he turned back and sneered at the motionless victim, "Enjoy your new home," before closing the door with a thud.

Dust particles danced in the slivers of sunlight that made their way through the porous exterior walls of the shed as they settled back to the ground on and around Anna. For several moments, nothing else stirred in the tiny room. The air was stale and tepid as the early morning sun hadn't yet heated the small building to unbearable conditions.

Scurrying along the floor next to the south wall of the building a small gray mouse guided itself with its twitching nose in search of a morsel to eat before disappearing through a knothole that led to a much larger connecting building with a common wall. Curious eyes on the other side of the wall peered through chinks and slits in the wood in an attempt to see who, or what had been placed in the attached building. When nothing stirred or revealed itself, the eyes lost interest and went in search of other things.

The minutes spanned into hours as the temperature rose significantly in the small building, and still Anna didn't move. A loud commotion could be heard on the opposite side of the wall as something or someone roused the inhabitants from that portion of the building and moved them outside where sounds of vehicles roaring to life mixed with harsh voices barking out orders greeted them.

The noise continued for several minutes before growing faint as the vehicles moved off and away from the buildings.

Large black flies buzzed around Anna's head and body, but it did nothing to move her from her spot on the makeshift bed. The heat went from hot to unbearable as the corrugated steel roof on the small building bore the brunt of the midday sun and transferred it to the inside of the little sweat box.

Finally, as the sun began to set on the western horizon, Anna began to stir. Slightly at first with stiff and jerky motions that became more pronounced as time passed on. Moaning deeply, Anna raised her hand to her throbbing head as she struggled to move into a sitting position. The room spun and nausea filled her senses, immediately causing her to lie back down. Dazed and confused, she tried to figure out what was going on but could recall very little.

Anna whimpered out, "Jay, are you there? Jay?" With great care she continued to trace back and forth with her fingers over the large bump on the back of her head. She could feel the dried blood in her matted and tangled hair but couldn't recall how she had been hurt or what had happened to her. All she knew for certain was her head throbbed and she was extremely sick—too sick to move, rendering all else moot in her life.

The pain was severe and time passed slowly until she mercifully slipped back into a pain-numbing sleep wrought with tormenting dreams and frightful images. External noises of the returning vehicles and individuals barking orders only added content to her dreams as her mind integrated the sounds into her subconscious thoughts. Even the sounds of voices only feet away through the thin wall separating the two rooms failed to rouse her from her sleep.

Finally, after a long and fitful night, Anna's eyes opened as she attempted to scan the small room she occupied. Confusion and fear filled her mind as she tried to figure out exactly where she was and what had happened. Her body was stiff and ached from lying on the hard surface.

Rolling to her side, and with some difficulty, Anna was able to rise back into a sitting position. The room spun from dizziness as she tried to focus on anything to gain her bearings. There was very little noise, only sounds of people or animals breathing heavily in their sleep somewhere on the other side of the wooden wall separating the two rooms.

Focusing on the noise, she moved gingerly toward it, each inch exacting a terrible toll on her weak and shaky body. Every little movement intensified the severe throbbing in her head as she made her way across the dirt floor to the common wall. Darkness pressed against her from all sides and elevated the fear in her chest as she continued to inch forward.

Finally, her hand touched the smooth, worn wooden wall that formed a boundary of her small prison. Leaning her upper body and head against the wall, Anna began to shake uncontrollably. She could feel warm tears of fear and pain as they ran down her cheeks before dripping on the ground. Try as she might, she was unable to ebb the flow.

She cried out into the darkness, "Jay, where are you?"

She had never felt so alone or such despair in all of her life. Nothing made sense to her as she frantically scanned her memory for any clue that might spark a memory of what had happened to her or why she was locked alone in a dark and solitary room. The smell of dust hung in her nostrils and made her choke as her body began to shake with the sobs of emotion now overwhelming her.

She began to sob and cry out, "Jay, help me! Where are you? Where am I?"

Suddenly a quiet voice spoke to her through the wall, "You are in the dungeon! Don't cry. You are not alone."

Startled, Anna wasn't certain that she hadn't just imagined the words she had just heard. Her heart raced with fear as she tried in vain to peer through the wall to see who was on the other side.

"Who is it? Who's over there?" she demanded in a quiet but firm voice.

No one answered. Holding her breath and listening to the darkness, Anna waited for more words to be spoken, but none came. Finally, after several minutes she gained enough nerve to knock on the hard wooden wall and ask once again, "Who is there? Who was talking to me? Where am I?"

This time, after still no response, she banged on the wall with her fists, determined to get a response of some sort. "Who's there?" she demanded in a loud voice. "You better answer me, or I'll scream," she threatened.

"Be quiet! You'll get us beaten or worse if you keep being loud," the voice hissed back at her.

"Get us beaten by whom?" she whispered back. "Who is this, anyway?"

"We'll be beaten by Luis, or killed," the voice answered.

From the sound of the voice, Anna was sure she was talking to a boy, twelve, fourteen, but not much older than that. She scanned her memory in an attempt to determine who this Luis character was but could come up with nothing.

"Well, who are you, and what is this place?" she demanded with a little more force.

Silence was all that greeted her questions.

"I mean it, I'll scream."

"Please be quiet! Luis will come, and then we will all be sorry, you'll see!"

The fear in the voice on the other side of the wall had an unnerving effect on Anna as she reflected on his words.

"What is your name, and where am I?" she questioned, much quieter this time.

"If I tell you, will you be quiet and go back to sleep?"

The Unraveling   145

"Yes," she promised.

"My name is Carlos, and this is our home. We belong to Luis and do work for him. You are in the dungeon. That's where he puts us when we are in trouble if we are lucky enough to still be living after our punishment," he explained. "Now, please be quiet. I don't want to get into trouble."

"Thank you, Carlos," she whispered through the wall.

There was no response, and after a few minutes of waiting, Anna slumped down to the ground and closed her eyes. Her head was really throbbing, and she was beginning to feel sick once again. For the first time since her ordeal began, she remembered to pray. Pray for her, for Jay, for Carlos, and even for Luis.

She didn't know what kind of ordeal she had gotten herself into, but she knew it was all in God's hands now, and she laid it all at His feet. As she prayed, a reassuring calm came over her body as she felt the presence of the Lord. Before she knew it, she had dozed off.

A loud thud on the other side of the wall brought Anna awake and back to an upright position. It took her only seconds to remember where she was and the conversation she had had with Carlos just the night before. Now she could hear many voices, some shouting in anger as some sort of commotion was set off in the room next to hers.

"Get out of here! Hurry up, you good for nothings, you have work to do," Anna heard repeatedly on the other side of the wall. Every so often the words were punctuated with a large bang, almost like gunfire, but without quite the same intensity or loudness. As she listened, she could hear a hiss followed by a loud *crrack!* She finally decided it was a whip or some sort of rope being used on whoever was next door.

Her heart raced as she said a quick prayer for Carlos and the others on the receiving end of the whip. Cries of pain brought chills to her spine as she heard young kids begging for mercy from their tormentor.

It must be Luis.

In time all grew quiet and the dust from the other side began to settle back down to the earth. Questions ran over and over through Anna's mind as she tried to gain any memory of Luis, Carlos, or how she had come to be in this place. Specks and rays of light began to filter through the outside walls of her building, marking the beginning of a new day. Try as she might, nothing came to her mind or made any sense to her.

Maybe it's all just one big dream, she thought but knew it was anything but.

The wall crashed and the little building shook as the door to the dungeon was flung open, slamming against the side wall of the little room. Dust billowed up everywhere, making it difficult to see or breathe as Anna peered out of the darkness to see who was there. Light from the outside was blinding, and she raised her arms up in front of her face as a shield in an attempt to see who was there. Finally, her squinted eyes made out the outline of a large man holding a bull whip in his right hand and an evil smile on his scarred face.

This is Luis! This is Luis! her mind screamed as fear gripped her heart.

"Welcome to my home," echoed a deep and gravely voice.

Anna shrunk to the rear wall of the little shack and made herself as small as possible as nerve-wracking laughter erupted from the mouth of the man standing directly in front of her.

"My name is Luis, and you are my newest guest!" he roared while entering the small room. "Welcome to your new home!"

Paralyzing dread muted any response she may have had as her captor advanced toward her. She watched as the wooden door slowly swung more than halfway closed behind the man. Surging adrenaline rendered her unable to think and caused her heart to begin beating nearly out of her chest. *What is he going to do to me?*

"Lord, help me. Keep me safe," she prayed.

The Unraveling

Darkness once again filled the little room as Luis moved directly into what remained of the open doorway. The fading light matched the sinking feeling in her heart as evil laughter once again erupted from Luis.

Anna clenched her eyes shut as tightly as possible. *I shall fear no evil; I shall fear no evil; I shall fear no evil,* ran over and over through her mind as Luis raised the whip high over her head in a threatening manner. A sizzling hiss cut through the air followed by a deafening *crack!* that reverberated throughout the little room, followed by an evil laugh every bit as cutting as the sound of the whip itself.

Chapter 29

Blue skies and warm temperatures failed to raise Jay out of the dark glum he had been in since Anna's abduction. Two days had passed since she had been taken, and very little progress had been made in the search that was taking place for her. The terrible thunderstorms, remnants of Hurricane Geoff fresh off the Gulf of Mexico, had dropped so much water and wrought so much destructive havoc that virtually all of the roads within a hundred miles had been washed out in every gully or drainage ditch, preventing the federal police from even reaching the rural mission to begin their investigation into Anna's disappearance.

Several of the men had followed the faint car tracks found in the mud just outside the north gate of the mission in hopes of finding the whereabouts of Anna but had returned dejected, only to report the road had been washed out less than two miles down the road.

"The road is just gone!" Lupe tried to demonstrate with his hands the enormous size of the washout.

He added, "I don't know how anyone could have survived out there in that storm." He was unaware of the effect his words were having on Jay.

Jesse blurted out, "We'll find her!" It was more of an attempt to bolster Jay's spirits than to actually convince anyone that his words were true.

Everyone in town was somber at best. They all knew the odds were stacked against any of them ever seeing Anna alive again. Kidnapping was a problem in the region and very little help, if any, ever came from the federal government in cases like this. The fact that Anna was American normally would have increased her odds of surviving this ordeal since most Americans had resources and family with resources that were generally willing to pay a ransom, but any additional hope was negated by the fact she was a missionary. Mission groups generally refused to meet ransom requests.

"It just isn't good practice to give ransom for one of our people when they fall into evil hands. Once they know we are willing to pay a ransom, virtually every one of our missionaries would be in danger."

Jay could hear those words play themselves over and over in his mind. Words that had been spoken to both he and Anna during their orientation time at mission headquarters just weeks before.

"Besides, statistically missionaries are one of the safest, if not the most, safe group of people to go abroad. Bad guys generally know taking a missionary will yield them nothing but another mouth to feed, so they leave them be."

Bright yellow wildflowers dominated the desert landscape, results of the copious amounts of rain that had been falling all monsoonal season long. Everyone but Jay marveled at the vibrant color of the flowers, but he was too depressed to care.

"We see wildflowers like this maybe once every fifteen years or so." Jesse was attempting to draw his mind elsewhere, anywhere but on Anna.

Time had slowed to a crawl as the past two days seemed to have dragged on. Sleep was almost nonexistent for Jay and had come fitfully at best as nightmares of Anna being abducted played themselves out in his tired mind whenever he did manage to nod off. He had no appetite. Food had lost all of its appeal. His heart ached worse than it had ever ached before. Numbness filled his mind as depression and despair threatened to overwhelm him.

Jesse tried valiantly to encourage his friend repeatedly. "We have to keep positive and cling to hope and faith that God will keep her safe! He promised He would; the Bible tells us that."

"I hear what you are saying, but I just have a bad feeling about everything, the blood and torn dress, broken mug, all tell me Anna is not okay. I am just so afraid." Tears were running down Jay's puffy and swollen face.

Jesse felt helpless and had no answer that would help Jay with his grief. Despair filled his heart, as well as the hearts of most of the townspeople. It was a time of mourning and sadness even though they had known Anna for only a few short days. Already her impact on the mission had been huge. All they could do was pray. And pray they did, around the clock without fail as people lined the altars in the church praying for Anna's safe return. It was an amazing sight to behold and would have been extremely inspiring were it not for the circumstances that brought the people to their knees.

≈ ≈ ≈ ≈

The high desert sun coupled with the constant south wind had almost dried up the streets of the little village. Small, receding puddles still dotted the landscape nearly everywhere one looked. Some of the larger puddles had become seas of imagination as some of the children spent countless hours floating small sticks and paper boats across their surface.

In an attempt to take his mind off of Anna, Jay wandered the streets but avoided contact with any and all every chance he had. No matter the direction he began his walks, the end destination was always the same for Jay—at the north end of the mission compound, standing at the gate where he would scan the horizon in futility.

Somehow Jay had picked up a tag-along, a mangy black dog that seemed to have no owners. It following three or four steps behind him everywhere he went. At first, Jay tried to shoo the animal off but had finally given up when all of his threats and overtures had failed to do any more than send the dog ten or twelve feet out of his reach.

The Unraveling

"Suit yourself," he finally said to the dog as he turned and walked down the road, dog in tow.

～ ～ ～ ～

The minutes continued to tick ever so slowly as they waited with anticipation for the federal police to arrive. The power had been on and off, mostly off, ever since the storm, which made it difficult to tell the actual time since most of the clocks were powered by electricity. The lone satellite phone was iffy at best for some reason, so contact with the outside world was nearly nonexistent.

Over and over Jay continued to ask in desperation, "Where are the police?"

Patiently Jesse would reassure Jay, "They are on their way. I promise you. The roads are washed out, and they just aren't going to bring a helicopter in here or anything like that."

Jay asked with exasperation, "Why aren't they calling us? Nothing! We haven't heard a single word from them! Maybe they aren't coming at all!"

Jesse got up, walked over to Jay, and placed a calloused hand on his shoulder. "Jay, they are on their way. I promise you! Don't worry! They will be here and they will find Anna!"

His words lacked conviction, though, and did nothing to assuage Jay's fears and anxiety.

They were in the church at the makeshift headquarters, which had become an increasingly busy place. Several of the little old, toothless women had advanced on the two as they continued their vigil at the hard wooden table that doubled as a desk of sorts. Each one of the ladies carried a pot or container full of hot food. Jay motioned that he didn't want any, but the ladies wouldn't be deterred, even going so far as to heap his plate with the steaming food.

At first, Jay wasn't going to eat any of it but decided he had better after one of the ladies threatened to spoon feed him. The food was delicious, as usual, but Jay was too distracted to enjoy it. He was grateful, however, that one of the children brought him a Coke out of his house to drink. Even though it was lukewarm, the combination of caffeine and sugar seemed to perk him up just a bit. Jesse, on the other hand, attacked his food as if he was a man starved half to death. It took him very little time to polish off his plate of food and start on another.

High overhead, the fans turned in tandem and created just enough of a breeze to lift the corner of several pieces of paper scattered out across the desk but not quite enough to move them beyond where they lay. The breeze had just enough cooling effect to make sitting in the church on such a warm day tolerable.

Jay placed the last bite of a taco in his mouth when several of the young boys burst into the church. They were all excited and began speaking at once, and much too rapidly for Jay to understand. He did make out federal police, however, and his heart felt as if it had skipped a beat from the anticipation. Raising his hands in front of him, Jesse attempted to temper the excitement.

"One at a time, just one at a time."

Fransisco was the oldest of the group and after a short pause began explaining to Jesse that the federal police had finally arrived at the mission compound. His large brown eyes were opened wide, and the serious look on his young face would have normally tickled Jay, under different circumstances. Although he could make out a few words, Fransisco's speech was too fast for him to follow. Impatience started to build as Jay waited anxiously for Jesse to interpret the news. He didn't have to wait long.

With excitement evident in his eyes, Jesse quickly turned to Jay and stated excitedly, "The federal police! They are finally here!"

The Unraveling

Chapter 20

The small group practically ran from the church just in time to see a silver 4x4 Dodge Durango covered in red mud and grime turn the corner off of the main road as it drove toward them. Veering to its left, the Dodge drove out into the rocky soccer field and directly through a parting flock of white chickens in an attempt to avoid the water-filled ruts in the dirt roadway. The weight of the vehicle caused it to sink several inches into the rocky soil and wobble back and forth on the slick mud. The car left two long and deep divots in the soil as it continued on its path directly toward the group.

The midday sun was up and shining brightly and caused everyone to squint their eyes as they watched the vehicle approach, slow down, and stop just a few feet in front of them. It was extremely hot, and the humidity was high in the thin air of the high desert. Jay could see two men with mirrored sunglasses in the front of the car. He couldn't tell if anyone was in the back seat or not.

Practically before the car had finished moving, the man in the passenger seat opened the door and hopped out. He was wearing gray leather cowboy boots, new Wrangler jeans, a white shirt, and a stylish, skinny black tie. A golden badge was attached to the small black leather belt that held up his pants. His hair was black and wavy but had been cut short. The bright sun glistened off his hair and made it shine. Just looking at him, Jay could see that the man was very fit and guessed him to be in his midtwenties at most. The driver was a little more deliberate in his exit from the vehicle. He spent several moments rustling around in the console between the seats, retrieving a brown clipboard with several papers attached before getting out.

Jay sized up the man and noticed he was wearing an old pair of oxford shoes with scuffed toes, a pair of gray dress slacks that seemed to be a size too small, light blue shirt, no tie, and a black sport coat with a grease stain on the right lapel. This man had a receding hairline with a ring of shiny black hair circling a shiny bald dome. Hints of gray hair mingled with the black and that along with a slight potbelly indicated to Jay that this detective was probably in his midforties.

The older man raised his arms and stretched for several moments before moving toward the group. Each step the men took produced a suctioning noise as the sticky mud released its hold and caused them to take very pronounced steps as they moved forward. The younger man tried in vain to shake the sticky red soil from his boots but gave up after a few unsuccessful attempts.

The older of the two men spoke, "Greetings, my friends. I am Sergeant Lopes, and this is Officer Cruz. We are with the special crimes unit of the Federal Police of Mexico. Man, you are a long way from nowhere out here!"

Jay could see the distorted reflection of the group in the mirrored lenses that adorned both men's faces as they offered their handshake first to Jesse, and then the rest of the small gathering. Jesse introduced each one to them, and Jay was last as the detectives advanced directly to him.

Officer Cruz then asked, "Do you have somewhere we can go, somewhere to set up an interview room?"

Jesse motioned behind them. "Why, yes, we already have a control center of sorts set up in the church. Would that be all right?" Nodding that it would, the two officers headed toward the church without saying another word. They crossed the concrete sidewalk in front of the building and removed their mud-

The Unraveling   155

covered shoes before entering. The breeze from the fans was very refreshing at it played across their sweat-covered torsos.

Sergeant Lopes held out one of the fold-up chairs and offered Jay a seat. He and Officer Cruz took a seat directly opposite him at the long table. Without looking up, Sergeant Lopes asked the rest of the group to wait outside the church on one of the benches that sat against the building.

"We'll call you when we are ready to interview you."

Officer Cruz closed the large wooden doors behind the group before returning to the table. Noticing the concern on Jay's face, he explained, "We have to check out everyone's story, you know, to make sure they all match."

Sergeant Lopes went through a list of questions, name, age, birthday, etc., as Officer Cruz wrote the information down on one of the sheets of paper. The questions lasted several minutes, after which Sergeant Lopes folded his arms across his chest, slid his sunglasses to the top of his bald head, and sized Jay up for a moment or two without saying a word. The scrutiny made Jay very uncomfortable, but he did his best to return Sergeant Lopes's steady gaze.

"Now, son, I want you to tell me the whole story, and try your best to leave absolutely nothing out. Scan your memory for every detail. Somewhere in there is a clue that will lead us to your wife's abductors. It might be something that seems insignificant to you, but to us, that insignificant detail might be just the piece of evidence we need to solve this case."

Jay swallowed hard as Sergeant Lopes's words brought a small measure of comfort to his heart. Even though the two officers had done nothing, their mere presence was something he could grab onto, something on which to pin his hopes. For the first time since Anna's abduction, Jay felt a small tinge of confidence, even excitement, that all would be well even though something in his subconscious mind said exactly the opposite. He knew he should temper his hope and enthusiasm, but right at that moment he was much too tired and emotionally spent to even try.

For the next ninety minutes, Jay told his story, each and every detail he could remember to the two officers. Arms folded across his chest, Sergeant Lopes watched his face intently as he told his tale while Officer Cruz took reams and reams of notes. Both men waited patiently as Jay broke down in tears several times during the session, and they even offered him a paper towel as he painfully explained to them how he did not want to stay at the party while Anna returned to the house, but that Jesse practically insisted he do so, along with Anna, of course. This particular bit of information was of great intrigue to the two men, and they stopped Jay several times to ask him questions about Jesse and the conversation he had had with him that fateful night.

"You don't think Jesse had anything to do with this, do you?" Jay was in disbelief. The thought had never previously crossed his mind.

Officer Cruz continued, "Right now, anything is possible. We have to look at everyone as suspects until we are able to eliminate them by getting all of the facts."

The way Officer Cruz emphasized "everyone" indicated to Jay that that was exactly what he meant. Everyone, including even himself.

Jay swallowed again and continued the story where he had left off. Once again, the two officers showed considerable interest as he told them how Gabie and Rosanne had gone home with Anna, but instead of staying with her as they had been instructed to do, returned to the party. He was amazed at the feelings of anger and contempt he felt toward the two young ladies and realized that his feelings were becoming very apparent to the two officers.

Pausing for a moment, he asked again, "Do you think they were involved?"

For the second time, Officer Cruz explained to him that everyone would be a suspect until they had been given a reason to eliminate them.

"But I do have to say, their actions are at the very least, curious to me."

It took no more than a few minutes for Jay to finish telling the officers the rest of the story, and more than an hour answering questions that were asked of him, some over and over again to see if his story stayed consistent. When they were finished, they thanked him for his cooperation and asked him to not share any of what he had told them with the rest of the group. Officer Cruz escorted him back out of the church building and into the bright sunlight. Jay had to squint his eyes while Officer Cruz explained to the others he would need a few moments. More than ten minutes passed before he returned to ask Jesse to come in for questioning.

The session for the whole group lasted into the early evening hours, and the haggard look of each person as they emerged from the building was a true indication on just how thorough and emotional the questioning had been. Jay felt a tinge of guilt and looked quickly away as first Gabie and then Rosanne exited the church in tears.

Both girls blamed themselves for Anna's abduction even though Jesse did his best to assure them that had they not left, they too might have fallen victim to whoever had taken Anna. The girls nodded their heads in understanding, but his words did little to dampen the guilt they both felt. Jay knew Jesse was right. Even so, he still had hard feelings toward the girls. He knew his feelings were unjust and that he should ask God to forgive him and help him not have them, but his pride just would not allow him to do so.

Large, rolling thunderheads had been building all day and were now nearly upon the small village as the group waited for the officers to emerge from the church. Flashes of lightning could be seen as they arched across the dark clouds. Low rumbling thunder could be heard in the distance several moments after each flash. Finally, after more than an hour of deliberation, the two officers came out and dismissed everyone except Jay and Jesse.

"We need to see the crime scene." Sergeant Lopes led them to the silver Durango. "Get in; we'll drive you there."

The four of them climbed into the car and sat on the hot, black leather seats. The temperature inside was nearly unbearable, and Jay was thankful when Sergeant Lopes rolled down all four windows before turning the car around. They made their way back to the main road and turned north, toward Jay and Anna's house. The children were steeped in curiosity, and most of them ran after the vehicle as it made its way down the main road. The whole trip took only minutes as Jay directed Sergeant Lopes to the front of his house.

As the car rolled to a stop, Jay announced, "Here it is, home sweet home."

The four men got out and were met by the mangy black dog that had taken up residence on the sidewalk to the front door whenever Jay was not around.

Officer Cruz extended his hand out to the wary dog to sniff before turning to Jay. "A friend of yours?"

Jay shrugged and replied, "He just kind of adopted me for some reason, I guess. I've never petted him, though."

"Does he have a name?" Sergeant Lopes motioned toward the dog.

"As far as I know, he doesn't have one. I just call him 'dog.'"

They moved to the front door of the little rowhouse, and Jay moved out of the way after opening it wide for the officers, who warily entered. The house was exactly as Jay had found it the night Anna was abducted. Dried blood and the broken mug covered the floor near the bathroom. The two officers knelt down and examined every piece of ceramic from the mug and every bit of blood evidence they could find.

The Unraveling

Satisfied, they turned their search to the rest of the house. They looked in all of the drawers and cupboards searching for some sort of elusive clue, but Jay really had no idea what they could be looking for, nor did he ask. Their investigation inside the house took very little time. They searched the adjacent row-houses too, but that search failed to yield any clues either.

Sergeant Lopes then asked, "Can you take us to the gate where you found that piece of her dress?"

Once again they climbed back into the waiting car and drove the few blocks to the end of town. The gate was closed and there wasn't much to look at, other than the faint car tracks on the other side. Satisfied that they had seen all there was to see, they returned to the car.

Sergeant Lopes turned to Jesse as he turned the vehicle around. "Well, do you have somewhere to put us up around here?"

"Well, yes, we do, back at the church. We have guest quarters there. It's not much, but you are sure welcome to it."

"We don't need much. I'm sure it will be just fine."

They drove back to the church, got out, and went back inside. Jesse led them to the guest quarters in the rear of the building and showed them around.

"Like I said earlier, it's not much, but it does have two beds with clean sheets. The bathroom is down the hall. There's a refrigerator in the kitchen with some food in it, but I'll bring you your meals every day. We do have a satellite phone, which you are welcome to use at your convenience. Other than that, it's a pretty simple place."

"It'll be just fine," Officer Cruz stated warmly.

As they turned to leave, Sergeant Lopes cleared his throat. "Could we see the piece of clothing you found on the gate, please?"

"Oh yes! I nearly forgot." Jesse made his way to the makeshift desk in the center of the church.

He opened up a box and announced, "We have it right here," as he lifted out the torn corner of Anna's dress.

The colors were still vibrant and beautiful. Sergeant Lopes turned the cloth over and over in his hands.

Just the sight of the material caused a lump to form in Jay's throat.

"It's a very beautiful and unusual garment." Sergeant Lopes handed the cloth over to Officer Cruz.

"It's one of a kind, a handmade gift," Jay explained.

Officer Cruz set the piece of cloth down on the table. "Thank you all for your help."

"Now what do we do?" Jay asked the two officers.

"Now we wait," Sergeant Lopes announced firmly.

"Wait? Wait for what?" Jay had a hint of annoyance in his voice. He had already been waiting for the past couple days; now he wanted some kind of action.

"We wait for the kidnappers to contact us," Officer Cruz answered abruptly.

"Just sit here and wait?" Jay was unwilling to let it go.

Sergeant Lopes answered impatiently, "What would you have us do?"

"I don't know. You're the law enforcement. Maybe you could follow the vehicle tracks to try and find where they go." He added in frustration, "Something, anything but just wait!"

The two officers looked at each other and shook their heads before sitting down at the makeshift desk. Jay stared at them in disbelief. He couldn't believe their seeming lack of interest or urgency with the case. It was almost more than he could take.

"What are you doing?"

Jesse moved to his side and took him by the arm. "Jay, it's all right."

"No, it's not all right! That's my wife out there, and she's in danger! I want something done, and I want it done now!"

The Unraveling   161

In spite of his outburst, the two officers remained seated and began pouring over the notes that Officer Cruz had taken. Jay's outburst had absolutely no affect on them, which riled him even more. With a jerk of his arm, he broke free of Jesse's grasp and rushed across the room. In one fluid motion, he swept the papers the officers were looking at onto the floor and shouted, "Did you hear me? I want something done! Now!"

Veins of anger stood out on his temples as he challenged the two men. He didn't care if he had offended them; he wanted Anna back, and he didn't want to waste any more time.

Sergeant Lopes slowly got up and turned to Jay, while Officer Cruz bent to pick up the loose papers. Seeing what he was doing, Jesse quickly began helping him. Sergeant Lopes's eyes were drawn down into a controlled glare, although he didn't seem overly angry at Jay's outburst.

"Son, I'm going to ask you to please get hold of your emotions. I'm only going to ask you once." He stated this with an authority that left no room for doubt. "We are going to do what's best for Anna, and you should too. We are going to go over these papers to see if we can find any clues that we may have missed, and we are going to wait. Anything else would be an effort of futility. We won't find her on our own. We would waste countless hours trying and still be empty handed. If we go traipsing out across the country on some wild goose chase, we might not be here when they contact us. If that were to happen, the end result would not be good for your wife."

His words carried weight, and Jay's mind scrambled to find something to say. "How do you know they'll even contact us?"

"Because I've been through this game hundreds of times over the years, and that's how the game is played." He sat back down.

"Hundreds of times?" Jay was unconvinced.

"Señor, someone is abducted here in Mexico every thirty minutes. That works out to forty-eight people every single day. I'm part of a special victims unit that deals only with kidnappings. I know how they work and what to expect. I also need you to know and to understand what I'm about to tell you, eighty percent! *Eighty percent!*" he emphasized to Jay. "Eighty percent of the victims are either never seen again or are not recovered alive." He paused to let his words sink in. "Those are true and real statistics that you need to be aware of. For that reason, you need to listen to and do everything we ask you to. It's our goal to make sure she is one of the twenty percent."

Jay sat down hard as the weight of his words hit home. He could barely believe what he was hearing. "I'm sorry. I'm just so upset," he finally managed. "I'll do whatever you ask me to do."

"Now we will do what is best. Now we will wait…" Sergeant Lopes replied softly as he grasped the back of Jay's hand in his own. "Now we will wait."

Chapter 21

One day melted into another like a never-ending nightmare with nary a hint of Anna nor demand of ransom for her life. For Jay, the days were all the same: get up in the morning, wander around the compound, and avoid all human contact, check in with the police around noon, wander around some more, and dodge raindrops in the afternoons as the summer monsoons delivered daily thunderstorms. There was never any variation, never any need for it as his days were filled with a deepening despair and hopelessness.

During the first day or two, some of the children tried to engage him in games of hide-and-seek but gave up after all of their attempts failed to draw him out of his doldrums.

Jesse told Jay over and over every day while extending an invitation to him for prayer meeting, "Jay, you've got to have faith! For Anna's sake if for no other reason, you must keep the faith." At first Jay attended, but after a couple days, declined every offer extended to him. He couldn't really see much sense in going; God didn't seem to be answering his prayers anyway…at least that's what he told himself. Not that he didn't pray; he did pray, plead, more like it, with God to give Anna back to him.

Sometimes his prayers were laced with anger, other times they were filled with pleading and whimpering in hopes God would feel sorry for him and make Anna suddenly appear. Mostly, he played deal maker, promising God that he would have a better attitude, would go to any mission field for as long as God wanted with absolutely no complaining as long as Anna was brought back safe and sound. None seemed to work, which only deepened the dark pit in which he had descended.

Every day, he did receive a call from mission headquarters from Dr. Evanruud, who reminded him that thousands of people around the world were praying for him and Anna continuously and would continue doing so until Anna was returned safe and sound.

"Stay positive! God has a plan and will use this event for good!" the doctor told him every single day.

Although he was thankful for the call, he just couldn't seem to cheer up or gain even the slightest bit of hope. It wasn't that he didn't want to believe Anna was safe and would return soon, he did want to believe, he really did; but for some reason, whether it was the sight of the blood, the broken mug, or the fact that Anna had been sick ever since they had arrived in Mexico, something gave him a sick feeling in the pit of his stomach that grew day by day.

What if I never see Anna again? kept running over and over in his mind even though he knew he shouldn't think that way.

Day sixteen was shaping up to be just like the previous fifteen: hurry up and wait for some contact, any contact from the kidnappers. With growing frustration, Jay made his way to the north gate of the compound once again. This time, instead of stopping at the gate for a long, forlorn look across the horizon, Jay lifted the rusty bolt that secured the gate in place and opened it just enough to slide through to the other side. At first, he stayed very close, kicking around in the grass in an attempt to identify the tracks that had been left the night Anna had been abducted. All of the rains from the previous two weeks had erased nearly any sign that a vehicle had ever been anywhere but on the red dirt road. Closer examination, however, revealed a pair of wavy tire ridges. Though discovered by search parties days before, the sight of the tracks gave Jay a renewed and determined hope that Anna was somewhere out there, perhaps at the end of these very tracks.

Reaching down to the dirt, Jay swept away what little grass and debris that covered the tire marks. His fingers traced back

The Unraveling

and forth over the tire ridges. After several moments, he got back to his feet and began to follow the nearly indistinguishable tracks as they moved off through the rocky terrain. He covered vast stretches that held no tracks or sign that a vehicle had ever passed by, which triggered a heightened sense of panic inside of him, only to have his heart soar at the discovery of the tracks farther up the roadway. Even though he knew the tracks had already been followed and that there would be no new revelation by following them again, just doing something made the time pass without the weight of Anna's absence collared around him like a heavy anchor.

Blasting out of the underbrush like a cannonball out of a cannon, a startled jackrabbit darted through the sage and mesquite that dotted the landscape. Its sudden burst startled Jay as he watched the wily animal dart away as fast as it could. The sheer size of the animal's ears induced a chuckle, the first since his current ordeal had begun. Picking up a rock, Jay tossed it in the direction the rabbit had gone before turning around to survey his surroundings.

The terrain was the same as that immediately around the mission compound, yet the mission was nowhere in sight. Reaching down, Jay picked a long-stemmed piece of bunch grass and placed it in his mouth and began rolling the coarse stem back and forth with his tongue. The taste and smell of the grass reminded him of his youth and countless days wandering the outskirts of his hometown on the Palouse. Memories filled with forlorn images of a simpler time long past.

Heat radiated up from the desert floor as the midday sun reached its apex. Wiping the sweat from his eyes, Jay decided to push on, at least for a while longer, *I don't have anything better to do,* he surmised to himself as he continued to follow the rough roadway and fading tracks. A sudden noise brought him up with a start as he strained his ears with all his might in an attempt to hone in on the source. Slowly, he turned in a complete circle in an attempt to determine if the sound had been real or imagined. Unable to detect any further noise, he pressed on in hopes of identifying more of the faint tire tracks.

After traveling no more than a few yards, the faint noise from before brought him to a complete stop. *Voices!* he thought to himself as his heart began to race.

Who could be out here? he wondered as he gingerly worked his way back toward the mission. Frightful images of kidnappers and outlaws began to build in his imagination, which in turn produced a nearly uncontrollable desire to bolt.

Running his hands through his black and sweaty hair, Jay took a long, deep breath to calm his nerves as he moved back down the rutted dirt road toward the mission as silently as possible. His eyes locked onto a dead mesquite branch about the size of a baseball bat just off the road, so he made his way through the sage and retrieved the makeshift weapon. It was sound and heavy and would make a great club, if need be. Just having it in his possession made him feel considerably better as he ran his hands up and down the rough piece of wood, checking it for any weakness.

Satisfied there were none, Jay propped the branch on his shoulder and crept down the roadway, staying as close to the nearby sage as possible. Once again, the voices brought him up short. Listening intently, he decided it was only one voice, and it sounded as if it was calling his name. Resisting an urge to call out, Jay picked up his pace and moved down the road toward the source. Anxiety, although diminished, still tore at his heart as he tried to imagine who could be out here in such a desolate place. The closer to the mission he drew, the louder and more clear the voice became.

"Jay, Jay, where are you?"

Whoever was out there knew him and was yelling his name. Even so, caution overruled as he suppressed the desire to call out in answer to the voice while he continued his slow and guarded approach. The closer he got to whoever was calling his name, the

The Unraveling   167

louder the call became, which made it easier to locate the exact source of the noise.

With cautious deliberation, Jay slid into the underbrush and made his way toward whoever was out there. Even though he was fairly certain it was someone from the mission, he slid the heavy club off his shoulder and held it in a cocked position slightly over his right shoulder, ready to use it should the need arise.

Looking through the dull green mesquite leaves, he could finally make out the slender outline of Calderone, one of the young men from the mission. He continued to watch as Calderone slowly meandered down the red dirt roadway toward Jay. Every so often, Calderone would stop, bend down, and move the loose dirt around on the roadway before calling out Jay's name. For a while, Jay couldn't figure out what the young man was doing but, after watching Calderone make his way along the road, realized that he was locating Jay's tracks in the disturbed soil.

He's definitely looking for me! Jay thought as he watched the young man for several more moments. Satisfied that Calderone was alone, and friendly, he waited for Calderone to close the distance between the two before answering the young man's call.

"I'm right here!" He watched the startled young man jump in his tracks and nearly turn tail and run.

"Señor Jay, where have you been?" Calderone's face was a map of concern.

Placing the club back on his shoulder, Jay smiled at the youngster. "I've just been out here exploring, following the old car tracks to see where they lead."

Calderone smiled and nodded in understanding. "Well, everyone has been looking high and low for you! We have all been very worried."

"Well, I'm a big boy; I can take care of myself. I don't need to be looked after constantly," Jay responded with a bit of irritation on his voice. "Besides, what does it matter to everyone?"

Taking a deep breath, Calderone smiled as his large black eyes lit up and opened wide. "Well, Señor Jay, I have news for you! It's Anna! At the mission. You must come quickly!"

Jay could hardly believe his ears. Tears began to fill his eyelids, and his heart began to pound wildly as Calderone's revelation sunk in. Anna! In the mission!

"Señor Jay, wait, there is more I must tell you." Calderone continued in vain as Jay pushed past the man and ran down the road as fast as his legs would carry him.

Chapter 22

The merciless sun beat down on Jay from above and heat radiated up from the earth, giving him a double whammy. Sweat stung his eyes, and his breath came in short, painful gasps as he struggled to take in enough oxygen, made all the more difficult because of the elevation of the high mountain plains. Rising a small hill, Jay was surprised at just how far he had traveled from the mission, which was still about a mile away. The sweat in his eyes made it difficult to see and was compounded by tears of joy and anticipation over the good news: Anna was in the village.

Clear waves of heat bent and wiggled their way across the horizon and added to the distortion effect as he tried in vain to peer through them, the sweat, and the tears, as the compound spread out before him. Deep ruts cut into the road from all of the previous rains made it difficult to run and caused him to stumble on several occasions and even fall on another. Impact from the fall caused sharp red gravel and loose rocks to tear at the skin on the palm of his hands and ripped gaping holes on the knees of his jeans as some of the gravel became imbedded in the flesh on his legs.

Bright red blood began to trickle and cut little channels through the red soil that was caked on his hands. Ignoring the pain, he wiped the dirt and blood from his hands on his torn jeans and continued to press on, oblivious to the yells of Calderone, who was chasing after him, waving his hands and arms over his head.

Sweat flowed profusely down Jay's face and into his eyes and mouth as he continued to run. With a swipe, he ran his hand across his head in an attempt to wipe the sweat away but instead left red smudges of dirt mixed with blood streaked across his forehead. The inadvertent smudges resembled Navajo war paint worn by Indian braves on their way to battle.

As he approached the northern gate of the mission, he could make out several people as they began to wave and point at him. Scanning the small gathering, he wondered where Anna was but decided she was most likely at the makeshift headquarters getting debriefed by the police.

Panicked anticipation began to build in his chest as he reached the gate, which was being held open by one of the local men. Smiles, laughter, and happy faces greeted him at first, but the happiness on their faces quickly melted into fear and concern the closer he got. Their reaction was puzzling, but he didn't have time to figure out what was wrong. Anna was back, and he would not rest until he found her.

He moved through the streets of the village as fast as he could push his body, and his heart pounded from the exertion of the run. His gait had morphed into a fast, jerky walk as his body objected to the pace he had kept. Even so, it didn't take him long to cover the distance of the small compound and turn the corner toward the church. No one but a few chickens were on the outside of the small building, and they scattered as he approached the open doorway. Several voices could be heard coming from just inside the church, but he failed to detect Anna's familiar tone. With renewed strength, he rushed into the building and scanned the room as his eyes struggled to adjust to the dim light.

Jesse rushed to Jay's side. "Señor Jay, what has happened to you?"

Officer Cruz and Sergeant Lopes raised half out of their seats at the sight of Jay. Ignoring the concern on their faces, Jay ran past them and peered down the hallway and demanded, "Where's Anna?" his voice tinged with panic.

Sergeant Lopez sternly commanded, "Señor Jay, calm down, sit down! Anna is not here."

The Unraveling   171

"Where is she?" he yelled as his crazed eyes searched every visible inch of the sanctuary.

Grabbing him by the shoulders and turning him around, Officer Cruz stated strongly, "She is not here! Jay, she is not here!"

Tears began to spill out of his eyes and run down his cheeks as Officer Cruz's words penetrated his heart. Disappointment and despair sapped his fatigued body as he slumped toward the floor. Only the strong grip of Officer Cruz kept him from falling to the hard concrete floor as Jesse rushed to his side and helped move Jay to an empty chair.

Jay began to sob disappointedly. "What do you mean? She has to be here! Calderone said she was here!" They all turned as Calderone burst into the building, sweating profusely and gasping for air. Seeing the young man renewed Jay's strength, and he lunged.

"Aaugh! You told me she was here! Where is she?" Jay yelled at the terrified Calderone, who was slumping back toward the open doorway of the church.

Acting as a barrier, Officer Cruz stood between the two men and wrapped his muscular arms around Jay's body as he continued his fight to reach Calderone.

"You need to calm down! Now!"

"He told me Anna was here! Why did you do that?" Jay sobbed, his rage subsiding.

Large veins stood out on the temple of Sergeant Lopes as he listened to Jay's rant. Then he answered sternly, "We sent him to find you, to tell you the news. No one knew where you were. You've been moping around here for the past two weeks feeling sorry for yourself instead of taking an active participation in the search for your wife while everyone here is doing their very best to comfort you and help in any possible way to find Anna. You haven't even checked in lately, so when we did get some news today, no one could even find you to let you know. Calderone was the only one who even saw you leave the mission, and he volunteered to go looking for you. If it was me, I would have let you just wait until you came back."

Jay dejectedly sat back in the chair. "He told me Anna was here." He sobbed again, but found no sympathy.

"I tried to stop you, to tell you it was only a note from Anna, but you would not stop or wait for me to explain; instead, you just began to run and I could not catch you. I yelled and yelled, but you would not hear me. I didn't know what else to do, so I followed you here."

Thwumph, thwumph, thwumph! The overhead fans churned the air in tandem, lifting the edges and corners of the many papers that lined the top of the desk. Placing his head in his stained hands, Jay began to slowly digest the news he had just been given. It was devastating to him, and he found it was difficult to accept, his hopes had been so high, only to have them come crashing down. Self-pity and sadness began to creep back into his heart as an overwhelming sense of helplessness nearly paralyzed his body.

The other men slowly made their way back to their chairs around the table and waited for Sergeant Lopes to share the note they had received from Anna's captors. Jay watched as the sergeant reached with slow deliberation to a small envelope in the middle of the table. The envelope was smudged and torn and, by its bulging appearance, had something of substance inside of it.

Squeezing the two sides of the envelope, Sergeant Lopes tipped it up and allowed the contents to spill out onto a clean white sheet of paper. "If you can get a grip on yourself, I'll read you the note and show you the evidence inside."

Sitting up in his chair with renewed interest and guarded hope, Jay eagerly waited and watched as Sergeant Lopes slid a smudged, handwritten letter out from under a long lock of hair and a piece of cloth about two inches square. With care and deliberation the sergeant slid the paper directly in front of Jay, who was already reaching for it.

The Unraveling

"Don't touch it. That's why I wore gloves," Sergeant Lopes commanded as Jay attempted to pick up the paper. "You can look at it, read it, inspect it, but do not touch it. We still need to check it for prints."

Proof of life! I have the American, Anna! She is alive and being well taken care of.

Enclosed is proof of life.

A lock of her hair and a piece of her dress.

Do exactly as I instruct, and Anna will be returned unharmed.

I will contact you with further directions!

Absolutely do not get the federal police involved, or you will never see Anna alive again!

Jay scanned the paper, reading everything on it over and over before turning his attention to the other objects in the center of the table. Rising from his seat, he bent down as close to the articles as he could possibly get without touching them. The cloth was definitely from Anna's handmade dress, the purple colors vibrant and distinguishable to only that one garment. The hair, although similar in color, could be just about anyone's. Only DNA testing would prove it was from Anna.

Drawing in as much breath as he could through his nostrils, Jay attempted to detect any smell of Anna on the two pieces of evidence to assure himself they were from her but failed to detect any odor other than common dust. Even if they were, it didn't prove anything other than whoever sent the evidence had had Anna at one time or another—a fact that was less than assuring to Jay.

Jay finally asked in a quiet voice, "Where did this evidence come from?"

"It was taped to one of the water bottles that are delivered here on a daily basis," Officer Cruz answered matter-of-factly.

"We'll be picking up Salino in the morning when he returns with more water, just to see what he has to say about this," Sergeant Lopes explained. "I don't think he is involved, though."

Nodding his head, Jay sat back in his chair and stared at the three pieces of evidence in front of him. The new information was less than comforting, although it did offer a little hope, if for no other reason than some sort of communication had finally been made by the kidnappers. Still, it left so many questions unanswered. Most troubling of all was the sentence that directed him not to involve the federal police or he would never see Anna alive again. Would the kidnappers have any way of knowing the police were already involved, and was there any way he could uninvolve them?

Rising to his feet, he made his way to the small washroom at the back of the sanctuary and turned on the light. The bare bulb hanging from the ceiling revealed to him why the townspeople had reacted the way they had when he entered the mission compound just a few minutes earlier. Staring back at him out of the mirror was a face stained red from clay and blood that had inadvertently been applied when he attempted to wipe the sweat from his eyes and face.

Using the hot water and a rag hanging on a towel bar, he spent several minutes attempting to clean up before returning to the others.

Many of the townspeople had now gathered just outside the open doors of the sanctuary. An excited buzz could be heard as they discussed the news. Many of them were asking through the doorway to hold a prayer meeting for Anna's safe return. Finally, Jesse got up and met the people at the doorway. They were all upbeat and happy, feeling that God was indeed answering their prayers. Returning to where Jay was sitting, Jesse explained to him what was going on.

"Everyone is here and wants to pray for you. It would be so good if you would agree to come and participate. Everyone here loves you and feels as if you are part of their family. What do you say, will you participate?" He practically begged Jay.

Sitting in contemplative silence, Jay continued to stare at the piece of dress and lock of hair on the table right in front of him. Realizing that those two articles very well might be the closest he would ever again get to the love of his life brought tears of sadness and frustration to his eyes. Taking a deep sigh, he wiped them away and stood up and answered quietly, "Why not?" He made his way out the door and into the throng of well-wishers.

"It may not help, but it sure won't hurt."

Jesse followed his young missionary out the door, concern over his well-being tugging at his heart.

Chapter 23

Strong winds whipped the dust through the sagebrush but did nothing to ease the stifling heat brought by the mid morning sun. Microscopic missiles of red sand and dirt kicked up by the assaulting winds stung Jay on the face and neck as he crouched behind the wall of the mission compound with Sergeant Lopes and some of the other men. They had been there since dawn, waiting for the return of Salino with his daily truckload of fresh, clean water.

Several of the children were hanging around like seagulls at a fish market, curious as to what was happening. On several occasions they had to be shooed away from the group of men in an attempt to not draw attention or reveal that a contingent of people waited in ambush just inside the city walls. Eventually they returned to a hovering pattern just far enough away to be an annoyance but not be run off.

Officer Cruz, Jesse, and a few other men were outside of the walls of the mission more than two miles away and were hiding in a small, sage-filled ravine through which the winding red road passed. They were the lookout and had constant radio contact with Sergeant Lopes at all times. Jay had a hard time understanding why they needed a lookout since the road had no detours or any other roads that bisected it but decided that the two professional lawmen knew what they were doing.

Time dragged on unmercifully, and just when it seemed Salino would be a no-show for the day, Sergeant Lopes's radio crackled to life. It was Officer Cruz.

"Subject approaching." The voice coming across the airwaves brought an apprehensive excitement to Jay's belly.

177

A few moments later, the radio blared to life again. "Subject has passed, is alone, and is making his way directly toward you."

Once again, excitement boiled up in Jay as the upcoming confrontation and the possibility of learning Anna's whereabouts drew closer to becoming a reality. Even though Sergeant Lopes felt they wouldn't learn anything new, the slightest possibility that Salino might know something of value moved Jay's hopes upwards a bit.

Jesse's words from the previous evening as they sat through the planning of this exercise would not leave Jay's mind. "Do not let your hopes raise falsely, my brother. I have known Salino most of my life. He is a very good man with a very good family. He could not be part of this conspiracy, of that much I am sure."

Jay was more than skeptical but did his best to hide his doubts. *Besides, at this point, I really can't trust anyone, not even Jesse.*

They could hear the truck long before they could see it, its tired engine whining loudly in protest at the difficult pull over several of the small hills that led up to the mission. Red dust rose in the air and streamed ahead of the vehicle, thanks to a stiff tail wind that announced the coming arrival of the long-awaited truck and driver. Jay moved his legs and wiped the course gravel from his knees in an attempt to keep the annoying pebbles from embedding themselves in his skin. For once he wished he had worn blue jeans, in spite of the intense heat. At least they would have afforded him a little protection from the sharp pebbles that covered the ground. He could feel his excited heartbeat in his throat and was surprised at how loud it seemed to him.

Grinding gears followed by several loud backfires that sounded like gunshots announced the arrival of the truck, which had no brakes and had to downshift to stop its momentum. With a final, loud boom, the truck stopped just short of the gate and was quickly enveloped by dust, which clouded around the men and gave them all a covering of fine, red material. It was an old Chevy Luv pickup with a flatbed in place of the box.

The body was nearly gone, rusted out everywhere. The front grill was missing and had been replaced by a piece of ripped corrugated cardboard. There were no side windows or mirrors. The headlights were gone, and in their place were two tin coffee cans painted red with a white circular pattern pinstripe that wound around the can and gave it the appearance of spinning. Each wheel was painted a different color, and each tire was a different size, the only constant being that they were all nearly worn bare. Shaking his head in amazement, Jay wondered what kept the vehicle from falling into a rusty heap.

A nerve-grinding clunk made by the opening of the driver's side door brought Jay's attention fully on the spindly man getting out from behind the wheel to open the steel picket gate. Jay was amazed at Salino's height as his body and legs unfolded from behind the wheel, revealing a man every bit of six feet. He was as thin as a rail and looked to be at least sixty years of age. A braided rope wound around his waist and took the place of a belt to hold up the baggy old jeans that were at least two sizes too big. An oversized, off white, long-sleeve cowboy shirt complete with rhinestones and pearl snaps in place of buttons, stained with sweat and constant use covered his upper body. The sleeves were rolled up above his elbows, revealing deeply tanned forearms as thin as sticks wrapped with wrinkly skin. Worn cowboy boots with holes on the toes adorned his feet, and a straw cowboy hat covered his head but not the long gray ponytail that hung down his back several inches. Small black eyes receded back into a wrinkled and toothless face with severely chapped lips and were dwarfed by bushy, silver eyebrows that looked out of place on such a slender face.

To Jay, it was if this man had stepped right off one of those gag postcards depicting weathered cowboys of the Southwest, which could be purchased at any bookstore across America. Shaking his head in disbelief, he watched as Salino stretched for several moments before limping toward the gate to open it. For

The Unraveling

some reason, fear gripped Jay's body and kept him from moving when the rest of the men sprung into action to confront Salino as he swung the heavy iron gate open. Sergeant Lopes gently but firmly placed his hand on Salino's forearm and informed him that he would like a word with him.

With sadness in his eyes, Salino nodded his head in agreement as Sergeant Lopes led him through the gate of the mission. The grizzled water peddler mumbled, "I knew you would be waiting. Please, don't let anything happen to my truck or the water."

"I'll have Officer Cruz bring it over to the headquarters," Sergeant Lopes assured Salino as he motioned toward the church.

Salino chuckled. "They'll have to push it to start it. It's kind of ornery."

Jay watched and was amazed at Salino's calm appearance. *Maybe he's an old hand at this game.*

They questioned Salino for the better part of an hour, but just as Sergeant Lopes and the rest of the men expected, learned nothing new, or of importance. Salino spent most of the time explaining to the group how two armed men had stood in the roadway no more than ten miles from the mission and demanded that he bring the letter to them. They told him that refusal to do so would not only bring his death but the death of his entire family as well. Jay watched as tears welled up in the old man's eyes as he relived this part of the story. Try as he might, Jay couldn't help but feel sorry for him.

"You see, I had no choice in the matter. I love my family and I knew they would do as they threatened; that's why I left the bottle of water here with the note attached to it." With downcast eyes, Salino turned to Jay, tears streaming down his cheeks as he spoke quietly, "I am so sorry, young man. These are bad people! I don't want anything to do with them or with this business! I can see no good coming from it."

With a lump in his throat, Jay nodded back at the old man and his troubling words. Looking out the open doorway, he could see a dozen or more children, heads sticking out from behind the doors as they tried to see what was going on inside the church. When they noticed him watching them, they whipped their heads back in hopes of avoiding a rebuke that would send them on their way.

The interrogation continued for another twenty minutes or so as the two police officers urged Salino to try and remember anything that might help identify the kidnappers. For the first time Jay realized he was not the only victim of these men. Fear for Anna's well-being began to grow inside as imagination of evil men doing terrible things began to run rampant through his mind. Even though he tried, nothing would stop the terrible visions of torture and beatings being inflicted on Anna by the masked men.

A high-pitched scraping noise reverberated throughout the concrete block building as Sergeant Lopes pushed his chair away from the table and stood up. "I've heard enough. You can go back to your rounds of delivering water." He offered his hand to the grateful old man.

Salino pumped the offered hand vigorously. "Thank you so much, Officer!" Turning to Jay with a little less enthusiasm, he offered, "And many blessings to you, young man." Jay nodded and watched as the old man made his way out the door and headed to his truck. Most of the men followed him and offered words of encouragement as the old man climbed in. It took several of the men to push the truck and several tries of popping the clutch to get the old jalopy running. With a bang, the truck roared to life, and Salino slowly drove away.

Jay lowered his head into his hands. What just hours before seemed so positive had now resulted in nothing more than unfulfilled hopes. Despair filled his heart as a heavy weight settled in on his hunched shoulders. *Why are you allowing this to happen to me, God? I'm here just as you asked me to be! Why couldn't you have had me taken instead of Anna? What am I going to do?*

The Unraveling

A warm and friendly grip on one of his shoulders failed to bring Jay up. "Brother, I know it seems hopeless, and nothing makes any sense, but God has a plan! He'll make good out of this, even if we cannot see how. Who knows, we may never know the good that is sure to come from this, but it will!"

Jesse's kind words settled on deaf ears and a heart that was unwilling to embrace the possibility that something good could ever be made of this mess. Self-pity, anger, and hurt were the only things that filled Jay's spirit.

"I just don't see it. I just don't!" Jay's emotional dam burst open, releasing a steady flow of tears. He wiped the back of his hand across his nose and then did the same to his eyes in an attempt to remove the tears. It did no good, however, as they continued to flow, and his nose stuffed up once again.

Rubbing his hand back and forth on Jay's back, Jesse attempted to comfort his young friend. "It's all right, just let it out. You'll feel better afterwards."

And flow out it did as Jay continued to cry in spite of his best efforts. More than ten minutes passed and nobody said a word. Finally, with a long sigh, the tears stopped and fatigue and a hollow empty feeling settled in on his soul. He was too tired to think about all that had and was happening in his life.

Slowly, the men made their way back to the table. Sergeant Lopes quietly studied the pages of notes he had taken while interviewing Salino as the others quietly watched and waited. Outside, the world continued life as normal as sounds of children playing, chickens clucking, and vehicles coming and going began to drift in through the open doors.

"What do we do next?" Jay finally asked without lifting his head.

All eyes fixed upon Sergeant Lopes as the hardened lawman answered, "We wait! That's what we do next. All we can do, really."

"That's all we ever get done! Wait, wait, wait," he mumbled under his breath.

Sergeant Lopes replied, "Yeah, and that's all we can do, if we have any hope of seeing Anna alive again." These were chilling words that cut straight to Jay's heart.

Chapter 24

The clouds flowed like a river in the sky, streaming in east to west one after the other, powered by the steady conveyor belt of wind as they waited to unload their heavy cargo on the terrain below. Their holds carried torrential rains, which were delivered with a vengeful force on the land and all it held. Streams and gullies were filled beyond capacity as angry runoff water, colored tomato soup red by the volcanic soil, surged up and out over the banks that held the raging liquid. The floodwaters cut new channels and gullies, which diverted the waters to low-lying areas that would never again hold a drop. Earlier rains had already saturated the hard and dry desert soil, which led to extreme erosion on the hillsides of the lightly vegetated land, while the flat areas turned to a sticky, muddy gumbo, which made travel a nuisance even for those going only a short distance.

For Jay, the relentless poundings served only to drive him into a depression that grew deeper every single day as communication from the kidnappers had become all but impossible. Even the ever-reliable daily water delivery had become sparse, forcing them all to ration as the roads became more and more difficult to navigate.

Somehow a replacement missionary, Jack McDonald, had been able to make it to the mission compound during the onslaught. The usually one-day journey had taken him five, and though he arrived frazzled, Jack was well received and was settling in quite nicely. At first it bothered Jay that a replacement had been sent, but Jack's genuine concern and care had eventually won him over and then some.

Jack was more than a decade older than Jay and had a fatherly presence Jay appreciated ever so much. It didn't hurt that he had brought two cases of Coke with him from Mexico City. "Jay, my man, what grand plan do you have for us today? What worldly problem needs solved?" was his standard greeting each morning.

At first, Jay would only nod and mumble, but after a few days he really looked forward to this new daily ritual. It wasn't much, but for some reason it was enough to keep him sane.

Ever since the monsoons had returned, Jay had spent most of his time in the church, waiting for word from Anna's kidnappers. Though the time passed slowly, there was really nothing else for him to do without going outside, which in turn meant getting drenched and covered with mud, neither of which was appealing to him. So wait he did, day in and day out, pacing around the room like a caged lion with nowhere to go.

"You need to get a book or something. You're driving me crazy," Sergeant Lopes told Jay nearly every day during his pacing spells.

Jay's retort was unchanging, "How can anyone read at a time like this?"

Sergeant Lopes and Officer Cruz, though weary of the ordeal, still held their daily vigil inside the church, waiting for a call or message that did not come. Though eager to head back to the city and their waiting families, the extreme isolation of the mission made it impractical for them to do so, and the continued onslaught of terrible weather made their decision to stay on day after day much easier.

Jay's morning was turning out to be a repeat performance: wake up, lie in bed, listen to the rain, lie in bed some more, get up around noon, look outside the double doors at the rain, the mud, the lake that covered the soccer field before heading to the kitchen to find a bit of nourishment, pace, pace and pace some more as worries and thoughts of Anna filled his head. This day was different, though. At first he wasn't sure why, but after tilt-

The Unraveling 185

ing his head back and forth, he realized he couldn't hear a thing. *Could it be possible? No rain?*

Springing from his bed, he moved quickly out of makeshift bedroom and into the large sanctuary, which was still being commandeered by the federal police. The *swish, swish, swish* of the overhead fans greeted him with a comforting serenade as he made his way to the wide-open, double-entrance doors and the sight of bright rays of sunshine as they splashed several feet onto the dirty concrete floor of the entryway. He raised his hands to shield the sun from his eyes as he made his way out onto the concrete veranda. A steady, warm, and brisk wind from the south had been hard at work for several hours and had nearly dried up all of the water that just the day before had covered the soccer field.

Wet, red mud contrasted by a brilliant robin egg blue sky greeted his eyes everywhere he looked as it glistened and shone in the bright sunlight. Flocks of white chickens stained red nearly halfway up their feathered bodies were busy scratching and clucking their way across the ball field in search of worms or other insects they could feast upon.

Children were beginning to move up and down the roadway that led to the church, kicking as they attempted to dislodge the sticky mud from their feet. Seagulls cawed their greeting as they competed with the chickens for stray insects or other morsels to satisfy their ravenous appetites.

Raising his hand to his head, Jay ran his fingers through the mop of hair that crowned his pale and slender face as he surveyed the budding life in front of him. A large smile broke out as he watched one of the boys slip and fall flat on his back in the muddy roadway. This sunshine was just what he needed to help him cope with another hopeless day.

A familiar voice brought him quickly around as he looked for the source. For a moment, he couldn't tell who or where it was coming from, but his large brown eyes quickly locked onto the now-familiar form of Jack McDonald running straight down the little road that led directly to the church and to him. Excitement rang out in Jack's voice, and Jay laughed at the sight of him trying to navigate the muddy roadway.

Way up in the air each foot went, far higher than normal in an attempt to clear the sticky mass of mud off of each foot before placing it back on the ground. Both of his arms were raised up, horizontal to the ground in an attempt to give him added stability. Jack's long, spindly legs; thin, tall frame; and long, sticklike arms exaggerated his movements and reminded Jay of a jerky, choreographed replica of a marionette play he'd seen during his junior high school years. The motions were deliberate and comical, though comedy was far from Jay's mind.

"Jay, my man, good news; great news, actually!" Jack exclaimed between breaths as he leaned up against one of the posts holding up the veranda roof.

Jack was not used to the thin, mile-high atmosphere and was gasping to take in as much of the precious air as possible.

"What, what, man? What's the great news?" Jay's patience was running thin.

Raising one hand as in protest, Jack bent half over in fatigue and took several long breaths before starting anew.

"Jay, we have news! You have news! I mean, it finally came! News that you were waiting for."

Rushing to his side, Jay grabbed hold of his new friend in excitement. "What do you mean, Jack? Something from Anna? What are you trying to tell me?"

Running his fingers over his face, Jack wiped the sweat from his receding hairline and rubbed his nose with excitement. Sad looking and small eyes were perched over top high, bony cheekbones, which jutted out more than usual and gave his face a more slender appearance. With all the dramatic flair of a Broadway actor, he raised one of his large, bushy eyebrows and proclaimed, "That's what I have been trying to tell you! If you'd just calm

The Unraveling

down and give me a moment, I could get a word in edgewise!"
Jack winked.

No longer in the mood for dramatic flair, Jay shook his friend.
"Jack, just tell me! What is the news?"

"All right, all right! We received a note from the kidnappers
this morning addressed to you!"

"This morning, how did it get here? I mean, I thought all the
roads were pretty much impassable."

Jack plopped down on the edge of the concrete sidewalk and
slumped his elbows onto his knees in exhaustion. "Well, we were
running out of water, and we heard that Salino was stuck in the
muddy roadway about two miles outside of the mission with a
load of fresh water, so Officer Cruz, Sergeant Lopes, Jesse, myself,
and some of the other men headed out to help him get unstuck."

"And? And?" Jay demanded as Jack stopped for breath.

"Well, we had to unload all of the water containers from the
truck, you know, to make it light enough to push out of the mud."

Jay exclaimed impatiently, "What about the note? Just get to
the point."

"That's what I'm trying to do, man! Let me finish the story!"

Jay was in no mood for a long story or a game of twenty questions. Even so, all he could do was wait.

"Anyways, as I was saying, we were unloading all the water
and on the last container we found a note inside of a plastic
Ziploc bag."

"And, and!" Jay demanded with an emphatic gesture as pronounced as he could make with both of his hands.

"And we opened it up. It was addressed to you."

Jay waited for his friend to continue, but Jack had told his
whole tale.

"What?"

Jack replied, "What, what?"

"What did the note say? What was in the letter?"

"I don't know," Jack had a hint of exasperation in his voice.

"What do you mean you don't know? You were there!?"

"*Was* there is the key word! I came running here as soon as I found out about the note!"

"You mean you didn't wait to see what it said?"

"No, sorry… I was so eager to get back here to tell you the good news that I just took off running back here as quick as I could."

Throwing his hands up in frustration, Jay paced back and forth. "Are they north or south of the mission?"

"Well, they're south, but they'll be here any minute."

Without a second thought, Jay leaped out into the sticky mud and began to run, slipping and sliding each step of the way.

"Jay, wait, they'll be here any minute. There's no need in running out to them!" Jack yelled at the back of his friend, but Jay was already well on his way.

Jay ran through the red-stained chickens, scattering them every which way, past the children playing, to the main road and turned to the south, ran through the gate at the south end of the mission, ran through a group of men with red-stained clothing who were busy pushing an old Volkswagen van out of the muddy ditch without so much as a simple hello.

Everyone he passed stopped what they were doing and watched as he navigated the treacherous muddy roadway until he was out of sight. Slipping first one way and then another, he made his way over a few of the small hills before finally intercepting Salino and the group of muddy men who had helped get the old water wagon out of the muddy hole it was stuck in.

What a sight they were to behold as Jay bent down and gasped for air. The men's clothing was camouflaged in red mud as were their arms, hands, faces, and even hair of some of the men, a testament to the difficult time they had in freeing the stuck vehicle. Fatigue and irritation lined their faces as they formed a small circle around him.

The Unraveling

"Jay, what are you doing out here now?" Sergeant Lopes demanded as his gruff voice matched the deepening scowl on his face.

He replied somewhat sheepishly, "I heard about the letter. I came as quick as I could."

Some of the other men began to grumble as they returned to the small truck, where they reclaimed whatever small patch of real estate they had just given up, too tired to care about the ongoing conversation between Jay and Sergeant Lopes.

"Yes, we did receive a letter, and I'm going to go over it with you as soon as we make it back to the mission and get cleaned up."

Undeterred by the firmness of Sergeant Lopes last statement, Jay pressed on. "Well, I'm here now. Can't we just go over it right here?" He wasn't sure, but he thought he could detect a reddish hue seep into Sergeant Lopes face underneath all of the mud. Feeling the rising tension, Jesse stepped between the two men before the situation intensified. "Jay, we are hot and tired. We will go over the letter when we get to the mission. We don't have far to go."

"I want to go over it now, before we go another step!"

Holding up his mud-caked hands, Jesse tried to reason with Jay, "I understand your position, Jay, but we are covered with mud from our heads to our toes. We have been working for over an hour to get this supply of water out of the mud and to the mission. We need to go get cleaned up before we go over the letter at the headquarters back at the church."

Unwilling to be reasoned with, Jay held his ground. "I want to go over the letter right here, right now!"

"Why you…" Sergeant Lopes's anger was reaching the breaking point.

Were it not for the presence of Jesse standing between the two men, Sergeant Lopes surely would have choked Jay.

"It's *my* letter about *my* wife, and I *want* to read it right *now!*"

The men stood at an impasse as the wind began gusting around them, bringing the green mesquite and sage to life as it shook and rolled on currents of warm air. Wrinkles of determination ran across Jay's forehead and sharp, clifflike brows accentuated angry dark eyes as he waited for Sergeant Lopes's next move.

Jesse was the one to act, however, as he continued to shield the two men from each other as the rest of the group watched on. With slow and deliberate movements, he raised his right arm and placed it around Jay's tense neck, turning him slightly away from Sergeant Lopes.

"Jay, listen now, we all are concerned about Anna and we all want to see her returned safely to you. That being said, we have to use care each time we receive word from the kidnappers. We cannot simply open the plastic bag the letter came in and remove the letter out here in the elements. We have to follow procedure so the officers can recover any evidence there might be. So you see, we cannot open the letter out here, not if we want to protect the evidence."

Jay practically yelled in response, "There was no evidence on the last letter to come and there won't be any now! Going back to the mission is just a waste of time when we could finally be doing something proactive! I'm getting so fed up with the whole thing! Waiting and waiting with no plan of action! I'm tired of it!"

For several moments balled clubs hung at the ends of Jay's arms and were taunt, ready to strike as Jesse's words of wisdom weighed on his heart. Though he didn't like them, nor like admitting it, he knew they were right and to do anything other than return to a controlled environment would be a foolish thing to do. Slowly his hands relaxed and his head hung down as he gave way to Jesse's reasoning.

"All right, but I don't like it. I really doubt there will be any evidence we can use."

Jesse led him to the truck and offered him a seat on the tailgate as far away from Sergeant Lopes as he could get.

The Unraveling

"We'll find Anna, and we'll bring her home! I promise you that, my friend!"

Jesse's words were filled with a lot less certainty than they were meant to carry and did nothing to bolster Jay's spirits as the little worn-out truck groaned and grinded its way into gear.

Once back at the mission, Jay paced back and forth like a caged animal searching for an escape as he waited for Sergeant Lopes and the others to get cleaned up from their muddy ordeal.

What could be taking them so long! Come on! Hurry up! Try as he might, he could focus on nothing other than the letter he still hadn't seen. The mere knowledge of its presence brought both great hope and extreme fear to his heart. Hope that somehow this ordeal he was now in would soon be resolved and fear that the resolution would not be favorable for either Anna or himself, with fear far outweighing hope by far.

"Jay, my man, it's a bright and sunny day, and I feel good!" Jack exploded through the exterior doors with a flourish. "Let's celebrate, brother! Good news is on the way!"

"I wish I had your confidence. I'm nothing but a wreck, standing around, waiting, waiting, and waiting. I can hardly stand it!"

"It's going to work out just fine, you'll see! God has His hand on things. He'll take care of you! Soon, Anna will be back and this will all be a distant memory. Trust God, He'll never let you down! He never has me, that I know, my friend."

The two men moved to the long, makeshift desk, more of a catch all, really, being used by Sergeant Lopes in his commandeered office and grabbed a seat opposite each other as they waited for the others to return. Jay grabbed a pen and began turning it over and over in his hands and couldn't help but smile a little at the sight of his friend who was wearing a white-and-red striped polo shirt that was buttoned all the way to the top. The red collar was in on one side and out on the other. The mop of hair on his head was still damp from his recently finished shower, and his face was red from a combination of hot water and outside heat. A silly, permanent grin was fixed on his face, and together with the red shirt and red complexion reminded Jay of the old television character "Howdy Doody."

"I'm so nervous, I can barely stand it." Jay took up their earlier conversation.

"It's going to work out. I'm sure of it," Jack reassured Jay with much confidence in his voice. "Just remember, God is in control!"

"I try to remember that, pray to Him all the time and try to trust Him completely. But to be honest with you, sometimes it just feels like He's not listening."

Jay's voice was quiet and sad as tears filled his eyes. Sharing his feelings wasn't something he was used to, but Jack was disarming and genuine so he felt like he could truly open up to him.

"That's just Satan telling you that. He wants you to think that there is nothing you, and more importantly, nothing God can do to help your situation. He does that all the time."

"I know, I keep telling myself that all the time. I just can't help but feel that way, though. No matter how much or how hard I pray, I feel nothing but hopelessness and despair. I am so scared for Anna. I can't imagine what she must be going through."

Hot tears began to stream down his flushed face as he confided in his friend. "I feel so guilty and get so mad at myself for being such a baby. I'm here, safe and sound, while Anna is the one that has to go through all of the hardship. I'm trying to be strong for her, for myself, but I just can't seem to get a handle on things. I don't know how much more I can go through. My mind keeps racing and racing, imagining all the terrible things that could be happening to her until I start to really believe they *are* happening to her. Then I get more and more depressed; it's all just a vicious cycle that I can't seem to break. To tell you the truth, I don't think I could even live without Anna. I just don't know what I would do if I were to lose her."

The overhead fans chugged away as both men sat in silence. Tears continued to flow freely down Jay's cheeks. Instead of repeating the same things over and again, Jack sat in silence and let his friend have an emotional release.

Slowly the other men began to trickle into the building. Jesse and Officer Cruz first, followed by Sergeant Lopes and a few of the other villagers. They were all busy laughing and joking, their moods having improved considerably due to the bright blue, cloudless skies, and warm south wind that was blowing. Jack joined in the friendly banter going around as they all took seats at the table, but Jay continued to hang his head as he tried to get a grip on his emotions. Sensing the emotional state of his friend, Jesse walked over and placed a silent hand on Jay's back in greeting before grabbing a seat between Jay and Sergeant Lopes.

"Well, we're all here, I think. Let's get this show on the road." Sergeant Lopes set the mud-stained, Ziploc bag on the table in front of the group.

All eyes, including Jay's, were focused on the piece of paper inside the baggie. It appeared to be a piece of torn paper from some sort of tan colored stock, possibly a manila envelope. Although it was hard to be sure, it appeared the paper had not been damaged by all of the rain or the water from the water bottle it had been taped to.

With great theatrics, Sergeant Lopes removed two clear plastic latex gloves from a box of a hundred he had retrieved from his vehicle before coming in. With deliberate care, he slowly slid one gently onto his right hand, holding the cuff of the pliable material with his left before repeating the process on his left hand. The skin-tight gloves formed to his hands like saran wrap, and he punctuated the task by releasing his hold of the cuff several inches above his skin, resulting in a loud *whack* as the contracting material met his hand.

Moving slowly, and with the care of a surgeon, he picked up the plastic baggie and slowly turned it over and over in his hands, examining every possible inch of the folded paper inside before slowly and deliberately forcing open the zipper on top of the plastic bag. Reaching inside with just his forefinger and thumb, and with all present leaning forward silently in their chairs in anticipation, he carefully pinched down on a corner of the tattered paper and removed the note with his right hand while holding the plastic baggy in his left. Satisfied there was nothing more to remove, he carefully placed the plastic bag in the center of the table and used both hands to carefully unfold the piece of thick paper.

Leaning forward as far as he could, Jay stretched out his neck in an attempt to catch a glimpse of what was written. Sergeant Lopes dark eyes moved back and forth with little reaction as he read and reread the words on the paper.

Hurry up! What does it say? Jay's mind screamed over and over as he watched and waited for Sergeant Lopes to either read the words on the paper out loud or allow the rest of the group the opportunity to do so. Butterflies filled his stomach as he edged as far forward on his chair as he possibly could, and he noticed the others were doing the same. Finally, with the same careful deliberation used earlier, Sergeant Lopes set the piece of paper down on the table for all to see but not touch. When Jay saw the writing and read the first few words, his heart sank.

Aug 5th 2010

Go to the large lizard and wait for instructions. Do so today. No police! Don't follow directions and the girl will die! Remember, we are watching you!

The simple note was handwritten and made no sense to Jay whatsoever. To make matters worse, the date on the top of the letter was four days prior. Panic began to fill his chest like an expanding balloon, making it difficult for him to breathe. His mind was numb with shock as he attempted to digest the note.

Large lizard, what in the world?

Finally Jay stated, "I don't understand what this means at all."

Sergeant Lopes's eyes met Jay's, and for an instant Jay thought he could detect discouragement in them.

Then Sergeant Lopes spoke with an air of confidence. "The large lizard can only be the dinosaur statue more than sixteen miles away. I can think of no other meaning."

The rest of the men began nodding their heads in agreement, and a foggy recollection of the marker began to form in Jay's mind. So much had happened over the past month and a half that he had completely forgotten about the monument that had been donated to the children of the mission from a church in Florida. Small as it was, hope began to surge back into his body at the possibility.

Jay kicked his chair back and away from him as he stood up, Jay exclaimed, "Well, let's get going!"

Frustration and anger began to build when none of the other men moved or seemed to share his enthusiasm. Taking a deep breath, he repeated his words, only this time with much more authority. "Let's get going! What are we waiting for?"

Standing up and facing Jay, Sergeant Lopes answered with the cold authority he held, "Tomorrow! That's what we are waiting for."

Jesse, Jack, and the others shared nervous glances as Jay and Sergeant Lopes squared off. Shaking his head in disgust, Jay could barely believe his ears as Sergeant Lopes's words sank into his frantic mind. "What do you mean tomorrow? Didn't you read the letter? If I don't do exactly as the letter says, Anna will be killed! It may already be too late!"

Large red veins stood out on Sergeant Lopes's neck, and his hands balled into fists as he took a step toward Jay and barked, "We are not going to try to reach that dinosaur today and that's final."

Jay was frantic. "I don't understand. Why not? What you are afraid of? Why you are waiting? If we don't act soon, Anna will be dead. You read the note."

Deciding to take a different tack, Sergeant Lopes retreated to his chair, took a big breath, and exhaled before extending his arms outward, palms up, almost as if he were praying. "Jay, you saw the road. It was treacherous. We just spent three hours going two miles, and the rest of the road is much more treacherous than the first two miles from the mission. Salino spent several days stuck between here and there on that road. The last thing I want to do is spend the next twenty hours or so digging our vehicle out of the mud. No, we'll wait till morning; let the wind and the sun dry the roadway before we try to reach the dinosaur. Even then, it'll probably be difficult." His voice was almost whiney and patronizing, which grated on Jay's nerves.

"You don't know that! We could try! What do we have to lose?"

"We're not going to try! I'm in charge of this operation; what I say goes!"

"But they'll kill her! Don't you understand! It's right there, plain as day! Read it for yourself! Are you dense or something? Scared? Maybe you're in cahoots with the kidnappers!" Jay accused in an attempt to keep the argument going.

Sergeant Lopes wouldn't bite. Mind made up, he folded his arms across his chest and began turning the note over and over in his hands with a greatly exaggerated faux interest in the piece, as if it would reveal some overlooked clue that might help them.

Deciding to take a different approach, Jay turned to the others at the table in an attempt to gain their support.

"Jesse…Jack…Officer Cruz… Any of you?"

All eyes remained glued to the table.

"I thought you were my friends, that you really cared about Anna and me. That's what you have been telling us ever since we arrived, anyways. Here you guys have been telling me you're Christians, telling me to trust God and all, but I guess it's all been a big show. When I, when *we* need you the most, you turn your back on me, on us. I see how it is! You all are a bunch of hypocrites!"

With an exaggerated motion, Jay threw the pen across the room as hard as he could and stormed out of the building. Tears of anger magnified the bright sun light and caused him to shield his eyes as he made his way to the welcoming shade on the north side of the building. Plopping down hard on the concrete sidewalk, he buried his head in his arms like a child throwing a tantrum and began to sob as despair filled his soul.

Fifteen minutes or more passed before Jay felt the presence of someone sitting down next to him. Though the tears had stopped, his face felt flushed with heat, and he knew it would be streaked, so he kept his head buried in his arms to prevent anyone from seeing him in such a state. A gentle and warm touch gave him a start and made him jump with surprise.

"Jay, I just want you to know, we really are here for you, man." It was Jack. "I know sometimes it seems like it's all you versus the world, but it's anything but, my friend! More importantly, you should always know that God is with you at all times. He wants to carry you through these tough times if you'll just let him! Even if I don't know anything else, I know that much is true."

Keeping his head buried in his arms, Jay's voice was muffled and sounded foreign when he replied, "What, did you draw the short straw and have to come out here to deal with 'Poor Ole Jay'?"

"Well, I didn't have to come out here, but I volunteered to. Not because I really knew what to say, but because I love you, man! You're my brother in Christ, and I want to be here for you."

"If you really want to be here for me, then you'll go with me to the dinosaur right now and not wait for morning."

Jack patted his friend on the back a few times before removing his hand. "Jay, I just want you to think about something. Really listen to what I'm saying. Sergeant Lopes is right; there is no sense in heading out now when all we'll do is fight the mud. You know and I know that it'll be way better traveling tomorrow. As a matter of fact, we'll get there just as quickly leaving tomorrow as we would if we left right now."

"How can you say or think that? We have everything to gain. We have Anna's life to gain! Waiting till morning could cost her life!"

"It's not going to cost Anna her life!"

"You don't know that! How can you say that? Do you have a direct line to the kidnappers? Do you have some sixth sense that can tell the future or something?"

Jack stood up and started to leave. "Try to calm down a bit, focus on what we are trying to accomplish; trust God to give you wisdom and courage."

Jack's words brought Jay to his feet like a wind-up jack-in-the-box. "Calm down? Calm down? You're telling me to calm down? This is my life! My wife's life we are talking about!"

What am I going to do? What am I going to do? This is the only question that kept running through his mind, a question for which he had no answer.

Chapter 25

Darkness blanketed the countryside, making it possible to move with ease around the small building without drawing attention to himself. A warm and steady breeze covered any noise he might make, though he was careful to be as silent as possible. *There's no need to telegraph my presence*, he thought as he picked each step with as much delicacy as one might use to pick a flower. Not that he had to sneak around. In fact, he could go anywhere he wanted to whenever he wanted without anyone asking a single question.

People feared him. No, he didn't need secrecy to do his bidding, but for this task—to study his prey, his foe, his adversary—he chose to go in silent anonymity in hopes of devising a strategy. The challenge excited him as he anticipated an impending confrontation—a confrontation of life and death, one he was determined to win no matter the cost.

Soft voices wound about, carried on the wind straight to his ears, igniting a smoldering hatred deep within his hardened soul. The voices were coming from the inside of the rundown building just on the other side of the wall from the interloper and caused him to raise his right hand to the hard leather hilt of a bull whip that wound about his body and rested on the waistband of his dark trousers. The thought of using his weapon on those inside stirred an excitement and deep hatred that fed his very being and created a destructive desire in him that was nearly impossible to control. The soft voices reaching his ears served no purpose in him other than to add fuel to the fire that raged within. It wasn't so much the singing that angered him but the songs being sung. Songs about hope and love and some character named Jesus; pure rubbish in his mind.

Somehow, this Jesus character was giving hope to the people within the walls—his people, his slaves. They had no business having hope in anything other than him. It was he who decided life for them—when they lived, when they died. It was he who gave them food to eat, water to drink, not this Jesus character they were singing about. Soon he would put an end to it; soon he would stamp out the false hope they had somehow found. Not tonight, though; tonight he was there for one purpose—to study the source of this new false hope, the one who was affecting and infecting his world with this Jesus.

Oh how he hated her for it! Even his guards were becoming tarnished by her stories. At first he was completely shocked and did nothing when he caught a couple of them listening to the ramblings of this girl as she taught the others, but now if he caught them loitering anywhere near her cell, he dealt with them swiftly, inflicting as much pain as possible to prevent them from becoming too comfortable with this new prisoner. Besides, sympathetic guards were the last thing he needed when running an operation like his.

Feeling his way along the rough walls of the building, it didn't take long for him to reach the spot he had in mind even though it was pitch black out. Sliding his hands along the rough exterior of the building, it was easy to locate the smooth, rectangular piece of wood that had been installed over top of the existing siding. With extreme care, and as quietly as possible, he slowly applied pressure to the piece of wood until it began to slide sideways on a set of makeshift tracks that held it in place. It had moved no more than six inches before revealing two round holes eyes-width apart. Carefully, he moved his head to the wall directly over the holes until his forehead rested against the side of the building and then lined up his eyes with the small portals leading to the inside.

One small candle lit the little dungeon but gave off very little light, just enough for him to see the outline of a young lady, the source of his growing resentment. The candles were a luxury that he hadn't wanted initially to let her have, but he relented when Rosalita convinced him it would provide opportunity for him to observe his newest prize whenever he wanted. Even though she burned the candle round the clock, he only visited in the middle of the night when no one else was around. Not wanting to give the impression that he was keenly interested, he avoided checking in during the daytime altogether but instead relied on daily reports from Rosalita after she had taken food and water to her, also a luxury far greater than he would have done for any other prisoner.

"She's American; the Americans will expect us to take care of her. Failure to do so will make them really come looking for us," Rosalita argued successfully.

What she didn't know was that he had no plans to ever return her to the Americans whether they met his demands or not, and so far they hadn't. No, he had much more sinister plans for her. Plans that excited him far greater than receiving any amount of ransom. So watch her he would, for now, until his excitement coupled with an extreme rage deep inside of him grew greater than even he could control. That day was a moment he yearned for with great anticipation, and now that day was near at hand.

Chapter 26

She knew he was there, could feel him watching her, feel the evil as it traced her every move. Even so, she continued singing "Jesus Loves Me" through one of the knotholes on the wall between her dungeon and the dungeon of dozens of young men on the other side. Anna had brought hope and love into their lives where nothing but despair and sadness had been. This song was theirs, an anthem for each to place in his own heart, and nothing could ever take it away from them.

"Tell us about the golden streets," Carlos begged through the wall as the song came to and end.

"Yeah, tell us, please, Miss Anna," dozens of other voices chimed in unison.

Needing no further prompting, Anna did just that, telling them of God, Jesus, and the Holy Spirit and of His love for each of them. She described in great detail heaven as she imagined it to be, golden streets, huge mansions with an abundance of food, and a place for each one of them.

Carlos whispered, "Tell us about Jesus and about our place in heaven." She did just that, explained to each of them how Jesus had died for each one of them, how He had risen and gone to heaven and would come back for each and every one who accepted Him as their personal Savior. "And no one can stop you from going with Him. No one can keep you captive any longer. You will all be made free in Christ! God is your Father in heaven, and He will always be with you. I can promise you that!"

Anna was in her element. The Holy Spirit was alive and speaking through her straight to the hearts of the boys on the other side of the wall. Even the knowledge of the evil just outside her dungeon did nothing to hinder her testimony of Christ's love. None of them had ever heard anything remotely close to what she was telling them, and they were hungry to hear more.

She went on to explain through the hole in the wall, "If you want salvation, want to have Jesus as your personal Savior and God as your Father, all you have to do is ask Jesus into your heart, ask for forgiveness for your sins, and pledge to live for Him."

The young men clamored to accept Christ as their personal Savior. "I want to accept Jesus. I want too. So do I." They all responded through the wall. "Please, Miss Anna, could I accept Jesus as my Savior? I want God to be my Father," Carlos exclaimed through the small opening.

"Carlos, you already accepted Jesus a couple nights ago. You don't have to continue to ask Him into your life."

"I know, but I just want to be sure. I don't want Jesus to leave me here, Anna. I would just die if He didn't take me home with Him."

Unmistakable tears of emotion rang out on their voices as they repeated after Anna the sinner's prayer. Anna herself was nearly overcome with emotion at the eagerness and sincerity of the group of boys on the other side of the wall from her.

She prayed silently, "This is what I trained all those years for. This is why I am here! Thank you, Jesus, for this opportunity to serve you."

The hard ground was unleveled, making it difficult to stay comfortable. Anna had to strain her neck to reach the knothole she was speaking through. "I love you guys! Jesus loves you too! I hope you know that."

"Sing us more songs, please, Miss Anna," Carlos begged through the wall.

"Not tonight. You guys need your rest. I'll sing more tomorrow! You guys just keep living for Jesus! He will never fail you. I promise you that. Now get some rest. Tomorrow will be here before you know it," she comforted them as if she were their very own mother, and for some she was the only mother any of them had ever known.

Turning toward the voyeur behind the two round holes in the wall, Anna smiled and did her best to make eye contact with whoever was on the other side before extinguishing her candle. She had met him once, her first day there when he had come into her dungeon, snapped his whip around over her head before harshly cutting off a piece of her hair and a small section of her dress. At the time, Anna was sure he would do things far more sinister, but just when it appeared he had worked himself into a frenzy great enough to make her fears reality, he turned and abruptly left the dungeon. She had never seen him again, except through the eyeholes on her exterior wall. That person, she had come to learn, was Luis, the "angel of death," as the others referred to him. Every day, she prayed for God to keep her safe from Luis but to also speak to his heart that he might find salvation.

"Everyone needs a chance to gain their salvation, even Luis," she reasoned with herself as she laid down on the hard wooden pallets that made up her bed. "Oh if Jay could see me now, wouldn't he be surprised?" Anna began her evening prayers and then a fitful night's sleep.

A forlorn sorrow stabbed her heart. Not for her own plight, but for Jay and the difficult time she knew he must be having.

"Lord, keep Jay safe and please comfort his heart. I know he must be just beside himself with worry and grief. Please, heavenly Father, let him know that you are with me and will keep me safe."

It was the same prayer she had prayed every night since her abduction. It brought her comfort to know God was with the one she loved.

~ ~ ~ ~

Shaking with rage, Luis slammed the piece of wood back into place over top of the eyeholes. Never before had he seen anyone so brazen. The desire to tear her limb from limb nearly overwhelmed him. *Who is she to smile at me, and with no fear at all!*

The Unraveling

he thought as he moved back away from the dungeon. *Surely she doesn't realize who she is dealing with.*

Anger, confusion, and hatred filled his head as he moved across the disheveled compound as hastily as the dark night would allow. The going was precarious due to the heavy monsoons that had plagued the entire region the previous couple weeks, and stepping in a residual puddle of muddy water only darkened his mood even more.

"I should have killed her a few days ago when we heard no response from the mission! At least that would have stopped all this talk about Jesus, freedom through Christ, and salvation!"

Sliding the whip off his shoulder, he began slinging it around over his head, back and forth, back and forth as he approached a more sturdily constructed building. Through the air it went, over and over again, before sizzling down on the center of the closed door with a loud *bang.* For the next several minutes, nothing but the singing air of the whip, followed by the violent thud, could be heard across the compound as Luis took out his frustration on the inanimate object. Deep gouges and gashes in the solid core wood plank door bore proof that this was a ritual that had been practiced many times in the past.

Skin wet with sweat glistened in the moonlight as he wound the whip back around his torso. The exertion did little to alleviate the rage that was boiling inside, at best tempering it to a controllable simmer. Working the hard steel latch, he opened the door and moved to the inside. Several candles flickered from the suddenness of the breeze and cast eerie shadows on the white stucco wall opposite the door.

The room was barren except for a hard wooden chair and an old, low day couch with shredded cushions. Sitting on the end farthest from the door was Rosalita. Her body was tense and ready to move quickly out of his way as he moved to the center of the room.

The warm night air from the open doorway was a welcome infusion of freshness in the musky staleness of the old building but did nothing to lessen the tension permeating the room. The snarled lips and furrowed brow on his face told her to stay as clear as possible…or pay the consequences—a lesson learned long ago, more times than she cared to remember.

With catlike quickness, he moved across the room and snatched for Rosalita just as she sprang from the couch to the far corner of the room near a hallway that led to a run down and empty kitchen.

"Luis, what's wrong? Did something bad happen?"

Lunging at her with his grimy hands, he roared, "I'll tell you what's wrong! That American you brought to me with promises of wealth! That's what is wrong. She has been nothing but trouble, and trouble is what I do not need!"

Dodging his advances, Rosalita moved to the opposite corner. "What do you mean? Did she try to escape or something?"

"Escape would be acceptable, even desirable, if you ask me. She is being much worse than that!" He moved slowly across the floor, directly at Rosalita in an attempt to cut down her possible avenues of escape. She was too quick to be trapped that easily, though, and quickly darted to the far corner of the room.

Luis remained near the center of the room, swiveling his body just far enough to face her at all times. This was a game they had played oftentimes in the past, and he had learned to put as little exertion in as possible, just enough to force her to move one way or another, knowing that decisions and movement would eventually cause her to make an error in judgment. Then he would have her.

In an attempt to buy time, Rosalita's mind ran through all of the scenarios that could possibly have happened to set his anger off in such a manner.

"What did she do?"

The Unraveling

Red eyes wild with anger glared at her as he took a small step forward and answered with malice in his voice, "She is being disruptive to the others. I hate her and all she stands for! She needs to die."

He smiled when her body tensed at his threat of death. It was just the psychological opening he needed. In one fluid motion he turned and headed for the doorway. "I'm going to kill her! Right here and right now!" he bluffed.

Moving as quickly as possible, Rosalita moved to the doorway and stood in front of it, knowing Luis could easily grab her. "Luis, wait! The money, don't forget the money! We'll have it soon, I promise you that!"

An exhilarating rush surged through his vessels as he snatched her violently away from the door with a python-like grip, drawing her body directly into his. Foul breath gagged her as she struggled against his hold for precious air.

"The promise of money is what put us in the predicament we are in. Besides, we have delivered our contact note, and for three days no one has answered! They are not going to answer! She is a worthless piece of dirt, nothing more than that; just another mouth to feed. No, I am going to kill her! Tonight!"

Much to her surprise, he released his grip on her, and she slipped to the ground as he started toward the door. Anticipation surged through his veins, and he smiled with delight when she reached out and grabbed him by his pant leg.

"Luis, the rain; that's why they haven't contacted us. The rains washed out all the roads everywhere. You have to give them time to respond before you do anything."

"The money is more trouble than it's worth!" he stated as he reached the door and began to open it.

The thought of losing the money, and a possible chance at freedom, was more than Rosalita could stand. Though she detested the man, she wrapped both arms around his legs and begged, "Please, Luis, wait just one more day! Then do what you will. In the meantime, I'll make it worth the wait," she teased in the most seductive voice she could muster.

Holding her in one arm, he grabbed her flowing black hair and pulled her head backwards, hard, till she thought her neck was going to break. "Why are you so interested in this girl? If I didn't know better, I would think you were plotting your escape, and with my money!"

"No, Luis, I would never attempt to escape. I love you," she lied as he kissed her exposed neck.

Throwing his head back, he roared with laughter at her last statement. "Love me? I suppose you do, in your own twisted way! We'll see if you still feel that way by morning," he stated as he closed the hard wooden door and half drug, half carried her down the hallway to one of the rooms at the end.

Currents of air once again moved the flames of the candles to and fro as they projected their mystical air dance on the white stucco wall.

Chapter 27

Towering above the terrain like a lone soldier or primeval sentinel, the purple behemoth's toothy smile and small front legs seemed out of proportion to Jay as he walked around the concrete base of the dinosaur replica. It was his third, slow trip around the statue as he searched in vain for some sort of note or message that had been left by the kidnappers. Anxiety was once again rushing through his veins like ice water as he realized this might not be the place the previous note from the kidnappers meant. Worse yet, the fear that someone else may have been there and taken the note, or whatever was supposed to be there for him, was beginning to cause him to hyperventilate with near panic.

How can this be happening to me? he thought to himself as he claimed a seat on the hard concrete pedestal right next to the dinosaur's right foot.

"I have to get a grip on myself. No one could have gotten here to take anything. It took us five hours just to navigate the roadway from the mission, and there's nothing else around here for miles. Besides us, Salino has been the only other traveler through the area." He reasoned with himself in an attempt to calm his tense nerves.

Large chips in the purple paint were beginning to pock the finish on the dinosaur, although they weren't really apparent unless one was sitting right next to it. A large crack had formed where the head met the neck, and it extended all the way around the replica and was all the more evident from moisture seepage; remnants of the monsoons that had passed through the region.

"What in the world are you doing clear out here in Mexico?" Jay asked the silent lizard. "You're kinda out of your element, just like me." He patted the cold body of the beast.

With slow deliberation, he scanned the terrain around the monument as carefully and as far as he could possibly see. The words of the note stood out clearly in his mind: *Come by yourself, and no federal police or Anna will die! Today!*

Though the others had reassured him that the kidnappers weren't really watching, they had all gotten out of Sergeant Lopes's silver Dodge more than a mile up the road toward the mission. Sergeant Lopes gave Jay a radio and told him to notify him if there was any trouble or if he found another letter, neither of which had happened.

"Oh, Anna, what am I going to do? Lord, please keep her safe! I couldn't live without her, Lord!"

The sun was at full strength and the temperature was blazing hot and amplified by rising humidity from a rapidly approaching weather front. Wiping the sweat from his brow, Jay jumped when his radio crackled to life, "Jay, this is Sergeant Lopes. Have you found anything?"

With slow reluctance, Jay removed the radio from the hem of his waistband and keyed the stiff mic. "No, sir, I haven't found anything. Yet!" He emphasized the last word.

"We're moving in, then. There looks to be a storm blowing in. I want to get back before it turns this road to a mud hole again."

Once again, panic began to fill his heart as he placed the radio back onto his jeans. "It has to be here somewhere," he exclaimed as he jumped back to the ground and began to circle the beast.

With each trip around the statue, he widened his arc until he was more than twenty yards from it. With careful deliberation he studied each foot of ground, looking for some sort of sign the kidnappers might have left. Nothing at all looked out of place amongst the sage or around the red gravel parking area that circled the entire dinosaur. Looking up the road, he could make out

The Unraveling   211

the images of Sergeant Lopes, Officer Cruz, Jack, Jesse as they crested a hill on the road more than half a mile away.

"It has to be here! It just has to!" He took one last scan of the surrounding terrain.

Defeated, he retreated to the front of the dinosaur and once again climbed onto the concrete base to reclaim his seat. Voices from the others drifted slowly on the wind and announced their impending arrival, which only heightened his anxiety.

"Lord, help me. Anna's life depends on it."

Defeated and alone, he leaned to the small plaque on the front of the statue, tracing his fingers across the raised words on the brass-colored plate. "From Four Lakes, Florida, huh? I wish we had gone to Four Lakes, Florida, and never left there!"

As he reread the plaque, he could see marred paint and loose material around the edges, almost as if someone had tried to remove it. Bending down to within no more than a couple inches, he continued his examination as rising hope filled his heart for the first time in days. Carefully, with the tips of his fingers, he applied pressure to one side of the plaque and nearly yelled when it moved sideways more than a quarter of an inch.

Spurred on by the small movement, he began applying even more pressure to the side and to the top of the plaque. His hands began to shake with tempered excitement when it began to pull away from the base more than a half an inch, revealing what appeared to be a dark plastic container directly underneath.

Taking a big breath, he pulled on the edge of the plaque with all his might and was surprised how easily it popped off into his hands. The lack of resistance nearly caused him to fall over backwards, and after regaining his balance, he gently removed the dark, hard plastic container from its hiding place. By its weight, he could tell there was something of substance inside the container, so he pried off the plastic lid to reveal a large satellite telephone receiver and a note that had been sealed in a clear plastic baggie, just as the others had been. It took only a moment's hesitation for him to decide to open the bag and read the note before the others reached him, knowing full well that Sergeant Lopes would not be happy.

Power on the phone and press send. We will be waiting for your call.

The note was simple and to the point. With no hesitation, he pushed the power button and prayed the batteries weren't dead. Relief filled his heart when the screen lit up and began going through its warm-up cycle. "Hurry up, hurry up," he urged while peeking around the dinosaur at the men quickly approaching. They were no more than a minute or two away, he estimated as he turned his attention back to the phone. Satisfied it was on, he said a quick prayer and pushed *send*.

∿ ∿ ∿ ∿

"Time is up. I'm going to go kill the girl now," Luis stated as he made his way out of the back bedroom and down the dark hallway of the small house. Two gray field mice scurried from the center of the room and disappeared through a small hole in the wooden floor near the far corner as he made his way toward the door.

"Luis, wait! You said you'd give her more time! You can't kill her now!" Rosalita begged as she followed, mere steps behind, wrapped only in a tattered and dirty blanket.

"I did give her more time. I gave her another night to live! Now her time has run out! I'm tired of this game," he exclaimed with a laugh.

Rosalita moved quickly and grabbed Luis by the shoulder. "No, wait! The money! I know they'll call and give us the money!"

Swinging violently around with his free hand, Luis's fist slammed violently into the side of her face and knocked her to the ground. "Leave me alone, or I'll kill you too!"

The Unraveling   213

With a sickening thud, her head impacted the hard wooden floor, making her woozy as the blanket slid from her bare body and revealed multiple scars and burn marks.

Grasping at the edge of the blanket, she slid across the floor and begged him to wait, "Luis, just one more day, please! One more day!"

Her begging was no more than an annoyance to him, and he threatened to whip her if she kept it up.

His small black eyes shone with excitement as he anticipated the torture and blood letting that was about to occur. Without a second glance, he worked the hard steel latch, opened the door, and walked out into the brilliant sunlight, straight toward Anna's cell.

∼ ∼ ∼ ∼

The phone was hot and felt foreign as he placed it to his ear and waited. The phone's speaker crackled as the antenna picked up a lot of static from the air. His heart pounded in his chest like a base drum, and a nervous sweat broke out on his face as he waited and listened for some sort of ringing, indicating a connection. "Please, please, please answer," he begged with a desperate tininess to his voice.

A dozen or so seconds passed as he began to bob his head up and down slightly with a nervous energy like he'd never before felt.

"This is it, this is life or death, come on, please, Lord, let her be alive."

To his surprise, he could hear ringing through the phone, which caused his heart to pound even more.

"Please answer, please answer, please answer."

∼ ∼ ∼ ∼

Sadness and desperation settled over her body like a rising fog for the first time in her memory. Tears began pouring from her eyes as she lay on the dirty floor in the middle of the room. All of her life she had remained so strong, relying on no one but herself no matter what Luis had thrown at her in an attempt to break her. And try he did, hundreds of times, torture so sinister that even the strongest man would break, but not her. She exhibited a will and inner strength far greater than that of any man he had ever known, so he kept her around to amuse himself and to abuse at will, which he did, and often.

She tried to get a grip on herself, hated that she couldn't, hated that she had placed hope in anything but herself.

"Never again," she vowed, gathering the blanket around and pulling herself to her feet.

She yelled out the open door at the back of Luis as he made his way across the compound, "Kill her! See if I care! Kill her slowly! Make her pay!" Her voice was sheer hatred, and at that moment Anna was the target, that and the life she represented, the life she now would never know.

"I don't care!" she screamed at the top of her lungs.

"I don't need you, don't need the money, nothing! I'll make it on my own!" She sobbed as she worked her way to the open doorway and looked out.

The bright sunny day was a contrast to the dark storm that raged within her soul. If she wanted out of this life, she would have to make it out on her own, she could see that now.

Her thoughts were interrupted by a high, foreign ringing, followed by a pause, then ringing again, which startled her back to reality. For a moment she was confused as she tried to remember the source but moved quickly to the kitchen when she realized the ringing was coming from the satellite phone on the old wooden crate that masqueraded as a kitchen table.

Practically leaping across the room with excitement, she grabbed it and began punching buttons in an attempt answer.

〰 〰 〰 〰

"Hello, hello, is anybody there? This is Jay! Jay Bilston, Anna's husband. Is anybody there?" The receiver on his phone was filled with crackling noises, almost as if someone was fumbling with the phone on the other end.

"Hello, hello, can you hear me?" he plead as loudly as he dared, knowing Sergeant Lopes and the others would be there any moment.

About to lose hope, his heart raced when he heard a voice on the other end of the line, "Wait!"

It was a female voice, and he couldn't be sure, but it sounded like Anna's.

"Anna, Anna, is that you?" he cried frantically into the receiver. "Anna, Anna, say something, anything."

Again a voice came on the other end of the line, "Wait!" was all it said as Jay began frantically calling Anna's name over and over again.

∿ ∿ ∿ ∿

With renewed determination, Rosalita moved across the compound in bare feet. In her left hand, she clutched the worn blanket tightly around her body, and in her right the black phone connected to Jay. There was no sign of Luis, so she pushed ahead even faster and her heart raced when she saw the back of him as he reached the side of the building that housed Anna and the others.

"Luis, wait!" she yelled as she continued toward him. "The phone, the phone, he's on the phone!"

Her words brought him to a stop, and she could see his shoulders flinch as they hit his ears. She wasn't prepared for what she saw next, his eyes were filled with intense hatred and a fiery intent to kill.

"Luis, it's the phone. It's the mission. They have finally called."

Her voice was barely more than a whisper as she thrust her arm carrying the phone as far from her body as possible toward him, hoping that he would take just the phone from her hand and not grab her in the process. From his right hand hung the long leather bullwhip, while his left hand was empty and clenched into a fist. For several seconds she could see no recognition in his angry eyes, but after a moment or two, he reached out and removed the phone from her shaking hand.

~ ~ ~ ~

There was something happening on the other end of the phone, of that much Jay was sure.

"Hello, Anna, is that you?"

Over and over, he said her name into the phone with fading hopes and the realization that he most likely would be caught by Sergeant Lopes before his call was finished. Just when he had given up hope, a voice cut through loud and clear on the other end.

"One million American dollars! If you want to see Anna alive ever again, one million dollars! Understand?"

Jay gulped as the words stung his heart. One million dollars was exactly one million more than he and Anna had. His mind raced as he tried to think of what to say next.

"One million dollars! Are you there?"

Not knowing what else to say, Jay blurted out, "How do I know if she is still alive? I need to know if she is still alive."

A sinister laugh came through the receiver of the phone and cut straight to his heart. "You don't, but this I'll tell you, you will know when she's not alive! Now, one million dollars. Does she live? Or does she die?"

Fear spread throughout his body like water from an artesian well. "Yes, I agree," he heard a strange voice say, knowing full well it was his own.

For several moments his words were met with silence, which made him fear the connection had somehow been broken.

"In three days, take one million dollars to the north of the mission. Go ten miles before turning east on a little trail that follows a small ravine. In that ravine, about one mile from the road, is an old rusty barrel. Place the money in a black garbage bag and place

The Unraveling

it in the barrel. After I have retrieved the money and counted it, Anna will be released back to the mission. Understand?"

Jay nodded his head before answering, "Yes, I understand."

"If you do not follow these directions exactly as I have told you, the girl dies!"

The open line went dead. Jay's body began to shake. As quickly as possible, he turned off the phone and placed it and the note back into the plastic baggie before returning it to the hard plastic container from which it had come. As hastily as possible, he placed it back in its hiding place and reinstalled the plaque over the hole, brushed away any residual sand and grit, and sat down.

No more than a minute passed before Sergeant Lopes and the others emerged from behind the purple dinosaur. He asked, "Jay, did you find anything?" as he approached Jay.

Doing his best to look disappointed, he shook his head no. "Nothing, and I looked everywhere too."

Officer Cruz and the others spread out and combed through the sage to see if they could see anything Jay might have missed. Sergeant Lopes maintained eye contact with Jay, though his eyes weren't visible through his mirrored sunglasses. Without flinching, Jay returned the gaze and did his best to look innocent.

Sergeant Lopes replied sternly, "I thought I could hear you talking to someone."

"Nope, I was just praying out loud," Jay lied, hopeful his short answer would suffice.

A low rumbling of thunder reached their ears and reminded them of the approaching storm. "Well, let's get back to the mission then before this storm hits and regroup. Maybe we will figure out what and where the note is talking about," Sergeant Lopes announced to the others without moving his eyes from Jay.

Rising from his seat, Jay moved quickly to the waiting Dodge Durango. "Sounds good to me." He opened the door and got in.

Jesse, Jack, and Officer Cruz quickly followed his lead. Sergeant Lopes didn't move but instead scrutinized the purple dinosaur for several more moments before moving to the rig, shaking his head the entire way.

∿ ∿ ∿ ∿

Without warning, Luis violently threw the phone as far over Rosalita's head as hard as he could. His eyes were pools of fire, angrier than she had ever seen, and for the first time in her life, her face was filled with fear as he focused them directly on her. Before she could move, he was on her, grabbing her by the back of her hair and dragging her toward the house from which they had come.

"Luis, Luis, they called. Aren't you happy? Luis, why aren't you happy?" There was fear in her voice. Just as she opened her mouth to ask again, the hard hilt of the long bullwhip came smashing back down into her mouth, breaking several of her front teeth.

"Is that happy enough for you?" he sneered at her.

Blood filled her mouth and made her choke as she struggled to keep up with her captor. "Did they refuse the ransom?" she finally managed between gasping for air and swallowing blood.

"Oh, they agreed to the ransom all right, and for that you will pay the penalty for the next three days! After that, Anna will pay with her life," he answered harshly as he half dragged her along.

Pain shot through her head from the broken teeth and the deathlike grip that felt as if it was pulling all of her hair out by the roots. At that moment she hated Luis, hated life, but more than anything, hated Anna.

The Unraveling

Chapter 28

The long and bumpy ride back to the mission was a trip of tortured silence, each man lost in his own thoughts as rain pounded the group from above. Depression and fear had moved in big time and taken up residence in Jay's soul as his missionary training concerning kidnapping scenarios ran over and over in his frazzled mind, haunting him all the while.

Never, never agree to a ransom; always remind the kidnappers that you are a missionary serving God; that you have no money or resources and that the Sponsor Ministry does not ever meet ransom demands. His instructor's voice echoed in his mind. *I cannot stress how important these instructions are! If the kidnapper thinks there is no hope of ever receiving a ransom, the odds are better than even that he, or they, will release the captive to move on to more lucrative venues. If they have been promised a ransom and do not receive it, it is almost guaranteed that the captive will not live to see freedom, and if their ransom is met, literally thousands of missionaries around the globe will immediately become victims of evil kidnappers once word spreads that ransoms will be paid for their lives, and the chances are good that the abducted still won't ever see freedom again. That is one scenario we just cannot afford to ever see happen.*

Dread and hopelessness pressed down on him like a giant hydraulic press that crushed old, wrecked cars. Paralyzing fear clouded his mind like a thick fog coming in from the ocean. To make matters worse, Sergeant Lopes continued to eye him with the same intense suspicion a father would his daughter's first date. Through it all, Jay did his best to act as normal as possible, a task that was proving to be nearly impossible.

The group of men gathered at the church to reorganize and rethink the meaning of the kidnapper's previous note. Frustration bordering on anger and even an overall sense of hopelessness had become the mood du jour as not one of them could think of any other place the kidnapper could have meant other than the dinosaur.

"That's the only giant lizard around. He had to mean right there," Jesse exclaimed, frustration rising.

"Maybe we missed something. We could go back there in the morning; take more people and completely scour the countryside around the dinosaur statue," Office Cruz offered. "It has to be there somewhere."

"Let's do it. Yeah, we'll go back in the morning! Good plan." All of the others, except for Jay and Sergeant Lopes, chimed in hopefully in an attempt to bolster everyone's spirits and for lack of any other idea.

Throbbing pain sent out slivers of light behind Jay's eyes as he turned a silver paper clip over and over in his hands while his mind raced to find a solution to the problem he had created. The desire to blurt out a confession was nearly more than he could suppress, although his pride would never allow him to do so.

The questions ran over and over through his mind. *What if they find the phone at the dinosaur? What if Sergeant Lopes has it analyzed for fingerprints and my own prints are detected. What will happen to Anna if I am unable to raise the money they are asking for? What have I done?*

"Let's get something to eat, rest for a bit, and then return here for more planning, and for some prayer time," Jack suggested to the group. "Right now, we're just banging our heads against the wall trying to figure this thing out."

Everyone was in agreement and voiced so, except for Jay, who failed to raise his eyes from the floor. *Prayer time; for what? It's not like God has been listening one bit. If He had, I sure wouldn't be here or in this situation.*

The Unraveling

After a quick prayer, the men dispersed to their homes, Officer Cruz and Sergeant Lopes with Jesse, who had extended an invitation to them for dinner. Returning to his makeshift room, Jay plopped down on his bed and buried his head in his pillow.

"Oh, God, oh God, oh God, please! What have I done? My Anna, she's going to die. God, please help me. Please help her, Lord. I can't live without her, God."

At that moment, time meant nothing as he poured out his heart, begging God to spare Anna's life; but try as he might, he just wasn't able to overcome the fear and despair that taunted and tormented his soul. Vivid and violent scenes played themselves in his mind as his imagination ran wild, and all with the same terrible outcome: Anna's death.

Startled by a noise, Jay rolled over to find Jack standing in his doorway. He had no idea how long his friend had been standing there nor how much he had heard. Fearing the worst, he could feel heat rising in his face.

"Hey, man, what's up?" he mumbled as he sat up, avoiding eye contact.

"I just came to check on you, brother. Are you all right?"

Jay nodded his head and did his best to keep tears from spilling out of his eyes. A lump had formed in his throat, making it impossible for him to answer, although he did manage some sort of affirmative grunt.

"Kind of a stupid question now that I think about it." Jack moved into Jay's room and sat on an old wooden chair directly across from his cot. "I just want you to know, God is in control even if it seems the opposite is true. You just have to cling to that knowledge and have faith that He is going to take care of you and take care of Anna."

Once again the tears began to flow from Jay's eyes. He wasn't sure where the tears came from or what part of his body produced them, but he was surprised that the well had not yet run dry. He had cried so much already.

He managed to finally blurt out, "I know, it just looks so impossible right now. I mean, there just doesn't seem to be one bit of hope."

"That's just Satan trying to trick you, buddy. He'll tell you stuff like that over and over to chisel away at your faith. Don't let him do it. God does have a plan and is in control no matter how impossible it seems."

Jay nodded his head, but inside he knew the situation was impossible. Even if the resources were available, logistics alone made it virtually impossible to get the money into Mexico from the States, out to the mission, and finally to the drop site.

"Jay, it's going to work out, brother. I've seen God do some pretty miraculous things in my lifetime! I know what he can do. Let's pray about it, if you don't mind. I guarantee you, God answers prayer."

Springing to his feet like he was shot from cannon, Jay nearly knocked Jack from the chair. His whole body shook with frustration, vessels stood out on his neck and forehead, and his large brown eyes constricted down into an angry stare. "You just don't get it, do you?"

He clenched his fists. "There's nothing you can do! Nothing I can do and nothing God can do that will help this situation. Pray! Feel free! Pray all you want, nothing is going to help!"

Stinging rain soaked him nearly the moment he stormed out the door. The cool water washed the tears from his face and felt good on his skin as he moved aimlessly away from the church. Like a blind man, he stumbled awkwardly toward the soccer field, vaguely aware that someone was yelling his name before falling flat on his face in the rain-soaked red soil.

"Aughhh, why? Why? Why?" He yelled out to the storm, to God, or to whoever would listen to his brokenness, making no attempt to get up out of the mud.

With no regards to the rain or mud, Jack ran out to the ball field and helped Jay to his feet. "Brother, it's going to be all right!"

The Unraveling

Wrenching himself from Jack, Jay stood face-to-face with his friend as rivulets of red soil ran down his face. "You just don't get it, do you? It's not going to be all right at all! God's not going to help, no one is going to come riding in to save the day! Anna's going to die! It's that simple, man! Why can't you just get it? I can't take it anymore!"

"Jay, I know you are stressed, but you've got to get hold of yourself. In a little bit, we'll regroup, go over the last letter, and figure out where we need to go to hear from the kidnappers. I'm sure Sergeant Lopes already has something figured out." He grabbed Jay by the upper arm.

With a violent twist, Jay wrested free. "There is nothing to figure out, okay? We went to the right place. I found the phone, called the kidnappers, and agreed to their terms!"

Shock spread across Jack's face like ripples on water. "What do you mean you talked to the kidnappers?"

Contempt and anger contorted Jay's face as he spit the words out at his friend, "On a phone. I talked to them on a phone that had been left there by the kidnappers, all right?"

As both men faced off the dark sky began giving way to light as the fast-moving clouds thinned considerably.

"Where was the phone? None of us saw it."

"I put it back, behind the plaque on the dinosaur before you guys reached me."

"Why didn't you tell someone? Why have you been carrying this all by yourself?"

"Because I didn't know what else to do. I knew Sergeant Lopes would be irate with me for not waiting for him to inspect the phone and all, so I just called. I couldn't stand waiting any longer. Now I've messed everything up."

Bright rays of sunlight began to break through the clouds, and the rain all but ceased to fall. Seagulls hopeful for a free meal began to amass just to the south of them.

With a heavy sigh, Jack reached out and grabbed Jay by the arm. "We'll figure this out. Let's go tell the others what happened."

Defeated, Jay was unresponsive for a moment but relented by allowing Jack to lead him back to the church. Even though the situation seemed bleak at best, just getting the secret off his chest had lifted a load of guilt and despair off his shoulders.

After cleaning up, the pair made their way to the command table just as the others returned from their meal and afternoon siesta. Although a serious air could be felt, the mood was much lighter than before lunch. Sergeant Lopes hardly reacted when Jay confessed to the group all he had done. Finally, he leaned forward in his chair and picked up a black ballpoint pen. Stabbing the air with authority, he directed his ire at Jay.

"You! You have ruined this investigation. Anna's blood is now on your hands! I knew in my heart you found something there at that statue! I could sense it. Now, you have ruined everything!"

Rising from his seat, Sergeant Lopes threw the pen onto the middle of the table. The round cylinder bounced into the air like a rock skipped on water, barely missing Jesse's right ear. "I have had it! The rain! The mud! The remoteness of this place! And now this spoiled excuse for a man! I am just finished!"

The air was thick like a wet wool blanket and filled with a tension that weighed on each of them like a ton of bricks. Not one person moved or said a single word to stop Sergeant Lopes as he stormed from the building. Rising to his feet, Officer Cruz was unsure what to do, but it was a decision he didn't have to make. Returning as abruptly as he had gone, Sergeant Lopes marched back into the church and approached the table until he was directly across from Jay.

With raised arm, he shook his index finger directly at Jay. "We will finish this thing, but we will finish it my way! Do you understand me?"

Jay nodded his head in agreement.

"There will be no arguing, no second guessing, and absolutely no decision making on your part, understood!"

Again, Jay nodded.

"If there is any chance that she might be spared, it will be by the grace of God, that and whether you'll agree to carry out my directions. Are you willing to do that, to trust me completely?"

With a slow finality, Jay nodded.

Sergeant Lopes exclaimed with full authority, "All right, then, I'll outline my plan." Pausing to study each man's face, his gaze stopped on Jay. "Aren't you a praying man?"

Jay could feel his face flush with color as he nodded his head that he was. *A praying man.* He hadn't been called that before, not that he deserved to be. Instead of praying, he had spent all his time worrying, fretting, and feeling sorry for himself. This forced realization made him ashamed.

"Well, I believe prayer is our only hope now!"

Chapter 29

The small church was empty; Jay's reflection stared back from the glass window leading to the pastor's office—his office—like a pale ghost, almost there but not quite. At that moment, he realized that is how his faith is and has been, not just for this ordeal, but for the past several years of his life. A shadow faith. There, but not really. Sure, he was a Christian; at least, he called himself one. Not only a Christian but a member of the clergy, schooled and ordained to serve God and people. It was true—he did love God. But on his terms.

Visions of his past ran through his mind like a grainy movie—grumbling, complaining, always questioning the plan God had for his life: *why he had to be a missionary; why he had to go to Colorado Springs; why he had to travel to Mexico.* The memories haunted him anew as he relived each and every one of them. In that instant, he knew he had been living a lie. How could he effectively minister to the lost when his own faith was lacking?

This realization brought tears to his eyes once again. How could he effectively live a simple, Christian life without faith? How could he ever hope to have God guide his steps if he couldn't or wouldn't trust Him to lead down paths that were best for his and Anna's lives—even when those paths were contrary to what he thought were best in his own heart?

All were questions that had been haunting him over the past two days. Most of that time had been spent in prayer by him, Jesse, Jack, and a vast majority of the people from the mission. Jay was amazed by everyone's sincerity. He noticed very few dry eyes in the church as everyone came to pray for Anna's return. During that time, Jack had hardly left his side but supported his friend and brother in Christ with hugs, prayer, support, and a caring ear, for which Jay was becoming more and more thankful.

"Why has God allowed this to happen?"

Jack gave Jay an inquisitive glance as if to ask if he really wanted an answer. "Well, my brother, I don't have an answer. All I know is sometimes God allows us to go through a Job moment for His own glory. Call it a test, a journey of faith, I guess, to strengthen our own dependence on Him or to reveal His own glory in each of our lives. All I know is it is happening and God is with both you and Anna. Now, are you going to trust Him to guide your path no matter the outcome, or will you let doubt and fear dictate and tear down that which God wishes to build up?"

Jay paused to allow the question to sink in. "Do we really have any other choice?" He was afraid to think of any outcome other than Anna's safe return.

"Well, this scenario is going to play itself out, that's for sure. That isn't really the question. The question is, are you going to trust God wholeheartedly no matter the outcome, trust Him to watch out for your very own best interest and Anna's very own best interest even if it contradicts what you think is best?"

To that, Jay didn't have an answer. More than anything, he wanted to say yes, that no matter the outcome he would trust it was in his and Anna's best interest and how it pertained to God's plan for their life together. If he said yes, he knew he might be lying.

"Well, I like to think so. I hope the only scenario we have to go through is the one where Anna returns unharmed. That's what I'm praying for."

"That's what we're all praying for, brother! That's what we're all praying for."

~ ~ ~ ~

Now he was alone, the finality of the moment nearly more than he could stand. In his right hand he clutched a note, handwritten to the kidnappers on a folded white sheet of paper. A note he had written and rewritten dozens of times, hoping and praying the words he was saying would speak to the hearts and minds of the kidnappers, even though it seemed less than likely. A note asking simply for Anna's immediate release, a note that explained they were just poor missionaries, were there doing God's work, trying to improve the lives of the Mexican people, and had neither money nor access to any resources.

In his hand was the key to his future, Anna's future, their future together. In his hand were words of life or words of death, at least that's how it felt. The weight of that knowledge or perceived knowledge was taking its toll on him as was evident by the dark pools under his large eyes.

It had been well over a month since Anna's abduction, and it seemed more like a lifetime ago to Jay. Returning to the table, he glanced over the diagrams Sergeant Lopes had drawn of the drop site. After sharing the directions the kidnappers had given him, Sergeant Lopes had wasted no time in finding the drop site and scouting the surrounding area. It was a wide-open area devoid of any vegetation or outcroppings he or any other law enforcement could hide in until the kidnappers came.

"They couldn't have picked a better spot to make a drop site. There is basically no way we can survey it without being seen. We'll just have to make the drop and try to anticipate which direction the courier goes, although we don't want to stop him or spook him. If they suspect we are interfering, Anna will be killed for sure."

None of the plans or meetings held by Sergeant Lopes had given him much hope. Part of him was glad the ordeal was going to be over once and for all, even though he feared the end result.

"Faith means trusting God even when all seems impossible in our lives, not just when we think we know the outcome." Jack had repeatedly told him that over the past forty-eight hours.

The Unraveling

Jay said a quiet prayer as his shaking hands slid the note into a small parcel envelope. "Well, God, I guess it's all in your hands now."

Sergeant Lopes burst through the open doorway in a flourish but paused just short of the table when he saw Jay sitting silently, waiting for the others to return.

"Jay, I know this is hard for you, but you have to understand, there just is no other way. You have to believe me when I tell you that. I want Anna returned safely just as much as you do."

A large knot of emotion filled Jay's throat, making it impossible for him to answer, so he simply nodded his head in agreement. Moving to the table, Sergeant Lopes sat across from Jay, picked up the envelope, and removed the letter. Apparently satisfied with the contents, he refolded the letter and placed it back in the envelope before returning the package to the cluttered tabletop.

He offered in approval. "Very well done. Short and to the point."

They waited several more minutes for the others to join them, but when all failed to show up, Sergeant Lopes jumped up, grabbed the letter, and ordered Jay to follow.

With determination and an unmistakable excitement in his step, Sergeant Lopes moved outside the church and headed straight toward the silver Durango that was parked just off the sidewalk. The sun was bright and forced Jay to raise his arm over his head in an attempt to shield his eyes from the glare. He could make out the voices of Jack, Officer Cruz, and Jesse mingled with others he did not recognize.

They too were heading toward the Durango, and all seemed very upbeat, even excited.

"Well, it's about time to head out," Sergeant Lopes commanded.

Officer Cruz, Jesse, and Jack all piled in the opposite side of the vehicle and waited as Jay scanned his surroundings. Soft wispy clouds like white down feathers dotted the swimming pool blue sky. Children once again were playing soccer in the ball field with a ball made out of some old rags taped together with duct tape. Several people were walking about on the red dirt road that led directly toward the church, each going about his or her own business, unaware of the critical drama being played out right there in their own mission. With a reluctant sigh, Jay reached his long fingers to the door handle of the Durango and got in next to Jack, who looked uncomfortable, even comical, with his long legs folded nearly to his chin.

The trip to the drop site was made with very little conversation by anyone in the vehicle. Once the location was found, Sergeant Lopes handed Jay a plastic bag that contained the envelope and letter.

"I put an additional paper in there with the satellite phone number to the mission in case the kidnappers want to open up a more direct dialogue. I figure it can't hurt anything."

Nodding his head that he understood, Jay made his way down the side of the steep ravine by following a faint trail that had been walked into the hillside by wildlife or cattle long ago. It didn't take him long to spot the rusty barrel at the bottom of the ravine. A knot of emotion welled up in his throat as he made his final descent. Arriving at the barrel, Jay raised the bag containing the letter to his mouth and kissed it. "I love you, Anna," he managed to whisper before dropping the note into the barrel.

With a rustle he heard it hit the bottom of the barrel, and he bowed his head and said a quick prayer. Slowly he made his way back up the steep trail.

The mood was somber at best as the men suspiciously scanned the horizon in every direction for any sign of the kidnappers. Officer Cruz held a riot control shotgun in his hands for protection, not that it would do any good should they come under fire in spaces as wide open as these.

Sergeant Lopes reached for the car door. "Well, we've done all we can do. Let's get back to the mission and wait."

The Unraveling   231

"We could say a quick prayer," Jack countered, ignoring the glare from Sergeant Lopes.

No one said a word for several moments before Sergeant Lopes relented. "Suit yourself. We have nothing but time to kill anyway."

The small group gathered together as Jack led them in prayer for Anna's safe return, Jay's well-being, and for a hasty resolution to the crisis they were in. When they were finished, they all piled back in the Durango and made a quick retreat back to the mission. Jay watched out the rear window as the red dust streamed up into the air and couldn't help but feel as if he was watching his life go up in dust.

Chapter 30

The small rodent scurried back and forth, whiskers twitching to and fro as it nervously searched for a new escape route. From across the room he watched it and waited, knowing the little creature was experiencing the final tormented moments of its short life. An evil laugh, born somewhere within the soul, built up and spilled forth from his mouth like a rancid cloud of doom as the mouse tried in vain to enter the small hole he had plugged with a wooden dowel just moments before.

Tired of the game, he filled the air with sizzling and cracking by subtly moving the wrist of his right hand back and forth. Almost instantly the long leather whip sprung to life and sang a song of death before singing its final, crackling serenade. With a loud *crack* the end of the whip found its mark and removed the rodent's head cleanly from its twitching body. A small pool of blood spilled out of the body onto the floor as he coiled his whip back around his torso.

"Just a sample of what's to come." He kept his eyes on the pooling blood. "When I return, the Anna girl will experience me like she could never imagine, and then she will die."

"Really?" He felt the weight of her astonished stare, black and as deep as space itself. "What about the ransom, the promise to return her to the mission?"

With annoyance in his voice he mumbled, "What about it? I could care less about the money! I already have everything I need."

"But they will come after us. They'll keep looking until they have found her."

"Oh, they'll find her all right! I guarantee you that."

233

Sensing his growing annoyance with her line of questioning, she let the subject drop, just grateful she would soon have a break from him. The previous few days had been pure hell for her. Fresh bruises and burns that covered much of her body proved the abuse, not that anyone would or could do anything about it.

Moving across the hard wooden floor, he grabbed her flowing black mane and jerked her head straight back till she thought her neck was going to break. Dirty and spindly arms flew out from her lap straight from her side as she attempted to maintain her balance. If she hadn't been sitting in one of the old wooden chairs, she would have fallen straight to the floor. With an equal force, he pressed his filthy mouth down onto hers until the metallic taste of blood filled his senses. The familiar flavor excited him as he released his iron grip from her hair and moved toward the door.

"Just think how much fun we are going to have," he sneered as he paused in the open doorway. "Soon I'll be back, and then I'll have two to play with; double my pleasure." He cackled at her apparent displeasure. "What's the matter? Doesn't Rosalita like the thought of sharing Luis with someone else? Don't worry; you won't have to share for long! Just a day or two. Then I'll kill her."

Rubbing her hand across her mouth, Rosalita wiped the blood from her bitten lip. An untamed anger flashed across her eyes like lightning across the night sky. Seeing the anger in her expression brought a roaring response form her tormentor. "Oh how I wish I had a little more time. I can see you are in one of those combative moods! Stay just like that and I'll kill her tonight, after I have the money. Who needs two to play with when I have one like you?"

"Not if I kill her first," Rosalita whispered as she watched Luis move across the compound and get into a waiting Jeep.

She screamed, "I'll kill her, kill you, take the money and get clear away from here forever! Then we'll see who is laughing last!"

Rising gingerly from the chair, she surveyed the injuries to her body. It was painful to move, and the fresh burns throbbed to the point she could barely stand it. With shaking hands, she pulled the old sack dress over her head and moved to the couch to gain a little rest before Luis returned.

"I'll take a short nap and then kill the girl. When Luis goes to get Anna, I'll cut his throat, take the money, and leave." She smiled, realizing that it sounded far easier than it really would be. "Today Anna will be dead, Luis will be dead, and I will finally be free!" The thought brought a fading smile to her tired face as she drifted off to sleep.

Chapter 31

Strange shadows spread out their quicksilver arms and wrapped themselves around her throat and squeezed. Struggling did no good, and she could feel her life ebbing away. Panic filled her mind and paralysis gripped her body as screams of terror built up deep within, only to die as they reached the tongue. A white flash of pain erupted just behind her closed eyes, which produced a lingering agony that grew in great intensity. *So this is what it feels like to die.*

With a jerk, her eyes snapped open. It took only a moment for her to gain her bearings, and when she did a panicked, annoyance flooded her mind. The waning light coming through the window told her dusk was nearly over; she had slept away the whole afternoon.

Pain from her dream, or perhaps the cause of it, remained in her head, just behind bloodshot and weary eyes. A dull sleepiness still clouded her mind, and her arms moved stiffly as she raised her fisted hands and vigorously rubbed her sleepy eyes. "Aaugh! How could I have slept so long? Luis will be back any time!"

Rising from the old worn couch was difficult as her body protested with pain with every little movement. It felt as if she were one large bruise caused from nearly three straight days of torture and abuse, the likes of which she had never gone through before. Luis had been merciless as each abuse led to an even greater one, fed by his ever-growing desire for sadistic pleasure.

Though he tried, his actions did nothing to break her spirit but instead produced a growing hatred that bolstered it and produced an equally burning hatred for Anna. It was Anna whom she blamed, though she had had no part in any of this. Anna's mere presence had brought about an increased violence in Luis, of which she was the recipient. For that, she had decided, Anna would die, and it was she who would take her life, thus denying Luis his most anticipated pleasure.

After that, she would somehow entice Luis enough for him to let his guard down, just enough to give her the opportunity to kill him, take the ransom money, and flee forever. Kill Anna, kill Luis, take the money and flee, or die trying; either way, she would finally be free of the only life she had ever known.

Stopping just inside the kitchen, Rosalita picked up one of the nearly empty liquor bottles sitting on a makeshift table and downed the small quantity of alcohol that barely covered the bottom. The liquid ran down her throat and produced a burning sensation clear into her empty stomach. A choke escaped her lips as she vigorously shook her head. Moving to the door in the growing darkness, she felt around the small end table.

Slowly she moved her hand across the top, down the side, and finally felt along the bottom until her fingers came to rest on something cold and metallic resting on a hidden ledge. Reacting with a triumphant gasp, she acted as if she had just discovered an old friend as she retrieved a six-inch dagger from its hiding place and placed it in a small pocket in her filthy and worn dress. *Boom, boom, boom,* went her heart as she began implementing the plan she had formed so long ago.

Moving through the door and into the outdoors, she paused just long enough to gaze at the dark storm clouds growing in the night sky, a scene that reflected her angry mood. Satisfied no one was around, she moved quickly across the rough ground, unaffected by the pebbles and other debris that pressed against the soles of her bare feet. It had grown dark enough that she had to navigate the grounds by memory, instinct, and sound. The smooth hilt of the dagger rested in her right hand, the cool firmness of the weapon gave her a sense of power and steeled her resolve.

The Unraveling

Sensing as much as seeing the large building housing Anna and the other prisoners, she moved to her right and followed the smooth trail that led down the side Anna was being held in before turning the corner to the barricaded door that led to her unit. The sounds of voices singing "Jesus Loves Me" fanned the embers of hatred that flowed inside of her and made her all the more anxious to carry out her plan.

The night was devoid of any light as the heavy cloud cover masked stars and moon and eliminated the normal residual light from the receding sun. The complete darkness added an eerie composition, which she welcomed as she struggled with the heavy bar barricading the door. Little slivers of light produced by Anna's lone candle shone through the fractured and shrinking wood that made up the walls to the building.

Even though she was being as quiet as possible, the singing had ceased as the inhabitants had either heard her approach or sensed something was wrong. With a final heave, she lifted the bar and swung open the crude wooden door. Inside, Anna sat on her wooden pallet, hands in her lap. Large worried eyes relaxed with relief when she realized it was Rosalita and not Luis who had come to visit her.

A surprised look spread across her face when Rosalita pointed the dagger at her and commanded, "Out, now! Hurry up!"

Pausing just long enough to grab the flickering candle, she did as instructed and moved out of the small, stale dungeon she had called home for more than a month. Curious and concerned eyes followed her every movement through knotholes in the wooden wall that separated the two rooms. No one dared say a word for fear Luis was near at hand.

With a quick prayer, Anna passed through the doorway and moved by Rosalita, who was brandishing the dagger in her right hand, punctuating its presence with small, quick jabs in Anna's direction. By the light of the candle, she could see a crazed and angry mood in her eyes that she had never seen before. The menacing look birthed a small fear in the pit of her stomach that began to grow as Rosalita shoved her in the back and told her to move down the building several feet to the door of unit housing the young men.

"Open it!" She removed the candle from Anna's shaking hands. "Now!"

Craning her neck, Anna tried to look around at her surroundings, grateful to be outside in the fresh air.

With the heel of her fisted hand, Rosalita hit Anna on the back of the head as hard as she could when she realized what Anna was doing. The force caught her by surprise and nearly knocked her from her feet. "I said hurry, and I meant it!"

Regaining her balance, Anna struggled against the heavy steel bar that barricaded the door. At first it didn't budge, but after several moments, and with all the force she could muster, the bar slid from its moorings and sprung free, allowing the door to swing outward several feet.

Rosalita ordered, "Go in!"

"What are you going to do?" Concern rose in Anna's voice.

"Go in, now!"

Seeing no other options, Anna obeyed the order and moved beyond the doorway and into the much larger room. Dozens of sets of large, dark eyes belonging to the faces of the young men she had befriended gazed upon her for the first time since her abduction, and she could tell they were just as surprised and uncertain of what was happening as she was.

"In there, hurry up!" Rosalita punctuated her order with a shove from behind.

Following her instructions, Anna moved forward as the group of boys shrank away from her. "What are you going to do?"

Rosalita ignored her question and shoved her from behind again forcing Anna to move to the center of the room. The dirt floor was uneven and caused her to fall to her knees. She prayed

The Unraveling

silently for God to protect her and to be with Jay no matter the outcome before rising to her feet.

Rosaltia hissed, "Turn around! Turn around now!"

Slowly, Anna turned to face her assailant. The snarling lips and steel glare that dominated Rosalita's face shocked her and made her take a step backward in fear and shock.

With deliberate care, Rosalita placed the flickering candle on the dirt floor and began tossing the sharp dagger back and forth before moving just inches from Anna's face. "I'm gonna slice your throat!" She became excited as fear spread across Anna's face. "But first, I've got other plans for you."

Numbness seeped into Anna's brain as Rosalita's words sunk in. Unsure what to do or say, she said the only thing that came to her mind. "God loves you, and I love you, Rosalita! We really do!"

The words stopped her in her tracks, and for a moment Anna could detect a flicker of uncertainty in her eyes. "You don't have to do this. Don't have to listen to what Luis tells you. God has a plan for your life. He loves you and wants you to come live with Him in heaven." She was emboldened by Rosalita's weakening resolve.

Shaking her head with anger, she slammed the hilt end of the dagger down on Anna's cheek, knocking her to the ground. "Shut your mouth, you witch! I'm not fooled by your tricks and stories of spirits and demons! You might be able to fool these slaves, but you aren't going to fool me!"

Pain filled Anna's senses as she struggled to maintain consciousness.

Rosalita screamed, "Get up!"

Mustering all of her strength, Anna rose to her wobbly feet and faced Rosalita. Tears of pain and fear coursed down her face as she cupped the rapidly swelling contusion on her right cheek.

"Now, for the fun part, I'm going to let these animals have their way with you, rape you over and over so you can know a little of the torture that I go through! Then I'm going to kill you!" She snarled, motioning to the dozens of filthy young slaves watching. "Now, take off your dress! Do it!"

Panic filled Anna's heart and made it difficult for her to breathe as her mind raced in an effort to think of some way out of the predicament she was in. Annoyed with her lack of movement, Rosalita moved across the floor and firmly applied the dagger to Anna's throat. The sharpness of the blade sliced through the outer skin and produced a trickle of blood that began to flow down her neck.

She threatened coldly, "Either do what I say, or I'll kill you right now!"

Anna knew Rosalita meant business. With trembling hands she lifted the distinctively colored custom dress from her body and raised it over her head. She could feel the eyes of the young men as they surveyed every inch of her body. Bile rose in her throat and nearly caused her to vomit as she folded the once beautiful dress over her arm.

"Give me the dress! You aren't going to need it any longer! I'll keep it!"

"Please, Rosalita, you don't have to do this."

"I know! I *want* to do this!"

Slowly, Anna presented the dress to Rosalita with trembling hands. Eerie shadows from the dim candle danced back and forth across the floor and onto the far wall like spirits, watchful and eager for the show that was playing out before them.

Anna was shocked when Rosalita carefully set the dress on the dirt floor and quickly lifted her own filthy, sack dress from her naked body with absolutely no sign of shame for her nakedness. The scars, bruises, and burns that covered her body horrified Anna, and for the first time she understood the suffering Rosalita must have endured for most of her life. The realization brought fresh tears to her eyes as Rosalita tossed her old dress to the ground at Anna's feet.

"Now, take off the rest of your clothes! It's time for these pigs to have their way with you!" Anna didn't move. "I said take them off!" she screamed at Anna as she slowly slid the straps of her bra from her shoulders.

Rosalita's slitted eyes were filled with anger and excitement but grew wide with fear as the sound of a roaring engine caught her ears. "Shhh! Listen!" She raised her hands to her mouth, signaling for them to remain silent.

As the sound of the engines grew louder, Rosalita's body began to tremble. Taking a step toward Anna with the dagger at throat level, she contemplated slitting her throat before deciding there was not enough time to do so without getting caught in the act.

"I'm leaving. You can do with her what you want—she's yours! Luis is going to kill her anyways. You might as well have some fun before that happens."

Moving quickly, she backed to the solid wooden door, pushed it open, and slid out into the enveloping blackness beyond while Anna and the mob of young men watched her go.

Anna prayed quietly. "Thank you, Jesus! Please keep me safe, Lord."

Several moments passed and no one said a word. Covering her body with one hand, Anna reached down and scooped up the dress Rosalita had been wearing only moments before. She moved back a step or two from the young men as they began to murmur the instructions Rosalita had given them just minutes before. Emboldened by sheer numbers and by the fact they were now alone, several of the young men began to advance menacingly toward Anna with a look of desire raging in their eyes. Holding the dress in front of her body, Anna backed to the wooden wall that separated the two cells.

"Get her! Yeah, get her clothes! Hurry up!" Several of those hanging back yelled at the more brazen men as they approached her.

"Stop it, get back! Luis will kill you if you touch me!" Anna yelled as the group continued its advance on her.

For a moment her warning and the mention of Luis's name had the desired effect as the young men stopped in their tracks, but only for a moment before fleshly desire and lust won out and the men renewed their advance. Just as it appeared they would reach her, a young man near the back of the throng began to yell. "Stop! Stop what you are doing right now! This is wrong and you know it! This is the one that has taught us about God, Jesus, and heaven. We aught to all be ashamed of ourselves."

Never had she been as grateful as she was at that moment. She prayed silently, "Thank you, Jesus," while sizing up the young man who had come to her rescue.

The boy was slightly taller than the others, rail thin, with dark eyes that looked too large for his thin face. A flat and wide nose sat perched just above his large mouth lined with dark yellow teeth. A stringy mop of black hair covered his head and nearly covered his eyes on the front while hanging nearly to his shoulders in the back. His clothes were barely more than rags and did little to hide just how malnourished he really was.

One of the others challenged, "Who made you boss?"

"Yeah, that's right!" the others chimed in.

"Nobody made me boss. It just isn't right, and you know it! If you are going to get to her, you're going to have to come through me." He challenged with clenched fists as he stepped in between Anna and the rest. "Besides, she's right. If we touch her, Luis is sure to kill us!" He added the latter to give his argument teeth.

Grumbling could be heard throughout the group, but no one stepped forward to directly challenge the young man. Slowly, the mob dissipated as he stood guard over Anna. He told her over his shoulder, "Get dressed. No one will bother you now."

Anna wasted no time doing as directed and quickly dropped the raggedy dress over her head and onto her petite frame.

The Unraveling

"Thank you so much," she exclaimed to her new protector while extending a hand. "I'm Anna, and you must be?"

"I'm Carlos," the young man said as a Cheshire cat grin spread across his face. "I already know who you are."

"Of course you are." Anna recognized his voice from the talks through the wall. "Just consider this our formal introduction."

Carlos led her to the other side of the cell, a common area covered with wooden pallets that had been placed to create a floor on which they all slept. She noticed that each person had either cardboard or some sort of plastic sheet wrap material in their own personal area to sit and sleep on. Their accommodations were less than poor—stark and bleak at best.

"Here, you can have my spot," he offered. "I'll sleep on the ground next to you, that way no one will bother you," he added loud enough for the others to hear. "If they do bother you, just let me know, I'll deal with them."

Anna smiled at his bravado and thanked him for his generosity. Sitting down, she motioned for him to join her. "What do you think Luis will do once he finds me here?"

"I don't know, probably beat someone." Anna heard the fear and sadness in his voice. "He doesn't need much of an excuse to beat us."

Anna gently placed her hand on Carlos's forearm. "Let's pray about it, then."

Carlos agreed, and many of the others gathered around as Anna began leading them all in prayer, many for the first time in their lives.

～ ～ ～ ～

Spurred on by fear, Rosalita crept up the smooth path to the edge of the rustic building that housed the prisoners. There were no more sounds of engines, and she feared she might be too late to make it back to the house before Luis did. Cursing under her breath, she drew comfort from the feeling of the dagger in her right hand and the absolute darkness that blanketed the compound. Though the darkness made moving about difficult, it gave her cover that she otherwise would not have had.

The soft dress she had confiscated felt good on her body as she ran her left hand over the surface of the garment. Her hand stopped when it passed over something small and hard near the waistband. With enthusiasm, she searched around until her hands discovered a small, hidden pouch pocket. Working her fingers through the fabric, her heart began to beat rapidly as they came into contact with something cold, round, and hard.

It soared when her fingers grasped tightly to Anna's wedding ring that had been hidden there. Although it was too dark to see, Rosalita knew it was more beautiful than anything she had ever worn in her entire life.

Emboldened, she began to sneak in the direction of the house, picking up speed as she went.

"Tonight is going to be the greatest night of my life," she told herself over and over and, for the first time, felt that nothing could or would go wrong.

Sounds of voices stopped her dead in her tracks as she strained with all of her might to pinpoint their location. She wasn't sure if what she heard was real or imagined but decided it must have been her imagination when she failed to detect any other sounds. Satisfied, she continued to move across the compound under cover of nothing but the night itself.

Bright flashes of lightning lit up the night sky, revealing the rundown house no more than a hundred yards away. Fearful of being seen, she began to run as fast as her legs would carry her in hopes of reaching her destination before another bolt lit up the sky. Her heart pounded with excitement and fear the closer she got to the house. The dagger felt good in her hand and gave her a sense of strength and assurance as she steeled her mind toward the task she had set for herself: kill Luis. At that moment, nothing else mattered, not Anna, not the dress, not even the ring she was now wearing on her finger.

The Unraveling   245

With a sudden and vicious crash, Rosalita's focus went from hopeful elation to a life struggle for breath as some unknown object struck her on her back, directly between her slender shoulder blades. The blow sent her reeling face first onto the hard dry ground and sucked every bit of wind from her lungs. The protective dagger went flying from her hand and clattered against the ground out of reach and out of sight. Her hands clawed at the ground in agony as her mind struggled to make sense of what had just happened to her.

"Try to escape from me, will you?" a familiar voice screamed over top of her. "You're more trouble than you're worth!" it bellowed, followed by a vicious stomp directly in her back.

"And to think, I was going to keep you around, have some fun, maybe let you live! You are so ungrateful."

Luis raged over her, stomping her back, violently kicking her sides, even stomping on her head as his anger roared out of control.

"You're not worth anything to me! Not worth anything to anyone! Even the mission said to keep you! They wouldn't pay a single cent for you! Missionary! Humph! You ain't nothin! Hear me? Nothin'!"

Dim lights from flashlights held by the guards danced around Rosalita as she tried to raise her head. Time after time she tried to speak out, to scream out that it was she and not Anna who was being attacked, but each time she attempted to raise her head, Luis stomped on it. Her world was spinning out of control as consciousness began to thankfully slip from her grasp. Blood began to stain the colorful dress as the skin on one side of her neck was peeled away from her flesh by the hard sole of his boot. The sight of blood only egged him on more as he continued to stomp the life out of her frail body.

"So you want to go back to the mission, go back to your husband." He taunted over and over again. "I'll tell you what; I'll give you a ride there right this minute."

With determination in his step, Luis made his way to the Jeep. With angry determination he threw the vehicle in reverse and backed violently to within feet of Rosalita's prone body lying facedown on the ground. Driven by a violent lust, he grabbed a thick rope from the trunk area and moved to Rosalita's body. Grabbing a handful of hair, he raised her head just enough to slip a noose around her neck. Her body convulsed as she moaned. He moved to the Jeep and tied the other end of the rope around the ball of the hitch. Vaguely aware of what was happening to her, Rosalita clutched at the rope with her left hand in a futile attempt to free herself.

"Want to go back to the mission? Well, then, let's get going!" He released bloodthirsty roar as the Jeep sprung to life down the bumpy desert road. Almost instantly the rope grew taut and wrapped around her outstretched arm several times as the angry truck dragged her down the road and out of sight of the entire camp.

Crestfallen eyes of the guards followed the dim beams of light shining from their flashlights as they traced a smooth path of bloody dirt that led away from a round patch of bloody soil where the Anna they had come to love had just lain. Overhead, lightning lit up the night sky, followed almost immediately by a booming clap of angry thunder, a perfect compliment for such a violent night.

Jack stretched out his arm and squeezed the back of Jay's shoulder as he encouraged his friend. "What do you say we stretch our legs a bit, get a bite to eat? It'd do our souls some good."

Jay shrugged his shoulders with indifference. They had spent the better part of two days since delivering Jay's note, sitting at the make-shift desk at the headquarters, eyes glued to the satellite phone in hopes that the kidnappers would call and tell them to come pick Anna up. So far there had been no word, a fact that seemed to push Jay into a depression that grew deeper with the passing of each and every minute. The stormy weather only added to his doldrums, not to mention the fact it had hindered Sergeant Lopes from tracking the kidnappers after they retrieved the package from the drop site, a fact that added a great amount of annoyance and distress to Jay's tormented soul.

To his credit, though, Sergeant Lopes had been out scouring the countryside ever since with Officer Cruz and a few others from the mission in an attempt to locate either the kidnappers' hideout, or at least some sort of sign that might indicate which direction they might have headed once the ransom had been picked up. So far no mentionable progress had been made.

Jay rubbed the sleep from his eyes, stretched his arms, and grabbed the phone to check the screen one more time in hopes someone had or was calling even though the phone had not been out of his sight for two days. "I guess something to eat wouldn't hurt anything. Besides, there's nothing else for us to do."

Dark shadows circled his red and weary eyes and, coupled with two days' growth of dark beard, made him look ten years older.

They made their way to the front of the church where Jesse had prepared a table with tortillas, cheeses, juice, fruit, and salsa for anyone attending the prayer vigil that was still going on around the small wooden altar. Any number of people could be found praying on Anna's behalf any hour of the day, a fact that brought a little hope to Jay's hopeless world.

The fresh corn tortillas made Jay's mouth water, and the homemade salsa was one dish he couldn't imagine not having now that it had been introduced to his diet. The cheese was some sort of soft cheese made from goats' milk right there at the mission, and although it had a sharp, almost pungent taste, he had grown to enjoy it in small quantities.

The food did wonders for his stomach, not to mention his mood, as he and Jack visited about life in general. Jack had grown to be a friend from God that Jay just could not live without, although he found himself yearning for times of old spent with his best friend, Bill, and spiritual mentor, Chet, both back in Pullman, Washington.

The two finished up their snack and headed outside to see if it was still raining. Puddles dotted the landscape once again as the land had suffered assault after assault of monsoonal storms like none could remember. To make matters worse, the constant cloud cover and gusting winds during the previous two days made satellite phone reception hit and miss at best, a fact not missed by Jay's troubled mind.

The two took turns skipping rocks off the largest puddle just in front of the church and were soon joined by several of the children from the mission, who quickly mastered this new and wonderful game. It was a good distraction for Jay, and before long, thoughts and worries of Anna had completely left his tormented mind.

The fun continued throughout the afternoon, and even a couple cloudbursts failed to dampen the spirit of the two men and half a dozen kids as each tried to best the other skipping rocks.

The Unraveling   249

The sound of an approaching vehicle halted the fun as all eyes tracked the rapidly approaching silver Durango.

Jay watched as Sergeant Lopes climbed slowly from the vehicle and moved to the concrete sidewalk under the front veranda. He couldn't help but notice the usually stiff and official sergeant was now standing somewhat hunched over with his hands in his pockets, chin resting on his chest.

Jay's stomach began to twist and burn with fear as he reached the concrete and moved to within several feet of the sergeant. By the time he stopped, less than three feet separated the two as Jack brought up the rear and stood directly behind Jay.

Sergeant Lopes kept his eyes fixed on a small crack that ran across the concrete sidewalk between the two of them. "It's Anna. We've found Anna."

Jay's knees weakened with fear and nearly buckled at Sergeant Lopes's less-than-enthusiastic answer. An awkward moment of silence only added to the growing fear and despair that were raging inside.

"Where is she? Where is Anna?" He heard a strange, nearly falsetto voice come out of his mouth.

"She's dead! They killed her!"

If Jack hadn't been standing directly behind to catch him, Jay would have fallen hard to the concrete.

Jay couldn't speak; he was a motionless lump of despair, half-lying, half-sitting on the rough concrete sidewalk. Silence as thick as wool wrapped itself like a thick fog around the mission grounds as word of Anna's death spread across the campus. There wasn't one dry eye as everyone openly mourned their loss. Even Sergeant Lopes, who had never met Anna, shed a tear.

Hatred and anger filled Jay's heart and gave him enough strength to rise to his feet. He turned to Sergeant Lopes. "Where is she? I want to go see her."

"We found her a couple miles down the road, in the ditch."

"Take me to her."

"No, you can't see her!"

"What do you mean I can't see her? She's my wife! I demand that you take me there right now!"

Sergeant Lopes held his hand out in front of Jay. "I said you can't see her! You will just have to wait here."

"Wait for what? If you don't take me there, I'll walk."

Without warning, he moved beside Sergeant Lopes and tried to run for the city gate. Grabbing him from behind, Sergeant Lopes took him down. Jay's arms flailed wildly about in an attempt to strike Sergeant Lopes so he could get away.

He screamed through his tears, "Get off me, you thug! Get off me now! She's my wife, and you can't keep me from her!"

Sergeant Lopes held him firmly in the mud. "If you calm down, I'll let you up, but you're going to have to calm down first."

Jay's body racked and shuddered with emotion as tears poured from his eyes. The pain was too great for him to speak, and for several minutes he lay there and sobbed. It took him some time to gain his composure, and when he did, he told Sergeant Lopes that he would stay calm. With outstretched hands, Sergeant Lopes helped him to his feet and extended a hand as a gesture of good will. Jay contemplated for a moment before taking the sergeant's hand in his own.

Jay stated quietly but firmly, "I still would like to go see her."

"Sorry, my friend, I cannot take you there."

Jay paused for a moment as his mind churned through his options. "As an American citizen, I'm asking that you take me to see my wife, also an American citizen."

"Jay, you don't understand. I can't take you there. I don't know how to tell you this, but they killed Anna and dragged her for a long distance." He paused long enough to allow this new bit of news to hit home. "I am going to guess that they dragged her for more than twenty miles. You can imagine the damage done to her body."

The Unraveling   251

Shock hit Jay like a wooden club and sent his emotions reeling once again. "Then how do you even know it was her?" He was scared and hopeful at the same time.

"Well, we first found the rope that was used, and this was stuck between the strands of woven material."

Reaching into his pocket, Sergeant Lopes pulled out Anna's wedding ring and handed it to Jay. Tears once again gushed from his eyes and distorted the inscription he had had printed on the inside of the ring before they were married.

"This doesn't mean anything! Someone could have stolen it from her."

Sergeant Lopes returned to the Durango and retrieved a clear plastic bag from the floorboard. "We also found this."

Though dirty, Jay could make out a piece of blood-soaked fabric about eight inches in diameter. Through the grime, he could see the vivid and unique color pattern of Anna's handmade dress.

"There's more." Sergeant Lopes stated quietly continued as he returned to the Durango and retrieved another bag. Inside was a piece of scalp with long, nearly black hair—Anna's hair.

This new and gruesome evidence hit Jay the hardest. "What about the rest of her?" The horror of the thought took his breath away.

"Well, we are still looking. When a body has been dragged for that great a distance it tends to not stay intact. With a desert full of predators, we might not find much more than this. Of course, we'll do DNA testing, but here in Mexico it can take up to two years to get the results back."

"It's her; she would never let anyone get hold of this ring. The dress and the hair…" his voice trailed off as a new wave of sadness was overtaking his feeble senses.

A crowd had gathered around Jay as eager onlookers strained to see what was in the bags. All the noise, all the shock and horror of the moment finally caught up to him as he dropped to the ground and vomited.

Chapter 33

The remainder of the previous day had been most difficult for Jay as person after person came to give him their condolences. Sergeant Lopes disappeared back into the field to check on the men that were still out searching for Anna's remains. When he returned, he announced that he would be leaving in the morning for Mexico City but would be back in a few days to check up on the investigation.

Jay interrupted the startled sergeant, "I'm going with you. I'm going to leave and never come back." His tone left no room for argument, though many tried. After making several calls to mission headquarters, a return plane ticket to Dallas, Texas; Denver, Colorado; and finally Spokane, Washington, was secured, making it possible for Jay to go home. It was decided that Jack would fly with him as far as Dallas, where one of Jay's family or friends would meet him to escort him the rest of the way home. Sergeant Lopes allowed him to keep the wedding ring, even though it went against the federal police investigation policy.

Repeatedly the people approached Jay. "You've been through too much! You're too tired! What about all of your belongings?"

Choking back tears, Jay replied, "I'm going home and that's final! You can keep the stuff! Give it away! That part of my life is over anyway!"

～ ～ ～ ～

The sounds of birds welcoming the sunrise brought Jay back to consciousness, though his personal nightmare continued to rage in his head. Pain like none he had ever known before ate at his heart like tigers feasting on prey. He sat up on the edge of his cot and stretched. Noticing Jack sleeping on a mat on the floor, he did his best to rise from the cot and leave the room without disturbing him. *Sometimes it's just best to be left alone,* he thought as he made his way out of the church.

A brilliant, red sunrise marked the eastern sky and forewarned of an approaching storm system sure to strike later in the day. Nevertheless, it was a beautiful sight to behold, which he would have enjoyed had circumstances been different. Looking up to the sky, he wondered to himself about God and how someone so loving could allow so much pain and sadness into the lives of those most obedient to His will.

He whispered to the morning sky, "Maybe you just aren't real."

Thoughts of Anna swirled around his mind and soul as he surveyed the horizon and the beauty of the sun. He knew she would have been in awe, praising God for such a beautiful sight had she been there to witness it, a fact that made him even more forlorn.

"Did you get any rest last night?" Jack suddenly asked from behind.

Jay shrugged his shoulders but was unable to respond. He turned away from Jack in an attempt to hide his emotion.

"Hey, man, it's all right. It's good for the spirit to let your emotions out. That's why the Israelites grieved for a set period of time, to help their souls. Today we think it isn't macho if we show emotion, but it's something we were made to do. It's a process God has given each and every one of us so we can live and get on with our lives."

Ignoring an impulse to go off on his friend, Jay simply nodded and said nothing. Instead he focused his attention on Sergeant Lopes's silver Durango as it made its way to the church. Both Sergeant Lopes and Officer Cruz got out of the vehicle and approached Jay. "I know it's early, but we have a long way to go, and you two have a flight to catch."

"It can't be early enough for me. I can't wait to get out of this godforsaken country."

The men helped Jay grab a couple of duffle bags of clothes from his room. For a moment he contemplated leaving the chrome framed picture of he and Anna on the little shelf above his cot, but after second thoughts, grabbed up the picture and placed it his bag too. Without looking back, Jay walked from the room and headed straight for the car. There would be no sad good-byes, no forlorn farewells, no adioses, no second thoughts. Just as he was placing his bags in the back, Jesse approached from the village. The gray mop of hair, all disheveled, and red in his eyes told Jay he had just gotten up and hurried to the church to tell him good-bye.

"Señor Jay, you are family to us! We will always have a place for you here and a place for you in our hearts!" Tears pooled in his eyelids. "I know you don't want anyone telling you this, especially right now, but what has happened is for God's best plan for our lives. I will be praying that you have the faith and will one day be able to see what I say is true. God only wants what's best for you."

Anger filled Jay's heart at the words he had just heard. "If you want to go on believing that by allowing the one you love the most to go through the suffering she had to go through is all in God's best plan, you go right ahead! I don't see any possible way it could be the best for me or for her, and I don't see any way a God of love could or would ever allow this to have happened."

Jay climbed into the seat directly behind the driver, closed the door, and stared straight ahead. The image staring back at him out of the driver's rearview mirror was shocking, to say the least. He barely recognized who the thin, pale face with red and tired eyes, unkempt hair, and overall sour image belonged to. Shaking his head, he wondered what had happened to the life he had once loved.

Sergeant Lopes and Officer Cruz said their good-byes and climbed in the car with Jack, who promised Jesse he would soon return. No one said a word as Sergeant Lopes turned the key and brought the vehicle to life. With a wave, he put the car in gear

The Unraveling

and headed out through the streets of the mission and finally out the main gate, down the road that led to Mexico City.

Chapter 34

The morning brought a cocktail of stale air, the pungent aroma of bacteria-induced body odor, and disturbed dust, but Anna eagerly inhaled a lung full, just happy to be alive. Memories of the previous evening's activities had haunted her the whole night long and afforded her little more than short cat naps between violent nightmares filled with Rosalita and Luis.

"Lord, thank you for another day! Please give me wisdom today, help me to witness to these young men, and please be with Jay. Comfort him and reassure him that I am just fine."

A lump of emotion filled her throat with her thoughts of Jay. She could hardly imagine the trauma he must be going through, not knowing where she was at or if she was safe. "Lord, he's in your hands. Keep him safe."

Slivers of sunlight squeezed through every little void that the shrinking wood fiber had left on the eastern wall and told her it was indeed morning. The natural light was enough for her to scan around her new cell and over the still-sleeping young men. Her eyes paused when they came to Carlos, the young man who had saved her life, or at least prevented terrible things from happening to her the night before. An immense hunger for God burned in his soul, and he spent much of the night quizzing her about Jesus, God, salvation, and heaven. Tears of sorrow and anger rolled down his thin cheeks as she told him the story of Christ's crucifixion.

He had asked her repeatedly, "How could they do that to such a loving man?"

When she told him how Christ had risen from the dead, tears once again began to flow, but this time tears of joy. Even though she had shared the plan of salvation with him and the others many times over the past several weeks, Carlos never grew tired of hearing about it. His thirst and wonder for the Word made her heart soar and affirmed in her heart why God had placed her here.

A loud banging followed by the heavy barricade being lifted brought the whole group out of their slumber. "Get up, you worthless scum. Time for work!"

The voice belonged to one of the guards. Anna tried to make herself as small as possible in hopes of avoiding detection. The sleeping mat she was on was on the outside of the throng of beds, so her efforts were for naught. In fact, she was the first person Jalle made eye contact with, which stopped him dead in his tracks. In an instant the angry and determined expression on his face morphed into one of fear as his whole body began to shake.

"Ghost, she's a ghost, a ghost!" he cried out as he backed out of the door and slammed it shut.

No one knew what had just happened. All eyes searched around in an effort to locate whatever ghost Jalle was referring too, but no one could see anything remotely close to a ghost. It took Anna a while to figure out Jalle had been talking about her. Worry filled her heart as she wondered what would happen to her once they figured out she was no longer in her own cell.

"God, it's in your hands now. I just have to trust you will keep me safe."

The room was abuzz about a ghost and what the day had in store for them. It didn't take them long to find out as Jalle returned with some of the other guards to show them the ghost he had seen. They could hear him through the walls; his voice was high pitched and strained as he led the others to the front of the barn. Anna's heart raced at the sound of metal sliding on wood as the barricade was lifted out of its stay.

The large wooden door began to creek open ever so slowly as first, curly black mops of hair, and then round faces of fear belonging to Jalle, Robello, and a few others poked out from behind the door in an attempt to catch a glimpse of the ghost. Their eyes widened as round as silver dollars at the sight of Anna sitting on her mat with the others. *Slam,* went the door, followed quickly by scraping of steel against wood as the bar locking the door was slammed back in place.

They listened to the voices of the excited and fearful guards as they talked about Anna's ghost while moving rapidly away from the building. A smile spread across her face as her gaze stopped on Carlos's bright and understanding eyes. For some reason the guards thought she was dead, and now they thought she was a ghost. The realization elicited a small chuckle from the two as they shared in their revelation.

An excited and concerned murmur spread throughout the room as the slaves voiced their concern over what would happen next. Nothing but severe thunderstorms kept them from tending the precious crop of drugs Luis was growing, and even then he sometimes made them stand out in the weather just for humor's sake.

Rosalita's warning that Luis was going to kill her kept running through Anna's mind as suspense-induced indigestion filled her stomach and brought the taste of bile to the back of her mouth. She had no idea what she would do or say when and if he showed up but prayed that God would protect her and give her wisdom in the event he did come to check on her "ghost."

It wasn't very long till they could hear the scared voices of the guards as they returned and once again opened the door. They could hear the voice of Jalle as he rambled on about Anna's ghost until someone or something abruptly silenced him. For a moment, an awkward and tense silence filled the air before a much braver Luis stepped through the open doorway, whip in one hand and bottle of tequila in the other. His appearance was every bit as menacing as Anna remembered, and she and the rest shrunk back in reflexive fear.

The Unraveling

With trembling bodies they watched him approach to within a dozen feet or so before stopping. Keeping his eyes on Anna, he took a long drink of liquor from his bottle and carefully set it on the ground at his feet. With his free hand, he removed a flashlight from the waistband of his trousers and fixed the bright beam of light on Anna.

With cautious deliberation, he moved first right and then left as far as he possibly could without getting any closer to her than he already was. Anna could see that his eyes were bloodshot from either lack of sleep or from the consumption of too much alcohol.

Without warning, he flicked his wrist and cracked the bullwhip above her head, and in spite of herself, Anna ducked down and shrieked a little with fear. Her outburst seemed to have the same effect on Luis as it did on her, and he stepped back several steps and turned as if to flee. "She is a witch! She is not a ghost! A witch that has turned Rosalita into herself!"

Anna was shocked by his statement and did nothing to respond. She could hear a murmur spread through the guards as they began backing through the open doorway. "What have you done with Rosalita?" Luis demanded with shaking voice. "What have you done with her, witch?"

Unsure what to say or how to answer, Anna shrugged her shoulders and said the only thing that came to her mind. "Get us some food, please. Get us some drinking water too."

The sound of her voice was more than Luis or the guards could stand as they made their way back out of the building and slammed and locked the door. They must have truly believed she was a witch and were truly fearful of what she might do, because in a very short time they returned with food and water for all of them. Anna curbed her desire to speak out, to tell them she was not a witch, realizing that their perception of her might be the only thing saving her life, at least for the time being.

Chapter 35

The nervous mood persisted for three days, and with it came a cloud of worried anticipation that felt as if it could burst at any moment. Never before had the young men had three straight days of food, water, and no work, and they knew it would not last.

Though worried, giddiness filled their hearts as they basked in the leisure, hopeful that it would not soon end. During that time, Anna spent much of the time praying with and for each and every one of them. She used the time to share God's Word and plan of salvation for their lives. For many, the hope she gave them was the only hope they had ever known, and all who had not already done so accepted Jesus as their personal Savior.

All of the guards took time to check on them and to bring food and water. Each was scared that Anna was a witch or evil spirit, so they got in and out as quickly as possible. Sometime during the second day, Anna was able to convince Jalle that she was not a witch. During her time in solitary confinement she had grown to know him and had even witnessed to him on several occasions. At first he was suspicious, but soon his suspicion gave way to emotional relief as he shared with her all that had happened to make them think she was a ghost. Sadness filled Anna's heart as she learned of Rosalita's fate. Luis was convinced she was a witch, however, and for that reason kept as far away from Anna as possible.

About once a day, after drinking an ample amount of alcohol, he would garner up enough nerve to come barging into the cell, cracking his whip, but not close enough to injure any of the inhabitants. Each time, Anna could tell he was intoxicated by the way he moved and by his overall filthy appearance. Not that

261

he was clean by normal standards, but now his hygiene was visibly worse.

Slurring his words, he would yell and accuse Anna of being a witch, of turning Rosalita into herself. Each time he would demand Anna return to the dead so Rosalita could come back to him. His whip menacingly cracked the air, a show of force meant to let her know he meant business. Each time he moved close enough to harm them, Anna stood up and faced him until he became unnerved and left.

They could hear him rant and rave outside the building, hear his whip crack over and over as he took his frustrations out on something. Anna prayed it wasn't one of the guards.

Daylight had given way to night, and Anna had lit three candles. It was a privilege for the men, a luxury they were not used to. Many of them stared at the flickering flames, mesmerized by exotic and synchronized movements as they responded to drafts in the air. With a soft voice, Anna sang "The Old Rugged Cross" and "Amazing Grace" over and over until some of the men joined in. They were already learning the words, placing them in their hearts and minds to cherish and draw strength from for the rest of their lives no matter their circumstances. Outside their dungeon, a commotion broke out, and they could hear the frantic voices of the guards as they discussed something but were unable to decipherer a single word. Everyone grew quiet as mice, their large brown eyes barometers of the fear that was raging inside their hearts.

What's going to happen? The question raged through their collective minds.

Suddenly, the door to their cell burst like an exploding water balloon, and Jalle rushed frantically inside.

"Miss Anna, Miss Anna, you must leave us right now! Luis has been drinking all day, threatening to come here and kill you. The only thing that has kept him away has been his fear of your magic. Now he's too drunk to worry about anything at all other than killing you! You must go right now, before it is too late! If you don't, we will not be able to do anything to stop him."

Sweat dripped from Jalle's troubled face, and his lower lip trembled. It was a huge risk for him to come here; if Luis caught him it meant certain death. Anna's mind was blank; uncertainty filled her heart as she tried to think of what to do or say.

She began to pray silently. *Lord, please help me.*

"Come on, you have no time to spare. You must leave here and head south through the wilderness; there are less roads for him to search for you there. If you don't go now, it will be certain and painful death. He is in a rage that will not be satisfied until someone dies."

Carlos and some of the others pulled Anna to her feet. "Go, Anna, please go!" They were pleading fearfully as tears stained their faces. "We'll cover for you until we know you've had enough time to get away."

A surreal fog filled her mind and shock at the suddenness of her new and imminent danger prevented her from thinking straight. Thick black clouds lined the sky, covering any light the stars and moon would have offered. A constant warm breeze picked up her long black hair and spread it across her face; her body trembled in fear.

"Stay heading in this direction; go as fast as you can. We will try to convince Luis that you disappeared and hope to at least stall him long enough for you to be safe."

She asked fearfully, "But where will I go? Is there a town out there?"

"There is no town for hundreds of miles, but there are people living out there. God willing, you will find them."

"But I have no water, no shoes, no light, nothing. What will I drink? How will I survive?"

Jalle hesitated for a moment. "Well, you'll have to trust your God to provide. If you stay here even long enough for me to get you these things, you will be killed by Luis."

The Unraveling   263

Several loud *cracks* could be heard, followed by raucous bellowing as Luis began his drunken pursuit of Anna.

"Hurry, he'll find you in no time if you don't go! Be careful, there are some bluffs about two hours travel by foot. They aren't that high but high enough to hurt you seriously or even possibly kill you!"

Anna nodded her head and said another quick prayer asking God to protect her. "Thank you, Jalle, for your help,"

Quietly, Jalle replied, "No, thank you, Miss Anna. My heart is happy for the first time in my memory. Maybe one day soon we will meet again in the heaven you told us about."

"I'm sure of that, my friend. God bless!"

With a slight shove from behind, Jalle sent Anna on her way out into the night, out into the wilderness. Though she had been set free, her heart was heavy with loss as she left her new family behind. Several loud *cracks* told her Luis was not far behind, so she ran blindly into the black night.

Chapter 36

Light did not exist in this place. The still blackness was devoid of life, yet he was there, waiting, unseen, and alone; a killer more black than night itself—a monster, really—misshapen, grotesque to look at, not that anyone ever laid eyes on him. He was created to kill, and he knew it, accepted the fact with no remorse or concern either way. It was who he was, his purpose in the world in which he lived. Not many ventured his way. When they did, he made quick work of them before feasting on their remains.

He had survived all these years because he was good at what he did, perhaps the best ever, though lack of peers made it impossible for him to ever know. Not that it mattered; it didn't in the least. His heart had no room for pity for his victims. To him they were simply unfortunate travelers who had happened upon the wrong route of travel, random victims of fate.

Rarely did he leave this place. When he did, it was only for a very short distance before he returned to his known surroundings. Familiarity bred comfort and safety, which he cherished.

The utter blackness of this night beckoned him out into a world he seldom traversed. Keen senses honed by a life spent in blackness were at full alert as he moved carefully about. Though to some, his movements would have seemed lumbering—cumbersome, even—to him they were adequate enough to complete the job of death with skill and efficiency.

This night, nothing moved but for a slight rustling of leaves on the nearby sage, movement caused by the gusting wind. Visibility was zero, just as he liked it. With careful deliberation he moved across a small, sandy clearing as quickly as possible to avoid any unwanted detection, though the likelihood was remote at best.

Carefully and patiently he checked the wind for indication of any interlopers and could detect none. There was an air of complete solitude, just as he liked it.

Still, something seemed wrong to him. Every sense on high alert, he readied his weapon and prepared to battle to the death. Still nothing moved, no sound in the air, no vibration in the ground, no scent on the wind, nothing. An edgy unease began to stir within his mind as he moved slowly about, probing the wind for clues to his unseen foe. Usual nerves of steel were giving way to a more primal instinct to flee, an urge he suppressed as he moved about in a slow circle, guarding against any sudden onslaught or surprise attack. Nothing approached, a fact that only heightened his anxiety. He moved his weapon back and forth and stood still as the night in an attempt to detect even the slightest disturbance. Several minutes passed, and then he felt it.

At first a vibration so small he wasn't sure it was real, followed by another and another, each stronger than the one before, stronger even than any he had ever felt before. Uncertainty of what the threat was or the danger it posed rendered him incapable of making any rational decisions. Panic seized his psyche, and against every ounce of self-judgment and control, he gave way to the primal instinct to flee.

Back to the safety of his dark and solitary cave, back to where he was king. His mind screamed at him to go as he darted out into the small sand clearing. Instantly it was upon him, a force larger than any he had ever known or seen before. From above it came with a vengeance. Instincts once again took over as he threw up his weapon in self-defense. The impact was strong and clean, and he felt it penetrate deep into flesh of whomever or whatever pressed down on him from above, extinguishing every bit of life from his tense body.

~ ~ ~ ~

Falling head over heals on the hard sand, Anna screamed as she blindly groped for her right foot. Intense pain like none she had ever before felt caused her to gasp as it shot sharply up her leg and into her thigh, her lungs complained with every labored breath. With her right hand, she felt the bottom of her foot for the source of the pain. Her hand clamped onto something large and slimy, something that has embedded itself into the flesh just in front of the heel of her foot.

"It's a scorpion," she announced to the air between labored breaths.

Struggling to her feet, she pressed on, fear over what was behind trumping all pain from her new wound. It seemed as if she had been running for hours, though she was fairly certain it hadn't been that long.

The shooting pain intensified with each difficult step as she continued south, or what she thought was south. "Please, God, help me! Please help me!" she sobbed over and over between breaths.

An intense light flashed behind her eyes, and her mind spun as if on a merry-go-round as her body fell hard to the sandy ground and slid to the bottom of the steep ravine next to a scraggly mesquite growing from the desert floor. Once again, stillness returned to take its place next to the darkness pressing down from above.

Chapter 37

All eyes stared intently at the three candles and the dim flames they produced as they lapped hungrily at the air. The faces of the young men were masks of fear as they listened to the loud cracks of the whip just outside their building. Anna had been gone for more than an hour, and so far Luis had done nothing more than storm into the building, whip in one hand, bottle in the other in search of her. With laser eyes of anger, he scanned across the huddled mass. Those same cutting eyes morphed into large orbs of fear and shadows of doubt when he realized Anna was nowhere to be found.

"She's disappeared or hexed herself into one of you," he slurred accusingly at the group as he backed out of the cell, only to return every fifteen minutes or so to see if Anna had reappeared.

Each time, the group stayed huddled and silent in spite of his rants. It was during those departures that Carlos took the initiative to lead the young men in quiet prayer, asking God to keep Anna safe and to keep them all safe from Luis and the violence he represented. Following each prayer, a nervous calm would return for a while before being broken by his sudden and violent intrusion.

"Where is she?" he would roar at them, still too afraid to approach lest she suddenly appear. Not one person uttered a word.

Snapping the whip over their heads, he threatened them, "I'll kill you, each and every one of you until I find her!"

No one budged as his psychotic onslaught raged on. Each appearance brought a show of greater violence and less fear as the consumed alcohol muted his concern over Anna's perceived witchcraft.

But then, as suddenly as it had begun, the whip cracking came to an end, forcing them to endure several minutes of fearful silence. Their hope was that Luis had worn himself out for the night or drunk himself into an unconscious stupor. Carlos wondered what had happened to Jalle and said a quiet prayer for their new friend. If not for him, Anna most certainly would be dead by now.

Everyone jumped as the door to their cell exploded open to reveal a crazed Luis. An eight-inch dagger with a bone handle was clenched between his teeth, and he slowly unwound his leather whip from his shoulder. His wide and insane eyes were white with anger as if he were in some sort of trance, and his black and bushy eyebrows were scrunched down into a *V* that nearly touched—a product of a scowl that jutted out over his menacing eyes.

Slowly, he moved into the cell and headed straight for the young men sitting on their mats as fear raged in their souls. Collectively, they shrunk back away from him as far as the wall of the building would allow.

He promised the frightened group, "Tonight you will die one by one until the American witch is given over to me! Tonight!" A viscous smile nudged itself onto the corner of his mouth and completed the crazed look on his face as he moved to within a few feet of the men. "Which one of you will be first?" He enjoyed the looks of their faces and squirms of fear from his captive audience.

His eyes scanned the group for any sign of weakness, but seeing none, his glare fixed on Carlos. "You, there! You were always hanging around the American, letting her sleep on your mat! Where is she?"

He roared again, louder. "Where is she?"

The smell of his foul breath reached all the way to Carlos and the others, nearly gagging them as they stared straight ahead.

"Come here, you! I want some answers, and you are going to give them to me!" He pointed to the young man.

The Unraveling

Slowly Carlos got up from his mat and walked to within feet of Luis. "Lord, please give me strength," he prayed silently.

He roared, "I'll cut you belly to nose if you don't tell me where she is!"

Carlos watched as Luis hurled the knife with his right hand. Twisting and turning, it soared past his head with a hiss, barely missing his right ear before sticking with a vibrating thud into the wooden wall directly behind him. "I swear to you, one by one you'll die until I start getting answers!"

No one even blinked or moved a muscle in hopes Luis would not soon turn his rage on them. Carlos stood his ground, his thin and frail body shaking like a leaf with fear in anticipation over Luis's next move.

With a flick of his wrist, the deadly whip sprung to life. Exhibiting deadly accuracy, Luis brought the shredded end sizzling home on Carlos's right shoulder. The impact sent sharp pains through his arm and neck and knocked him to the hard earthen floor. Turning to his stomach, Carlos began to crawl away from Luis, but the venomous whip struck him on the back over and over.

Pieces of his shredded clothing soaked with his own blood began to fly through the air. Sweat and splattered blood covered Luis's angry face and body as he worked the whip over and over.

Luis raged between blows, "Tell me where she is!"

Even if he wanted, Carlos could do nothing but shudder and writhe in pain. Up and down his body the whip went, shredding and cutting with each and every blow. Tears of sorrow and anguish poured down the faces of the others as they watched in horror at the scene unraveling before them. Never had they seen Luis so violent and intent as now. Never had they seen the crazed look as the one that adorned his face.

"Tell me!" he screamed in a horse and foreign voice. "Tell me where she is!"

Reaching out in front of him as far as possible, Carlos clutched at the hard soil in an attempt to pull himself away from the madman at his back.

Luis's breathing was labored. His thirst for violence had never been so great. His skin glistened in the candlelight from sweat that was pouring from every pore of his body. Each blow brought exhilaration like none he had ever experienced before.

Light began to fade from Carlos's awareness, and confusion clouded his mind. Garnering his final strength, he raised his head and was surprised to see a brilliant light emanating from overhead. Insurmountable joy filled his heart at the realization of what was happening.

"Thank you, Anna, for showing me the way! Thank you, Jesus, for being the way! I'm coming home!" he whispered as his spirit soared to the arms of God.

Unaware of what had just transpired, Luis continued his assault for another fifteen minutes, striking Carlos's limp body over and over again with as much force as he could garner. A peaceful calm enveloped Carlos's slender face and an everlasting joy was apparent for all to see in his fixed and glazed eyes.

Throwing his bloodied whip to the ground in exhaustion, Luis stumbled to his right, bent down, and retrieved the half-empty bottle of alcohol from the ground. Then he stumbled out of the cell and into the dark of the night.

Chapter 38

You could hear them before you could see them—one humming old folk songs, the other braying along either in protest, or harmony. Both were off key. The thin line of dust kicked up by their feet was visible if one strained one's eyes hard enough. It too announced their arrival ahead of time.

"Git up there, Pedro. We don't have all day," the withered and dusty old man in striped pants ordered his pannier-laden mule. Braying in protest, the large gray beast with white hair around his nose and mouth seemed to slow even more, if that was possible.

Removing the oversized hat from his head, Chino swatted the animal on his rump. "I said git up there."

With a hop, Pedro kicked out his back feet, narrowly missing the legs of the old man who was walking just behind. They were a cantankerous pair that had practiced this process of travel for some time, repeating it over and over again as if choreographed for some elaborate production—an odd sight in the desert, as out of place as an oasis, but here they were.

Sharp hills laden with mesquite and sage made up the landscape, broken up by reddish white sand dunes thrown in every here and there, placed seemingly by some abstract artist with no rhyme or reason or form. A small, worn path snaked along the contours of the hillside, created from a century or more of use by those few people that subsisted in a country as hard as this.

"Git up there, old mule," Chino chided his partner as they followed the path around the corner of the hill. "We got to git these supplies home," he added in hopes it would encourage his counterpart to pick up the pace.

They had been on the rugged trail since before dawn in hopes to beat at least most of the heat. Now the sun was full in the sky, and they still had over a third of the way to go until they reached the little shack Chino and his family lived in. Just ahead, the trail rose sharply up the steep hill and crossed over a saddle in the box canyon. Both man and beast knew once they were on the other side, it would be nothing but downhill the rest of the way, making their travel much easier from there on out.

Just as the trail began to ascend, Chino spotted something out of place under a crooked old mesquite tree just ahead, no more than ten feet off the trail.

"Whoa there, boy! What we got here?" he asked.

The old mule brayed and came to a stop. "I know it's a person. I ain't blind," Chino replied.

Moving as close to the edge of the trail as possible, the old man moved back and forth and peered down at the prone and still figure.

"Well, it's a she, and she ain't from around here, I can tell just lookin' at her."

Satisfied, he moved back to the mule, removed his hat, and wiped the sweat from his eyes. "Well, let's git on up there," he bellowed out while swatting the beast on its rump.

Much to his surprise, the mule didn't budge but instead let out several long brays in protest.

"Well, I ain't taking her. She ain't from around here, and I ain't gonna git involved. The last thing we need is some sort of trouble, so we're going to mind our own business and head on home. Now git up there."

Still the beast refused to move.

Shaking his head, the old man moved to the front of the animal and pulled on his halter. "We just can't afford any trouble, besides there's supposed to be some bad sorts around here. My guess is they'll be looking for her, and if we take her, they'll come looking at our home. No, we ain't gonna take her; now let's git on up there," he explained to the suddenly obstinate beast.

Pedro laid his foot-long ears back on his head and scrunched his lips up, revealing his large, brown, stained teeth in protest. Nothing Chino did or said convinced the beast to move away from the helpless figure below. Resigned to the fact the animal was not going to move, Chino opened the heavy baskets draped over its back and removed a canteen of water and a handful of grain before walking back to the front of the beast.

Exaggerating his movements, Chino unscrewed the cap from the canteen and took a long drink, accentuating it with a loud sigh. "Now, look here, you dumb animal. If you follow me, I'll give you a bit of a drink and a handful of grain."

Moving backwards, one step at a time, he coaxed the beast up the trail to the top of the saddle before stopping to give it a drink. After the drink, he let it eat the grain out of his hand as he scratched behind the animal's ears.

"Trust me, it's just best we move along and mind our own business. Besides, we barely have enough for the family to eat and drink, let alone a whole other mouth to feed. She'd be nothing but trouble anyway, and we'd have to nurse her back to health, assuming she would even live long enough to get her home with us," he reasoned.

Satisfied that he had made his point, Chino returned to the pannier and placed the canteen back inside before closing and tying the flap with a long leather strap. Raising his head, his hopeful eyes scanned the thin, wispy clouds, hopeful to see signs of cooling rains that might possibly be coming his way, but there were none. Instead, blinding rays of sunlight reminded him just how hot it really was as he moved to the back of the beast. "Get on up there," he bellowed to the animal.

Pedro refused to budge.

"I said, git on up there now," he repeated the command, this time a little more forcefully.

For the next ten minutes, Chino tried everything he could think of, but nothing he did made any difference as Pedro refused to move even a single inch. Finally, resigned to the fact it was going to be Pedro's way or no way at all, he gave in, turned the mule around, and returned to the girl at the bottom of the hill.

"I'll take her, but I'll tell you this much: if she lives, she's gonna have to share your grain!"

If Chino didn't know better, he would have sworn that Pedro's braying reply was indeed a chuckle.

Returning to the pannier, he removed a chunk of canvas and some leather banding. After searching the area, he was able to locate two fairly straight pieces of mesquite, which he used to build a makeshift travois that he hitched to the mule before turning his attention to the girl. He was surprised at how light she was and equally surprised that she was still breathing. Slowly he moved her to the travois and strapped her on.

Shaking his head, he felt her right leg, which was swollen to nearly twice its normal size and was quite red. The hot sand stuck to her face and hair and gave her a ghostly appearance. Carefully, he checked her foot and found the source of the apparent infection.

"Scorpion sting, and a bad on from the looks of it," he announced to himself.

Opening her mouth, he forced some water down her throat and waited while she sputtered and choked before repeating the process. "My name is Chino, and this here is Pedro. Nice to make your acquaintance," he announced as Anna mumbled and choked some more.

Removing his hat, he slapped the mule on his rump and gave him the order to "git on up the hill."

This time, Pedro responded with a loud bray and even had a noticeable prance in his step as they crossed the saddle and headed down the other side.

The Unraveling   275

Chapter 39

Jay gazed out the rain-streaked window of the large airplane as it taxied down the runway and came to a stop. The elation he normally would have felt when arriving back in Washington was absent. It had been replaced with an apathetic attitude fed by exhaustion and sorrow. He'd been traveling the past forty-eight hours with nothing more than cat naps along the way, and he hadn't eaten much either.

Bill clapped him on his back and announced to his friend, "Yo, dog, we made it!"

Jay simply nodded his head without talking or making eye contact with his tattooed and pierced buddy from home. Bill was a reformed drug addict who was on fire for the Lord and had committed his life to helping other addicts break free from the chains that bound them. Five years earlier, he had started and run the "Turning Leaf Ministry," whose mission it was to break the chains of addiction through the restorative power of Jesus Christ. Armed with nothing more than Jesus's love and an obedient spirit, Bill had not only started the ministry but expanded it into two neighboring cities. Surprisingly, Bill had not talked as much as he normally would have, for which Jay was grateful. They had rendezvoused at Dallas, and after short introductions between Jack and Bill, had boarded a flight for home.

They deboarded the airplane and headed down the concourse toward the luggage terminal. Bill had no luggage, and Jay had carried his two duffel bags of clothing onto the plane, so waiting was not necessary. They moved to the parking garage and found Bill's old forest green Subaru parked between a black Escalade and red Ford Escape. Before Jay knew it, they were out the garage and on their way down State Highway 195 toward home.

Rain fell from the summer sky and halted all harvest in the massive wheat fields that lined either side of the roadway. The rolling hills were golden and brown with either ripe grain or freshly tilled fields. Large red or green combines sat abandoned in the fields, waiting for dryer weather so they could finish gobbling up the plump kernels of wheat. A touch of nostalgia tugged at Jay's heart as he surveyed the once familiar geography and replayed memories of happier times.

They drove down the hill that led into Pullman and stopped at the light at the bottom. Bill's long hair danced in the wind from his open window. "Man, I just love the smell of summer rain," he announced as they turned on Grand Street and headed north to Bob and Nancy Rosemont's. Nancy and Bob were Anna's aunt and uncle, and it was their home in which he would be staying. They had been owners of the only lumberyard in town but were retired now. Jay had worked for them for years prior to going into the ministry. They were like a second set of parents to him.

Normally, he would have stayed at his own parents' home. They lived just a town away, but they were gone on a six-month commitment to the Gulf States. They belonged to a group called Habitat for Humanity United, and they traveled around the country building low-cost homes for the poor.

Bill pulled the car into the driveway behind Bob's maroon Chevy truck and shut it off. Late summer purple, blue and red flowers lined the drive and small sidewalk leading up to the house. A handmade "God Bless This House" plaque rested above the entry door next to an American flag, which was dancing on the wind. Several hummingbirds hovered around the red bird feeder just outside the kitchen window with white "tic tac toe" grid work. Brown shutters next to the window were beginning to look nearly black in the fading light. Dusk was just settling in, but it was still light enough for Jay to make out two new tattoos on Bill's arm. One was a picture of a cross with scripture under it and the other a lion with scripture under it too. Bill held up both arms for Jay to inspect, "Check out my new scrips, man!" Jay nodded and leaned his head against the headrest.

"Dog, you haven't said ten words the whole trip. What up, man? I mean, I know your life is turned upside down and all, but it's me, the Billster. I love ya, man! I know you probably don't feel like talking right now, but know in your heart, I'm here for you anytime."

Tears filled Jay's eyes as they scanned the dirty red floor mat at his feet. "Thanks, Bill, I know you are. I just don't know what to do or say anymore. My whole world is in turmoil. I don't feel like living. Man, it hurts so bad, hurts like someone is reaching into my chest and squeezing my heart. I can barely breath. I can barely sleep. I can barely move. I'm a mess and don't know what to do about it. My life is an absolute nightmare."

Large and random drops began to hit the windshield with a splat. Bill reached over and placed his right hand on Jay's shoulder and could feel his friend's body shake with silent tears. Both were quiet for several minutes, content to listen to the pounding rain. "Dude, you've just been through an unbelievable situation. Part of you has died; you're supposed to feel pain and misery. God created us to be able to grieve. It's part of the normal healing process. Just don't try goin' macho on us. We're your fam and we love ya, man! Take your time, let us love on ya, dude! Just trust God! He'll take care of you and let you know what you're supposed to do next. You can trust the ole Billster, the Big Man upstairs always comes through."

Jay's shoulder tensed under Bill's hand. Inside, a fire raged that he could barely contain. Every conscious fiber in his body wanted to strike out in verbal anger at his friend, but he maintained control. The last thing he wanted to hear or needed to hear was that God was going to take care of him, had a plan for his life, loved him, or would make the best out of his situation.

God had let him down and made him question his whole faith. Now he was alone after having given up everything for a God that had forsaken him.

They watched the yellow lights come on inside Bob and Nancy's house as dusk gave way to night. Several of the neighborhood streetlights flickered on simultaneously, casting their bluish white beams of light down the street. Almost instantly a cloud of flying moths and insects swarmed around the source of the light, diving and darting around as if performing some sort of ritualistic street light dance.

Reaching down to his side Jay undid his seatbelt. "Well, I can see Bob peeking out at us every now and again. Maybe we should get inside."

"Right on! Knowing Nancy, we'll be forced to strap on the old feed bags as soon as we walk in the door, not that I'm complaining or anything."

Bill undid his belt and started to open his door. "Bud, I hope you know, I got your back and God really has your back. If you need to talk or when you want to talk, the Billster will be right here for ya, just a phone call away."

Jay could feel the emotional heat rising on his neck and face. "I know, and I appreciate it. I really do," he stated through clenched teeth.

Jay followed his friend up the chipped and worn sidewalk, hesitated for a moment, and with a big breath opened the door and went inside for an emotional reunion he wished desperately he could avoid.

The Unraveling

Chapter 40

It had been one of the most difficult weeks Jay had ever spent in his entire life. Nancy made over him as if he were an injured child when all he wanted was to be left alone. To make matters worse, a collage of pictures representing Anna's life hung on the wood paneled wall in the living room of Nancy and Bob's home. It was virtually impossible for him to move anywhere throughout the house without being reminded of her life and reminded that part of his heart had been ripped out of his chest with her death.

Their home church held a memorial and life celebration service for Anna a week after Jay had arrived home. Planning the event was too difficult emotionally, so Jay's sisters stepped in and, with Nancy's help, planned the entire event. It was a nice service but felt odd since there was no casket or burial as was customary for most funerals.

The church was completely packed with dozens of people standing the entire time at the rear of the sanctuary. The usher placed Jay at the front of the church with the rest of the family, which was customary. Tears streamed down his face as images of Anna at various stages of her short life were projected onto the screen at the front of the church. An equal amount of tears flowed from his eyes as the pastor began his eulogy, but this time they were tears of anger. The pastor spoke at length about God, Anna and Jay's commitment to Him, and the faith they exhibited in stepping through the doors God had opened in their lives, even if it meant death.

"I know Jay, and I know how much he loves God. I also know it will only be a matter of time before he's moving back through those doors of service, no matter where they might lead, in antici-

280

pation of the great blessings God has in store for his life. Though these are heart-wrenching times, and the loss we all share a part of are beyond any human comprehension, we can rejoice in the knowledge that Anna is praising and worshiping today in the arms of her Lord in heaven. A knowledge that makes life bearable, joyful even, and answers the question we all have asked so often these past few months, why? Why now and why Anna? It just made no sense to any of us. Questions we may well never be able to answer until we ourselves are in fellowship with Anna at the very throne of God. So in closing, I will thank you, Anna, for the testimony that is your life, and thank you, Jay, for your faithfulness and obedience to God's call. We are richer today for having had both of you in our lives."

Jay's mind went numb as people went through the line to give him their condolences. It amazed him the number of people that wanted to know what he was going to do next, as if losing his wife was like losing a job. When the end of the line snaked through, he was more than thankful and quickly took the opportunity to slip out of the building for some alone time.

It was a beautiful late summer afternoon on the Palouse punctuated by a deep blue sky absent even the slightest hint of a cloud. Jay sat on a little bench just outside the door to the church and removed his shoes and socks and rolled up his slacks a few inches before moving to the brilliant green, manicured front lawn of the church. Slowly he moved around the yard, enjoying the feeling of the cool grass on his feet and wondering in amazement at the contrast in worlds that his life was now part of—this one, peaceful and filled with plenty; the other hard, violent, and lacking in almost every area. Thoughts of Anna swirled around in his mind as he moved about the yard—her smile, her hair, her inner beauty that affected and infected everyone it touched.

"How could you take her from me? I did everything you wanted me to do. I just don't understand," Jay prayed to God. "My life is ruined now! I hate you, God. I am so angry toward you. Everything you have promised is a joke. My life is a sham, a laughingstock. Nothing has turned out the way if was supposed to! I just want to die!"

He felt bad for telling God he hated Him, maybe even a little scared that God might smite him right where he stood. Part of him hoped He would, hoped that his life would end right there, at that place and at that moment. Despair like none he had ever known filled his heart.

A voice he knew caused him to jump a little. "Jay, how are you doing, son? I've been pretty worried about you, tried to call several times."

Turning quickly, Jay wiped his eyes before facing his old friend Chet. "Sorry, guess I've been pretty much preoccupied lately."

"That's all right; I figured you had other things going on. I've just been worried about you, thought we could go get a Coke or something."

The two men embraced. "I miss her so much, I just want to die."

Chet patted his friend on the back. "I know it seems like your world has come to an end, my friend, and part of it has, but I just want you to know, it's going to get better, you'll see."

"But why Anna? It just doesn't make any sense to me? We were there to spread God's Word, and instead of blessings, she lost her life."

The two men separated, and Chet scuffed the ground with his foot while several people left the church and did their best to avoid eye contact with the two. "I know it doesn't make sense, probably never will, and I also know you have to learn somehow to trust God. He has allowed this to happen for a reason."

Slowly Jay shook his head no. Turning away from his friend, anger and resentment began to build in his heart. Taking a deep sigh, he reached down and picked up a piece of landscape rock that had somehow made it into the grass and tossed it back and forth between his hands. For several moments, neither man said anything as Jay did his best to control his tongue.

"Well, I appreciate everything you're saying, really I do, but I just don't think God really cares all that much. If He did, He never would have allowed Anna to die. From now on, I'm going to place my trust in me. At least that way I'll know what I'm getting into beforehand and know whom to blame afterwards."

Chet stood motionless and quiet. Tears returned to his eyes when he heard the words of his friend. "Well, I know you're going through something that most people your age never have to go through. I understand your anger, resentment, and sadness. I also know that deep in your heart, you know the truth about God and truth about faith. I just hope you don't let the bitterness that's building in your heart destroy all that God has done in your life. I'm here to tell you, it just isn't worth it."

With anger, Jay threw the rock across the road and watched it bounce clear to the wall of the neighbor's house. "Please don't lecture me about bitterness until you've lived a day in my shoes! And another thing, I'll tell you about the truth and faith. The truth is Anna is dead, I have no wife, I have no money, and I have no life all on account of faith, and that's the truth! God deserted us in our greatest hour of need. I'm not going to give Him that chance again."

A stunned look crossed Chet's face as he ran his thick fingers through the thin gray hair that failed to cover his head. The lenses in his gold-rimmed glasses magnified the red emotion that filled his eyes.

"Well, I can't say I can relate exactly to what you are going through...," he started slowly.

"That's right, you can't!" Jay added emphatically.

Several more people left the church and filed past the two men standing in the lawn. A few of the children tugged on their mother's dress and pointed at Jay. "Look, Momma, there he is."

The Unraveling

"Shush, don't point," each mother said with embarrassment as they whisked their kids to their car.

"Well, I'll tell you this much," he added now that they were alone again. "If you think you're the first person who has lost someone close, you have another thing coming. Plenty of people have lost loved ones—wives, husbands, siblings, children, or parents—long before they should have. You know what?" he asked. "They continued on with their lives, regrouped, trusted God, and became mighty men and women in the process," he added, pointing a finger at Jay. "Others, well, let's just say they gave up, let self-pity turn into bitterness and rage, and ruined not only their own lives but the lives of all they touched." He paused. "From where I stand, the choice is yours. I'm not saying you shouldn't mourn. But don't let this tragedy define the man God wants you to be."

Having said his fill, Chet turned and headed toward the church but stopped and turned around. "And one more thing, you're not the only one who is mourning the loss of a loved one today. Everyone here is mourning the loss of a loved one. We all loved Anna with all of our hearts. We love you too and want to show how much if you'll just let us."

Chet opened the door and re-entered the church as his words settled over Jay's heart like a weight. Even though he knew everything Chet had said was the truth, he couldn't bring himself to forgive God for what had happened.

I'll never allow myself to be vulnerable like this ever again in my life, he vowed to himself as he slipped his feet into his socks and shoes. With a sigh, he opened the door to the church and went inside. *Might as well join the rest of the mourners,* he thought as the door automatically closed behind him with a resounding thud.

It's all one big pity part anyway. He mimicked Chet in his mind, adding fuel to his bitterness.

A dark and ominous cloud hung over his head and forecast to all the destructive mood he was really in. Sarcasm filled his heart. *Another day in paradise.*

Chapter 41

Drip, drip, drip, drip. Anna's eyes flickered open at the annoying sound. *Drip, drip, drip.* Each one made her head throb. "Augh, where am I?" she questioned as she rose halfway up off her corn husk mattress before succumbing to a dizziness that clouded her senses and caused her to fall back to the bed. It was dark inside the little building; only one small crude window was visible, but it was boarded off with some sort of loose material that was flapping in the wind. *Drip, drip, drip,* water continued to fall from the thatch ceiling overhead, falling to the dirt floor where it was collecting in little puddles but missed falling on her, which was amazing considering the amount that was coming through the ceiling. It seemed more like a sieve than a real roof.

Moving her head ever so slightly, she could make out the rough walls, lack of furniture, several other husk mattresses, and a little stove in the center of the room. There was no stove pipe, and the ceiling directly over the stove had an opening about a foot in diameter that was covered with thick black soot, indicating the stove must vent through the roof without the aide of a stovepipe.

Her right leg and foot throbbed with a dull pain that refused to subside. Broken memories of Luis, Carlos, Jalle, and the others began returning to her mind, but she wasn't sure if they were real or a residual nightmare from which she had just awakened. One look at the dress she was wearing confirmed that her memories were real. Try as she might, she could not remember where she was or how she had gotten there. Thoughts of Jay filled her mind, and she prayed that God would keep him safe and reassure him that she was all right. The holes in her memory caused her heart

286

rate to increase as panic began to grow inside. She suddenly had a great urge to get up and run as fast as she could back to the mission. She took several deep breaths and forced herself to calm down and then asked God to keep her safe wherever she was.

Pain started to build behind her eyes and caused her to close them. In no time, she slipped back into a fitful slumber, only vaguely aware of the voices that seemed to be coming from directly above her. Opening her eyes, she smiled at the funny face that was no more than inches from her own. It was old and wrinkled with no teeth and was bordered with nearly white hair that poked out like straw from under a kerchief. It reminded her of the fake "shrunken heads" she had seen as a young girl in one of the *Ripley's Believe It or Not* Museum her parents had taken her family to on a family vacation. This time the head was connected to a tiny neck and a proportionately tiny body, and it was talking to her.

"There, there, child, you'll be all right. Just take a drink of this," the old lady said as she forced some of the bitterest liquid Anna had ever tasted into her mouth from a crudely made cup.

The broth was warm and caused her to choke several times before she turned her head away in revulsion. "It may not taste that good, but it's good for you. It'll get you back on your feet in no time. Now, drink the rest of it."

Anna could feel her head being turned until her mouth was once again in line with the cup. Once again bitter liquid was forced into her mouth as she gagged the last of the bitter liquid down. In an attempt to remove the horrid taste from her mouth, she swallowed and gulped several times, but the aftertaste was nearly as bad as the drink itself.

"Now you can get some more rest," the little old lady told her as she made her way to the makeshift door.

Anna could feel her eyes growing heavy again but managed to turn her head toward the back of the departing lady. "Where am I, and who are you?"

The Unraveling   287

A strange and warped voice answered, but she was too tired to understand what it was saying as she drifted back into a deep sleep filled with peaceful dreams. When she awoke, she was startled to find four girls, varying in size and age, crowded around her bed. They were joined by two grown women, one the little old lady she had already met. All had on kerchiefs covering their fine black hair and were wearing threadbare dresses that were made of the same vivid yellow yarn, probably woven by one of the two older women.

"Where am I?" Anna asked groggily.

"You are here, in our home," the youngest of the girls announced to the giggles of the other girls.

"Hush, you let her be," the wrinkled old grandmother chastised the others with a wave of her hand. "She needs her rest."

"It's all right," Anna replied with a smile as she attempted to rise up on one elbow. "I asked where I was and she told me. By the way, I'm Anna."

The youngest little girl beamed back at her as she reached out and softly rubbed Anna's arm with her grimy fingers. "I'm Serena," the girl responded, "and these are my sisters, my mother, and my grandmamma."

The ice had been broken, and Anna listened as each of the girls introduced themselves. They were excited and happy to finally be able to visit with the stranger in their midst. Before long, she knew each of them by name—Serena; Sancha; Shoshone; Madia; the mother, Beatrice; and the grandmamma, Reina. They visited for a while before Reina instructed them all to leave her to mend and get some more sleep.

The days progressed, and as they did, Anna was able to finally get up and move around her new setting. The house was all alone, in a remote setting miles from any other people. Chino, his mother, wife, and girls lived there and tended a small herd of sheep, a few goats, four pigs, a dozen chickens, and a small garden of maize that they raised not only for their own use but for feed for the animals. What they grew they lived off of or traded with others for needs they could not provide. Their home was crudely built but provided shelter from the weather even though the roof leaked whenever it rained.

The family accepted her as one of their own, and she shared the gospel with them daily. Although they knew bits and pieces of the story of Christ, superstition and fear dominated their understanding. Within days, each had received Jesus as their personal Savior with a joy and hope they had never before known. Anna thanked God for allowing her to share the gospel with new people and was overjoyed at their response. *This is what it's all about,* she thought to herself as she taught the children "Jesus Loves Me," along with other several other Sunday school songs. "Thank you, Lord, for giving me this opportunity!" she prayed and marveled at the way God made things work for the good, even when the opposite seemed true.

Slowly, Anna regained her strength. She felt bad for eating a share of the meager food supplies the family had, but they would hear no arguments from her about it, insisting that she eat her fill first, even ahead of Chino, which was a great honor. Anna taught them how to bless their food, to thank God for all He had provided for them. They were eager to learn and listened to all of her lessons with great interest, eager to apply what they learned to their lives.

At the end of her second week with the family, Anna approached Chino. "I really need to get back to the mission. My husband is there, and I am so very worried about him. Do you know where the mission is?"

"Well, I know of the mission and about where it is, though I have never been there. I'm sure I could find it, though."

"Do you think you could take me there? I really need to get back. The people will all be worried sick."

With some reluctance, Chino agreed to take her back to the mission. "I'll take you back in one week, that way I'll know you are

The Unraveling   289

strong enough to travel, and the storm that is coming in will have passed by," he said while eyeing the building cloud bank. "The last thing we want is to get caught out there in an angry storm."

Anna counted down the days in suspenseful anticipation of Jay's and the rest of the people's reaction when she came riding through the gates on a mule. A smile broke out on her face at the thought of the festive party they would hold. Never once did it occur to her that everyone there thought she was dead.

Departure morning came long before the dawn as Chino prepared Pedro for the long trip. All of the family had risen to see Anna off, and not one dry eye could be found as they all gave their tearful good byes. "I'll be back one day, I promise. I'll bring some Bibles and some other good things that will teach you about God when I come," Anna promised.

Serena sobbed as she took hold of Anna's leg. "Please, Miss Anna, take me with you. I wanna go with you."

"I would if I could, but you need to stay here with your family, to help take care of them. They would all miss you so much if you left. Besides, I'll come back one day." Anna comforted the little girl while running her thin fingers through her thick black hair. "Plus, you need to stay here and tell anyone else you meet about Jesus. Tell them all about what I told you. That way they will be able to go to heaven one day."

Serena nodded as Anna hugged and said good-bye to each and every one of the family. "I love you. I'll never forget you! Don't forget about Jesus," she told them as tears of sadness and joy ran down her face.

Chino held the reins and started out leading the mule, with Anna riding sidesaddle down the narrow and dusty trail toward the mission. Tears of sorrow ran down her face while hopeful anticipation lifted her heart at the prospect of the joyful reunion to come. A small glow began to emerge on the eastern sky and continued to grow brighter by the minute, promising the birth of a new day and hopefully a new and brighter beginning.

Chapter 42

Two days on the trail had taken its toll on Anna as each dusty hill they climbed brought an elevated state of suspense and anticipation, while each hill descended served only to deflate expectations. Sticky, hot air, product of a rapidly approaching monsoon, made travel nearly unbearable, and she found her lightheadedness and sick stomach had returned with a vengeance.

Each drainage entered was a mirror image of the one just exited, or so it seemed to Anna—red soil, gangly mesquite trees here and there, sage nearly everywhere they looked, and no inhabitants to be seen. The long trip was starting to wear on Chino too, and he showed it with his grumblings and mumblings of discontent every step of the way. The only one that seemed to be unaffected by the trip was Pedro, who just kept plodding along without so much as a single one of his usual outburst or moments of obstinate protest.

Instead, he seemed almost eager to carry Anna on his back, and he soaked up the attention she gave him, scratching behind his ears, rubbing his neck, softly singing to him along the way. Several times, Chino complained to her that she was spoiling him, that he wouldn't be worth a thing once she was gone if she didn't quit spoiling him. She knew he was teasing her, though, and just smiled at his grumblings along the way.

They made a wide berth of the area in which Chino thought Luis was operating his drug outfit. The last thing either of them wanted was to accidentally run into him or any of his thugs out there in the wilderness. Anna was grateful for the safety, even though the wide berth meant an extra day's travel, she agreed to it wholeheartedly.

Dusk was setting in as they approached the top of a long drainage they had been in for more than half the day. "Well, I'm not sure we're ever going to find this mission of yours. I just don't know which direction to go or how much longer to look. I don't like being away from home for this long. One never knows what will happen out here in the wilderness," Chino told her dejectedly.

Nodding her head that she understood, Ann said a silent prayer asking God to guide their paths home. Thought of traveling back to Chino's home stirred a fear in her heart that had been looming just under the surface for most of the day. For one rare moment, despair over her plight began to take root in her heart, and she even questioned God's will for her life. It was a thought and feeling she quickly relinquished to God, knowing full well that it was Him that was guiding her.

"I think we should find somewhere to hunker in for the night," Chino announced while surveying the area for any possible cover.

"Can't we just go over one more hill? We're almost to the top anyway," Anna pleaded.

Her request brought about a renewed round of grumbling from Chino as he removed his old, worn, large-brimmed hat from his head and scratched his long, greasy hair. "I don't really see what it will gain, but I guess we can," he agreed.

So on they went, up the final thousand yards or so before cresting the flat top mesa. They traveled till the sun began to set, and they could see the new valley spread out for miles in every direction below them. Raising his hand, Chino halted the mule and Anna as his eyes squinted down and attempted to focus on something on the valley floor, nearly two-thirds of the way across.

"There's something down there out of place, but I can't tell what it is," he announced with wonder in his voice.

Anna strained her eyes to make out whatever Chino was looking at, but her eyes failed to do any more than detect the object that was somewhat larger than the surrounding terrain. "What do you think it is?"

"Not sure. It looks like there are a few roads down there, or big trails at least. I guess we can amble that way for a bit and see if we can make it out any better."

They traveled till darkness forced them to stop and were disappointed that neither of them had been able to make out the landmark they were heading toward. Though she knew it wasn't reasonable, fear began to build again in Anna's heart as she worried they might be heading toward something Luis had built out there in the desert. Once again she prayed for God to keep them safe and to direct them away from any danger.

Chino was determined to head for home in the morning but reluctantly agreed to travel just a little farther in hopes of identifying whatever was out there. Anna prayed as she quietly sang as many hymns as she could remember. Though it was hard, she placed it all in God's hands, deciding whatever happened would be His will. A peaceful calm settled over her heart as she watched the brilliant stars overhead and listened to the heavy and even breathing from Chino as he slept. Thoughts of Jay once again filled her mind and gave her a touch of homesickness as she fondly recalled the past events of their short life together. With a smile on her face and a tear in her eye, she thanked God for giving him to her and asked Him to keep Jay safe before nodding off to sleep for the night.

Rising rays of sunshine told them they had overslept and roused them from their makeshift beds. Anna walked down the trail for a ways with her eyes focused on the large structure they were heading toward as Chino prepared Pedro for another day of travel. The temperature was already climbing, and she could tell it was going to either be a scorcher, or a monsoonal thunderstorm was going to develop as she made her way back to the disassembled camp that was now folded and tucked away on Pedro's back. Graciously she accepted a small corn tortilla Chino offered her for her meager breakfast before climbing back aboard the

The Unraveling

beast, which was letting them know just what he thought about traveling in the heat for the fourth straight day.

Down they went, into a long valley filled with sage and rock and nothing more. Dust kicked up from Pedro's hooves filled Anna's nostrils and made her yearn for a bath, something she had not experienced for longer than she cared to remember. The abrupt descent in elevation caused them to lose sight of their landmark, much to Anna's dismay. To make matters worse, Chino's mood had soured considerably, and he was threatening to turn around and head for home every few minutes. Through it all, Anna continued to remain positive, praying and singing softly hymns of praise to her Lord.

The vastness of the coulee they were in amazed Anna as hour after hour slipped past with seemingly very little progress being made. Ominous thunderheads tinged with grays and blacks boiled and roiled overhead as humidity rose on the air and made Chino once again take up the grumbling and threats to turn around and head for home. Finally and mercifully they climbed the far hill of the coulee and were amazed as the hot and lonely desert revealed the most beautiful sight Anna could have hoped or imagined.

In the valley, no more than half a mile away, a large and purple behemoth sentinel rose up from the desert floor and pointed the way toward the elusive mission they were seeking. Never in her wildest imagination had she ever thought a sixteen-foot purple dinosaur would bring her as much joy as this. With excitement on her voice and tears running from her eyes, Anna explained to Chino where the beast had come from and that it pointed the way to the mission.

Finally, for the first time in a long while she felt as if she was nearly home as they plodded their way up and around the marker. Their spirits were raised considerably as they headed down the long road for home and for the love of her life. She could already imagine the look on his face when she rode into the mission.

Chapter 43

More than two weeks had passed since the memorial service for Anna. For Jay it seemed more like an eternity. Each new day brought a despair and gloom deeper than the one before as he sought refuge in the upstairs bedroom in Nancy and Bob's home, Anna's old bedroom, to be exact. For most of the day he would keep the heavy curtains closed and burrow under the covers to avoid contact with anyone from the outside world, even Bob and Nancy, emerging just long enough to drink some water or use the restroom. Even though sleep eluded him, the majority of the time he stayed hidden and alternated from feeling sorry for himself and being mad at God for the way his life had turned out. Thoughts of death and dying were becoming frequent topics in his mind, and he welcomed the thought of his life coming to an end.

On at least six different occasions Bill had come by and even come into his room, just to sit with Jay, never saying a word. Sometimes he would sit for hours, while other times he would stay for just a few minutes before praying for his friend and then leaving. It was aggravating to Jay, and he decided the next time Bill came over he would ask him to just leave.

Darkness roused him from the security of his covers as he glanced over at the digital alarm clock by his bed. 2:34 a.m. his clock glared at him in an aggravatingly red light. Pangs of hunger tugged at his stomach, a feeling he was not used to anymore. For most of the past two months, his appetite had left him; and when he looked in the mirror, he could see it was taking a toll on him. When he stepped on the scale, it revealed that he was down to his sophomore year in high school weight, which was much too light for a full-grown man.

Rising from the bed, he slipped a bathrobe over top of the lightweight sweats he was wearing and headed down the stairs to the kitchen. The hard linoleum floor was cold and felt good on his hot, bare feet as he made his way to the refrigerator. Deciding what to take was difficult at first until he spotted a six-pack of Coke and several cold barbecued hamburgers left over from the evening dinner.

After retrieving a couple of each, he returned to the kitchen table, sat down, and began to eat. The sharp bite of the Coke felt good on his throat and nearly made him choke as the cold liquid burned all the way into his stomach. The hamburgers tasted good, but he felt full after eating only half of one of the round disks of protein. A voice from behind nearly made him jump over backwards with fright as Nancy came into the kitchen and turned on the light.

"Thought I could hear someone, or at least a mouse out here," she announced pleasantly enough.

"Sorry," Jay muttered under his breath as his chin sunk down onto his chest and his eyes focused on the white lettering on the can of Coke sitting right in front of him.

"That's all right. You can help yourself anytime you want. I hope you know that."

Jay nodded that he did as Nancy made her way around the table and took a seat directly opposite him.

"We just wish you'd want to help yourself a little more frequently and maybe even when we are all awake," she added quietly.

Jay nodded but still said nothing.

"I hope you know, tons of people care about you and are worried sick over you."

Once again he nodded and grabbed his Coke from the table and took a big drink.

A large stack of unopened mail sat on the table in front of Nancy. With both hands, she pushed the stack toward Jay. "They've stopped by, sent all of these cards and letters, called non-stop. I just don't know what I'm supposed to tell them anymore."

A football-size knot of emotion filled his throat as he shrugged his shoulders and shook his head with an indifferent air.

"You can't just hide away for the rest of you life like some hermit. Sooner or later you have to move on, as hard as that seems."

A warm heat began to rise through Jay's neck into his face as he fought to maintain control.

With his right hand, he slammed the partial can of Coke down on the top of the table, hard, spilling some of the dark brown liquid in a little pool next to the letters and cards. "It's my life; I don't see why people can't understand that and just leave me alone!"

"People have invested a great deal in your life, both yours and Anna's life. We have a vested interest in your welfare. We love you and love Anna too. If we were any different, had any less concern for you than we do, it just wouldn't be normal," she replied calmly. "I know you need to grieve and that all people grieve differently, but we need to grieve with you, we need to hurt with you, we need to love on you to help get you through the process. Can't you understand that? The path you are on leads to destruction. I can see it, you can see it, and everyone else can see it too."

"I. Don't. Care! It's my business and my business alone! I didn't ask to be in this situation, did nothing to deserve what I'm going through, and I'm just plain brokenhearted and mad! I just want to be left alone!"

A tense silence followed Jay's outburst.

Then Nancy said, "Well, I hear what you're saying, but what about Anna? What about God? Do you think your behavior is honoring either one of them?"

Jay shot up from the table so quickly, the chair he had been sitting on tipped over and slid across the floor. "For your information, Anna's dead! I don't see how what I do or don't do affects her in any possible way. As for God, well, I don't even want to go there! Why should I honor Him? It's because of Him that I'm in the situation I'm in! I didn't see Him honoring my obedience during all of this. I just don't know what He wants from me? I've given Him everything, all there is to give—all my money, my future, my wife. There's just nothing left to give!"

Tears of frustration streamed down Jay's face as he moved to the doorway leading back upstairs. "I'm sorry, Nancy. I am just so upset. I do love you, love Bob, love so many people. I just don't think you understand just how much I hurt."

Tears streamed down Nancy's face too as she got up from her chair and made her way to where Jay was. "Jay, we all hurt too, more than you can ever imagine."

"How do you deal with the pain? I just don't see how you deal with the pain."

"We don't deal with it; we give it to God. It's all we can do; that and draw comfort from the knowledge that Anna is in a better place."

"I've tried to remind myself of that too. I just can't see how being apart from me is being in a better place. It's just not fair!"

Nancy placed her hand on Jay's back. "Well, honey, life just doesn't make sense all the time, and even if we don't want to admit it, heaven is a better place than here no matter our circumstances."

She could feel Jay's back as it convulsed with each sob. "Besides, you just need to trust God and know in your heart that even though you don't understand why this happened, and maybe never will, God has a plan and will make something good come out of this. He always brings good from all things."

Once again Jay erupted in anger. "Just what good could ever come of this? Tell me, Nancy, just what possible good could ever come about because of Anna's death?"

With mouth agape, she watched him storm up the stairs and slam the door. His outburst brought a fresh round of tears flowing from his eyes. She started to follow him, but just as she reached the stairs a voice stopped her in her tracks.

"Let him go. There's no talking sense to that boy right now. He's going to have to cool off some before any more can be said," Bob said from the doorway to their bedroom. "Sorry, I heard pert near the whole conversation, all the ruckus woke me up," he explained as Nancy rushed crying to his arms.

"I'm just so worried and sad. I don't know what to do or say."

"You already said and did all you could. We'll just keep praying for God to speak to his heart. Besides, your words will sink in once he cools off. Now come back to bed. Sitting out here and worrying won't accomplish a thing. If he's not better by tonight, I'll have a sit down with him."

Together they returned to their rooms to attempt to search for enough peace in their hearts to get a bit more sleep, a task that seemed much greater than it had just minutes before.

Chapter 44

Morning came slowly for Jay, who lay on the bed with his head buried under his pillow. It had been several hours since his outburst at Nancy, and he was just as frustrated and upset now as if it had just happened.

Not one person understands, he thought angrily.

It's all God this or God that! I'm so tired of it!

The despair that came with Anna's memory was suffocating to him, and even when he tried to focus on something else, his mind kept tracking back to the life he had shared with her.

Sounds from downstairs told him Nancy and Bob were up and around, which caused him to climb under the covers to feign sleep lest they should come check on him. The last thing he wanted was to have a repeat of his earlier conversation. His heart raced every time the noises become louder, indicating a possibility of visitors; but thankfully for him, none emerged.

Rising from his bed, he peeked out the window when the familiar sound of the kitchen door opened and closed, followed shortly after by the sound of an engine starting. Relief washed over him when Bob's maroon truck backed out of the driveway with both he and Nancy in it. It looked as if they were dressed up, and Jay guessed that it must be Sunday and they were headed to church.

Moving from the window to the small study desk, Jay opened the drawer and removed a piece of white copy paper from inside and retrieved a pen that had been sitting in a little catch-all shelf designed to hold pens, pencils, paper clips, and the like. He closed the drawer and quickly scribbled out a note on the blank paper and signed it.

Dear Bob and Nancy,

Thank you so much for all you have done for me. I love
you and am so grateful to have you in my life. I am going
home for three or four days to my parents' house. I need
to be alone. Please don't try to contact me or send any one
after me. I just need some time to myself to get my head
straight! Once again, thanks for all you have done.

J

A thick and eerie silence filled the room and made Jay uneasy as
he scurried about, shoving as many of his clothes as he could find
in one of his duffel bags. His dark eyes gleamed with a sheen of
purpose as he scanned the room before heading down the stairs
and into the kitchen. Everything was peaceful, clean, and in order
as if none of the previous night's events had ever taken place.

A partially eaten coffee cake with crumb topping sat out on
the counter, inviting Jay to grab a piece. Nancy had even left
several cups of coffee in the pot, which was turned on just in
case Jay should happen to come down and want some. A tinge of
shame and sadness filled his heart as he recalled the way he had
exploded at Nancy the night before, but he pushed it out of his
mind and replaced the feelings with the anger of his own loss.

With deliberate action, he removed the handwritten note
from his pocket and read its contents one last time before placing
it writing up on the center of the kitchen table before moving to
the kitchen door. He paused just long enough to scan the house
where so many fond memories lived before heading out with duffel bag over his shoulder to another stage of his life.

The Unraveling   301

Chapter 45

Though familiar, his parents' home was cold and uninviting as he moved through its rooms. A hidden key under a fake rock on their patio had let him into the house, and even though there was nothing wrong with him being there, he felt as if he were intruding or even trespassing. Family pictures that lined the walls held captive a simpler, more carefree time and brought a tinge of yearning in his heart. With his fingers he traced over the familiar kitchen table where he had shared many meals with family and friends, while memories of the past flooded through his mind with such clarity and depth they could have just happened yesterday.

From the kitchen to the living room he went, picking up little knickknacks and doilies that had been part of his life so many years before. Cascading emotions overtook his senses and caused him to weep uncontrollably as he went through each memory. A solid oak mantle stood straight and true over the fireplace and held statues and awards given to his parents and siblings for various reasons over the years. A wedding picture of he and Anna had been placed front and center and brought so much pain in his heart he turned it picture down on the mantle before moving on.

Down the hall he went and into farthest room at the end. The air was cool and smelled dusty and stale as he clicked on the seldom-used overhead lights. Green shag carpet, matted and worn, felt strange under foot as he moved around the room. Old board games were stacked forlornly one on top of the other and were caked with years of accumulated dust. An old console television lined one wall. Two old and worn recliners sat facing the television in anticipation of a show that would never again play.

Paying little attention to the other contents, he moved to the wall farthest from the door and stopped at an old, upright cabinet with an etched glass front full of pheasants flying from cover on one edge and whitetail deer from a cornfield on the other greeted his eyes like a long-forgotten friend. Many an hour of his youth had been spent staring at just that scene with hopeful daydreams of the day it would become reality.

Numbness had settled over his mind and body as he tried the latch on the cabinet. It was fixed and locked as he jiggled it back and forth. He paused a moment before running his slender fingers up the side of the cabinet and across the dust-covered top until he felt a hidden key lying there in wait. Retrieving the key, he unlocked the case and turned the lever. The door sprung open, revealing a full array of guns and ammo on the other side. Under the rifles and shotguns was a small cabinet. Slowly and deliberately he opened both doors to reveal a shiny-cut nickel revolver. It was his dad's 44 magnum. A ribbed 6 1/2" ported barrel was highlighted with a red dot front sight. The black grips were inviting, and he picked it up. It was heavy but well balanced and felt good in his hand.

A Smith and Wesson emblem was etched into the dull steel on the right side of the gun's frame; the cylinder was full of hollow tip bullets. Carefully, he tucked the pistol under his arm and closed first the lower and then the outer cabinet doors before locking them. With his free hand he placed the small key back in its hiding place and retreated from the room, turning the lights off as he went. Once back inside the kitchen, he wrapped the gun in a small dish towel and placed it in the duffel bag amongst his clothes.

Paranoia filled his mind and he peeked out the windows several times to make sure no one was watching or coming to get him. Satisfied, he went to one of the kitchen drawers and pulled out a piece of scrap paper and pen. With a sigh, he wrote a quick note and folded it.

> Dear Mom and Dad. I love you so much!
>
> Thank you for all you have done and all you have been to me and for me through the years.
>
> I don't want you to worry about me or my life.
>
> I am going to a better place.
>
> Love, your son,
>
> Jay

Jay took one last look around; his eyes gleamed with resentment and sad determination. Tears welled in his eyes as he realized this would be the last time he would visit this place. He dashed away the tears and opened the outside door. Pausing one last time, he attempted to grab onto something, anything that might keep him there, but found none. With a renewed sense of purpose, he closed and locked the door and replaced the key in its regular hiding place before heading down the empty street and out of sight.

Chapter 46

For three days he moved across the country, drinking water from the spigots of houses along the way. From Palouse, through Potlatch, clear to Plumber and beyond he traveled, nearly to St. Maries before turning east on Mountain Road in the heart of the Benewah.

Lack of food and water added to the confused state his mind was in, and images of Anna haunted him constantly, adding to the pain and agony that tore at his heart. The long, warm late summer nights were spent huddled out of sight of the road, usually in some kind of outcropping where the odds of detection were minimal at best. This night would be different. This night he would reach his destination.

The road he was on was dirt and had seen little use for some time. The dust was several inches deep and was powdery and light, billowing up around his feet with each step, the smell of dust reminding him of his time at the mission. Night was closing in, which made it difficult to see any landmarks that might trigger his memory. Beautiful and rugged evergreen mountains rose up all around him, some spilling out nearly onto the road he was traveling. Dust clung to the needles on the trees and dulled the glossy greens underneath.

He'd been on the road all day long and was surprised that his destination was still not in sight. Fear was beginning to grow in his heart that he had picked the wrong road but was quickly quenched as he rounded a bend and the narrow mountain gap opened up into a familiar, large grass meadow. There was just enough evening light for him to make out an old dilapidated cabin at the far end. Picking up his pace, he moved off the road and cut through the grass on an old game trail that led directly to the cabin.

It had been constructed from logs the pioneers had harvested from the forest more than a century before. Weather and lack of repairs had taken their toll as one corner of the front was collapsed since last he had seen it. Empty windows and door gave it an eerie feel that sent shivers up his spine. Weeds and trees grew up around and through it, making it barely possible for him to circle the small building. In his mind, he could imagine it in pristine shape with clear ground all around where the children once ran and played.

"Well, Anna, I made it. I didn't think I would for a while, but I did," he whispered to the wind.

Gingerly, he moved through the underbrush and then through the open doorway of the single-room cabin. The old wood floor was rotted out on one end but felt solid enough under his feet, so he entered. Litter covered the floor and bore truth of recent trespassers. With his foot, he scattered the refuse and sat down with his back against the wall, duffel on his lap. Slowly he opened the zipper and felt around until his hand made contact with the cold steel within. Grasping it in his hand, he pulled it from the bag and placed it on the floor next to him. Fear of the unknown tugged at his mind, and the pace of his heart quickened as he thought about where he was and what he was going to do. A silent voice mocked him, *Seek God, seek God.* It played itself over and over in his mind, and he fought against it with all of his will.

"I gave you a chance, God! Gave you my life, our lives! Look where it got me! I can't take it anymore!" he yelled at the voices in his head.

Pictures of Anna played themselves out, over and over, pictures in his memory. She seemed so real he could almost smell her.

A loud rustling outside the cabin brought him back to reality as he grabbed the pistol up from the floor. Adrenaline surged through his body, and his imagination ran wild as the noise grew louder. As quietly as possible he got up and crept out the open doorway. It was almost completely dark. Using as much stealth as possible, he moved around the building and peered into the bushes in an attempt to make out the source of the noise; his whole body shook with fear.

Unable to see anything, he moved closer still. A sudden and explosive movement caused him to swing the heavy pistol toward the source of the noise. Panicked, he fired three times into the brush. The noise from the pistol was deafening and echoed through the valley.

Nothing moved, and for several moments he stood, glued to the spot, gun leveled at the bushes. Finally, curiosity overruled caution and he moved closer step by step. Just as he reached the edge of the brush, the undergrowth erupted, knocking him to his butt. Rolling to his side, he fired blindly two more times at the noise but got a grip on himself as a mother raccoon, followed by three baby raccoons, ran past.

Every inch of his body convulsed as he came down from his adrenaline high. Disgusted by his fear, he kicked the ground in frustration and returned to the inside of the cabin. A full harvest moon blood red in color was rising in the night sky, and he was amazed at the amount of light it cast on the forest. Looking out the window opening, he could make out individual trees more than a hundred yards away and see individual meadow grasses as they glowed with a light from the sky.

Moonbeams shone in through the doorway and both windows and cast eerie shadows on the walls of the cabin. The light revealed two names carved into one of the logs on the opposite wall. Rising from his seat, Jay moved across the floor and affectionately ran his hand across the words: *Jay loves Anna*. He had carved it during their honeymoon, years earlier when the two of them had stayed in this very cabin for two nights. The property belonged to Chet and his family, and he had given them permission to stay there while they hiked around the mountains together.

The Unraveling

Tears poured from his eyes, and pain tore anew at his heart as he yearned for days gone by. "I can't take it anymore! I love you, Anna!" he whispered again as he staggered across the floor and reclaimed his seat on the floor next to his duffel bag. Evil forces began stirring twisted memories of conversations held with Nancy, Bill, Chet, and everyone else that cared for him.

You have to trust God! You have to place your faith in God! It's for the best! God will make something good out of your situation. God has mighty plans for you life!

They taunted him over and over, buzzing around his mind like some annoying and troublesome gnat that just would not go away. Sanity was slipping from his mind, and he welcomed it as he alternated from laughing to crying, back and forth, back and forth, arguing with the forces within. With shaking hand, he raised the pistol from his lap and traced the barrel back and forth on his face and around the edges of his mouth. *You'll never do it! You'll chicken out! You'll give in and let God run your life! Look at how that's turned out for you so far! You're nothing but a chicken! A wanna be! You're a loser!*

Over and over they taunted his mind, tempted him to take his own fate in his hands.

"Anna!" he cried out in despair.

Across the floor, a gray mouse emerged from the inside of an empty soup can someone had discarded years before. It moved along the floor, stopping every now and again as it tested the air with its twitching whiskers. Spying the animal through watery and bloodshot eyes, Jay trained the pistol on the little critter and followed it as it moved across the floor.

"Boom!" he shouted as he mock fired at the little animal before it disappeared below the rotted-out portion of the floor.

An insane laugh erupted from his lungs as he moved the barrel of the gun back to his head. Sweat dripped from his face as he nervously imagined what it would feel like, whether it would hurt, or if it would be so sudden he wouldn't feel a thing. Back and forth the barrel went, round and round his mouth. Finally, with all the determination he could muster, he placed the end slightly in his mouth and closed his teeth just over the front site.

"I'm going to a better place!" he told himself over and over again. "My pain is going to finally end! Anna, I'm coming home."

〜 〜 〜 〜

Several deer were busy feeding in the meadow as heavy dew fell from the sky. The September air was cool and damp and fore-warned of a rapidly approaching fall. Crickets serenaded the night sky, and the night air was alive with the sounds of croak-ing frogs as they basked in the light of the moon. The meadow teemed with activity as nature's nocturnal beasts came out to for-age and play.

Kaboom! The loud noise brought an instant quiet as each crea-ture sought immediate refuge. Unsure where it had come from, the deer ran a few feet this way and then a few that way as their ears twisted and turned back and forth in an attempt to pick up the direction and source of the noise. Satisfied the danger was gone, they returned to grazing on the tender shoots of grass on the floor of the meadow. The other creatures remained eerily quiet for several more minutes until first one, followed by another, and then another went back to their normal nightly activity of serenading the moon.

The Unraveling

Chapter 47

All of Eastern Washington was abuzz with the news. The headline in the *Daily News*, Pullman's own local newspaper, read,

> Missionary Raised from the Dead!

Several of the national news stations and publications picked up on the story, making Anna the talk of the country. Invitations were pouring in for her to make the rounds on all of the daily talk shows, with staggering amounts of money being offered for her exclusive story. Breaking news of Jay's disappearance and subsequent suicide letter only added massive amounts of fuel to an already-burning inferno.

Nancy and Bob found the note Jay had written and immediately called Chet and Bill to explain to them what was going on. They decided to honor his request to be left alone.

"Maybe that's exactly what he needs," Nancy argued successfully against Chet's better judgment.

Over the next couple of days, several of attempts were made to reach Jay by phone, but none were successful. After mission headquarters called with the good news about Anna's safe return, an all-out search-and-rescue effort was begun by family and friends. When they found what they believed to be a suicide note at Jay's parents', coupled with the missing handgun, an Amber alert was issued for Jay as all of the Pacific Northwest went into search mode for the missing missionary.

It took Anna three days to make it back to Pullman after reaching the mission. The Mexican Federal Police spent an entire day debriefing her. With the information she provided, they were able to locate the drug operation and liberate the young men being held against their will. Although their raid was successful, they were unable to locate Luis and were still scouring the countryside in search of him. When word of Carlos's death reached Anna, she cried and thanked God for placing him in her life.

Chino and Pedro were given a hero's welcome and were invited to move their entire family and animals to the mission compound to live. They were given a new hacienda built by a work and witness team from the United States. Serena vowed that when she grew up she was going to become a missionary just like Anna.

∿ ∿ ∿ ∿

"What if he's not there?" Anna asked.

"We'll cross that bridge when we get to it," Chet replied stoically.

The gray Tahoe crept up the dirt road, throwing up a plume of dust in the process. Rays of the afternoon sun shone brightly through the passenger side window and illuminated Anna's long hair, which had taken on an amber hue.

Worry lines stood out on Chet's forehead and made him look much older than he was as he strained to make out faint tracks in the dusty road through the dirty front window of his vehicle. "I'm not sure if those are human tracks or animal tracks," he mumbled to himself.

He opted to forego his sheriff uniform in lieu of blue jeans and a collared t-shirt since he was in Idaho, miles away from his jurisdiction, but carried his service revolver in a gun belt around his waist just in case. Billowing white clouds tinged with grays and blacks pushed up over the steep evergreen peaks that rose to meet them.

"Looks like a storm is brewing," Chet announced as he surveyed the growing formation.

Looking to the sky, Anna nodded, unable to speak; her heart pounded in her ears as the anticipation of a long-awaited reunion played out in her mind.

The Unraveling 311

"Lord, let him be there, and please, please let him be okay," she prayed over and over again.

Heavy dust caked itself to the windshield of the Tahoe as they bumped along the rough roadway and caused Chet to run his windshield wipers just so he could see. All of the accumulated dirt on the underbrush and trees along the rough roadway reminded Anna more of a moonscape than a forest setting. Despite the severity of the situation, Anna couldn't help but notice the majestic beauty all around her, and her eyes watered and heart sang thanksgiving to her Lord.

On and on they went down a road that seemed never ending until they finally rounded a bend that opened up into a large mountain meadow. Emotion welled up in Anna's heart as the dilapidated cabin came into view.

"Well, here we finally are," Chet announced with a mouthful of tension.

With a turn of the wheel, he pulled into the tall grass of the meadow and placed the vehicle in park. "Anna, when we get over there, I want you to stay in the car just in case," he explained. "I just think it will be for the best."

They drove across the meadow and parked the car about fifty feet from the front of the building. Blowing dust made it possible to see the gusting winds as they moved about the cabin, first that way and then this. Taking a deep breath, Chet got out of the car while Anna, with wide eyes glued to the open doorway, started to pray softly.

"Lord, please bring me through this trial. Whatever the outcome, Lord, carry me through. Thank you so much for all you've already done for me, Lord. Thank you for placing just the right people in my life just when I needed them most. Just strengthen me now, Lord, and carry me through this time. Keep Chet safe and please, Lord, let Jay be all right,"

The tall meadow grass was over Chet's waist, and his hands rubbed across the smooth heads full of tiny Timothy seeds as he made his way forward. "Jay, it's Chet! I have Anna! Are you here, Jay?" he yelled through cupped hands.

A knot of sadness and despair roiled in his stomach as he pulled a single, long stem of meadow grass from the ground and placed the picked end in his mouth. It had a slightly sour taste as he rolled the hard round stem back and forth with his tongue just as he used to do as a boy so many years before. Small seeds fell from the head from the motion and drifted slowly to the ground at his feet.

"Jay, are you there?" he yelled again before advancing toward the open doorway.

Anna covered her eyes and peeked through her slender white fingers.

"Jay, it's Chet and Anna. Are you here?" he yelled again as he reached the edge of the grass.

Thunder began to roll as the clouds continued their advance on the mountains and small meadow below. Chet wiped the sweat from his brow and looked around for something to throw inside the building. He picked up a softball-size rock and tossed it into the cabin and waited. It landed with a thud, and he could hear it roll to the far wall, where it stopped with a crash. The air smelled of dust and rain, which made him happy. Over the years he had responded to enough calls of human deaths where the individual hadn't been discovered for several days to know that a nearly unbearable odor of decomposition was always present.

Shrugging his shoulders, he motioned to Anna he was going to go inside the cabin. "Jay, if you're in there, I'm coming in!" he yelled as he began his advance.

Just as he took his first step toward the doorway, a filthy, emaciated figure burst through the opening. The man's eyes were wide and wild, his dark hair long and greasy. Grime and dust covered his entire body.

"Leave me alone!" he yelled as he waved a revolver back and forth at Chet.

The Unraveling

Instinctively, Chet's hand went to his own service revolver, and he drew it from its holster. It took him a moment before he recognized the man was Jay.

"Put the gun down, Jay. We don't want anyone to get hurt!"

"You leave me alone! I don't want to talk to you or anyone else! I just want to die!"

"Jay, I have Anna with me. She's alive! She's over in the Tahoe, Jay. We came to get you," Chet explained with as much authority as he could muster.

Sweat poured from his face as he watched Jay wave the gun back and forth. For a moment, he could see a hint of recognition in Jay's eyes as the gun wavered ever so slightly.

"Jay, it's Chet, you know who I am. I brought Anna with me. She's over in the car. Put the gun down and we can go see her."

The air was alive with electricity as lightning lit up the sky. Booming thunder echoed in the valley right on top of the amazing display of light.

"Jay, put the gun down," Chet ordered again.

Jay's eyes were wild with madness as he menacingly waved the revolver at Chet. "Leave me alone, or I'll shoot you. I'm not falling for any tricks!"

Chet lowered his gun and took a step toward his friend. "You'll just have to shoot me, then, because I'm not leaving you out here. I love you too much. We all love you too much. Anna is in the Tahoe. You have to believe me, man."

"Stop, I mean it, stop!" Jay yelled while taking a firm aim at his slowly advancing friend. "I mean it, I'll shoot!" he promised.

Tears filled Anna's eyes as she watched the scene unfold in front of her. "Lord, please speak to his heart and please keep Chet safe," she prayed over and over.

She watched with horror as Jay threatened Chet with the gun and was even more appalled when he set his stance to shoot his own friend. It was more than she could take, and she burst from the car.

"Jay, it's me. It's Anna! Stop it and put down that gun!"

For a moment she could detect a glimmer of hope and recognition in his red and wild eyes as he glanced her way.

"Stay back!" he ordered Chet, who continued to slowly advance on his friend. "Stay back or I'll shoot!" he threatened again.

"Jay, it's really me. It's Anna! I love you, Jay! I'm back. I'm alive. Please put down your gun."

Sensing his hesitation, Anna ran forward till she was no more than twenty feet away.

"Look at me!" she ordered. "It really is me!"

Large drops of rain began to fall from the sky as the three continued their tense standoff.

"Listen to her!" Chet ordered over the gusting wind.

"Stop it! I can't take it!" Jay cried.

"Jay, you put down that gun! We love you! I love you! I'm back from Mexico, from the mission. I'm alive and well. Put down the gun, and we'll go home. We'll be together! I promise you, Jay! I love you!"

Moving back a few steps, Jay looked first at Anna and then at Chet. The two continued their slow and steady approach, each talking to Jay, reassuring him Anna was real, that they were real and they were there to take him home. His mind buzzed with madness and confusion as he looked first at one and then the other. The girl sounded like Anna to him, even looked somewhat like Anna, but her hair was slightly off color, and she wasn't nearly as petite as Anna.

"Stop it! I can't take it! Anna's dead! I know she is. I was there! I'm going to kill you," he yelled at Anna, who continued to approach.

The scene seemed to play itself out in slow motion for Anna as she watched the man she loved pivot and swing the gun away from Chet and directly toward her.

"Noooo!" Chet yelled while raising his own revolver toward Jay and firing.

The Unraveling   315

The terror on Jay's eyes haunted her instantly as impact from the 357 slug slammed into his shoulder, spinning him around while the gun in his own hand dislodged from the force and flew several feet through the air. Jay's body twisted in the air before settling facedown on the hard ground.

"Jay!" she screamed over and over as she rushed to her fallen husband's side and turned him over.

Shocked that he had just shot his friend, Chet walked to the revolver and picked it up. "Empty," he said with a sick feeling before he bent over and wretched.

Rain began to beat down with force, washing the grime from the forest in the process. Wiping the mud from his face, Anna leaned down and attempted to breathe life back into the man she loved. Over and over she repeated the process while Chet rushed to the Tahoe and radioed for help. Warm, red liquid covered Anna's hands as she attempted to cover the gaping wound.

"No, God! Please!" She sobbed to the sky as rain pounded down from above.

The forest, the sky, the ground beneath all started to turn counterclockwise before going black as Anna slumped to the ground.

Chapter 48

Red, blue, and silver Mylar balloons bounced against the bluish green ceiling as they traveled currents of air like buoys on the sea. Anna watched them from her hospital bed as she recalled the crazy events of her life over the previous several months. Tears pooled around the edges of her large brown eyes as she thought of Jay, Carlos, and the rest of the people God had placed in her life. Her bittersweet thoughts were interrupted when Dr. Reaynos entered the room.

"Good news for you today! Both you and your boy are in good shape. Your blood pressure is nearly normal, and you are no longer spotting. If you continue to progress, you should be able to go home in a day or two… That is, if you promise to get some rest and promise to limit your guests. These past five days have been crazy; too many people."

Moving to her side, he checked her pulse and listened to her heart. "A baby boy. Do you have a name picked out?"

Tears welled up once again as emotion choked her words for a moment. Clearing her throat, she smiled. "Carlos Jay Bilston," she announced proudly. "I know the name's not very poetic sounding, but it's a name my baby can be proud of. I think he'll like it."

Nodding his head, the doctor smiled and took Anna's hand. "I know all you've been through. I just want you to know, you're an amazing woman. It's been an honor to have been your doctor."

"Thank you, I don't feel all that amazing."

"Well, you've been through a lot, and being pregnant really messes up your hormones. Trust me, you are amazing. You're an inspiration."

Anna nodded in embarrassment and was grateful when someone knocked loudly on the door.

"Yo, what up? Every time I come here I catch you lying down on the job, sista!" Bill teased as he walked through the door.

Smiling brightly, Anna reached her hand out and took Bill's in her own. "Doctor said I get to go home tomorrow if I'm good," she announced eagerly.

"Right on! Sounds like a good day."

Nurses and doctors rushed by Anna's open door as she and Bill caught up on news. He pulled up a chair and listened as she excitedly told him of all the people she had met while in Mexico. "I can't wait to go back there and share Jesus with those people. They are so desperate and lost. They really need Him."

"Well, the Bill-ster digs your moxy, that's for sure! From all the wild stories, I can sure see the Big Guy was really watching out for you."

Anna nodded as tears flowed from her eyes. "He was doing more than watching me. He was carrying me. If it wasn't for God, I wouldn't be here. Looking back, I am nearly overwhelmed by the way God guided my steps and the events in my life, especially when my circumstances seemed impossible to overcome. I did my best not to lose faith, and God never once failed me."

"Yah, He's been known to do that from time to time, especially if we let Him," Bill agreed.

Hundreds of get-well cards lined every inch of counter space. People had sent them from every part of the nation as news of her ordeal had been broadcast over and over on every news station in America and Mexico.

"Looks like you have a fan club," Bill said, motioning toward the letters.

"I have about a thousand more at Nancy and Bob's. Presents too. People are so weird." Anna giggled embarrassedly.

"They just want you to know how much you have inspired them! Nothin' wrong with that."

"I guess not, but what will I do with all the stuff?"

"Well, that's a good problem to have. I think you won't have any problem finding someone to help or a good home for most of the stuff. The rest, well, the Bill-ster is always ready to help a friend out."

Anna yawned and stretched. "I can't believe how tired I am all the time."

"It's not like you don't have a reason."

"But I've mostly slept for the past five days. You'd think I'd be rested up by now."

A chicken started to cluck as Bill's cell phone began to ring. "Cool tones," he explained as Anna giggled at the sound. "Let the Bill-ster get this, and I'll be right back," he promised as he left the room and closed the door.

Anna rolled to her side and stared out the window. She marveled at how green the grass and how vibrant the colors of the flowers that lined the parking lot were. It seemed that everywhere she looked, God was present, and she thanked Him for all the beauty.

She turned back over and smiled when Bill walked back through the door. "The Bill-ster has a small gift for you. Are you ready for it?"

"You didn't have to get me anything," Anna scolded.

"Dude, the Bill-ster does what the Bill-ster wants! You just need to be gracious and accept it."

"All right, all right,"

"Well, close your eyes, and promise not to open them till I give you the go ahead."

"Give me a hint, and then I'll close my eyes."

"Well, it's a big gift, it'll take up a lot of room, you can use it for a while and then give it away if you'd like. It only came in one color, and for the life of me, I don't know why you or anyone else would even want to have one around. But Chet and I got it for you to hopefully take your mind off the sorrows in your life."

The Unraveling

"Aww, you guys are so good to me."

Bill paused at the door, "Well, you're worth it, Anna! Your life is a testimony for so many people. Your faith is so strong and true. I just wish it could be something more. Just remember, the Bill-ster has limited resources. This really is the best I could come up with, so promise not to be too disappointed."

A half smile of embarrassment spread across Anna's face and her large eyes glistened with tears. "I don't know what to say. Thank you, Bill. I know that whatever it is will be great."

"Close your eyes then and no peeking," he commanded as he left the room.

Anna did as ordered and tried to imagine what her gift could be. Emotion once again spread through her body as she thanked God for such wonderful friends. A gentle breeze created by the opening of her doors raised her curiosity and nearly caused her to peek. She would have, too if Bill hadn't been there to admonish her not to.

The gift was large, and she could hear Chet and Bill arguing how to get it through the open door. "You should have opened both of them," Chet complained.

"Dude, it'll fit, just move your end all the way around."

Clanking and banging of wood against metal mixed with directions of "this way," "watch out," "hey," piqued Anna's curiosity even more.

"No peeking, you promised," Bill reminded her.

"Cross my heart," Anna promised.

They continued to maneuver and move things around, and Anna could tell whatever they were bringing her was large and cumbersome. Finally, when she didn't think she could stand it for another minute, Bill told her it was ready. Instant emotion overwhelmed as tears poured from her eyes.

"How—when—how did you do this?" she asked between sobs.

"It pays to have connections," Chet replied through tears of his own.

With her right hand, Anna reached out from her bed and took Jay's left in her own. Tears streamed down his face, but the emotion was too overwhelming for either of them to talk.

Seeing the question on Anna's eyes, Bill replied, "He improved so much over the past twenty-four hours, the doctors at Sacred Heart in Spokane let us transfer him down here to Pullman so he could be close to you."

Tears of joy flowed freely down everyone's faces as they hugged and laughed together.

"They said it's a miracle Jay's even alive," Chet told Anna as he filled her in on all that had been happening.

"His blood loss was severe, and he was so weak from all he had been through they didn't think they would be able to save him. They performed surgery on his left shoulder, inserted a few screws, and with a little therapy, he should be good as new in six months or so."

"He's as tough as shoe leather. I knew he'd be okay," Bill added.

"It's a good thing for both of you that I was able to raise Heart Flight. If they hadn't been able to fly into the mountains, and believe me, with the thunderstorm we were having, it was touch and go... Anyway, as I was saying, if they hadn't been able to fly in, both of you would have bled to death. Who would have guessed it would end up this way?" Chet chuckled to himself.

"But I didn't go in the helicopter," Anna argued.

"No, but the paramedics were able to give you a shot and get you stabilized until an ambulance was able to make it. First, they took you to St. Maries. Once you were stable, I had a transfer come up and bring you back to Pullman."

"I remember all that, silly. I wasn't in a coma or anything. I just knew I rode in the ambulance."

"Well, either way you can thank those folks from Heart Flight for saving both of you. I was a total wreck, nearly useless to either of you. I was able to put a compress on Jay's wound, but that's about it. The thunderstorm soaked all of us pretty good, but wouldn't you know it, just when I thought it would be impossible for the helicopter to make it through, it stopped raining and the clouds parted. Guess you have to chalk that one up to God."

Anna nodded her head in agreement.

"See there, dog, I told you the Big Guy has mighty plans for your life," Bill playfully told Jay.

Chet and Bill visited with Jay and Anna for a few more minutes before excusing themselves.

A happy but awkward silence settled into the room as Jay's large eyes locked on Anna's. Tears flowed freely from both and said what no words could. Finally, after swallowing the lump of emotion that had clogged his throat, Jay mouthed the words *I love you*. A raw and primitive emotion stole his voice as sobs of sorrow, joy, and wonder tore at his heart.

Anna swallowed to bring her heart out of her throat. "I love you too, so, so much."

For the longest time they held hands and said nothing, content to simply enjoy the moment. Several times Anna's nurse came to check on them, and by the sour look on her face they could tell she wasn't happy about having the added responsibility in her room. Anna's cheerful and uplifting disposition won her over, however, and by the end of her shift she was actually visiting and exchanging barbs with Jay.

At Chet's request, the hospital kept all visitors from their room to allow them as much private time as possible. "I think you too have some catching up to do," he announced with a wink.

Unsure where to start, Jay summoned his courage and cleared his throat. "Anna, I'm so sorry. I thought you were dead. I was nearly out of my mind with grief. I never would have hurt you. The gun was empty."

The words tumbled from his mouth and tears streamed down his face.

"Hush. I know you wouldn't have hurt me."

Silence filled the room again as Jay regained his composure. "I am such a failure; I failed you and failed God. I can't believe the way I acted. I don't deserve to even be mentioned with the word *missionary*."

"You're not a failure, Jay. You've just gone through a terrible ordeal. Most people would have reacted in the same manner."

"Maybe so, but I am supposed to be a man of faith. I don't think I've had faith in God for years. Besides, you're the one that went through a terrible ordeal. What I went through can't even be compared."

"You've had faith. You went to Mexico. That took a step of faith.

Jay shook his head no. "I went to Mexico because you went to Mexico. I didn't want to go there, didn't want to follow God's plan for my life, and didn't want to have to trust Him for anything, and I didn't. I grumbled and complained the whole time. That's not what faith is all about. I don't know how you or God can love me. I'm such a pitiful person. I'm surprised God didn't just let me die."

"Jay, God's not like that and you know it. He loves you more than any other person; loves each of us that way. There's not one of us that hasn't let Him down at some point in our walk with Him. Some let Him down all the time and He just keeps on loving us, speaking to our hearts, trying to get through to us. Just remember, He loved you and me enough to send Jesus to die for us. That's a huge investment He made."

"Faith is such a hard thing. I just don't know if I'm strong enough to give everything to Him."

The late-afternoon sun filtered through the window and glowed around Anna's head. "Jay, God doesn't want you to be strong. He wants you to be weak. So weak that you have to rely on Him, trust Him to guide your every step; to rely on Him to provide our daily manna. Faith isn't an easy thing. Even Peter sank, just remember that. It's what you do once you realize you've failed that matters. Give it to God, He's always there and will bring us through every one of life's obstacles if we let him. That's when we can truly see the blessings of life and the miracles He wants to perform in our lives every single day."

A deep thought struggled to push itself to the surface, but Jay was too tired to think. "I just hope you and God can both forgive me."

"He already has, Jay. He already has. As for me, well you'd better already know that answer."

Jay squeezed her hand as his eyes slid shut. Neither of them said anything for several minutes.

"Anna?" Jay asked with a gulp and a bit of hesitation.

"Yes, Jay?"

He took a gulp and fumbled for words. "Well, um. I need to ask you something. I mean, I'm not sure how to ask."

"Just ask, what is it?

"Well, I didn't know, um, well, I didn't know you were pregnant."

Tears of joy welled up in her eyes. "I didn't know either, until Reina told me."

"Who's Reina?"

"Well, Reina is…well, that's a long story for another day. Right now you just need your rest."

"Anna?" Jay asked sheepishly.

"Yes, Jay?"

Fear tore at his heart as he struggled to ask what was on his mind. "Umm, is it mine? I mean, I'm so sorry to ask you this, but the baby, is it mine?"

Anna smiled and answered with grace, "Of course it's yours! Who else's would it be, silly?"

Shame drove his eyes to the ground. "I'm sorry I asked you that. I just didn't know if anything happened to you while you were being held hostage."

A gracious smile spread across Anna's face. "Oh, Jay, I love you so much! God kept me safe the whole time! More than I could have ever imagined!"